BUFFY '97

JEREMY LAMBERT
MARIANNA IGNAZZI • MATTIA IACONO

Published by
BOOM! STUDIOS

Series and Logo Designer
Grace Park

Collection Designers
Veronica Gutierrez and **Marie Krupina**

Assistant Editor
Maya Bollinger

Editor
Elizabeth Brei

Special Thanks to **Sierra Hahn**, **Becca J. Sadowski**, and **Nicole Spiegel**.

Ross Richie Chairman & Founder
Jen Harned CFO
Matt Gagnon Editor-in-Chief
Filip Sablik President, Publishing & Marketing
Stephen Christy President, Development
Adam Yoelin Senior Vice President, Film
Lance Kreiter Vice President, Licensing & Merchandising
Bryce Carlson Vice President, Editorial & Creative Strategy
Hunter Gorinson Vice President, Business Development
Josh Hayes Vice President, Sales
Sierra Hahn Executive Editor
Eric Harburn Executive Editor
Ryan Matsunaga Director, Marketing
Stephanie Lazarski Director, Operations
Mette Norkjaer Director, Development
Elyse Strandberg Manager, Finance
Michelle Ankley Manager, Production Design
Cheryl Parker Manager, Human Resources
Dafna Pleban Senior Editor
Elizabeth Brei Editor
Kathleen Wisneski Editor
Sophie Philips-Roberts Editor
Allyson Gronowitz Editor
Ramiro Portnoy Associate Editor
Gavin Gronenthal Assistant Editor
Gwen Waller Assistant Editor
Kenzie Rzonca Assistant Editor

Maya Bollinger Assistant Editor
Rey Netschke Editorial Assistant
Marie Krupina Design Lead
Crystal White Design Lead
Grace Park Design Coordinator
Madison Goyette Production Designer
Veronica Gutierrez Production Designer
Jessy Gould Production Designer
Nancy Mojica Production Designer
Samantha Knapp Production Design Assistant
Esther Kim Marketing Lead
Breanna Sarpy Marketing Lead, Digital
Amanda Lawson Marketing Coordinator
Alex Lorenzen Marketing Coordinator, Copywriter
Grecia Martinez Marketing Assistant, Digital
Ashley Troub Consumer Sales Coordinator
Harley Salbacka Sales Coordinator
Greg Hopkins Retail Sales Coordinator
Megan Christopher Operations Lead
Rodrigo Hernandez Operations Coordinator
Nicholas Romeo Operations Coordinator
Jason Lee Senior Accountant
Faizah Bashir Business Analyst
Amber Peters Staff Accountant
Tiffany Thomas Accounts Payable Clerk
Michel Lichand Executive Assistant
Diane Payne Publishing Administrative Assistant

BUFFY '97, November 2022. Published by BOOM! Studios, a division of Boom Entertainment, Inc. © 2022 20th Television. Originally published in single magazine form as BUFFY '97 No. 1, Buffy the Vampire Slayer 25th Anniversary Special No. 1, Buffy the Vampire Slayer Free Comic Book Day 2022, Willow and Tara: Buffy the Vampire Slayer Vol. 8 Omnibus, Tales of the Slayers. © 2022 20th Television. BOOM! Studios™ and the BOOM! Studios logo are trademarks of Boom Entertainment, Inc, registered in various countries and categories. All characters, events, and institutions depicted herein are fictional. Any similarity between any of the names, characters, persons, events, and/or institutions in this publication to actual names, characters, and persons, whether living or dead, events, and/or institutions is unintended and purely coincidental. BOOM! Studios does not read or accept unsolicited submissions of ideas, stories, or artwork.

BOOM! Studios, 5670 Wilshire Boulevard, Suite 400, Los Angeles, CA 90036-5679. Printed in Canada. First Printing.

ISBN: 978-1-68415-877-5, eISBN: 978-1-64668-743-5

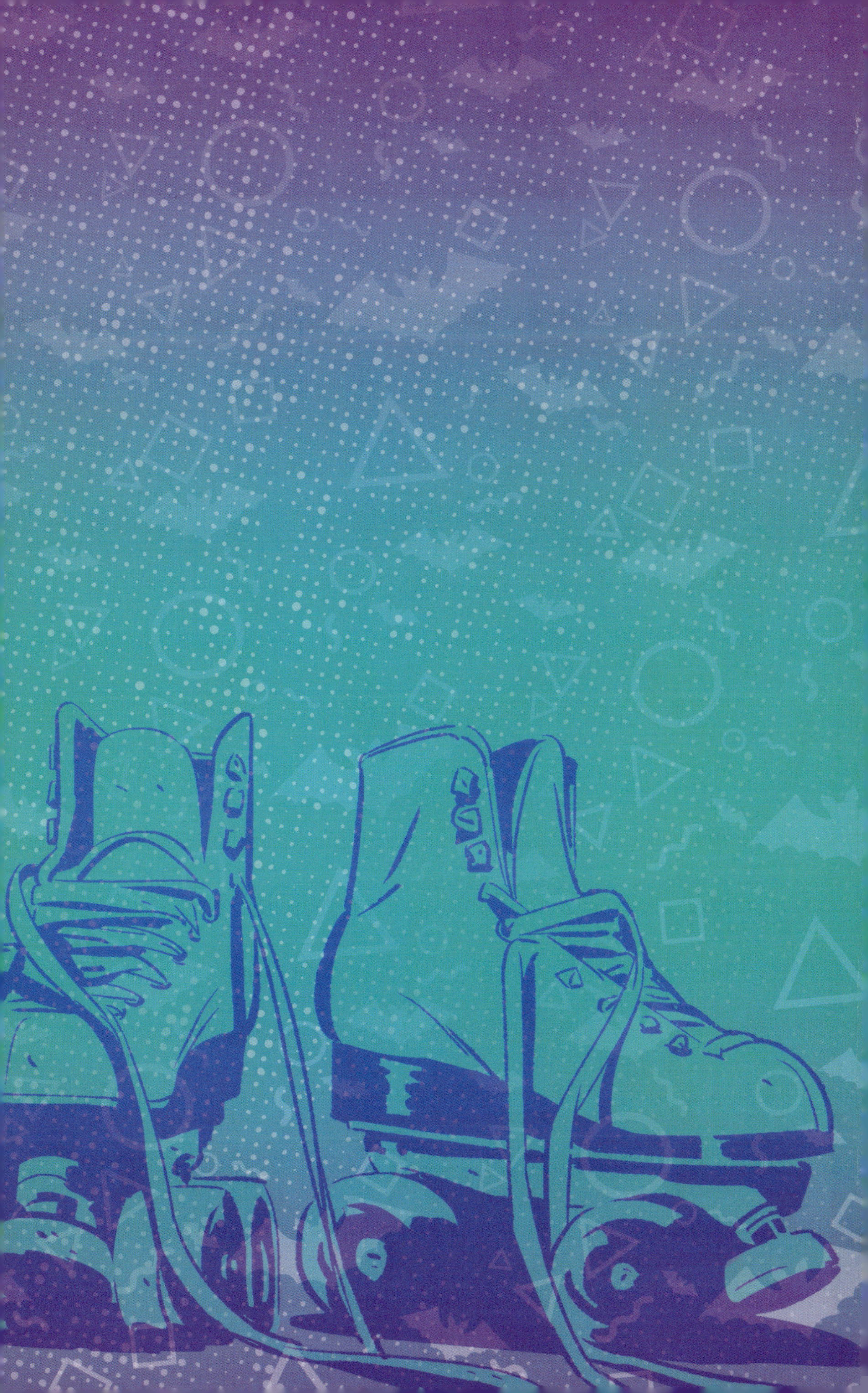

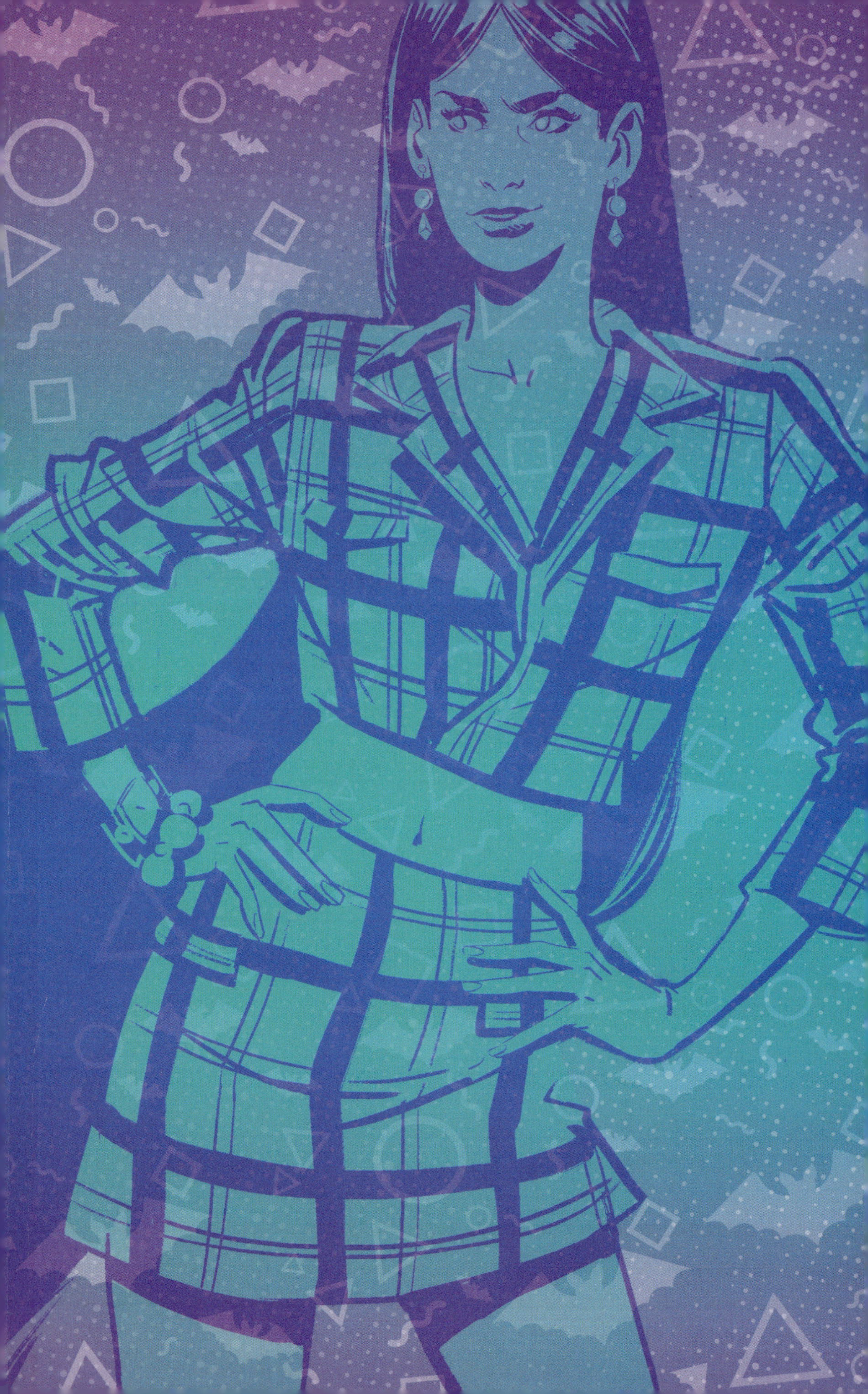

Created by
Joss Whedon

BUFFY '97
Written by
Jeremy Lambert
Illustrated by
Marianna Ignazzi
Colored by
Mattia Iacono
Lettered by
Ed Dukeshire

IS THIS WHAT I WANTED
Written by
Danny Lore
Illustrated by
Marianna Ignazzi
Colored by
Mattia Iacono

WILLOW AND TARA: WANNABLESSEDBE
Written by
Amber Benson
and **Christopher Golden**
Illustrated by
Terry Moore
with **Eric Powell**
Colores and Letters by
HiFi Design

THE INNOCENT
Written by
Amber Benson
Illustrated by
Ted Naifeh
Colored by
David Stewart
Lettered by
Michelle Madsen

WONDROUS & SURPRISING MAGIC
Written by
Lilah Sturges
Illustrated by
Claire Roe
Colored by
Roman Titov

MIRRORS DON'T LIE
Written by
Casey Gilly
Illustrated by
Bayleigh Underwood
Colored by
Heather Breckel

YEARBOOK
Featuring artwork by
Dan Mora, **David López**, **Gleb Melnikov**, **Eleonora Carlini**, **Marianna Ignazzi**, **Andrés Genolet**, **Hayden Sherman**, **Ornella Savarese**, **Valentina Pinti**, **Natacha Bustos**, **Ramon Bachs**, **Daniel Bayliss**, **Claudia Balboni**, **Cliff Richards**, & **Georges Jeanty**

Featuring colors by
Raúl Angulo, **Roman Titov**, **Cris Peter**, **Mattia Iacono**, **Eleonora Bruni**, **Patricio Delpeche**, **Gabriel Cassata**, **Jeromy Cox**, & **Dave Stewart**

Cover by
Jenny Frison

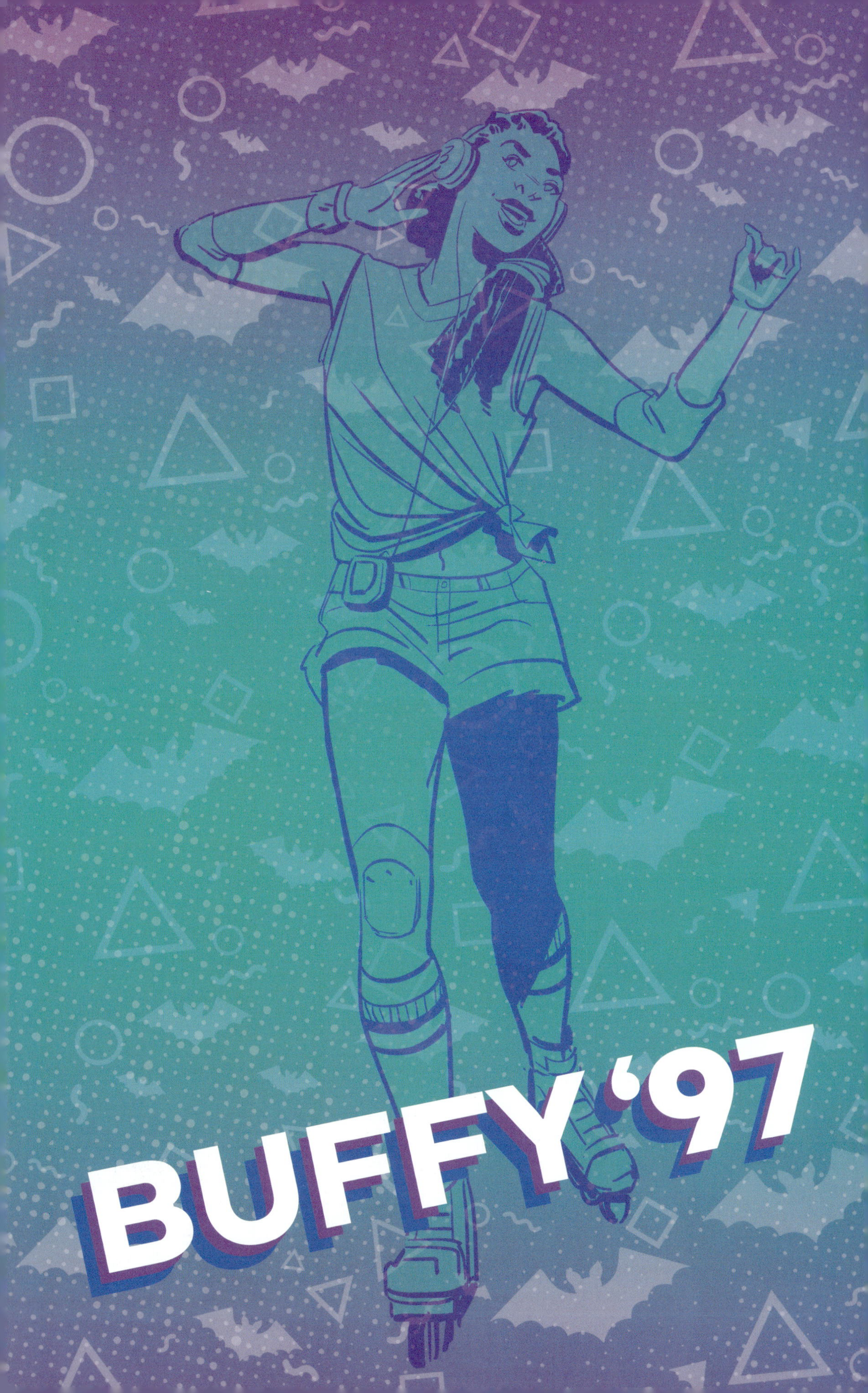
BUFFY '97

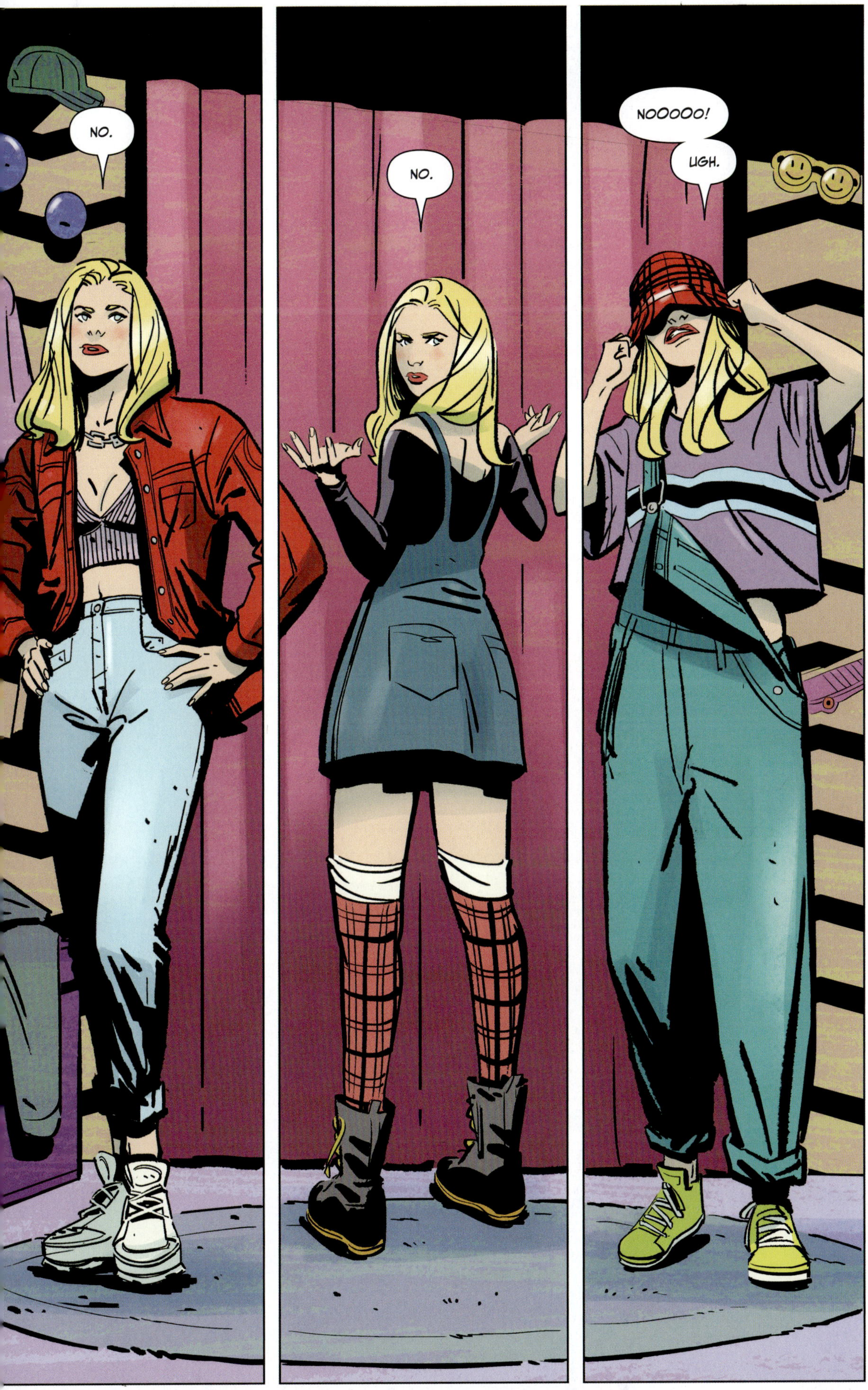
NO.
NO.
NOOOOO!
UGH.

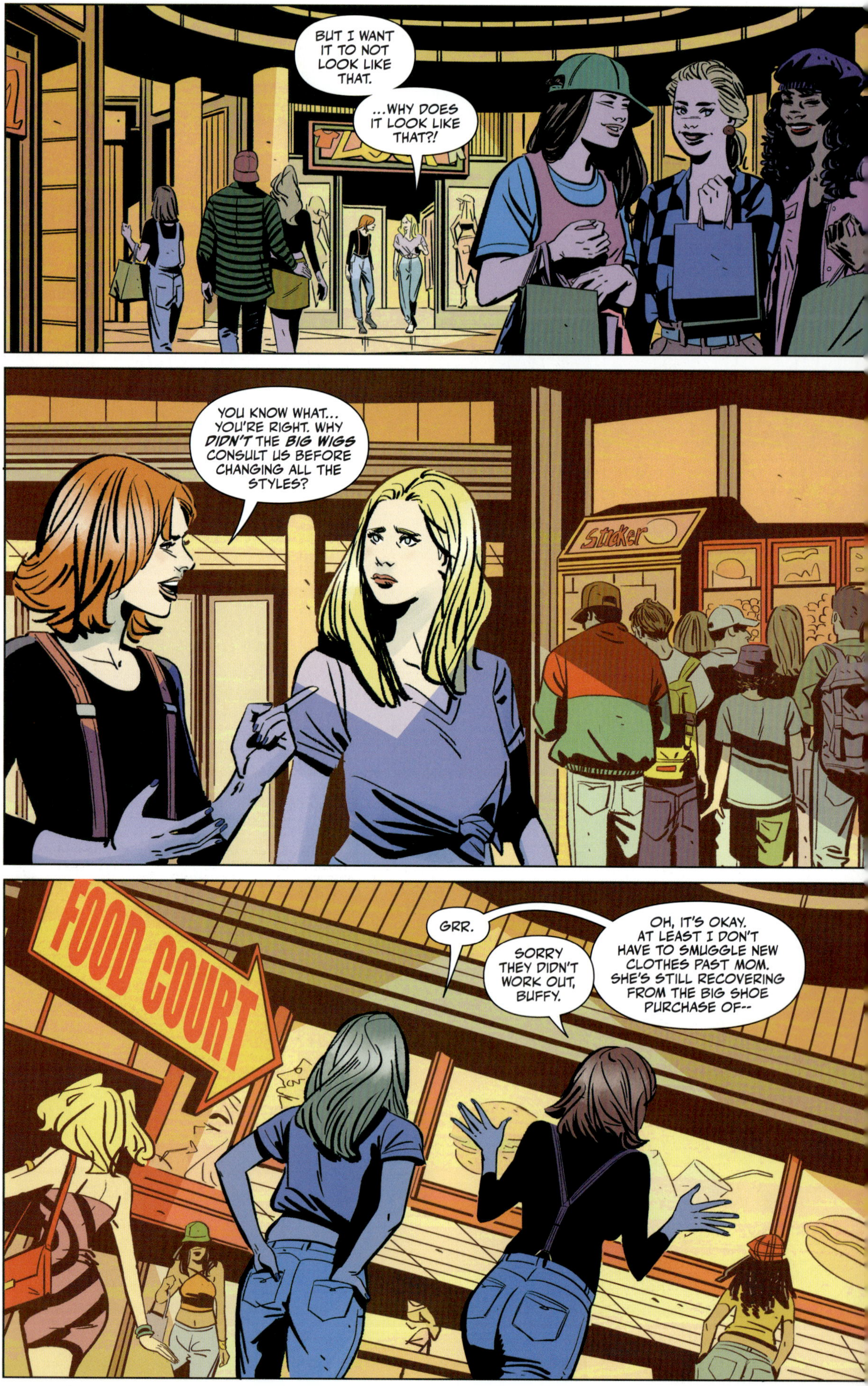
BUT I WANT IT TO NOT LOOK LIKE THAT.
...WHY DOES IT LOOK LIKE THAT?!
YOU KNOW WHAT... YOU'RE RIGHT. WHY DIDN'T THE BIG WIGS CONSULT US BEFORE CHANGING ALL THE STYLES?
Sticker
FOOD COURT
GRR.
SORRY THEY DIDN'T WORK OUT, BUFFY.
OH, IT'S OKAY. AT LEAST I DON'T HAVE TO SMUGGLE NEW CLOTHES PAST MOM. SHE'S STILL RECOVERING FROM THE BIG SHOE PURCHASE OF--

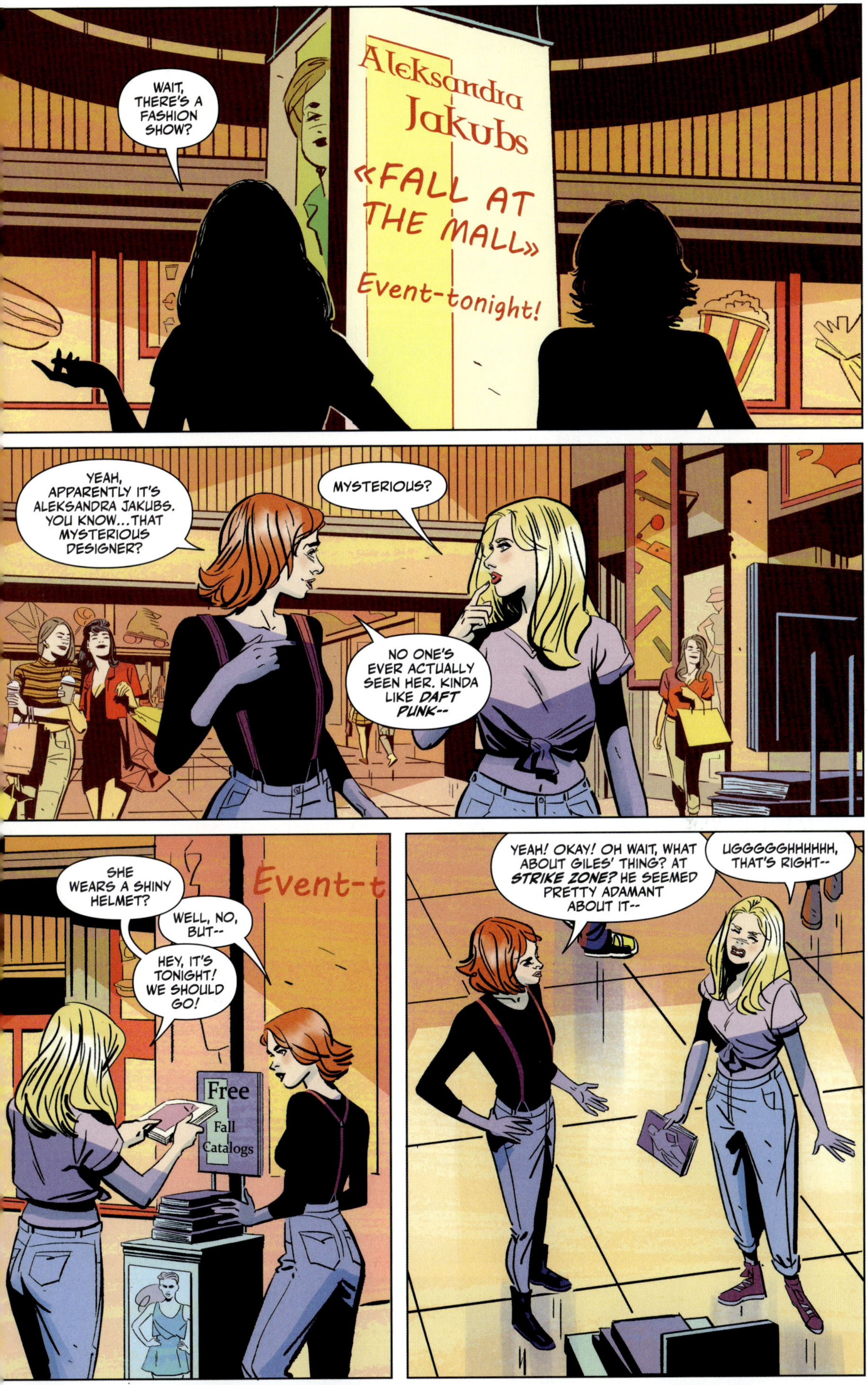
WAIT, THERE'S A FASHION SHOW?
Aleksandra Jakubs
«FALL AT THE MALL»
Event-tonight!
YEAH, APPARENTLY IT'S ALEKSANDRA JAKUBS. YOU KNOW...THAT MYSTERIOUS DESIGNER?
MYSTERIOUS?
NO ONE'S EVER ACTUALLY SEEN HER. KINDA LIKE DAFT PUNK--
SHE WEARS A SHINY HELMET?
WELL, NO, BUT--
Event-t
HEY, IT'S TONIGHT! WE SHOULD GO!
Free Fall Catalogs
YEAH! OKAY! OH WAIT, WHAT ABOUT GILES' THING? AT STRIKE ZONE? HE SEEMED PRETTY ADAMANT ABOUT IT--
UGGGGGHHHHHH, THAT'S RIGHT--

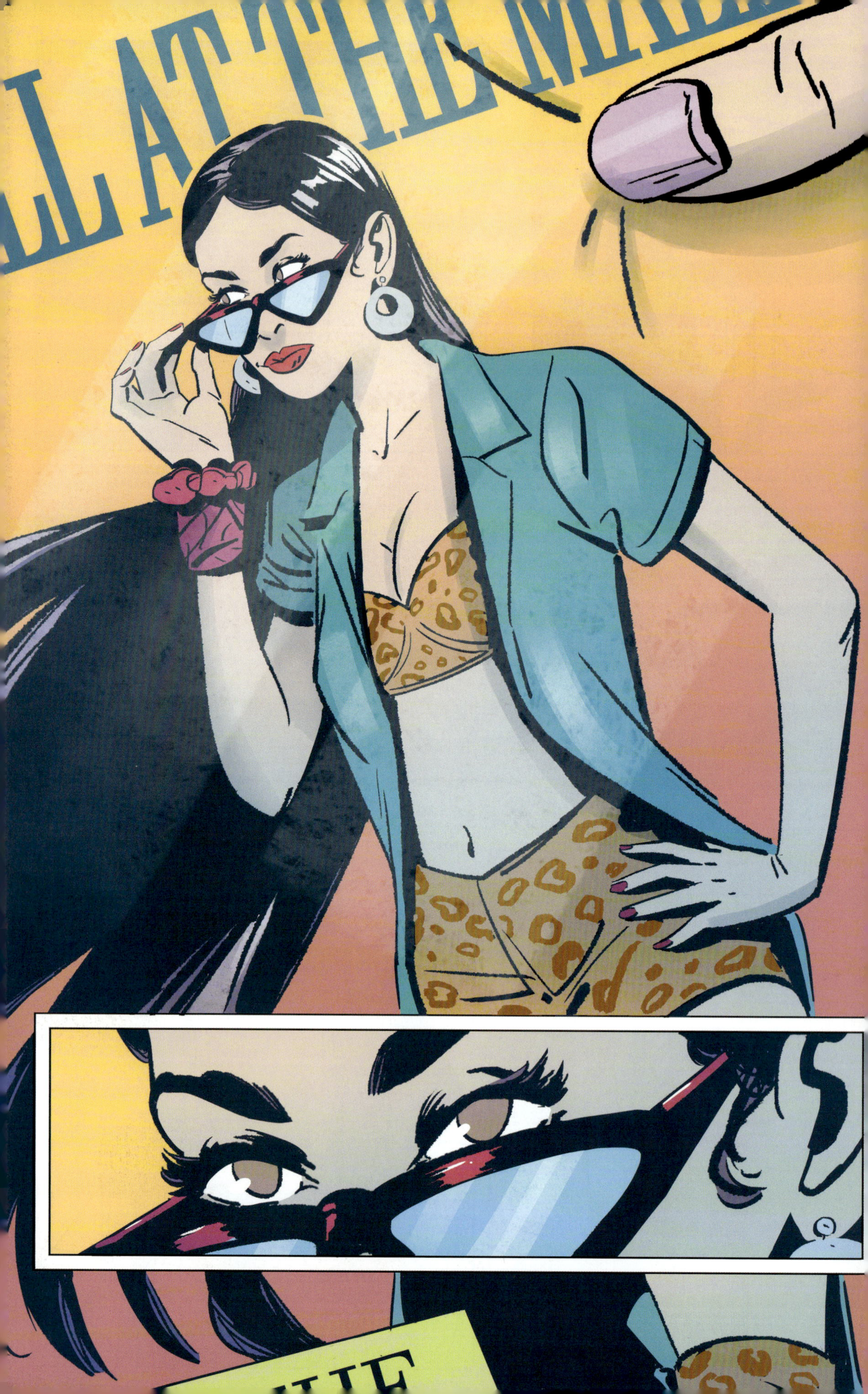

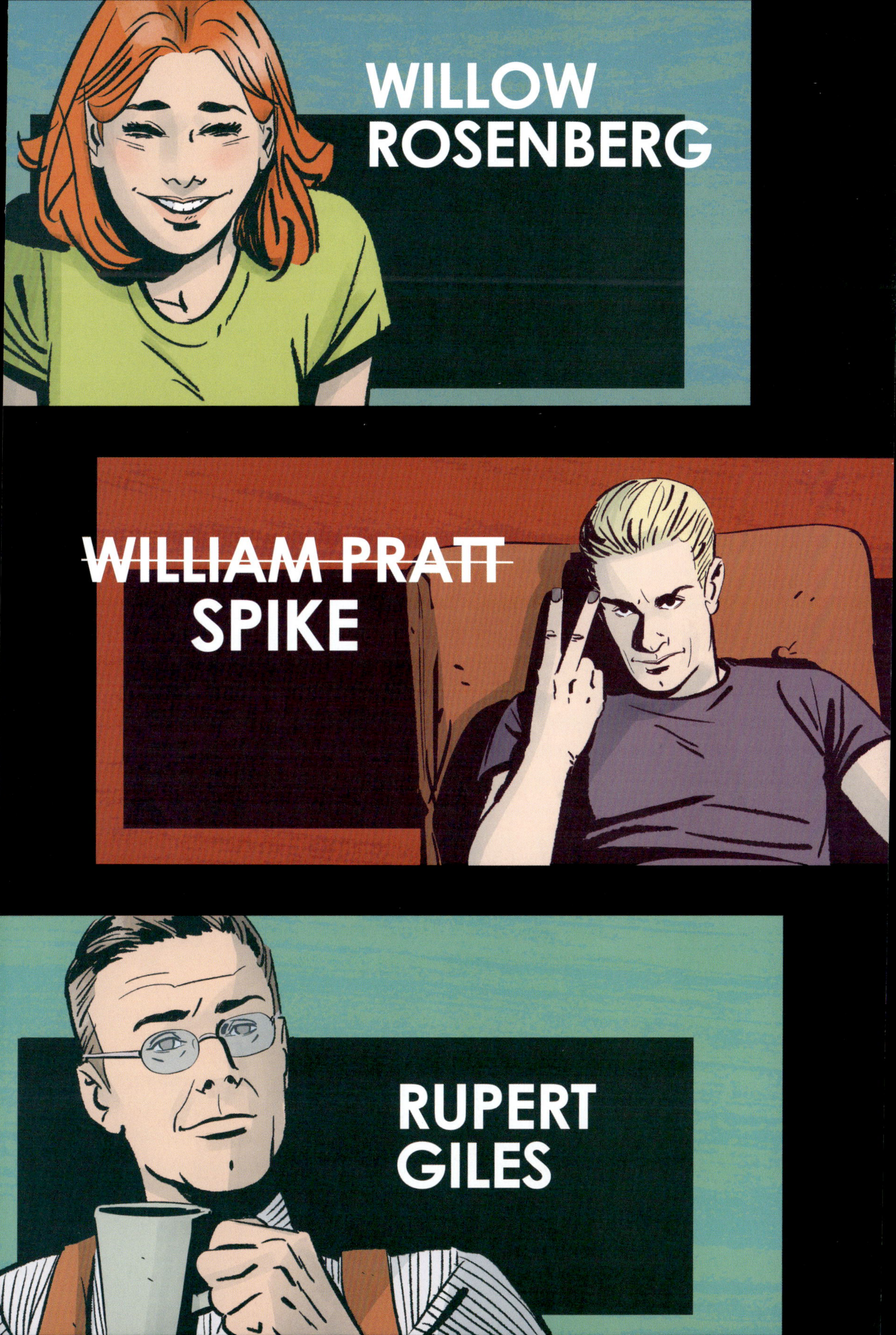
WILLOW ROSENBERG
~~WILLIAM PRATT~~
SPIKE
RUPERT GILES

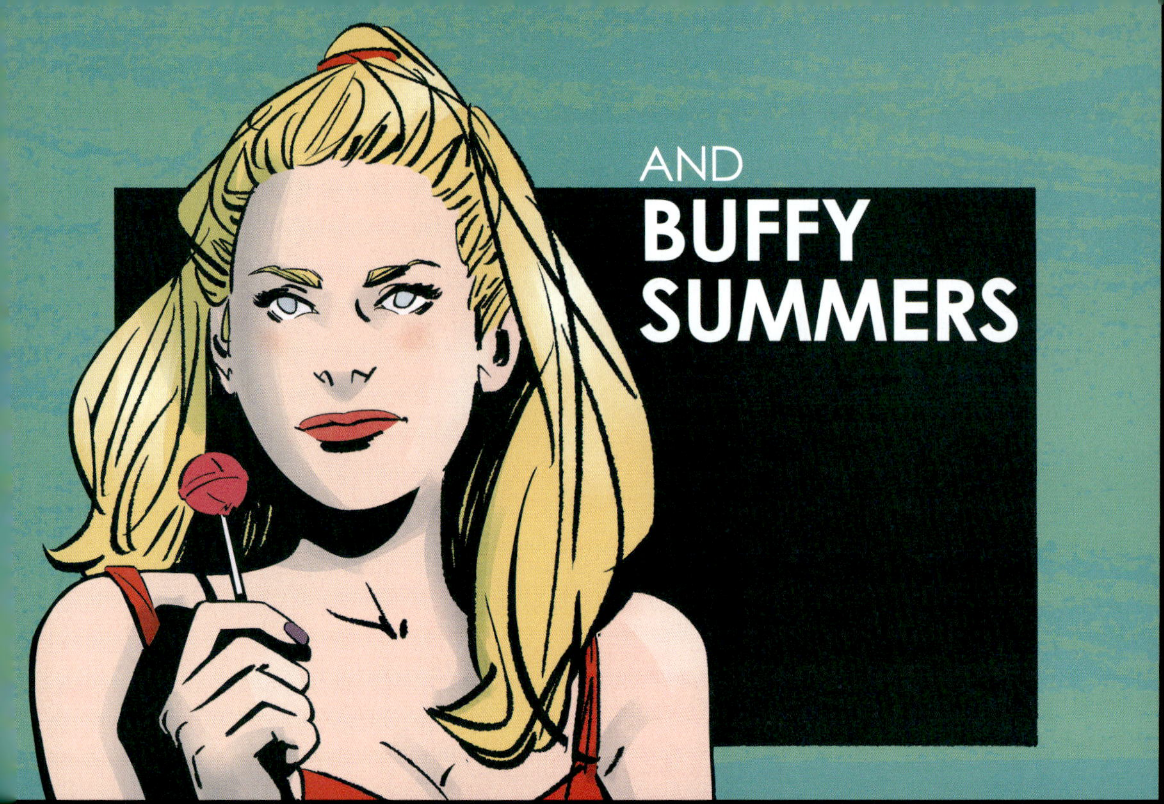
AND
BUFFY SUMMERS

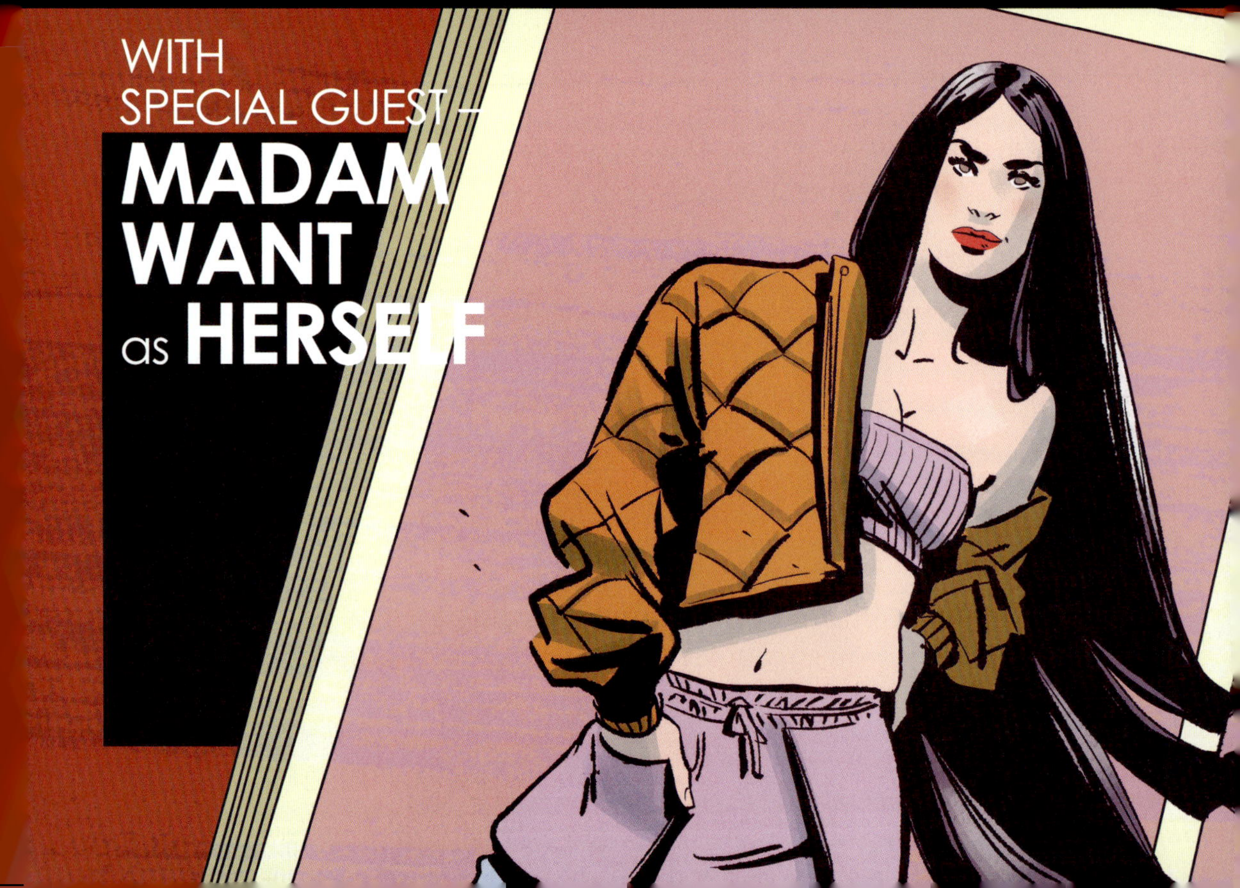
WITH
SPECIAL GUEST –
MADAM WANT
as HERSELF

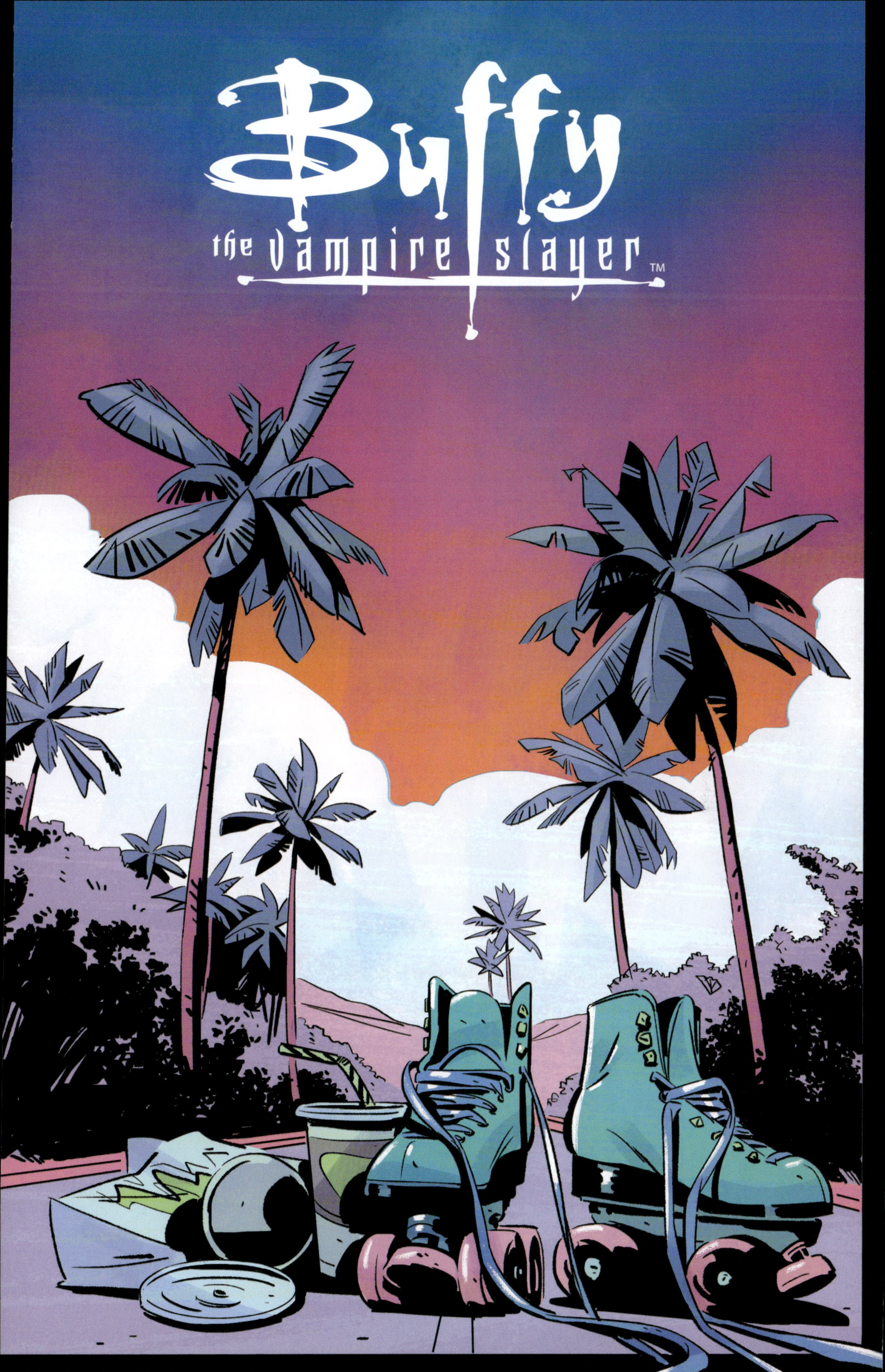
Buffy
the vampire slayer™

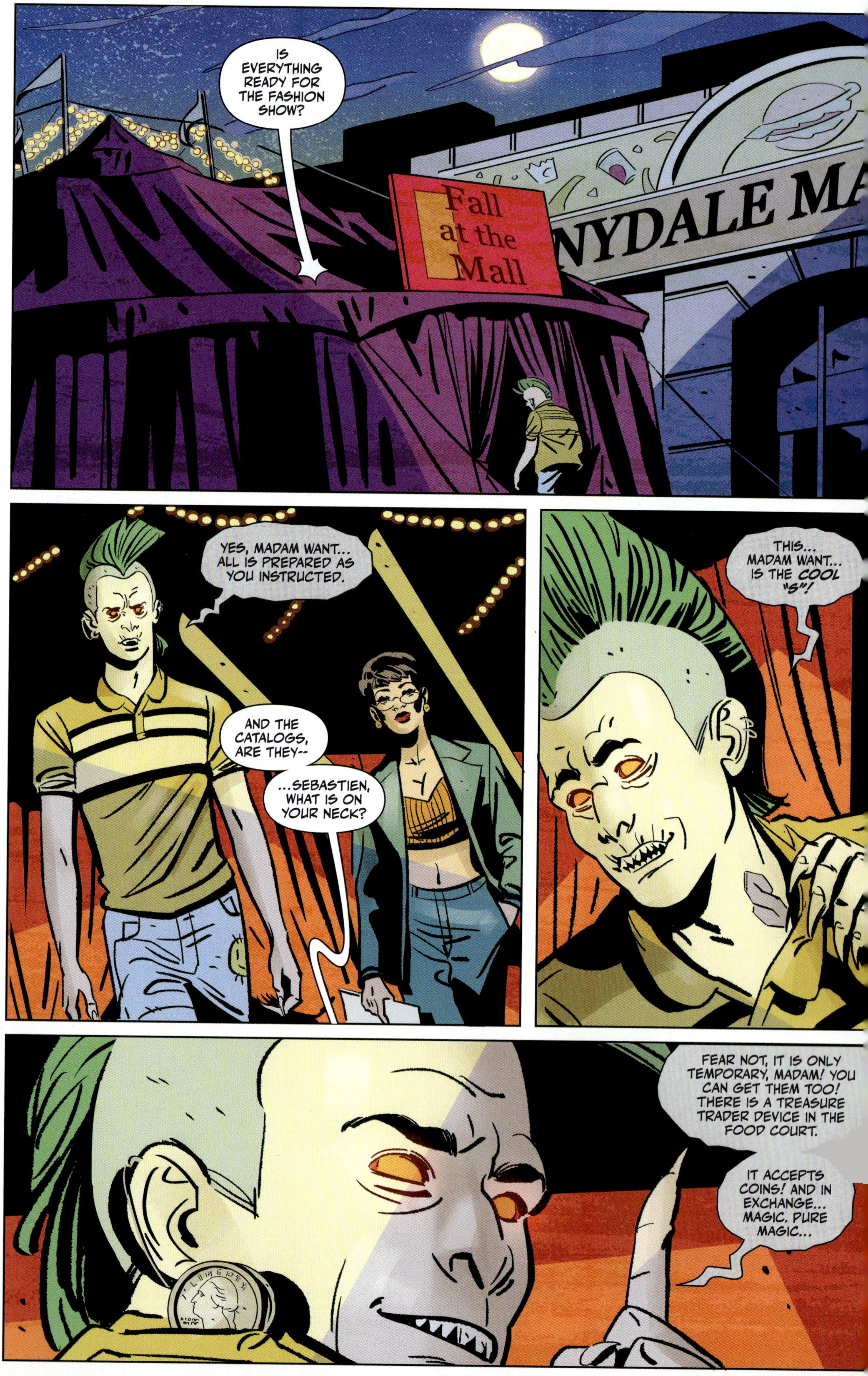
IS EVERYTHING READY FOR THE FASHION SHOW?
Fall at the Mall
NYDALE MA
YES, MADAM WANT... ALL IS PREPARED AS YOU INSTRUCTED.
AND THE CATALOGS, ARE THEY--
...SEBASTIEN, WHAT IS ON YOUR NECK?
THIS... MADAM WANT... IS THE COOL "S"!
FEAR NOT, IT IS ONLY TEMPORARY, MADAM! YOU CAN GET THEM TOO! THERE IS A TREASURE TRADER DEVICE IN THE FOOD COURT.
IT ACCEPTS COINS! AND IN EXCHANGE... MAGIC. PURE MAGIC...

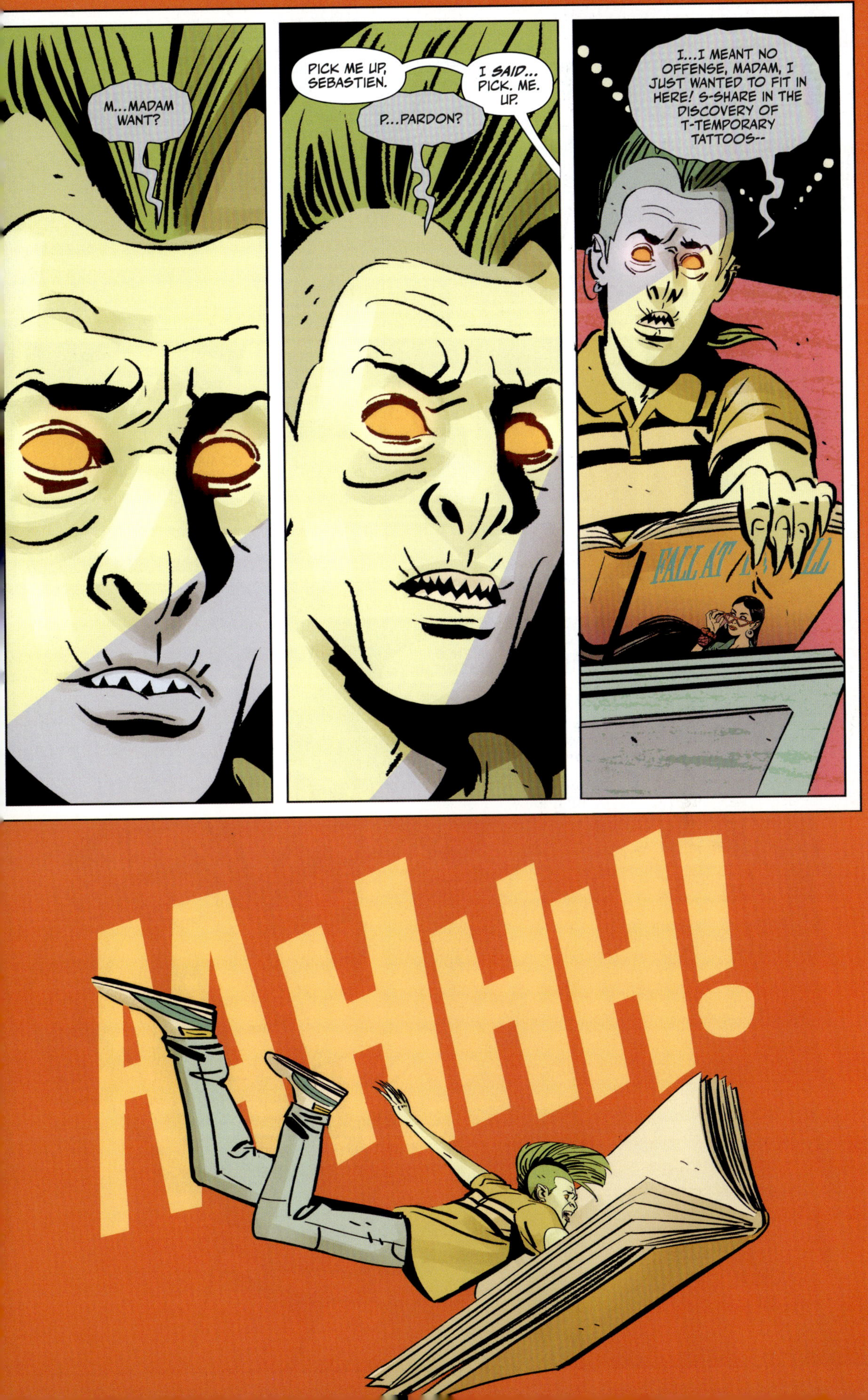
M...MADAM WANT?
PICK ME UP, SEBASTIEN.
P...PARDON?
I SAID... PICK. ME. UP.
I...I MEANT NO OFFENSE, MADAM, I JUST WANTED TO FIT IN HERE! S-SHARE IN THE DISCOVERY OF T-TEMPORARY TATTOOS--
AAHHHH!

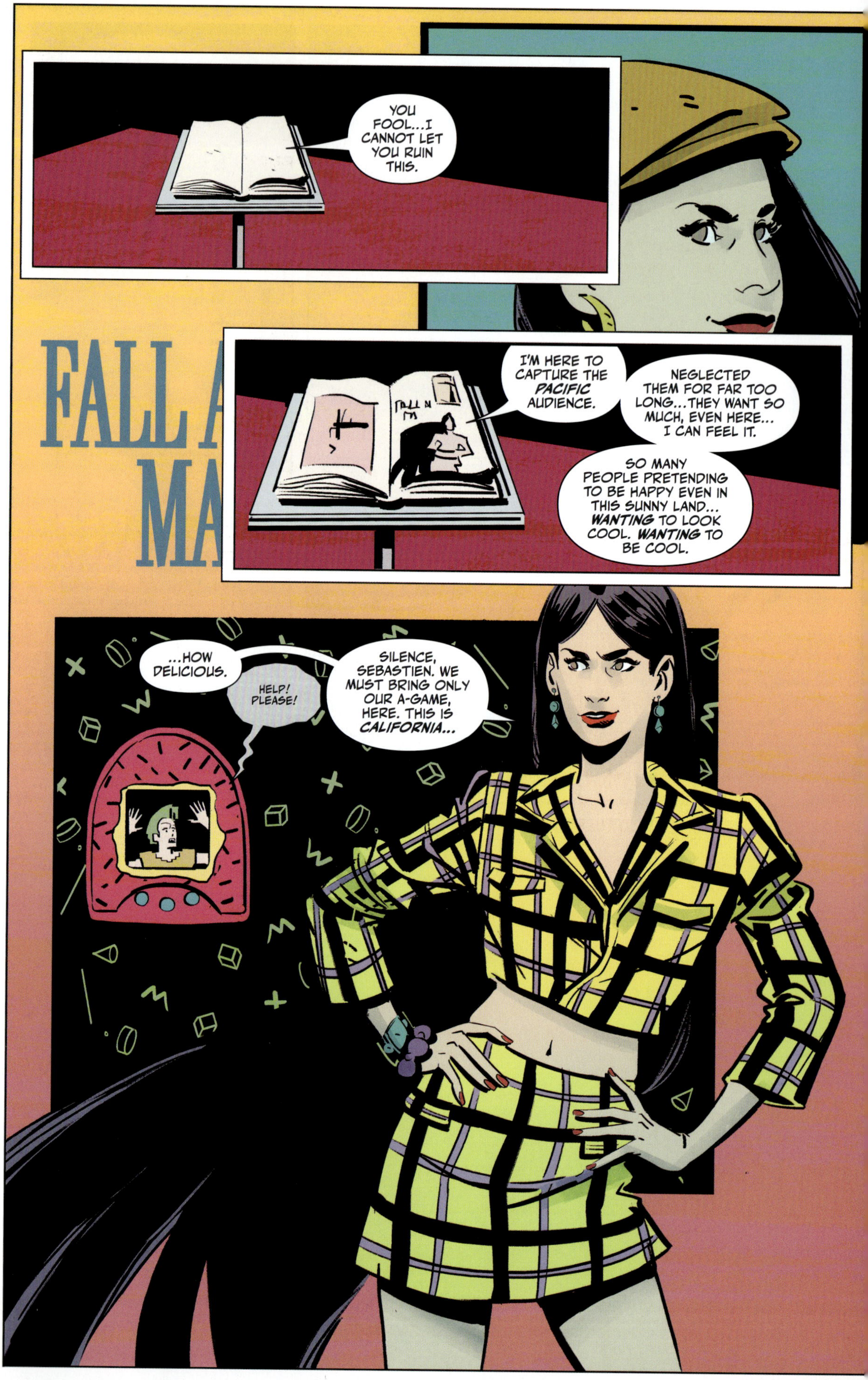
YOU FOOL...I CANNOT LET YOU RUIN THIS.
FALL A
MA
I'M HERE TO CAPTURE THE *PACIFIC* AUDIENCE.
NEGLECTED THEM FOR FAR TOO LONG...THEY WANT SO MUCH, EVEN HERE... I CAN FEEL IT.
SO MANY PEOPLE PRETENDING TO BE HAPPY EVEN IN THIS SUNNY LAND... ***WANTING*** TO LOOK COOL. ***WANTING*** TO BE COOL.
...HOW DELICIOUS.
HELP! PLEASE!
SILENCE, SEBASTIEN. WE MUST BRING ONLY OUR A-GAME, HERE. THIS IS ***CALIFORNIA...***

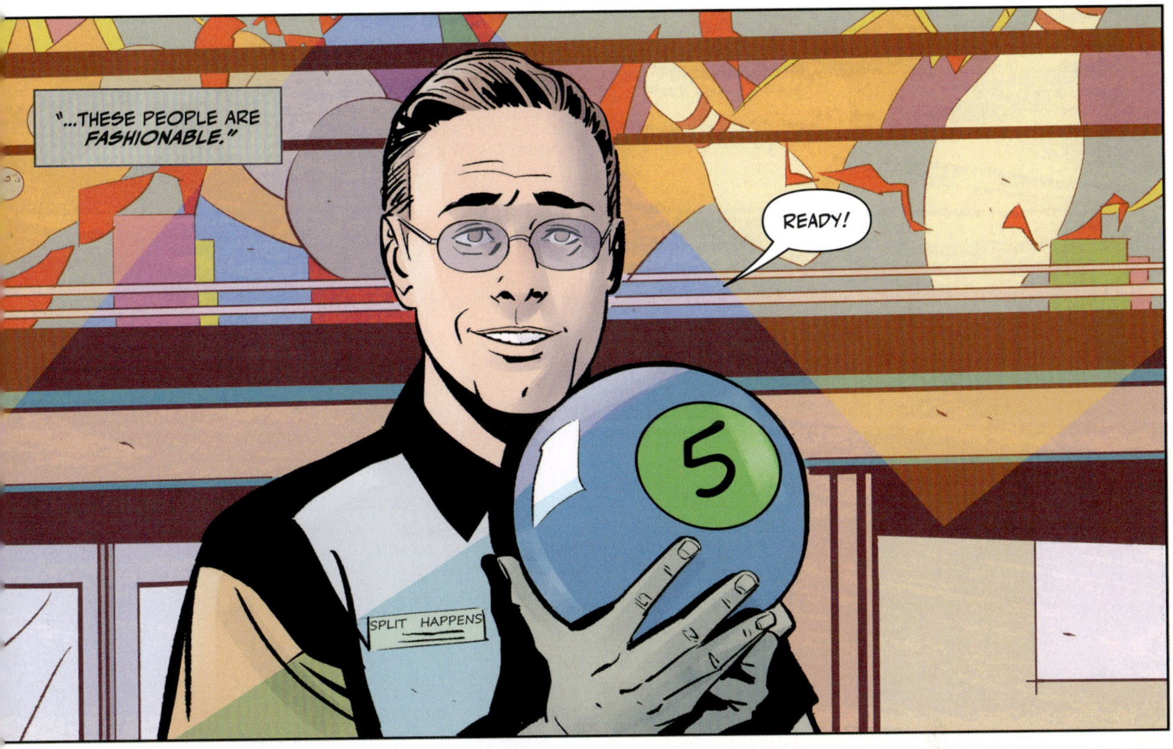
"...THESE PEOPLE ARE *FASHIONABLE.*"
READY!
SPLIT HAPPENS

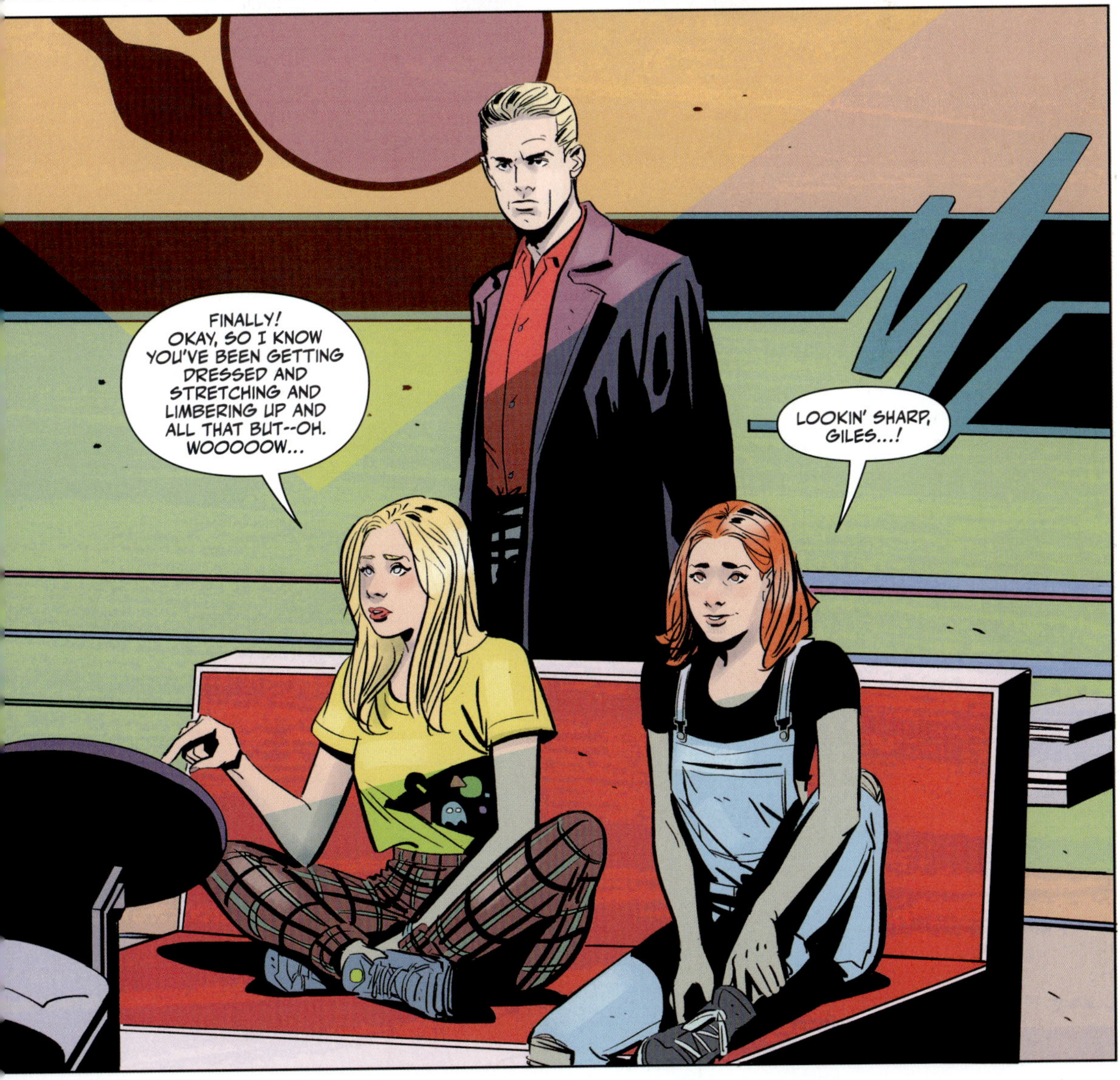
FINALLY! OKAY, SO I KNOW YOU'VE BEEN GETTING DRESSED AND STRETCHING AND LIMBERING UP AND ALL THAT BUT--OH. WOOOOOW...
LOOKIN' SHARP, GILES...!

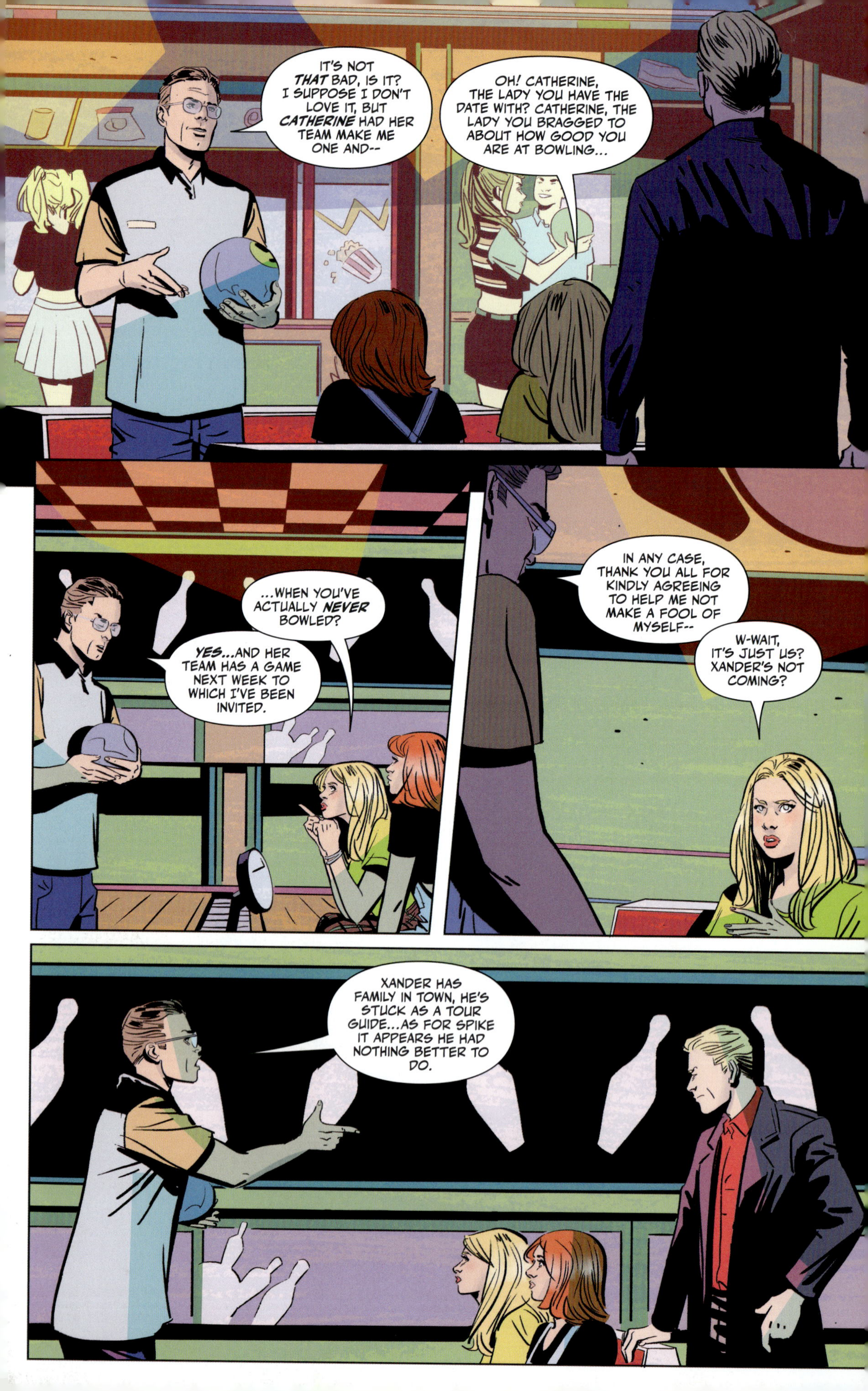
IT'S NOT THAT BAD, IS IT? I SUPPOSE I DON'T LOVE IT, BUT CATHERINE HAD HER TEAM MAKE ME ONE AND--
OH! CATHERINE, THE LADY YOU HAVE THE DATE WITH? CATHERINE, THE LADY YOU BRAGGED TO ABOUT HOW GOOD YOU ARE AT BOWLING...
...WHEN YOU'VE ACTUALLY NEVER BOWLED?
YES...AND HER TEAM HAS A GAME NEXT WEEK TO WHICH I'VE BEEN INVITED.
IN ANY CASE, THANK YOU ALL FOR KINDLY AGREEING TO HELP ME NOT MAKE A FOOL OF MYSELF--
W-WAIT, IT'S JUST US? XANDER'S NOT COMING?
XANDER HAS FAMILY IN TOWN, HE'S STUCK AS A TOUR GUIDE...AS FOR SPIKE IT APPEARS HE HAD NOTHING BETTER TO DO.

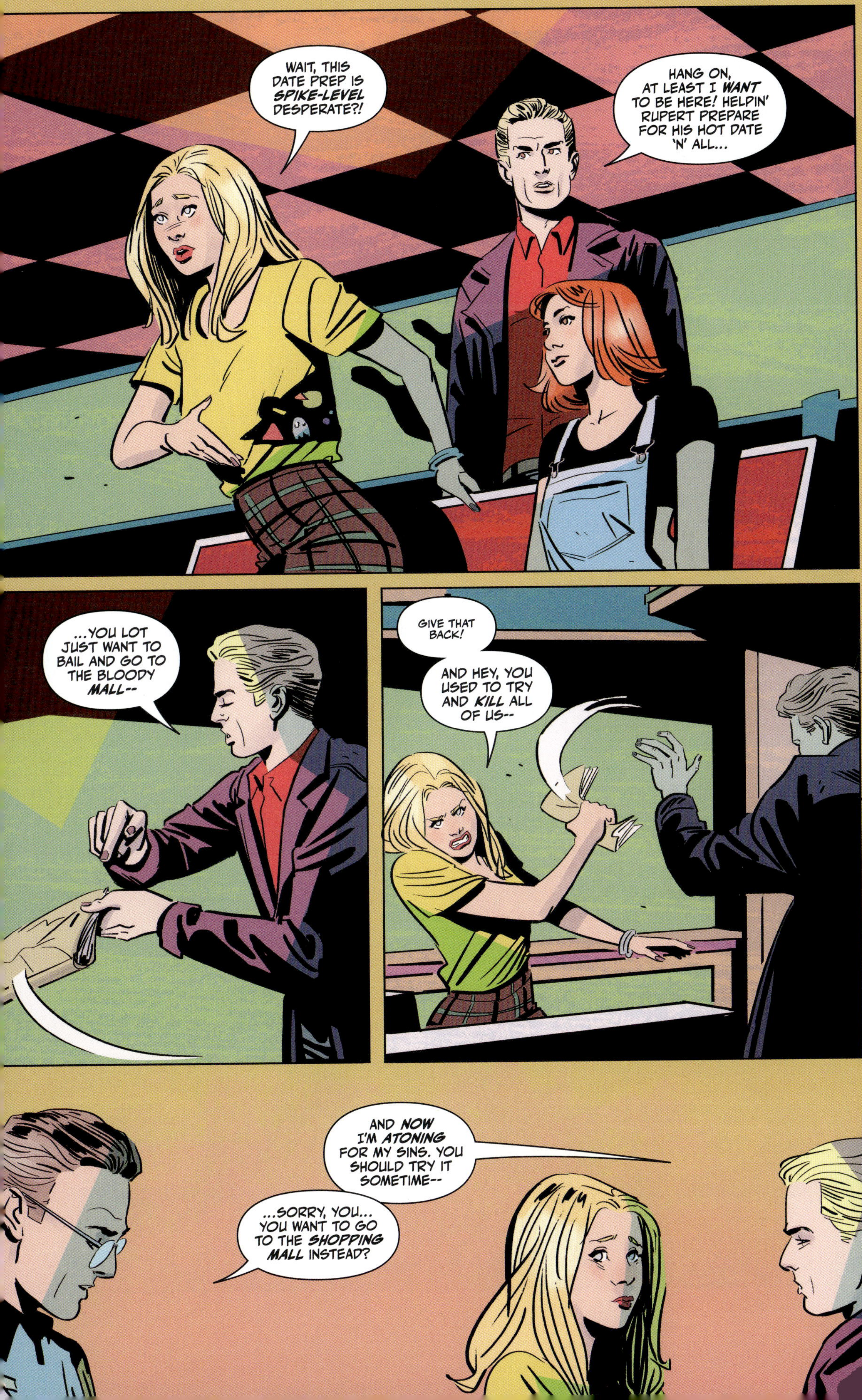
WAIT, THIS DATE PREP IS SPIKE-LEVEL DESPERATE?!
HANG ON, AT LEAST I WANT TO BE HERE! HELPIN' RUPERT PREPARE FOR HIS HOT DATE 'N' ALL...
...YOU LOT JUST WANT TO BAIL AND GO TO THE BLOODY MALL--
GIVE THAT BACK!
AND HEY, YOU USED TO TRY AND KILL ALL OF US--
AND NOW I'M ATONING FOR MY SINS. YOU SHOULD TRY IT SOMETIME--
...SORRY, YOU... YOU WANT TO GO TO THE SHOPPING MALL INSTEAD?

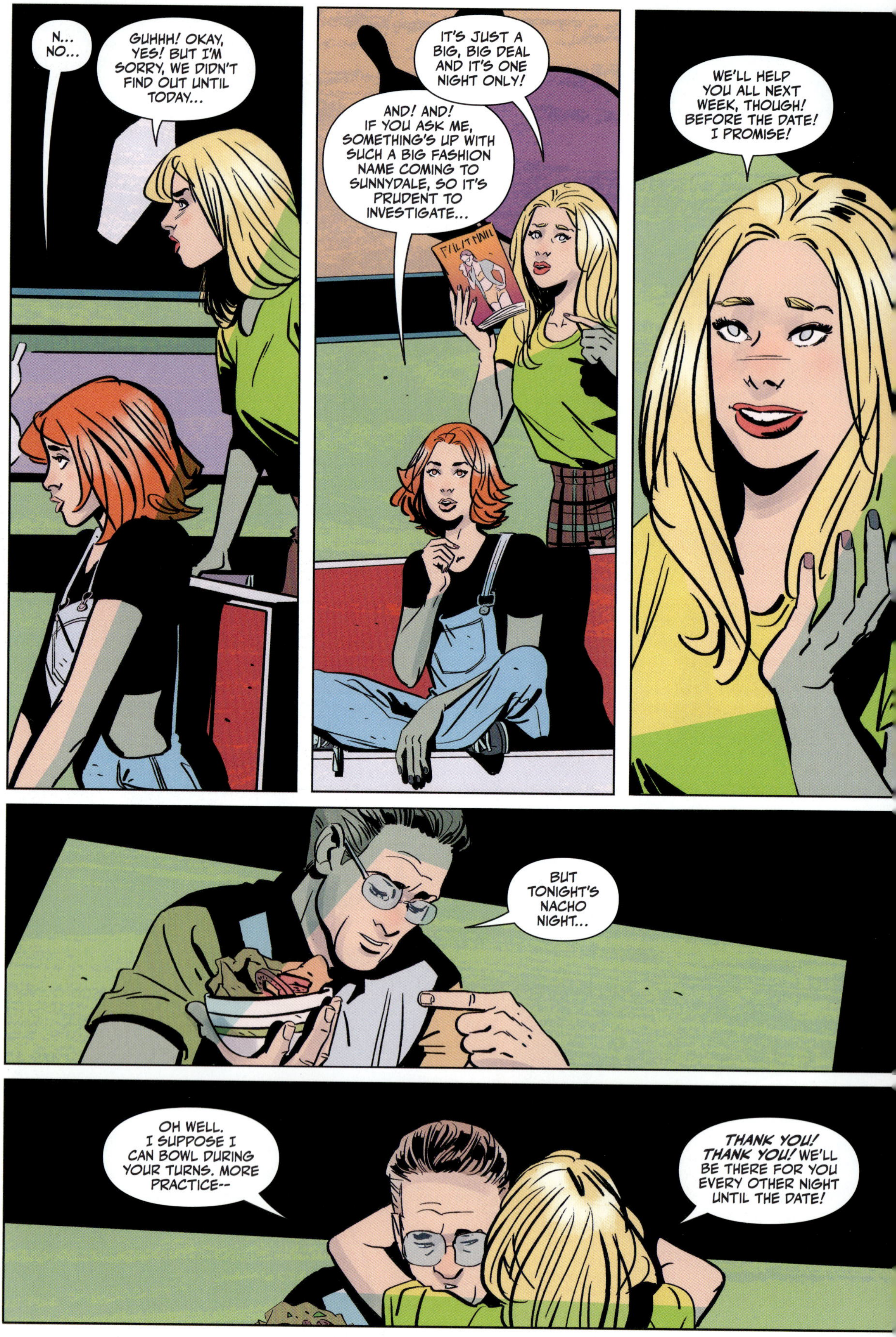
N... NO...
GUHHH! OKAY, YES! BUT I'M SORRY, WE DIDN'T FIND OUT UNTIL TODAY...
IT'S JUST A BIG, BIG DEAL AND IT'S ONE NIGHT ONLY!
AND! AND! IF YOU ASK ME, SOMETHING'S UP WITH SUCH A BIG FASHION NAME COMING TO SUNNYDALE, SO IT'S PRUDENT TO INVESTIGATE...
WE'LL HELP YOU ALL NEXT WEEK, THOUGH! BEFORE THE DATE! I PROMISE!
BUT TONIGHT'S NACHO NIGHT...
OH WELL. I SUPPOSE I CAN BOWL DURING YOUR TURNS. MORE PRACTICE--
THANK YOU! THANK YOU! WE'LL BE THERE FOR YOU EVERY OTHER NIGHT UNTIL THE DATE!

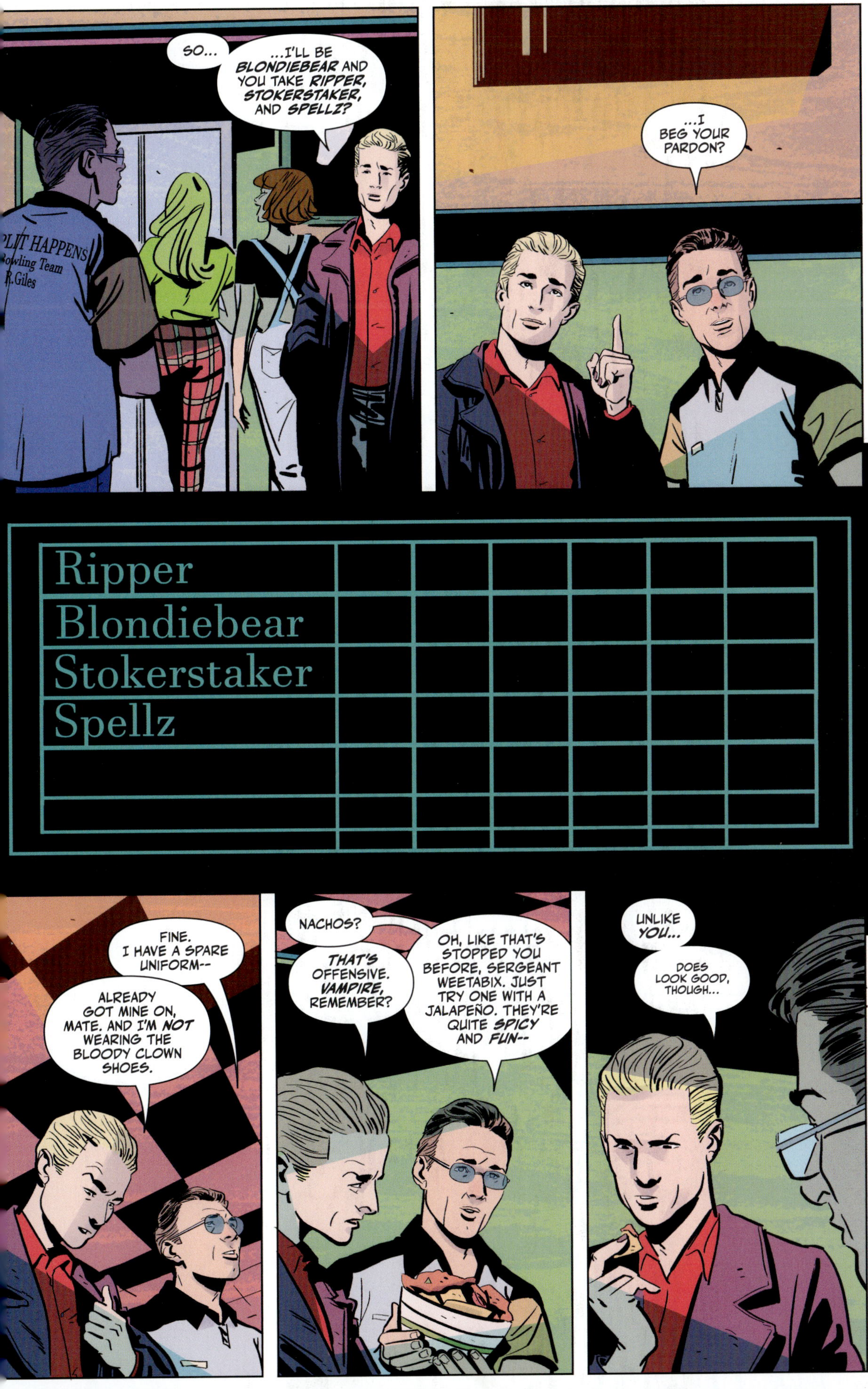
SO...
...I'LL BE BLONDIEBEAR AND YOU TAKE RIPPER, STOKERSTAKER, AND SPELLZ?
SPLIT HAPPENS Bowling Team R.Giles
...I BEG YOUR PARDON?
Ripper
Blondiebear
Stokerstaker
Spellz
FINE. I HAVE A SPARE UNIFORM--
ALREADY GOT MINE ON, MATE. AND I'M NOT WEARING THE BLOODY CLOWN SHOES.
NACHOS?
THAT'S OFFENSIVE. VAMPIRE, REMEMBER?
OH, LIKE THAT'S STOPPED YOU BEFORE, SERGEANT WEETABIX. JUST TRY ONE WITH A JALAPEÑO. THEY'RE QUITE SPICY AND FUN--
UNLIKE YOU...
DOES LOOK GOOD, THOUGH...

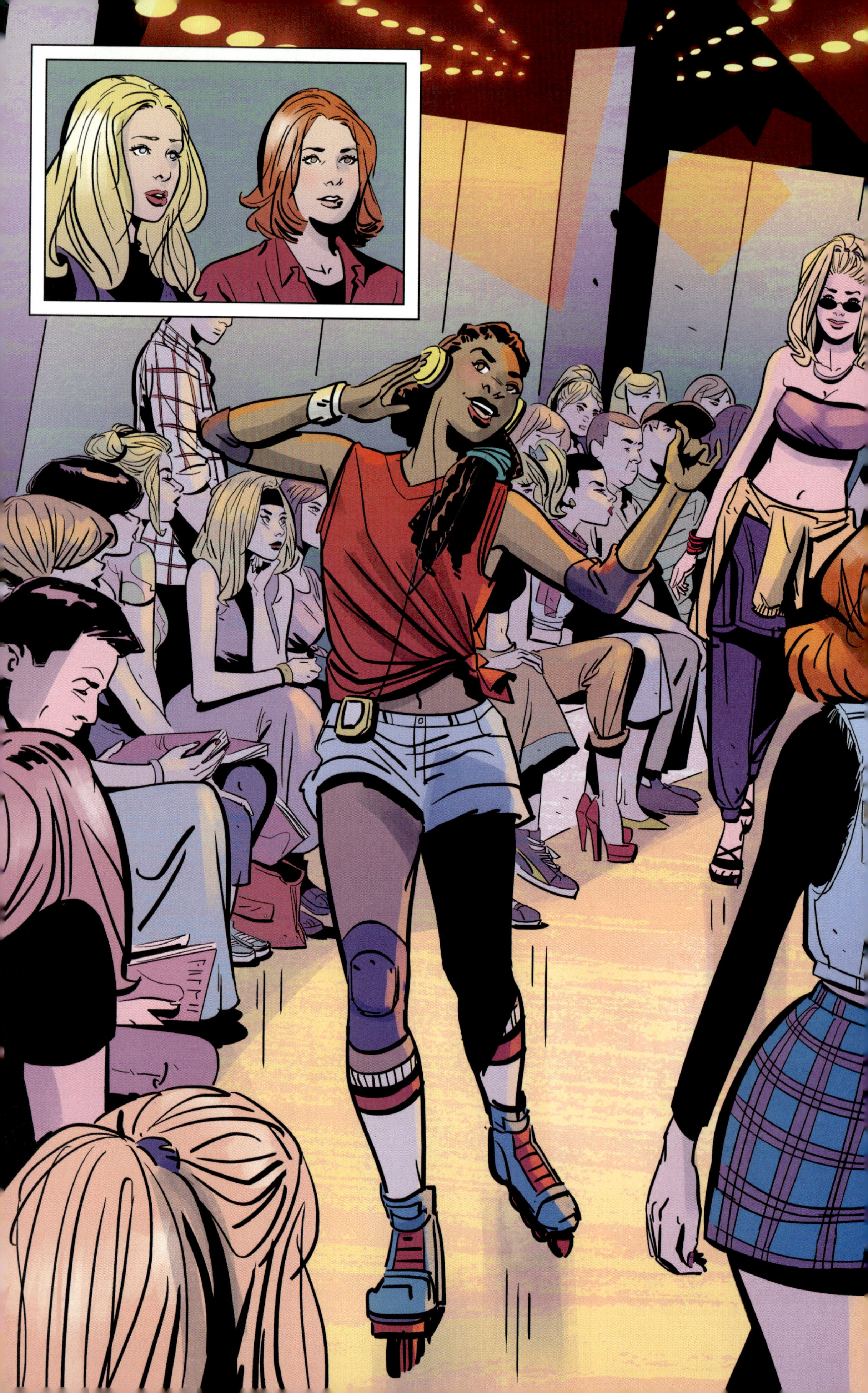

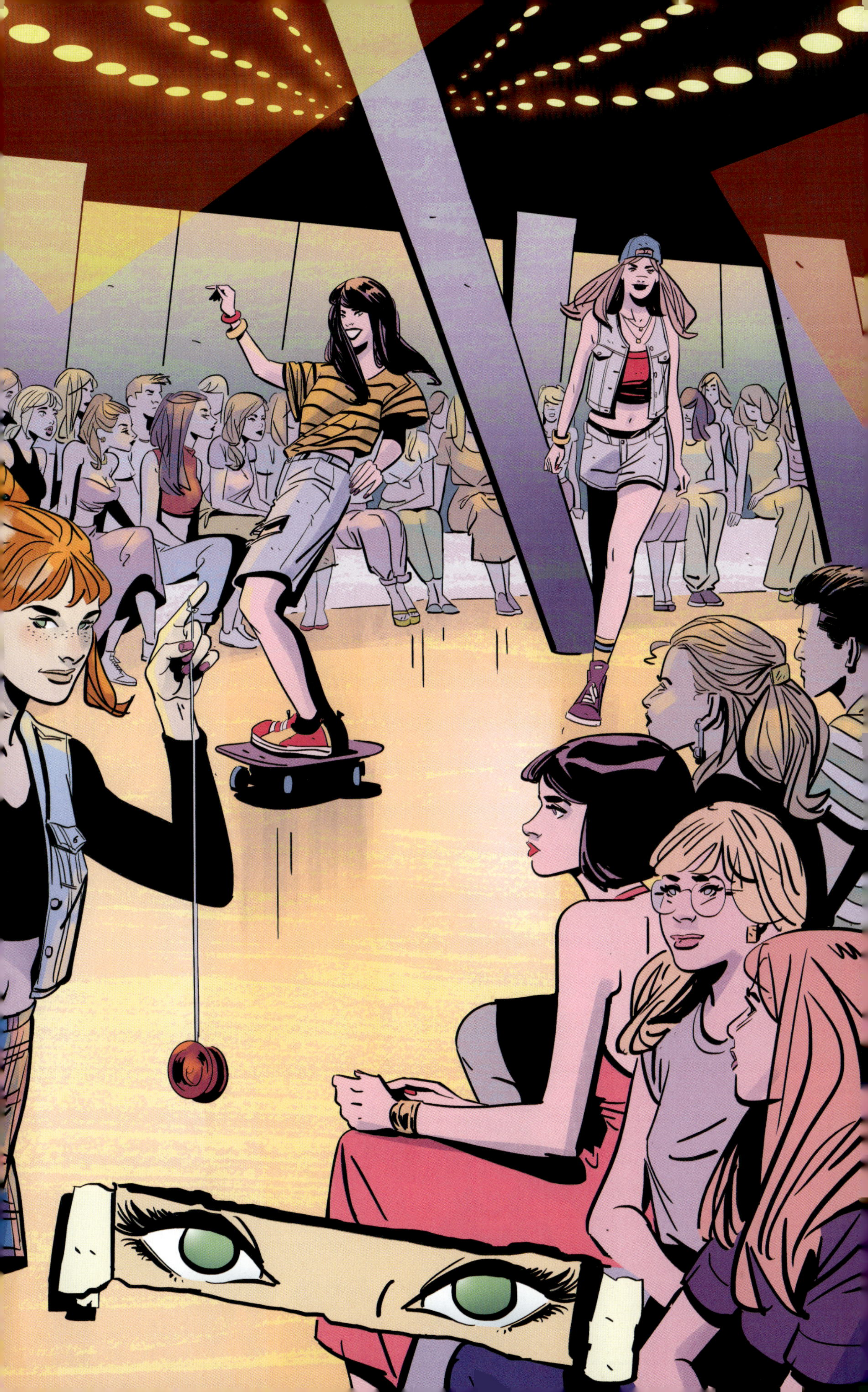

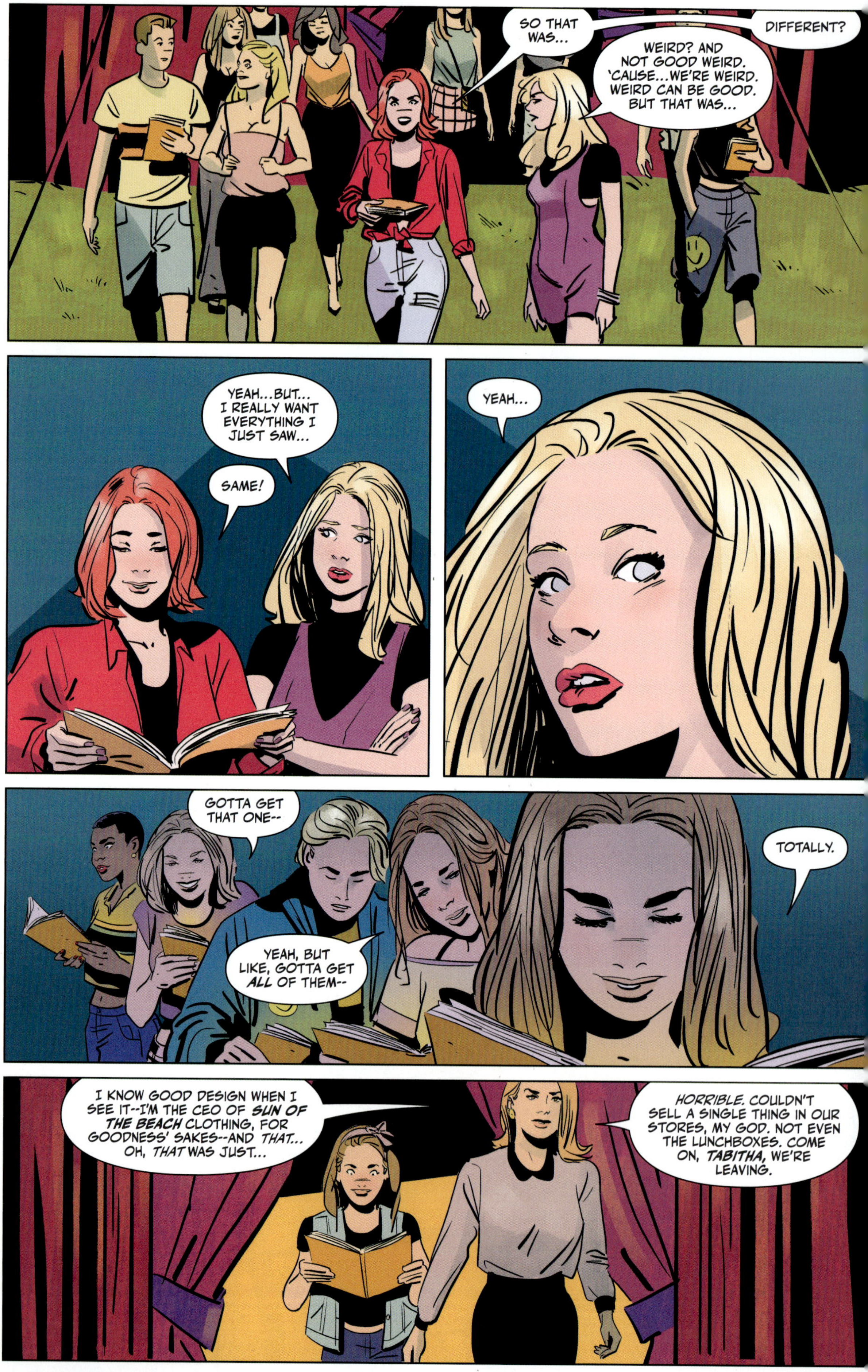
SO THAT WAS...
DIFFERENT?
WEIRD? AND NOT GOOD WEIRD. 'CAUSE...WE'RE WEIRD. WEIRD CAN BE GOOD. BUT THAT WAS...
YEAH...BUT... I REALLY WANT EVERYTHING I JUST SAW...
SAME!
YEAH...
GOTTA GET THAT ONE--
YEAH, BUT LIKE, GOTTA GET *ALL* OF THEM--
TOTALLY.
I KNOW GOOD DESIGN WHEN I SEE IT--I'M THE CEO OF ***SUN OF THE BEACH*** CLOTHING, FOR GOODNESS' SAKES--AND *THAT*... OH, *THAT* WAS JUST...
HORRIBLE. COULDN'T SELL A SINGLE THING IN OUR STORES, MY GOD. NOT EVEN THE LUNCHBOXES. COME ON, ***TABITHA,*** WE'RE LEAVING.

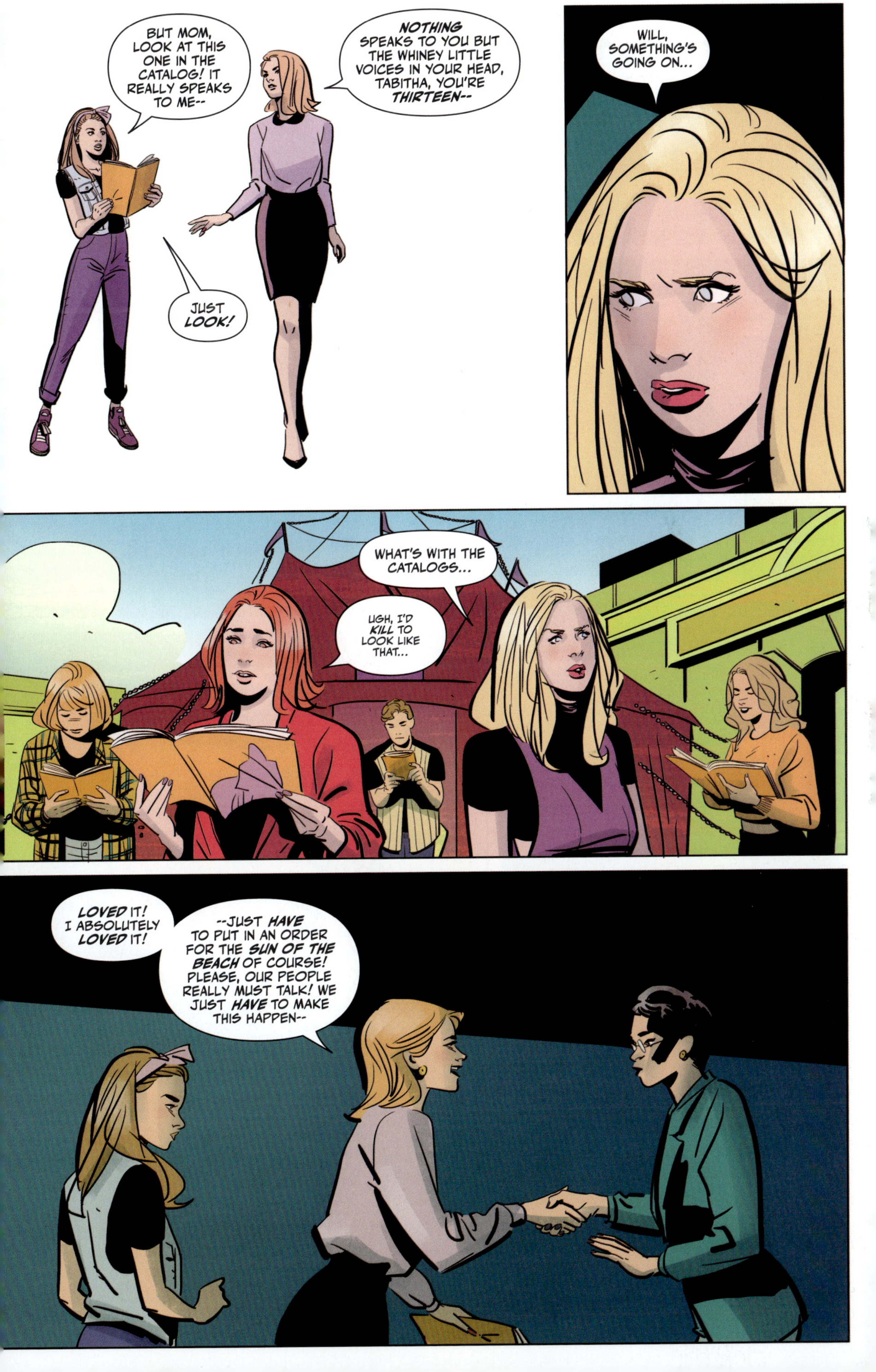
BUT MOM, LOOK AT THIS ONE IN THE CATALOG! IT REALLY SPEAKS TO ME--
NOTHING SPEAKS TO YOU BUT THE WHINEY LITTLE VOICES IN YOUR HEAD, TABITHA, YOU'RE *THIRTEEN--*
JUST *LOOK!*
WILL, SOMETHING'S GOING ON...
WHAT'S WITH THE CATALOGS...
UGH, I'D *KILL* TO LOOK LIKE THAT...
LOVED IT! I ABSOLUTELY *LOVED* IT!
--JUST *HAVE* TO PUT IN AN ORDER FOR THE *SUN OF THE BEACH* OF COURSE! PLEASE, OUR PEOPLE REALLY MUST TALK! WE JUST *HAVE* TO MAKE THIS HAPPEN--

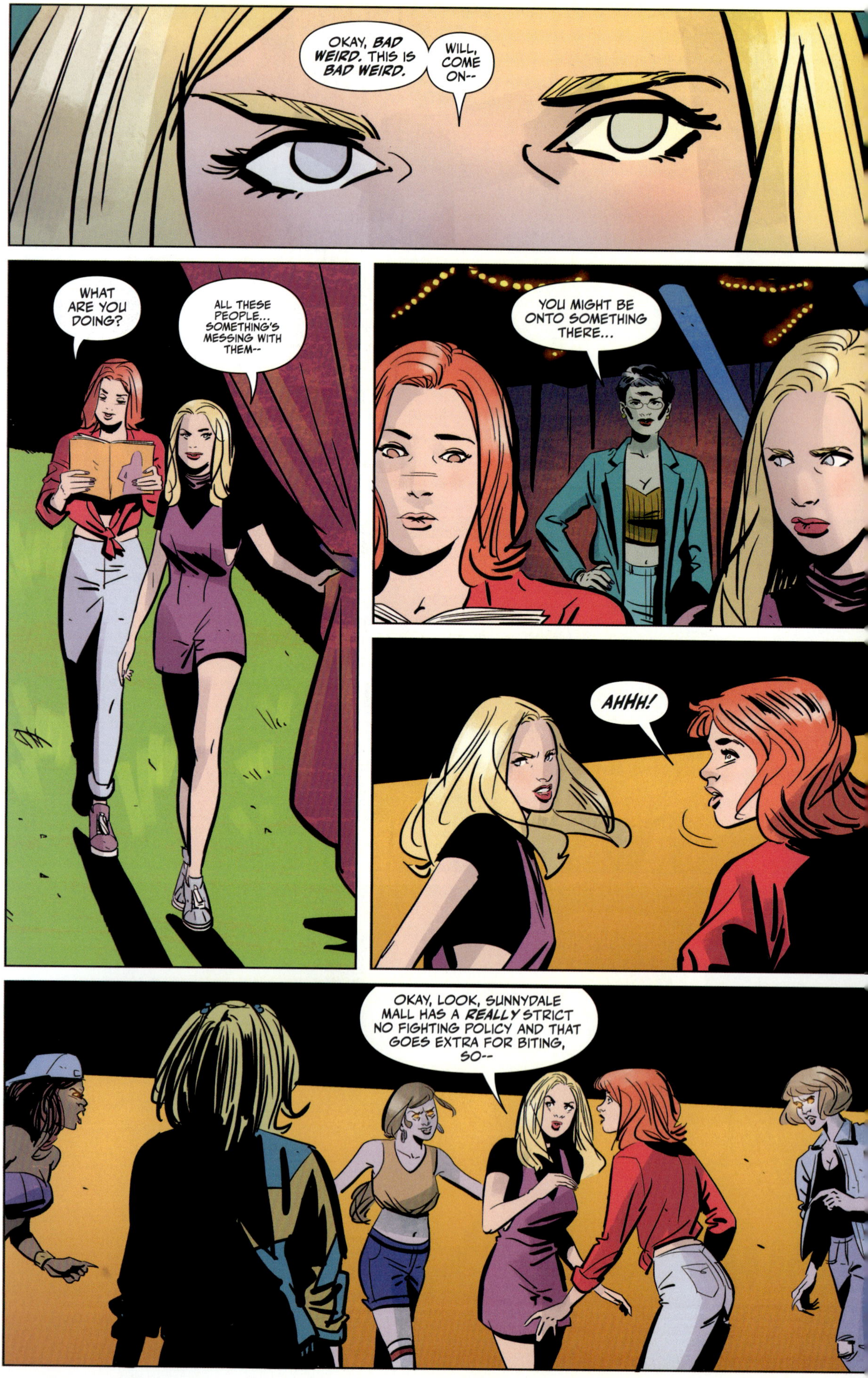
OKAY, *BAD WEIRD.* THIS IS *BAD WEIRD.*
WILL, COME ON--
WHAT ARE YOU DOING?
ALL THESE PEOPLE... SOMETHING'S MESSING WITH THEM--
YOU MIGHT BE ONTO SOMETHING THERE...
AHHH!
OKAY, LOOK, SUNNYDALE MALL HAS A *REALLY* STRICT NO FIGHTING POLICY AND THAT GOES EXTRA FOR BITING, SO--

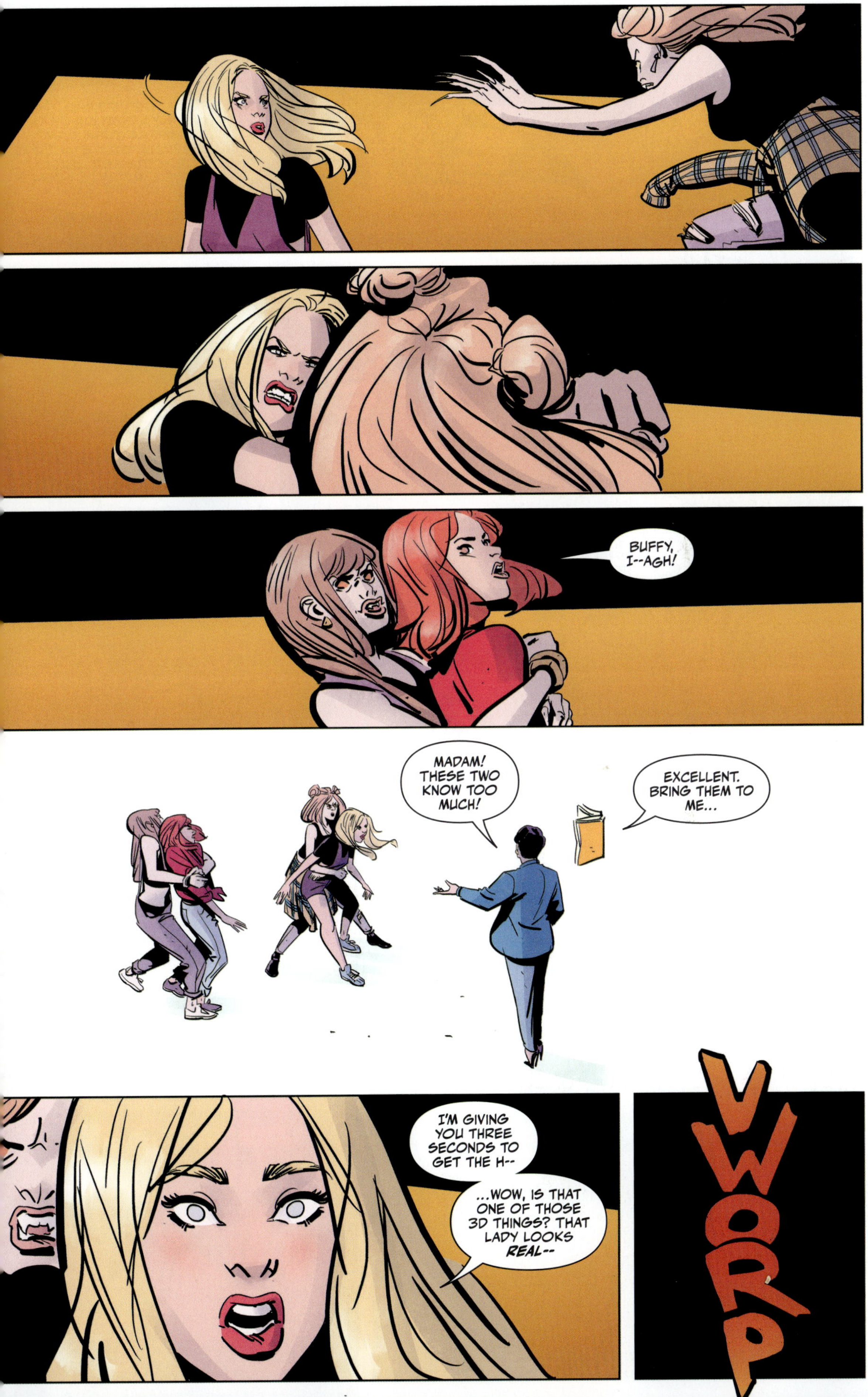
BUFFY, I--AGH!
MADAM! THESE TWO KNOW TOO MUCH!
EXCELLENT. BRING THEM TO ME...
I'M GIVING YOU THREE SECONDS TO GET THE H--
...WOW, IS THAT ONE OF THOSE 3D THINGS? THAT LADY LOOKS *REAL*--
VWORP

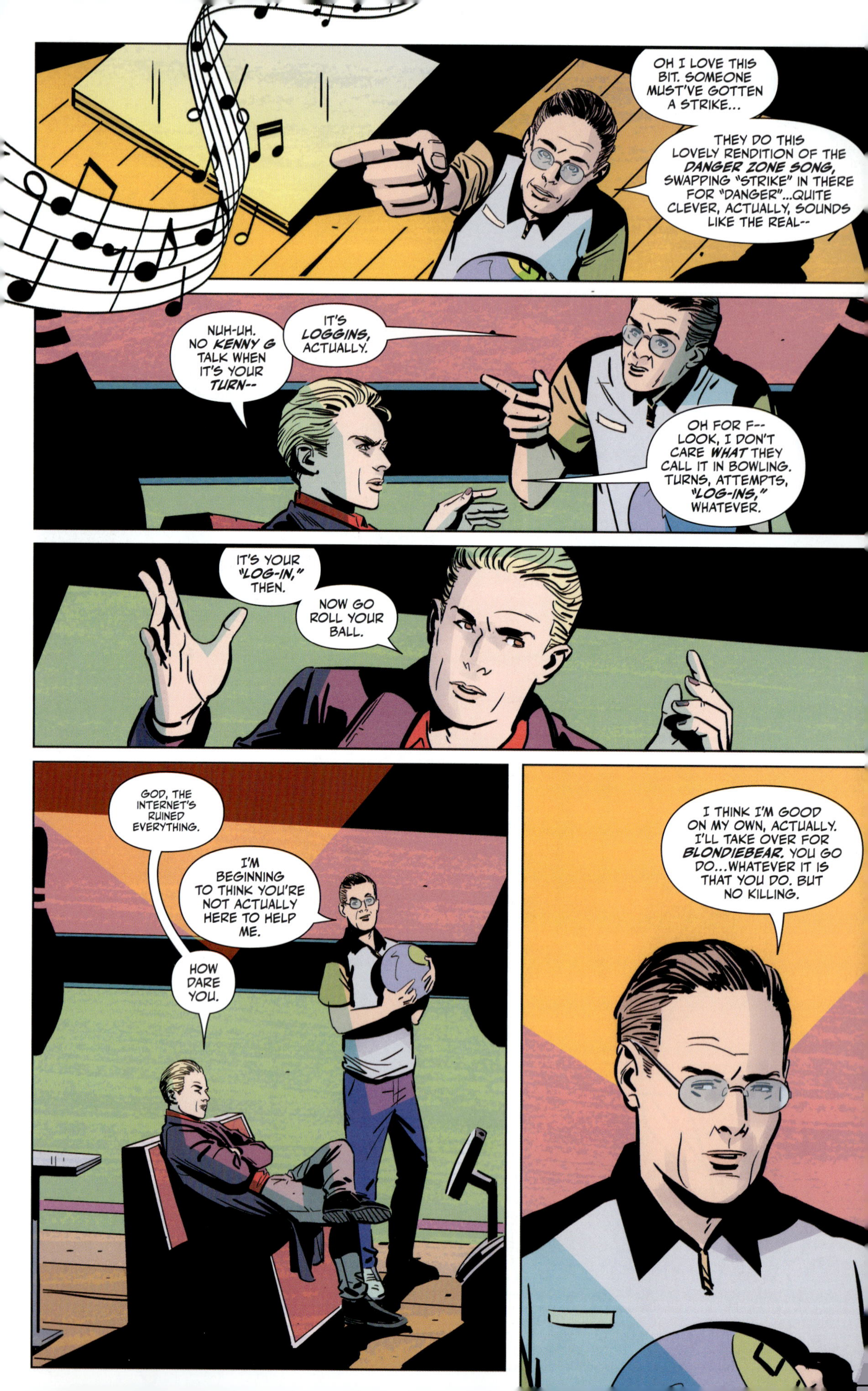
OH I LOVE THIS BIT. SOMEONE MUST'VE GOTTEN A STRIKE...
THEY DO THIS LOVELY RENDITION OF THE *DANGER ZONE SONG,* SWAPPING "STRIKE" IN THERE FOR "DANGER"...QUITE CLEVER, ACTUALLY, SOUNDS LIKE THE REAL--
NUH-UH. NO *KENNY G* TALK WHEN IT'S YOUR *TURN--*
IT'S *LOGGINS,* ACTUALLY.
OH FOR F-- LOOK, I DON'T CARE *WHAT* THEY CALL IT IN BOWLING. TURNS, ATTEMPTS, *"LOG-INS,"* WHATEVER.
IT'S YOUR *"LOG-IN,"* THEN.
NOW GO ROLL YOUR BALL.
GOD, THE INTERNET'S RUINED EVERYTHING.
I'M BEGINNING TO THINK YOU'RE NOT ACTUALLY HERE TO HELP ME.
HOW DARE YOU.
I THINK I'M GOOD ON MY OWN, ACTUALLY. I'LL TAKE OVER FOR *BLONDIEBEAR.* YOU GO DO...WHATEVER IT IS THAT YOU DO. BUT NO KILLING.

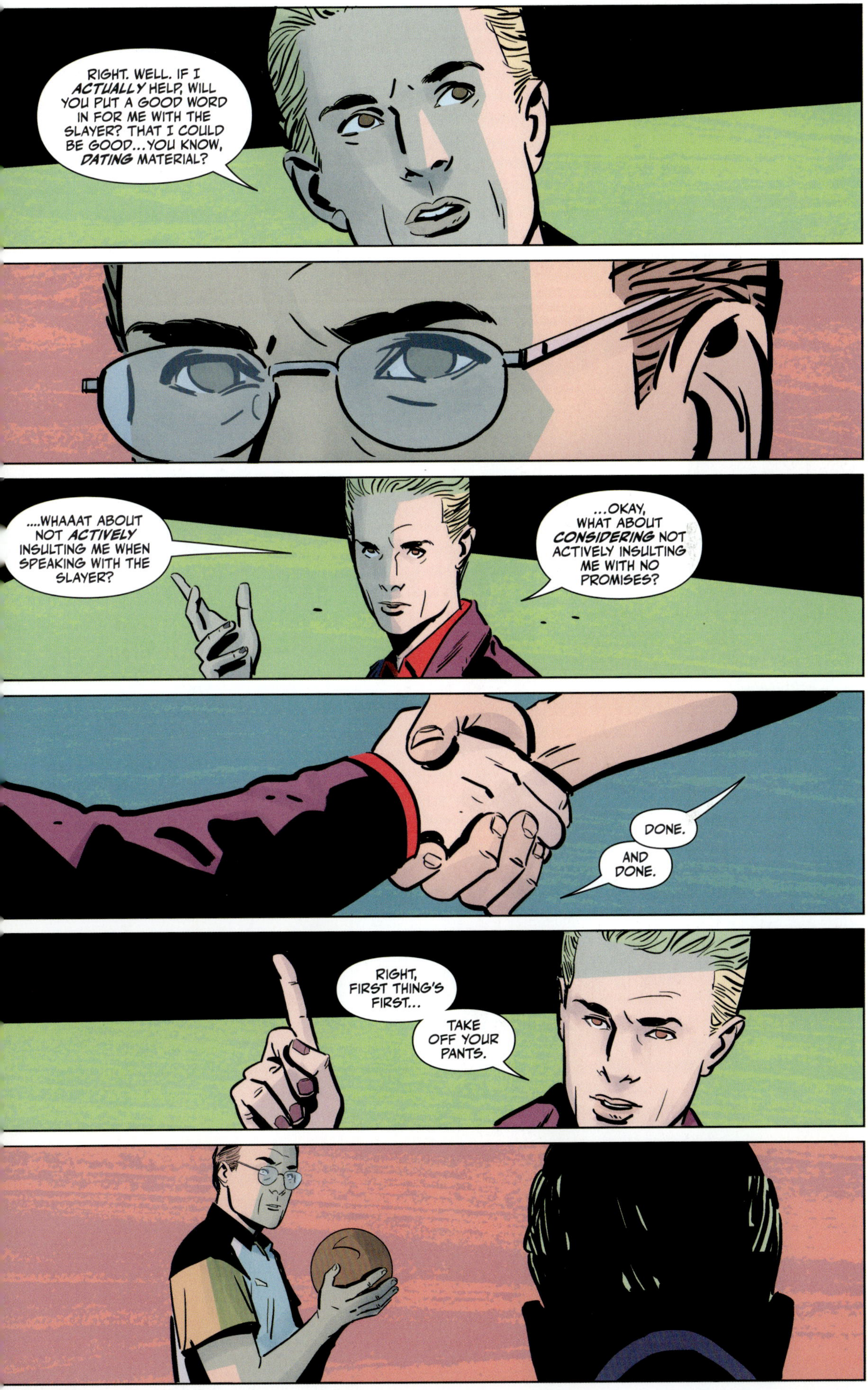
RIGHT. WELL. IF I *ACTUALLY* HELP, WILL YOU PUT A GOOD WORD IN FOR ME WITH THE SLAYER? THAT I COULD BE GOOD...YOU KNOW, *DATING* MATERIAL?
....WHAAAT ABOUT NOT *ACTIVELY* INSULTING ME WHEN SPEAKING WITH THE SLAYER?
...OKAY, WHAT ABOUT *CONSIDERING* NOT ACTIVELY INSULTING ME WITH NO PROMISES?
DONE.
AND DONE.
RIGHT, FIRST THING'S FIRST...
TAKE OFF YOUR PANTS.

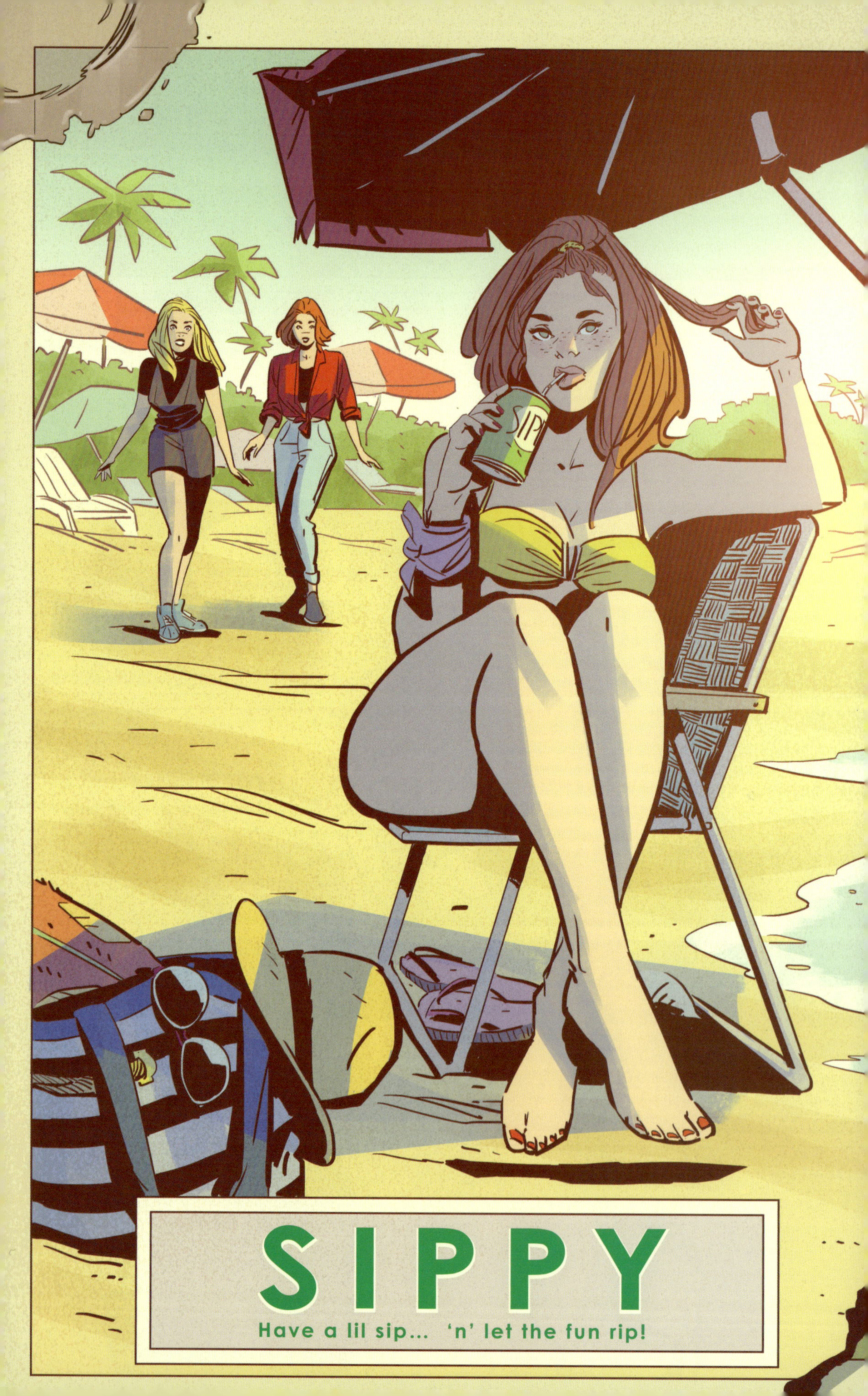
SIPPY
Have a lil sip... 'n' let the fun rip!

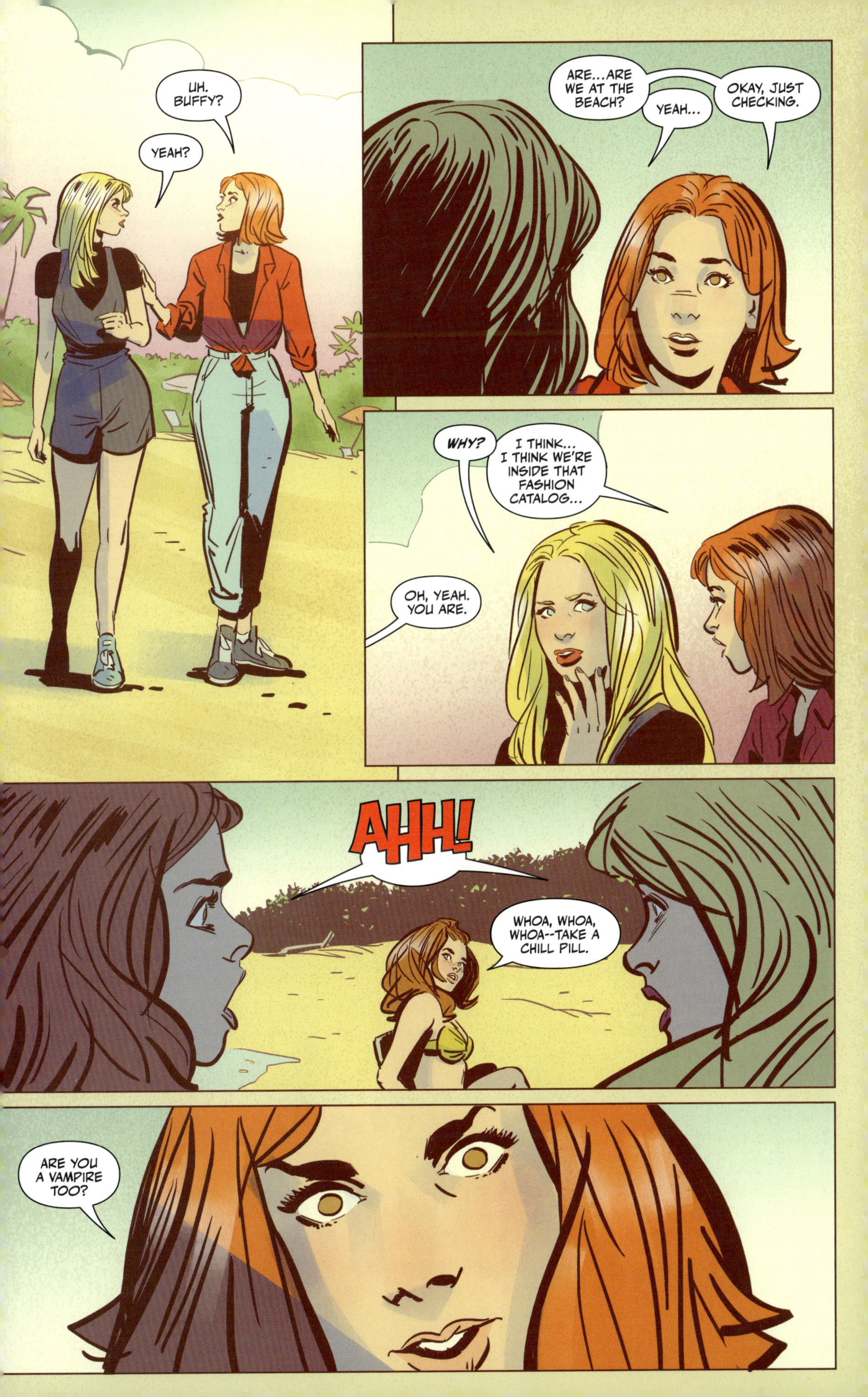
UH. BUFFY?
YEAH?
ARE...ARE WE AT THE BEACH?
YEAH...
OKAY, JUST CHECKING.
WHY?
I THINK... I THINK WE'RE INSIDE THAT FASHION CATALOG...
OH, YEAH. YOU ARE.
AHH!
WHOA, WHOA, WHOA--TAKE A CHILL PILL.
ARE YOU A VAMPIRE TOO?

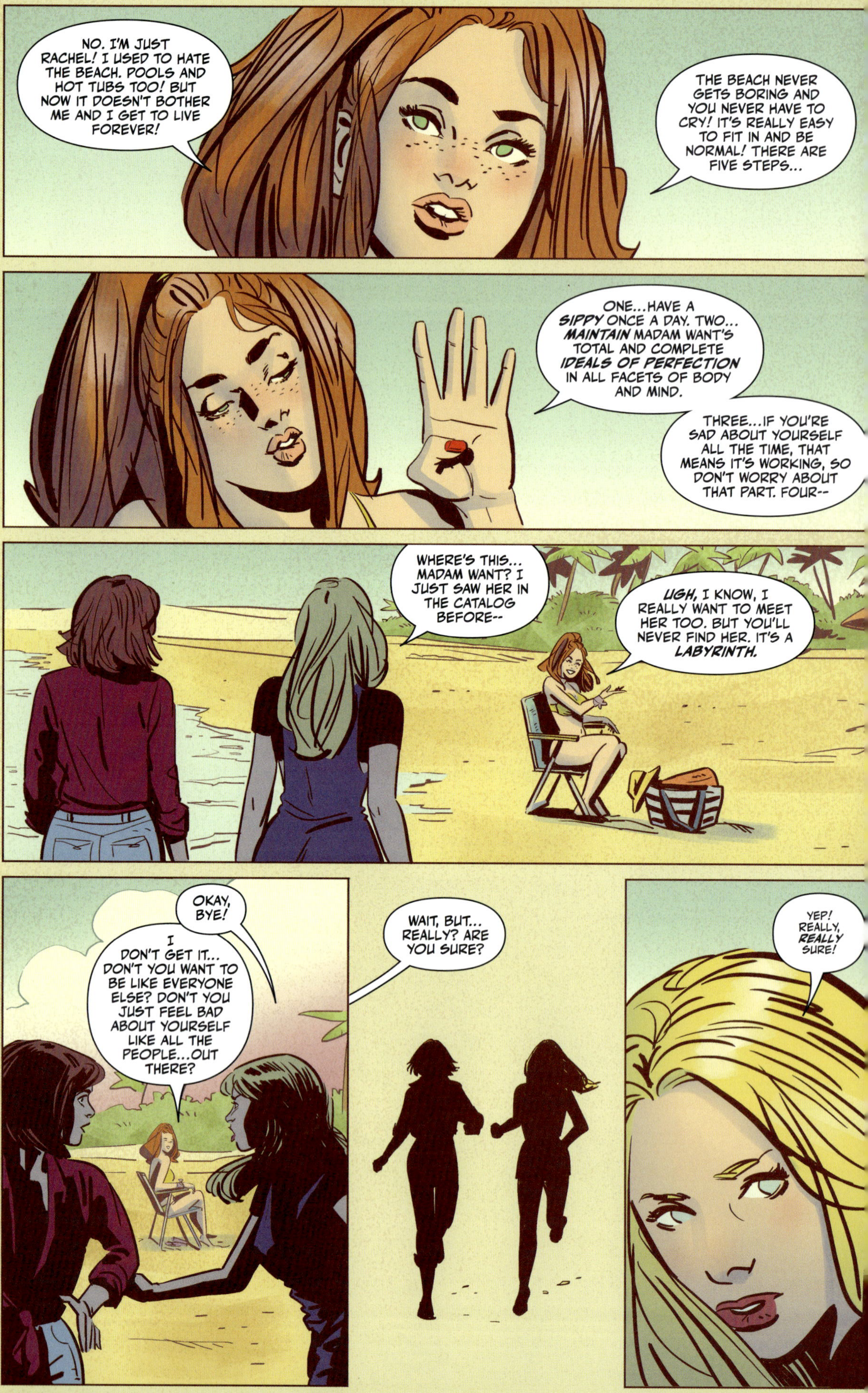
NO. I'M JUST RACHEL! I USED TO HATE THE BEACH. POOLS AND HOT TUBS TOO! BUT NOW IT DOESN'T BOTHER ME AND I GET TO LIVE FOREVER!
THE BEACH NEVER GETS BORING AND YOU NEVER HAVE TO CRY! IT'S REALLY EASY TO FIT IN AND BE NORMAL! THERE ARE FIVE STEPS...
ONE...HAVE A SIPPY ONCE A DAY. TWO... MAINTAIN MADAM WANT'S TOTAL AND COMPLETE IDEALS OF PERFECTION IN ALL FACETS OF BODY AND MIND.
THREE...IF YOU'RE SAD ABOUT YOURSELF ALL THE TIME, THAT MEANS IT'S WORKING, SO DON'T WORRY ABOUT THAT PART. FOUR--
WHERE'S THIS... MADAM WANT? I JUST SAW HER IN THE CATALOG BEFORE--
UGH, I KNOW, I REALLY WANT TO MEET HER TOO. BUT YOU'LL NEVER FIND HER. IT'S A LABYRINTH.
I DON'T GET IT... DON'T YOU WANT TO BE LIKE EVERYONE ELSE? DON'T YOU JUST FEEL BAD ABOUT YOURSELF LIKE ALL THE PEOPLE...OUT THERE?
OKAY, BYE!
WAIT, BUT... REALLY? ARE YOU SURE?
YEP! REALLY, REALLY SURE!

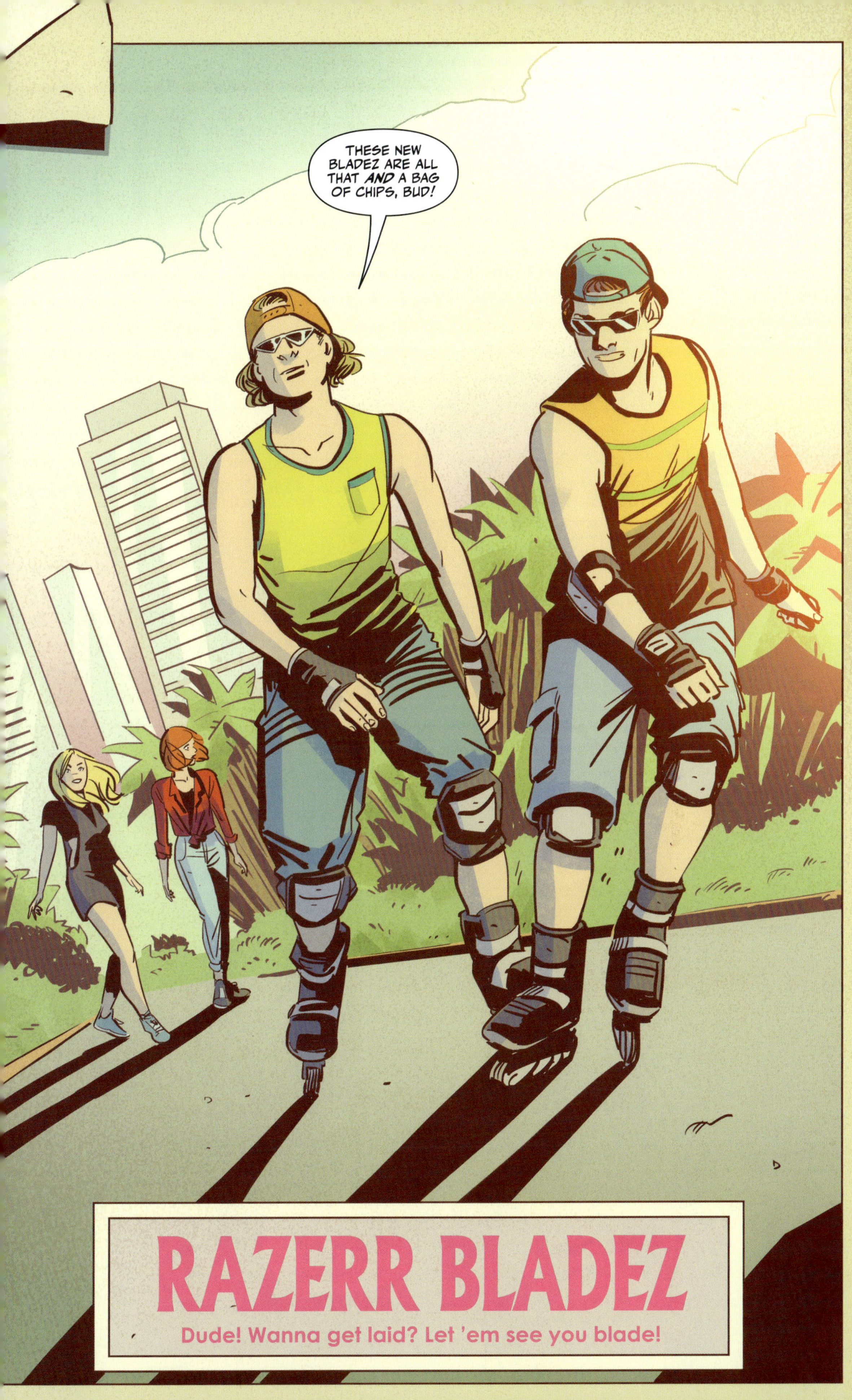
THESE NEW BLADEZ ARE ALL THAT AND A BAG OF CHIPS, BUD!
RAZERR BLADEZ
Dude! Wanna get laid? Let 'em see you blade!

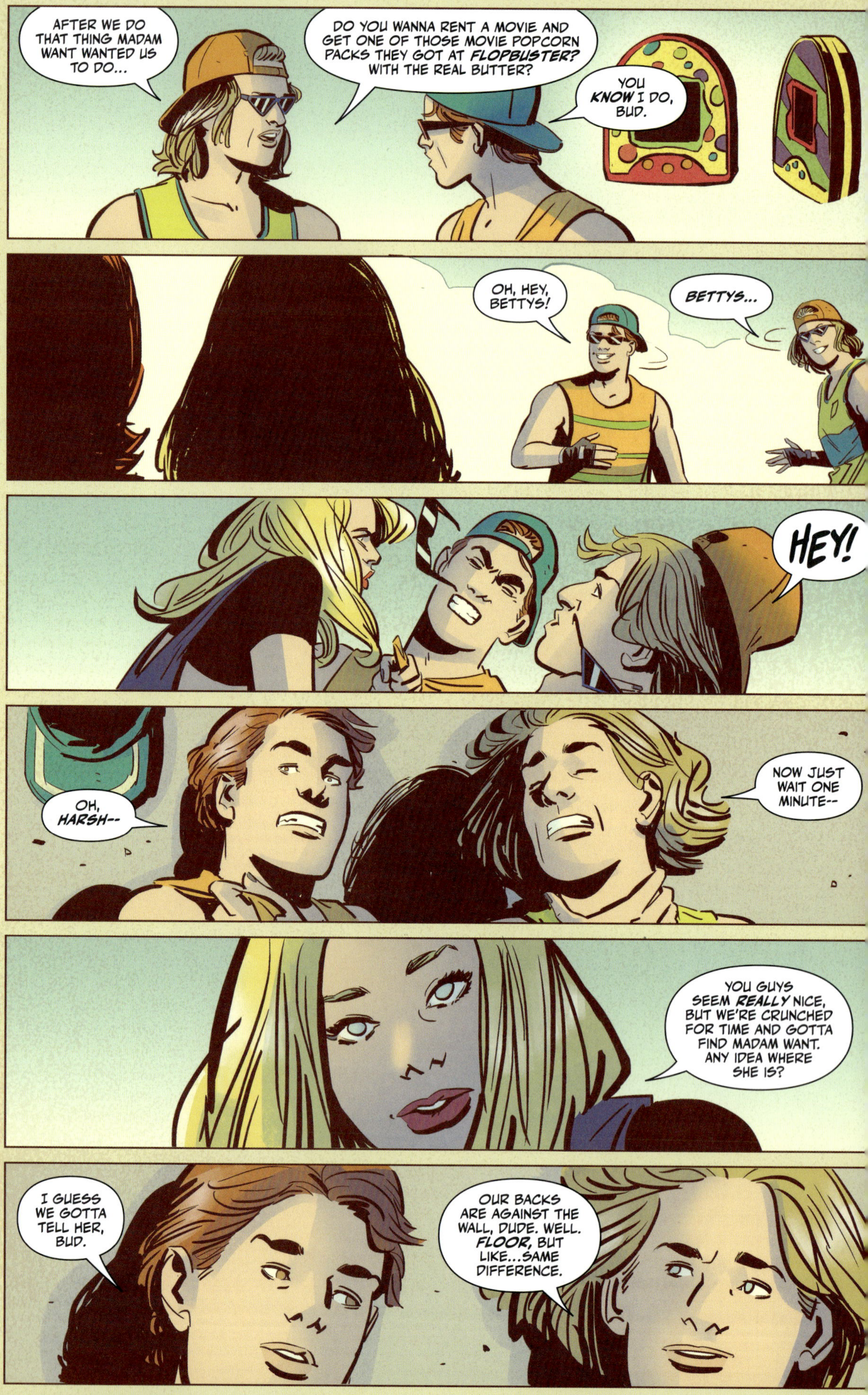
AFTER WE DO THAT THING MADAM WANT WANTED US TO DO...
DO YOU WANNA RENT A MOVIE AND GET ONE OF THOSE MOVIE POPCORN PACKS THEY GOT AT FLOPBUSTER? WITH THE REAL BUTTER?
YOU KNOW I DO, BUD.
OH, HEY, BETTYS!
BETTYS...
HEY!
OH, HARSH--
NOW JUST WAIT ONE MINUTE--
YOU GUYS SEEM REALLY NICE, BUT WE'RE CRUNCHED FOR TIME AND GOTTA FIND MADAM WANT. ANY IDEA WHERE SHE IS?
I GUESS WE GOTTA TELL HER, BUD.
OUR BACKS ARE AGAINST THE WALL, DUDE. WELL. FLOOR, BUT LIKE...SAME DIFFERENCE.

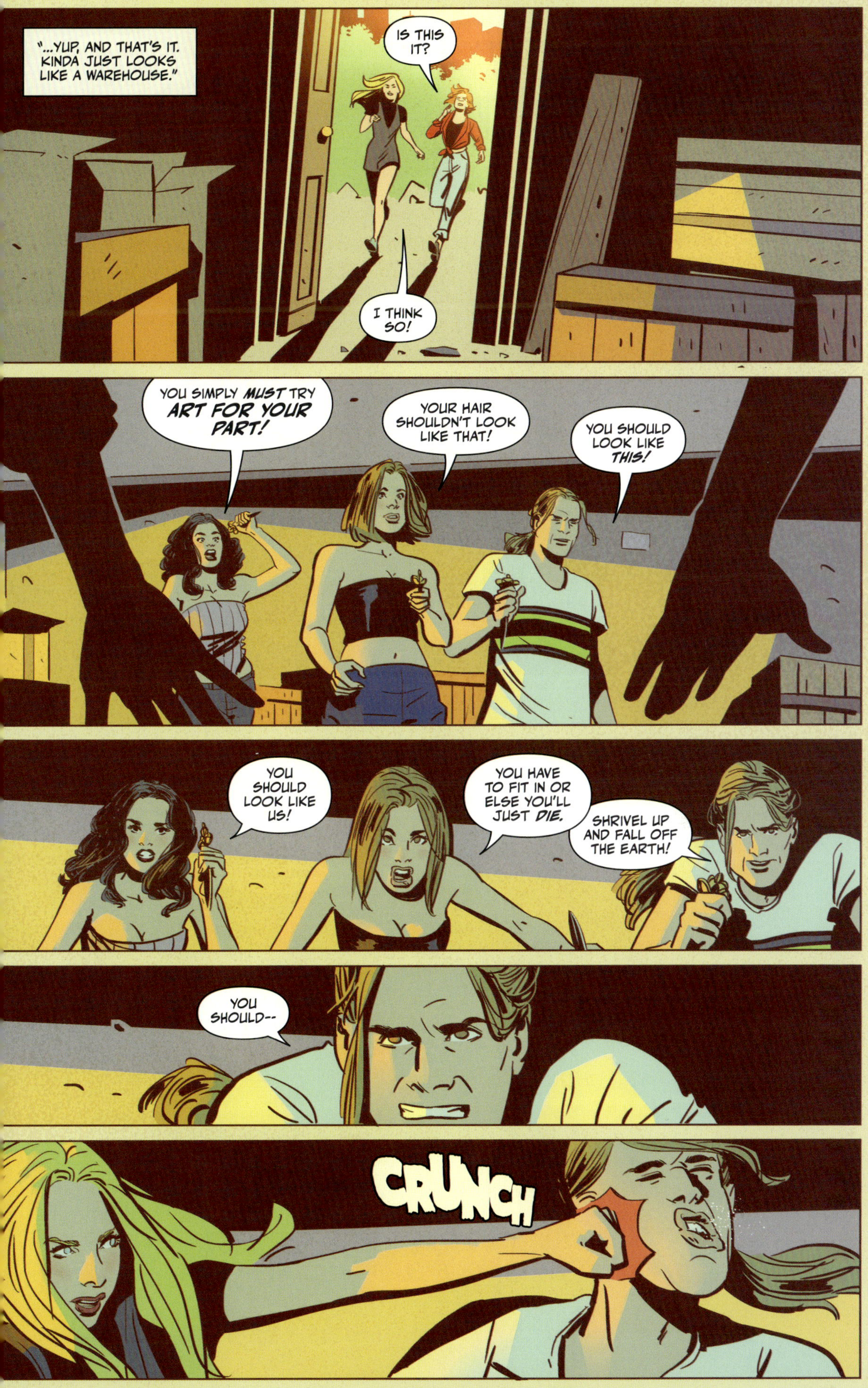
"...YUP, AND THAT'S IT. KINDA JUST LOOKS LIKE A WAREHOUSE."
IS THIS IT?
I THINK SO!
YOU SIMPLY MUST TRY ART FOR YOUR PART!
YOUR HAIR SHOULDN'T LOOK LIKE THAT!
YOU SHOULD LOOK LIKE THIS!
YOU SHOULD LOOK LIKE US!
YOU HAVE TO FIT IN OR ELSE YOU'LL JUST DIE.
SHRIVEL UP AND FALL OFF THE EARTH!
YOU SHOULD--
CRUNCH

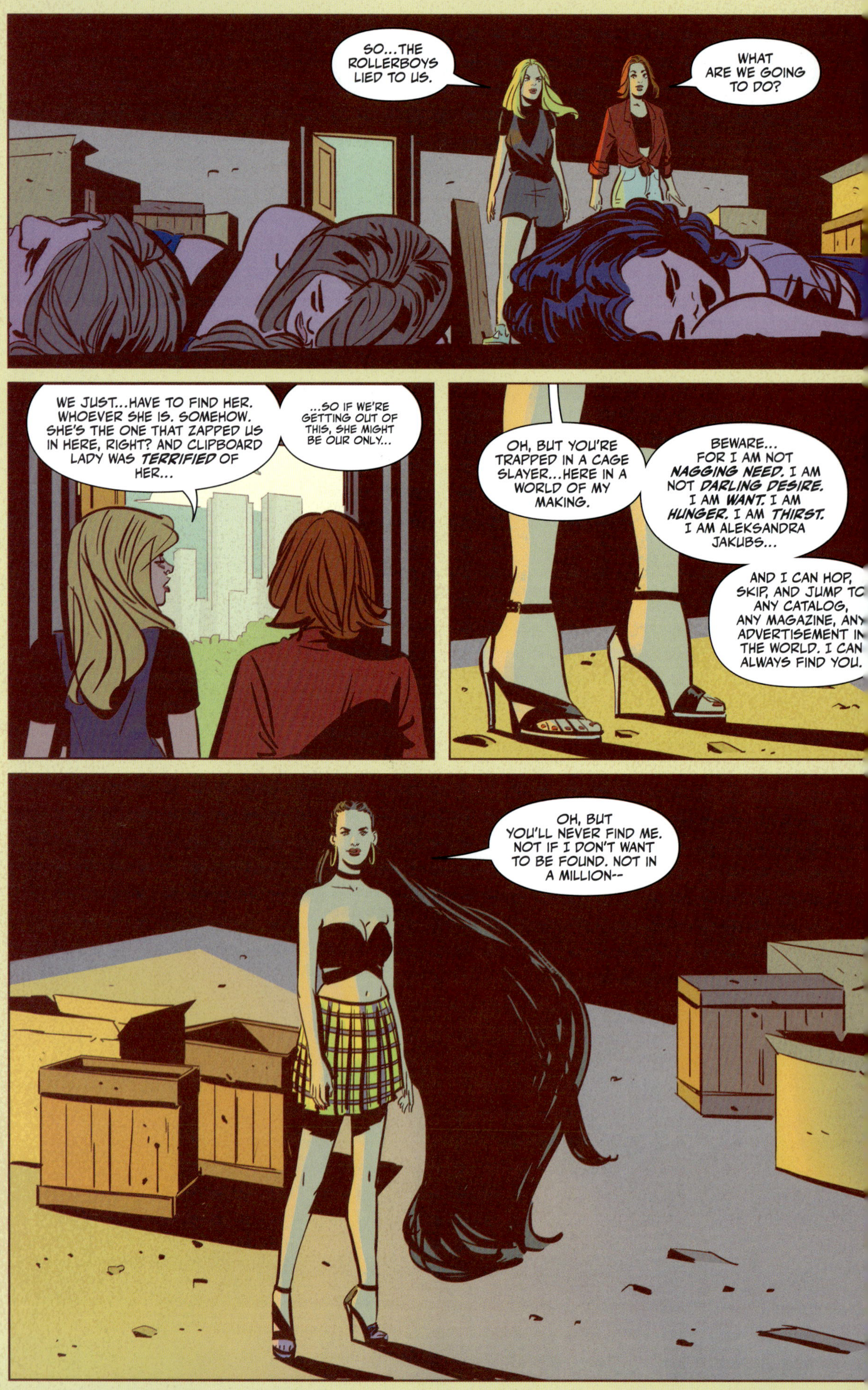

SO...THE ROLLERBOYS LIED TO US.
WHAT ARE WE GOING TO DO?
WE JUST...HAVE TO FIND HER. WHOEVER SHE IS. SOMEHOW. SHE'S THE ONE THAT ZAPPED US IN HERE, RIGHT? AND CLIPBOARD LADY WAS TERRIFIED OF HER...
...SO IF WE'RE GETTING OUT OF THIS, SHE MIGHT BE OUR ONLY...
OH, BUT YOU'RE TRAPPED IN A CAGE SLAYER...HERE IN A WORLD OF MY MAKING.
BEWARE... FOR I AM NOT NAGGING NEED. I AM NOT DARLING DESIRE. I AM WANT. I AM HUNGER. I AM THIRST. I AM ALEKSANDRA JAKUBS...
AND I CAN HOP, SKIP, AND JUMP TO ANY CATALOG, ANY MAGAZINE, ANY ADVERTISEMENT IN THE WORLD. I CAN ALWAYS FIND YOU.
OH, BUT YOU'LL NEVER FIND ME. NOT IF I DON'T WANT TO BE FOUND. NOT IN A MILLION--

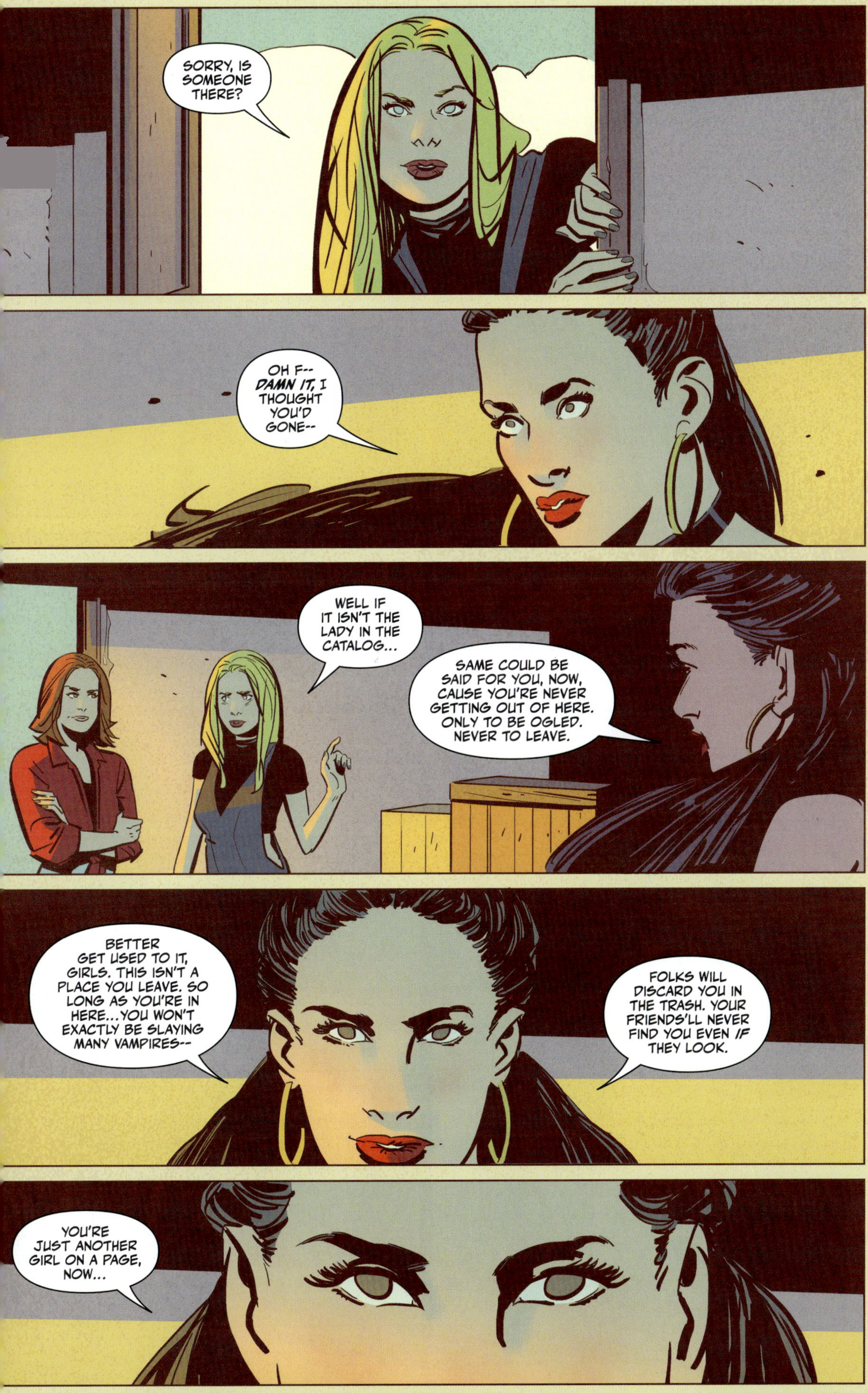
SORRY, IS SOMEONE THERE?
OH F-- *DAMN IT,* I THOUGHT YOU'D GONE--
WELL IF IT ISN'T THE LADY IN THE CATALOG...
SAME COULD BE SAID FOR YOU, NOW, CAUSE YOU'RE NEVER GETTING OUT OF HERE. ONLY TO BE OGLED. NEVER TO LEAVE.
BETTER GET USED TO IT, GIRLS. THIS ISN'T A PLACE YOU LEAVE. SO LONG AS YOU'RE IN HERE...YOU WON'T EXACTLY BE SLAYING MANY VAMPIRES--
FOLKS WILL DISCARD YOU IN THE TRASH. YOUR FRIENDS'LL NEVER FIND YOU EVEN *IF* THEY LOOK.
YOU'RE JUST ANOTHER GIRL ON A PAGE, NOW...

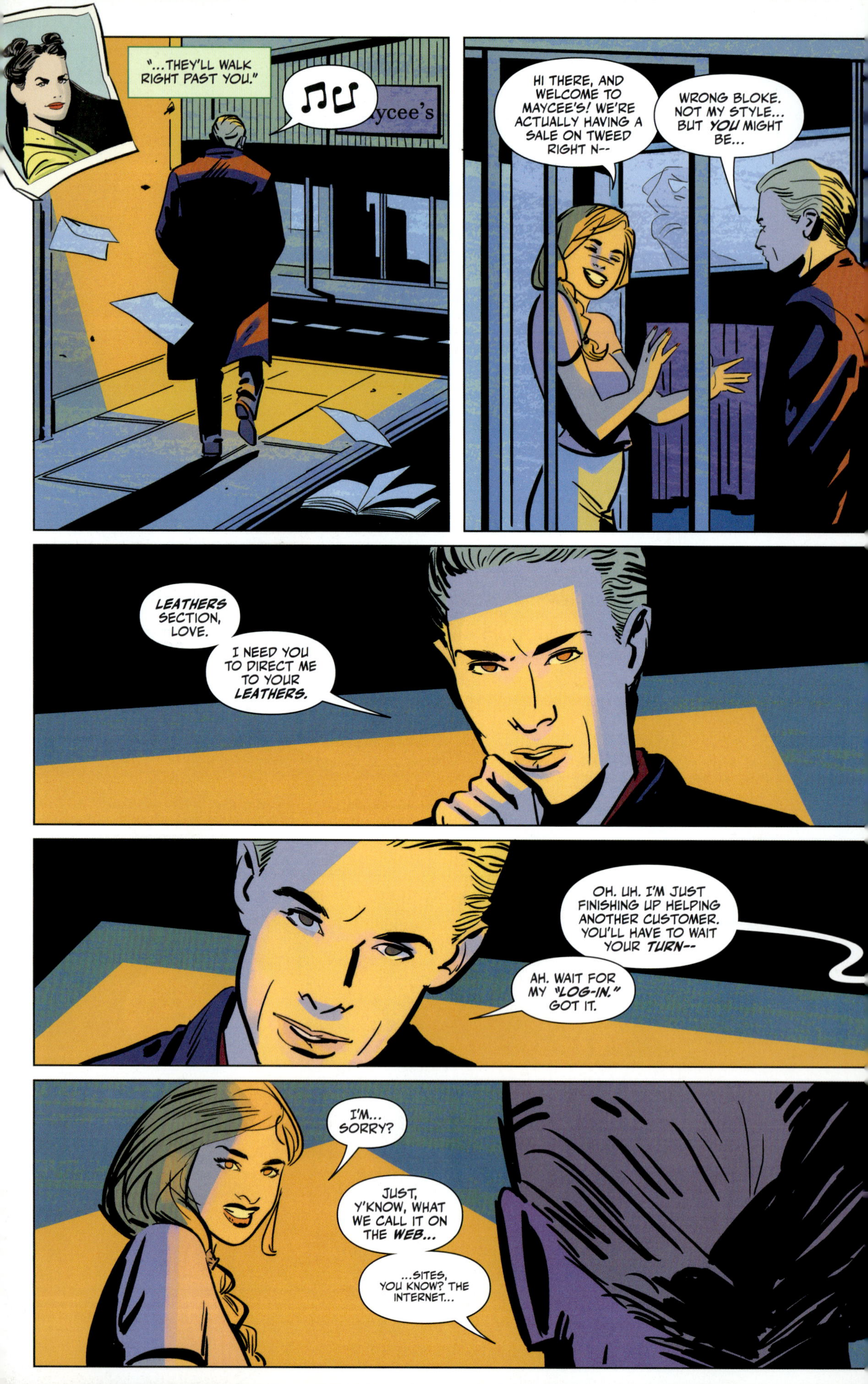
"...THEY'LL WALK RIGHT PAST YOU."
ycee's
HI THERE, AND WELCOME TO MAYCEE'S! WE'RE ACTUALLY HAVING A SALE ON TWEED RIGHT N--
WRONG BLOKE. NOT MY STYLE... BUT *YOU* MIGHT BE...
LEATHERS SECTION, LOVE.
I NEED YOU TO DIRECT ME TO YOUR *LEATHERS.*
OH. UH. I'M JUST FINISHING UP HELPING ANOTHER CUSTOMER. YOU'LL HAVE TO WAIT YOUR *TURN--*
AH. WAIT FOR MY *"LOG-IN."* GOT IT.
I'M... SORRY?
JUST, Y'KNOW, WHAT WE CALL IT ON THE *WEB...*
...SITES, YOU KNOW? THE INTERNET...

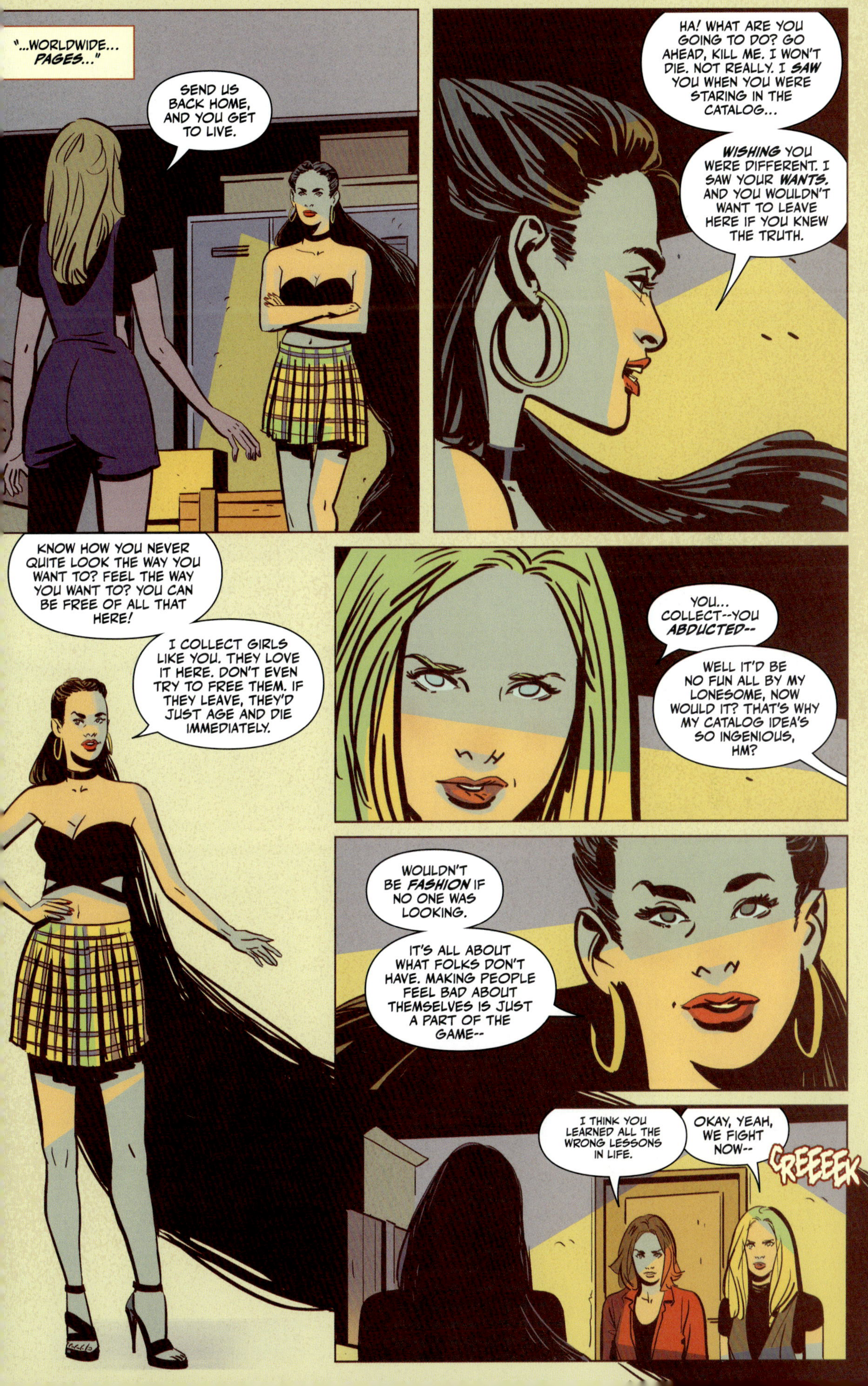
"...WORLDWIDE... PAGES..."
SEND US BACK HOME, AND YOU GET TO LIVE.
HA! WHAT ARE YOU GOING TO DO? GO AHEAD, KILL ME. I WON'T DIE. NOT REALLY. I SAW YOU WHEN YOU WERE STARING IN THE CATALOG...
WISHING YOU WERE DIFFERENT. I SAW YOUR WANTS. AND YOU WOULDN'T WANT TO LEAVE HERE IF YOU KNEW THE TRUTH.
KNOW HOW YOU NEVER QUITE LOOK THE WAY YOU WANT TO? FEEL THE WAY YOU WANT TO? YOU CAN BE FREE OF ALL THAT HERE!
I COLLECT GIRLS LIKE YOU. THEY LOVE IT HERE. DON'T EVEN TRY TO FREE THEM. IF THEY LEAVE, THEY'D JUST AGE AND DIE IMMEDIATELY.
YOU... COLLECT--YOU ABDUCTED--
WELL IT'D BE NO FUN ALL BY MY LONESOME, NOW WOULD IT? THAT'S WHY MY CATALOG IDEA'S SO INGENIOUS, HM?
WOULDN'T BE FASHION IF NO ONE WAS LOOKING.
IT'S ALL ABOUT WHAT FOLKS DON'T HAVE. MAKING PEOPLE FEEL BAD ABOUT THEMSELVES IS JUST A PART OF THE GAME--
I THINK YOU LEARNED ALL THE WRONG LESSONS IN LIFE.
OKAY, YEAH, WE FIGHT NOW--
CREEEEK

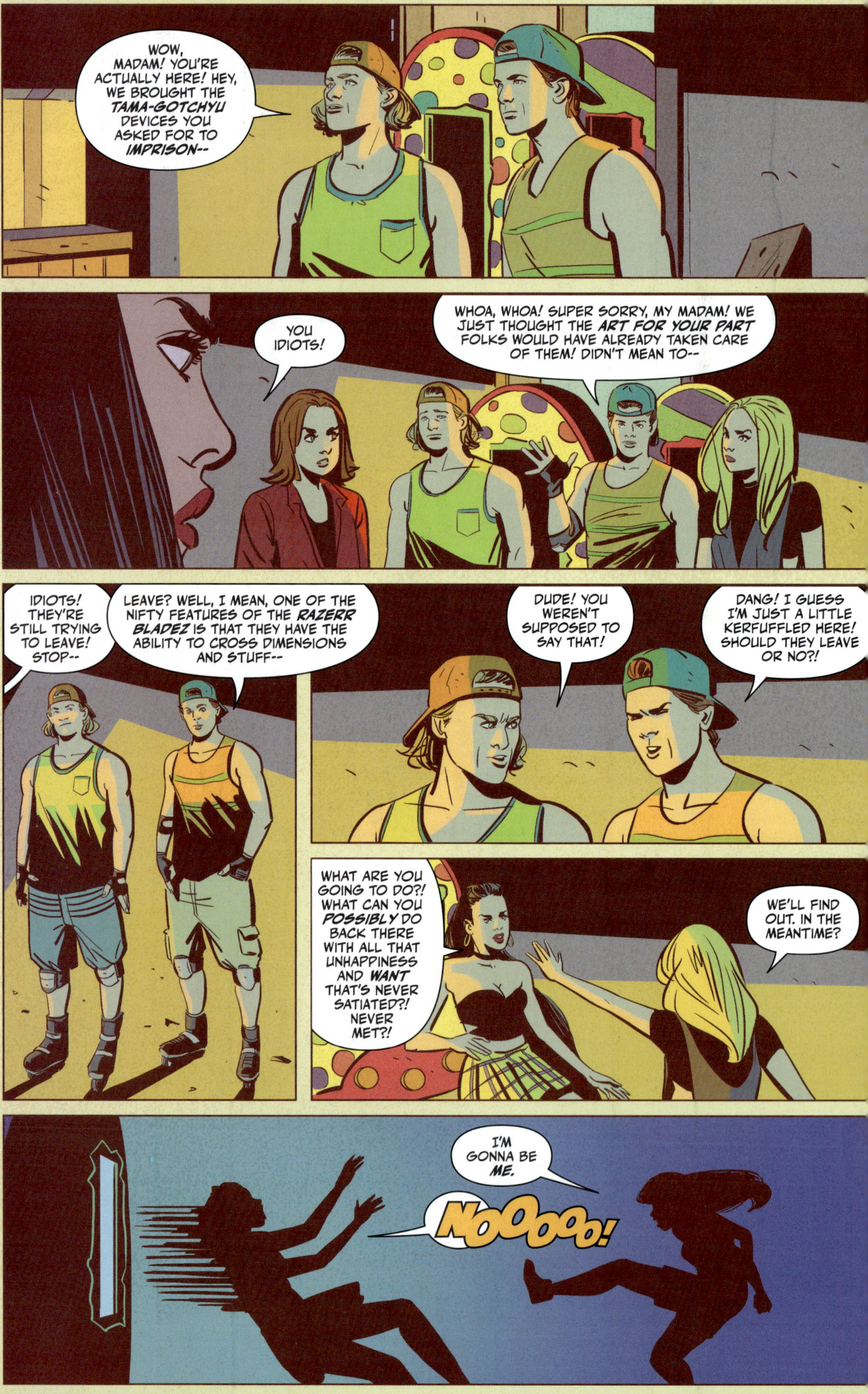
WOW, MADAM! YOU'RE ACTUALLY HERE! HEY, WE BROUGHT THE *TAMA-GOTCHYU* DEVICES YOU ASKED FOR TO *IMPRISON--*
YOU IDIOTS!
WHOA, WHOA! SUPER SORRY, MY MADAM! WE JUST THOUGHT THE *ART FOR YOUR PART* FOLKS WOULD HAVE ALREADY TAKEN CARE OF THEM! DIDN'T MEAN TO--
IDIOTS! THEY'RE STILL TRYING TO LEAVE! STOP--
LEAVE? WELL, I MEAN, ONE OF THE NIFTY FEATURES OF THE *RAZERR BLADEZ* IS THAT THEY HAVE THE ABILITY TO CROSS DIMENSIONS AND STUFF--
DUDE! YOU WEREN'T SUPPOSED TO SAY THAT!
DANG! I GUESS I'M JUST A LITTLE KERFUFFLED HERE! SHOULD THEY LEAVE OR NO?!
WHAT ARE YOU GOING TO DO?! WHAT CAN YOU *POSSIBLY* DO BACK THERE WITH ALL THAT UNHAPPINESS AND *WANT* THAT'S NEVER SATIATED?! NEVER MET?!
WE'LL FIND OUT. IN THE MEANTIME?
I'M GONNA BE *ME.*
NOOOOO!

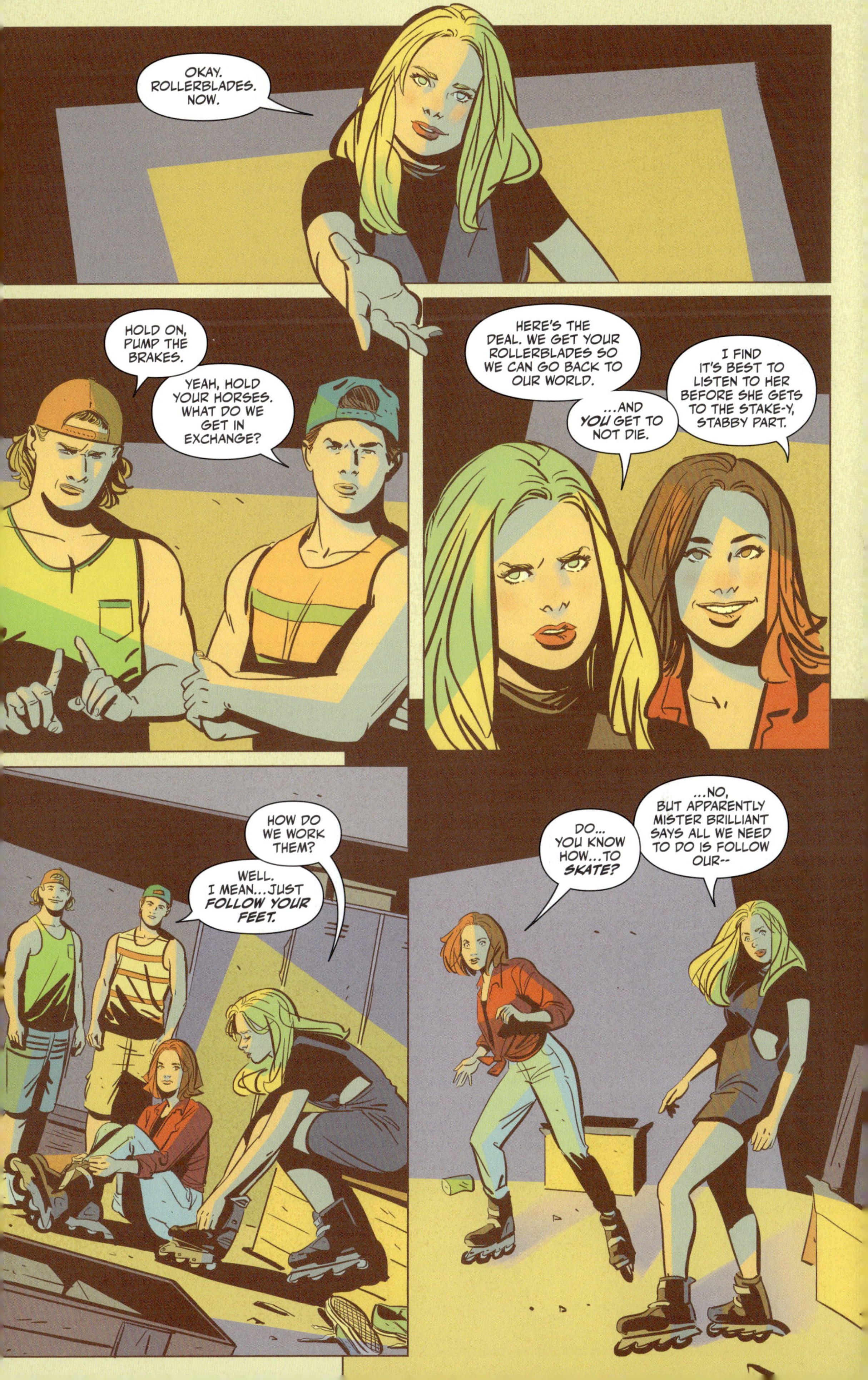
OKAY. ROLLERBLADES. NOW.
HOLD ON, PUMP THE BRAKES.
YEAH, HOLD YOUR HORSES. WHAT DO WE GET IN EXCHANGE?
HERE'S THE DEAL. WE GET YOUR ROLLERBLADES SO WE CAN GO BACK TO OUR WORLD.
...AND *YOU* GET TO NOT DIE.
I FIND IT'S BEST TO LISTEN TO HER BEFORE SHE GETS TO THE STAKE-Y, STABBY PART.
HOW DO WE WORK THEM?
WELL. I MEAN...JUST *FOLLOW YOUR FEET.*
DO... YOU KNOW HOW...TO *SKATE?*
...NO, BUT APPARENTLY MISTER BRILLIANT SAYS ALL WE NEED TO DO IS FOLLOW OUR--

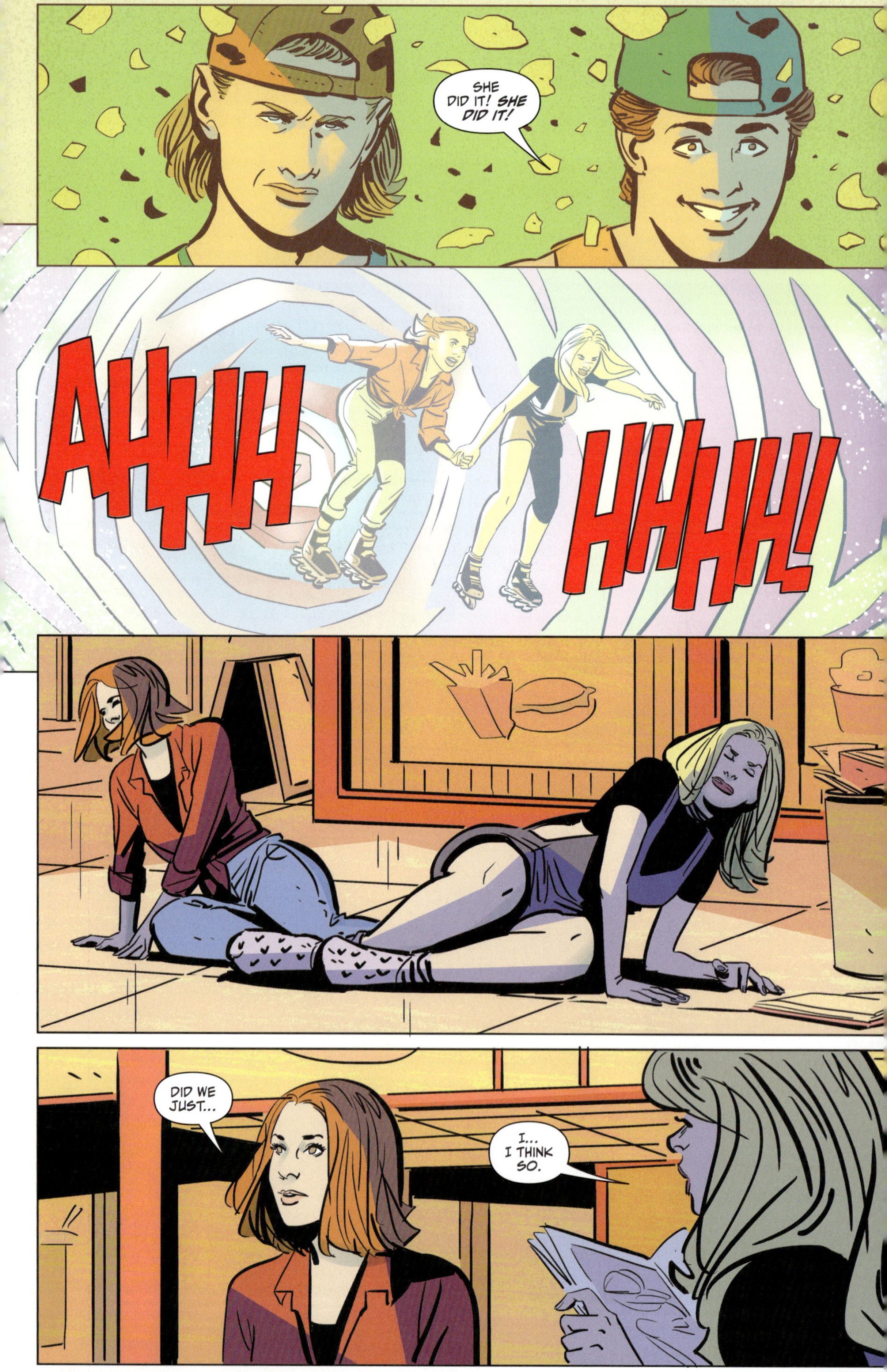
SHE DID IT! SHE DID IT!
AHHH HHHH!
DID WE JUST...
I... I THINK SO.

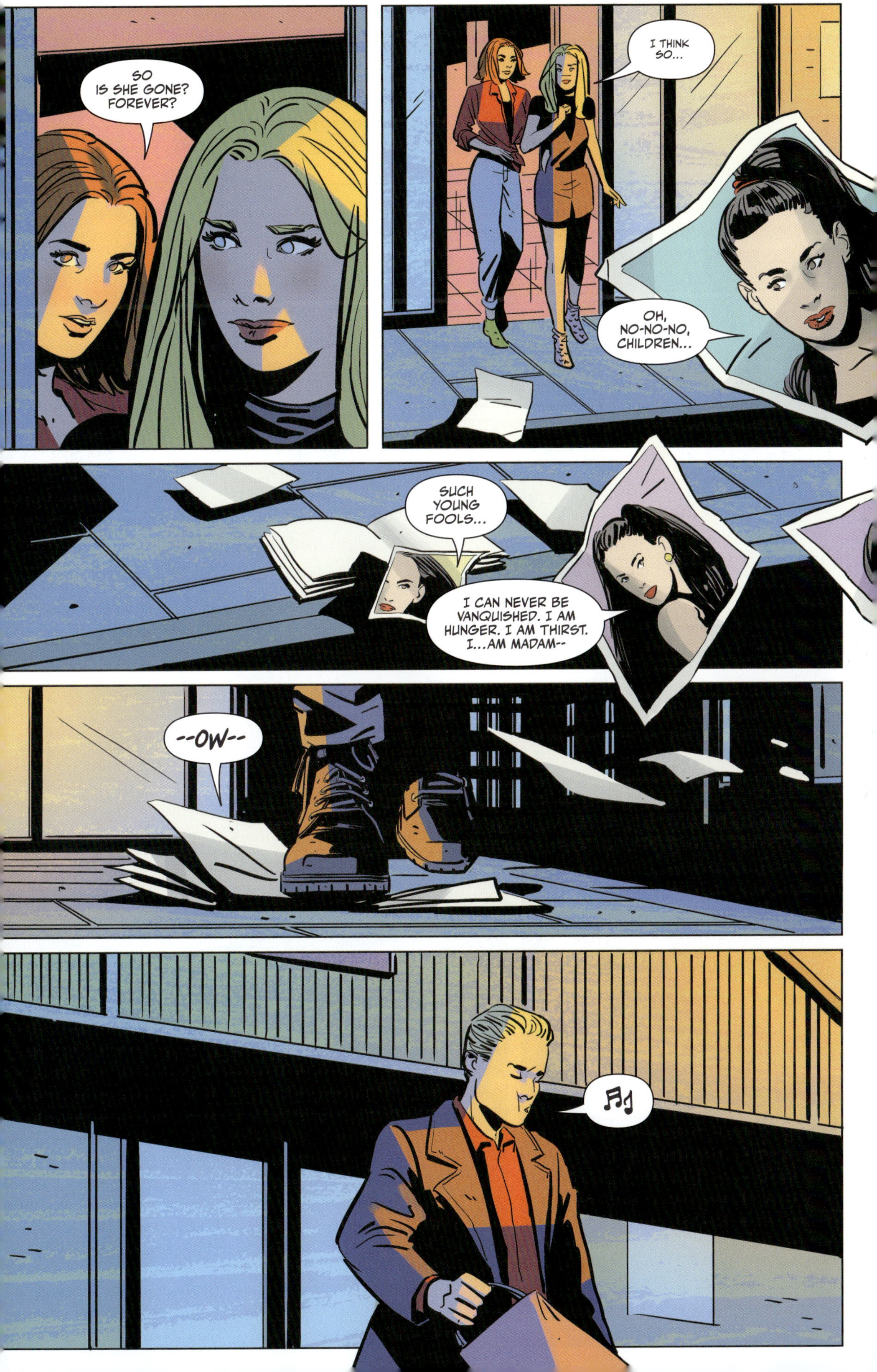

SO IS SHE GONE? FOREVER?
I THINK SO...
OH, NO-NO-NO, CHILDREN...
SUCH YOUNG FOOLS...
I CAN NEVER BE VANQUISHED. I AM HUNGER. I AM THIRST. I...AM MADAM--
--OW--

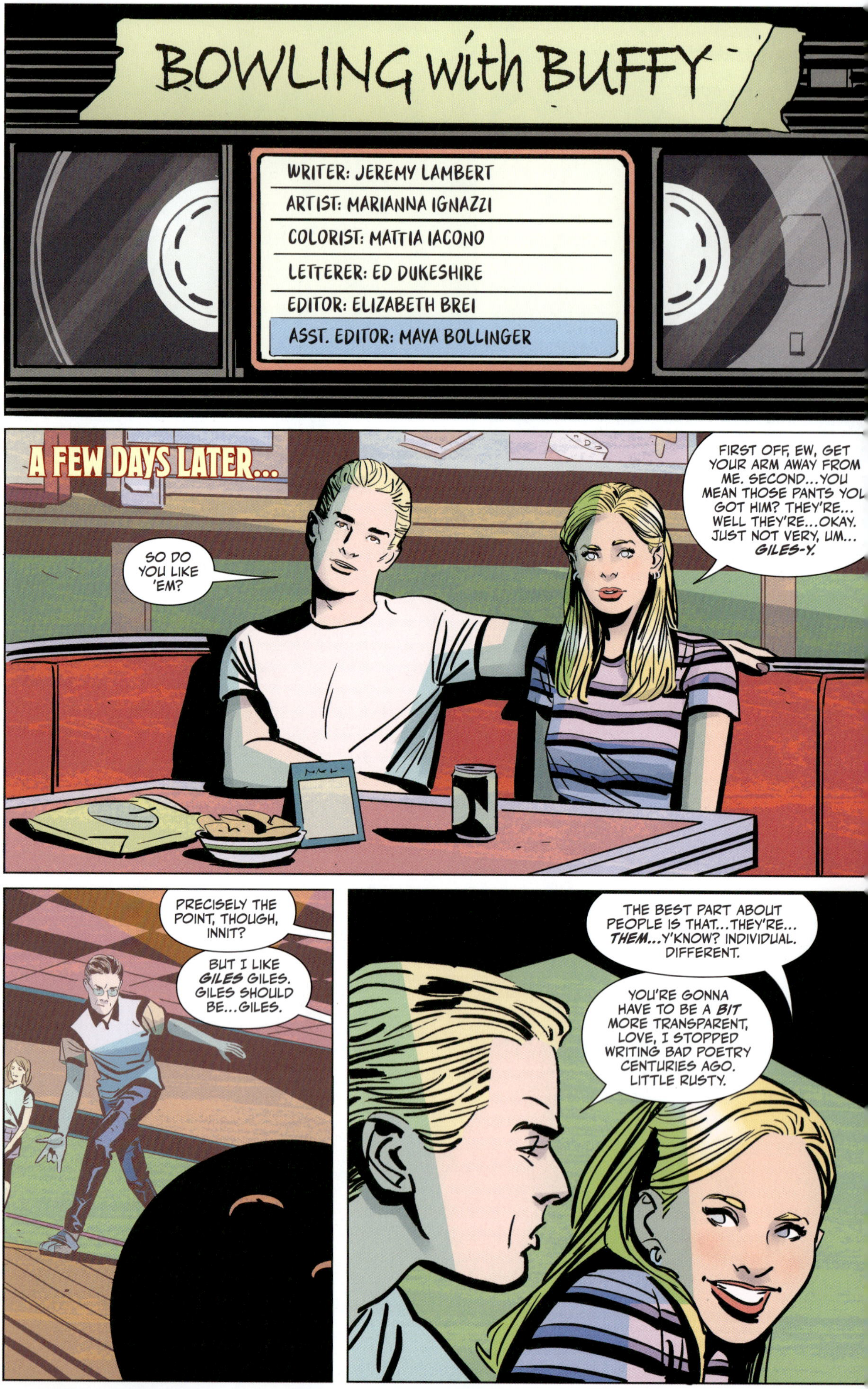
BOWLING with BUFFY
WRITER: JEREMY LAMBERT
ARTIST: MARIANNA IGNAZZI
COLORIST: MATTIA IACONO
LETTERER: ED DUKESHIRE
EDITOR: ELIZABETH BREI
ASST. EDITOR: MAYA BOLLINGER
A FEW DAYS LATER...
SO DO YOU LIKE 'EM?
FIRST OFF, EW, GET YOUR ARM AWAY FROM ME. SECOND...YOU MEAN THOSE PANTS YOU GOT HIM? THEY'RE... WELL THEY'RE...OKAY. JUST NOT VERY, UM... GILES-Y.
PRECISELY THE POINT, THOUGH, INNIT?
BUT I LIKE GILES GILES. GILES SHOULD BE...GILES.
THE BEST PART ABOUT PEOPLE IS THAT...THEY'RE... THEM...Y'KNOW? INDIVIDUAL. DIFFERENT.
YOU'RE GONNA HAVE TO BE A BIT MORE TRANSPARENT, LOVE. I STOPPED WRITING BAD POETRY CENTURIES AGO. LITTLE RUSTY.

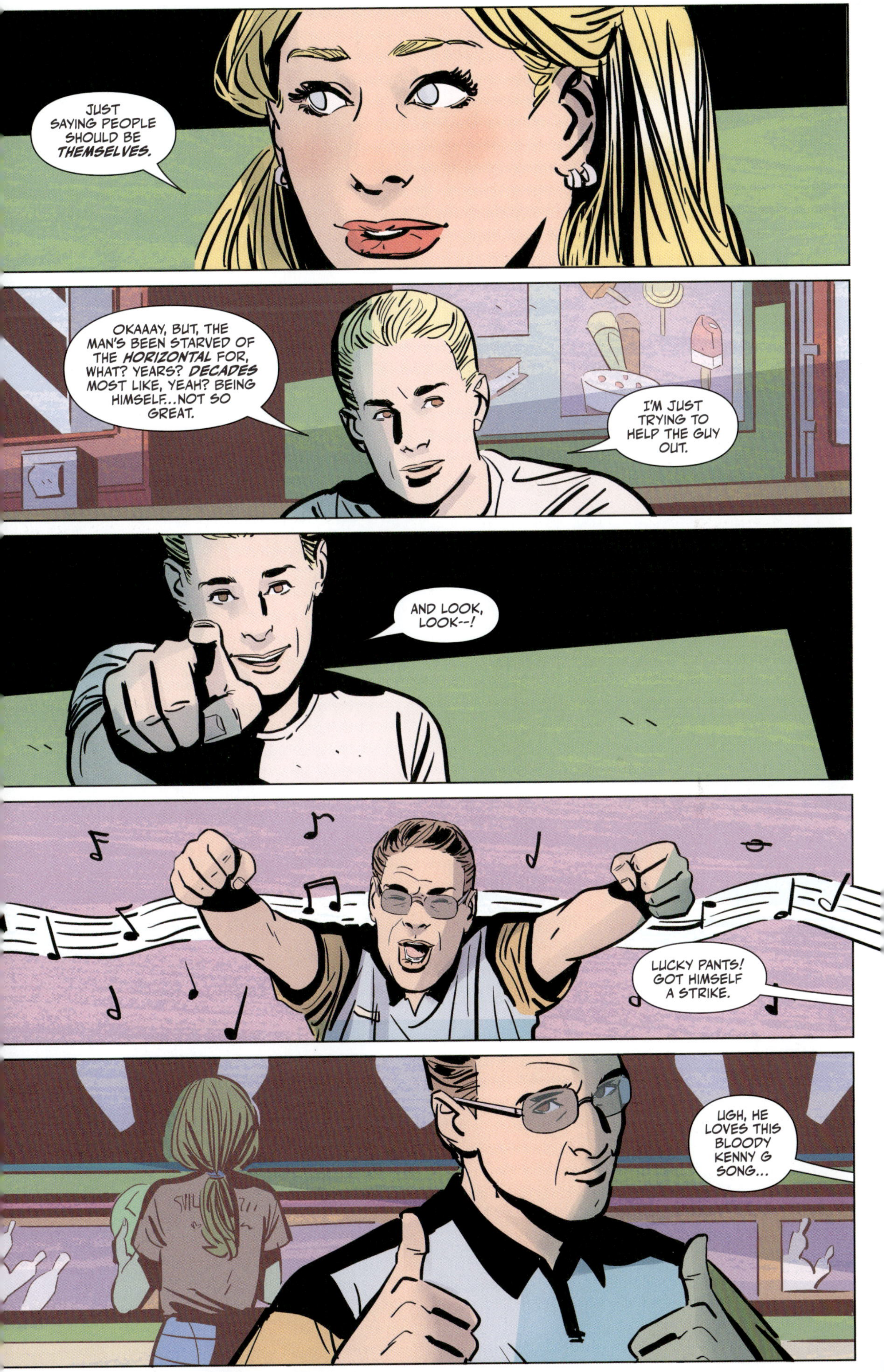
JUST SAYING PEOPLE SHOULD BE THEMSELVES.
OKAAAY, BUT, THE MAN'S BEEN STARVED OF THE HORIZONTAL FOR, WHAT? YEARS? DECADES MOST LIKE, YEAH? BEING HIMSELF...NOT SO GREAT.
I'M JUST TRYING TO HELP THE GUY OUT.
AND LOOK, LOOK--!
LUCKY PANTS! GOT HIMSELF A STRIKE.
UGH, HE LOVES THIS BLOODY KENNY G SONG...

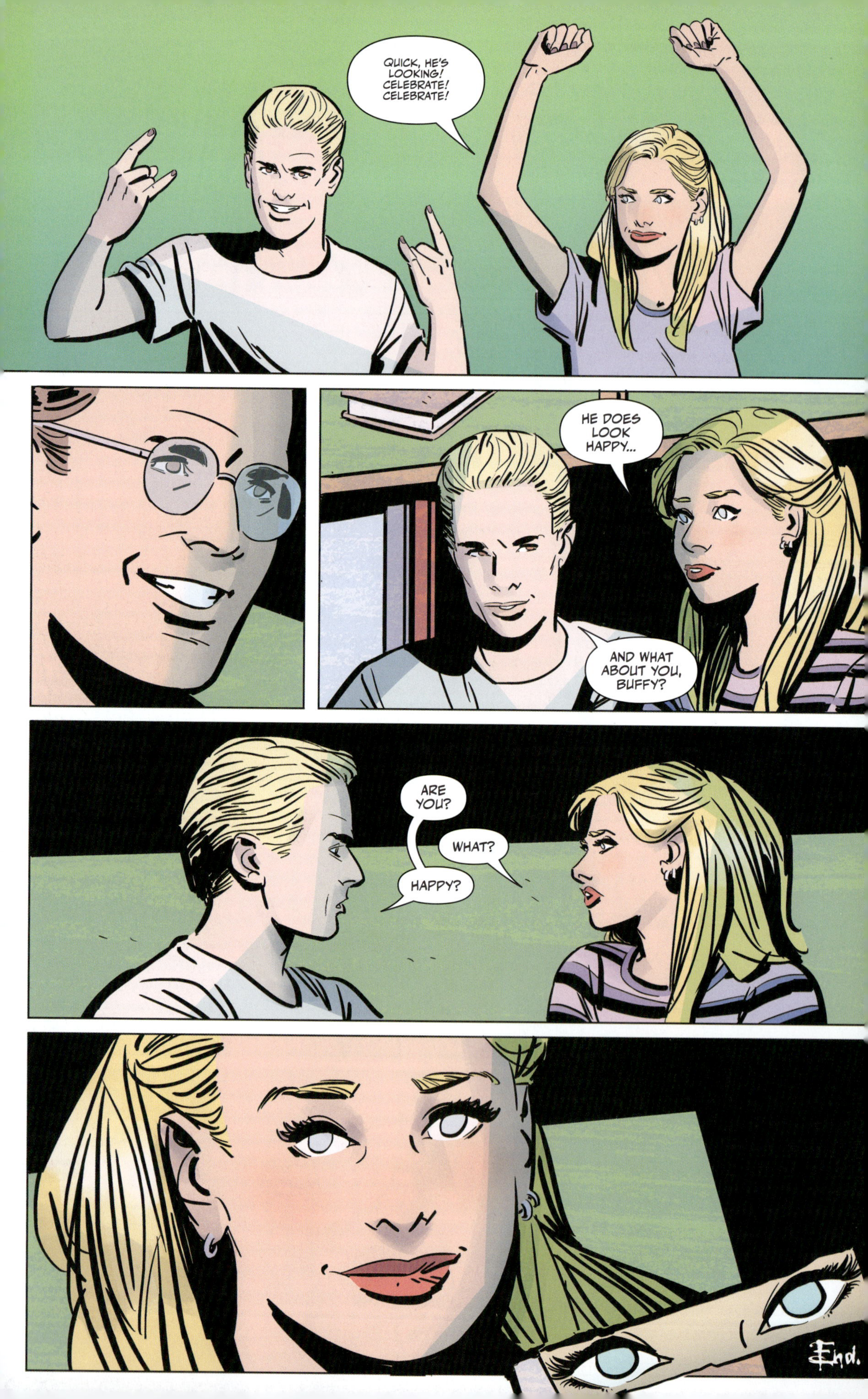
QUICK, HE'S LOOKING! CELEBRATE! CELEBRATE!
HE DOES LOOK HAPPY...
AND WHAT ABOUT YOU, BUFFY?
ARE YOU?
WHAT?
HAPPY?
End.

WONDROUS AND SURPRISING MAGIC

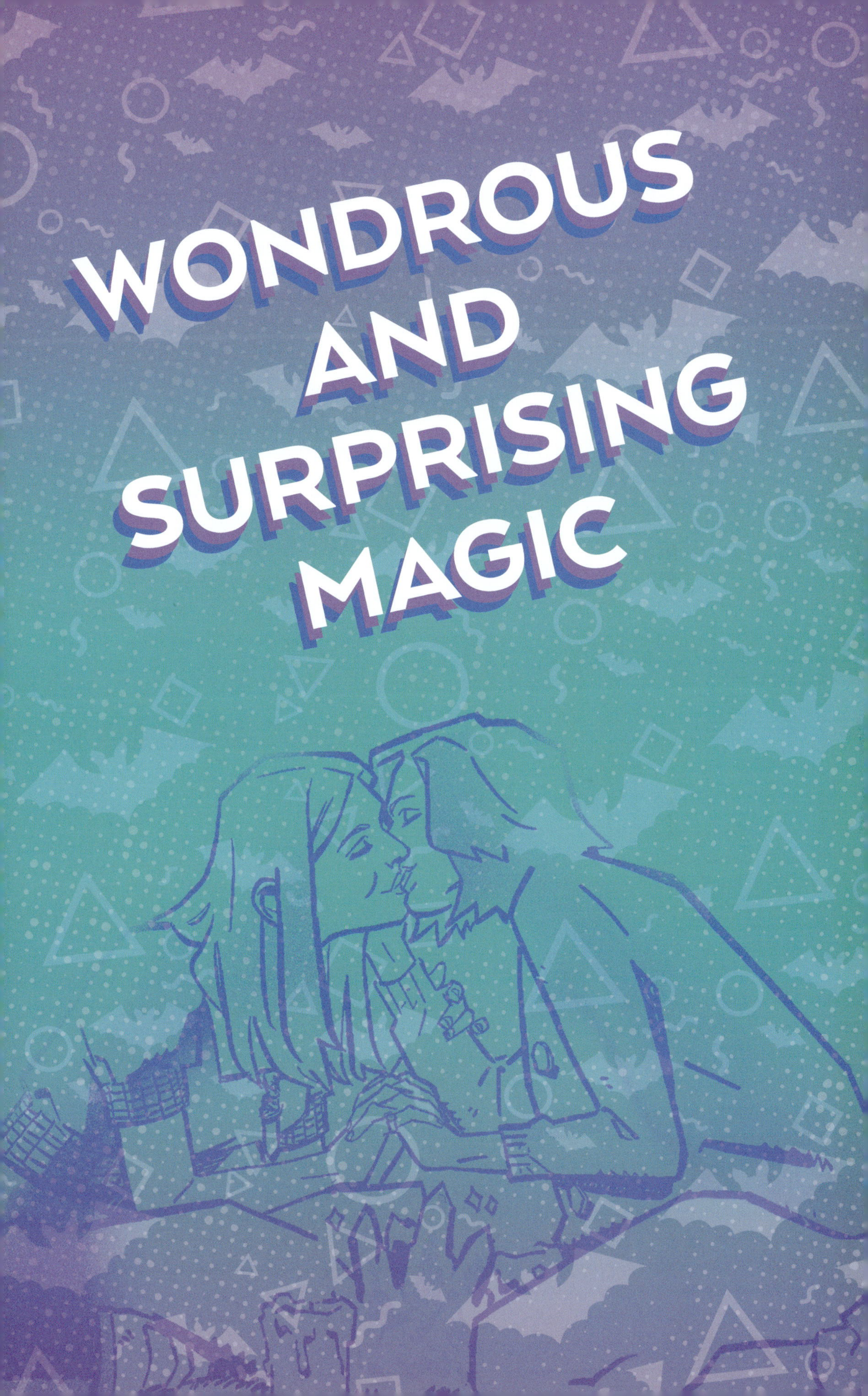

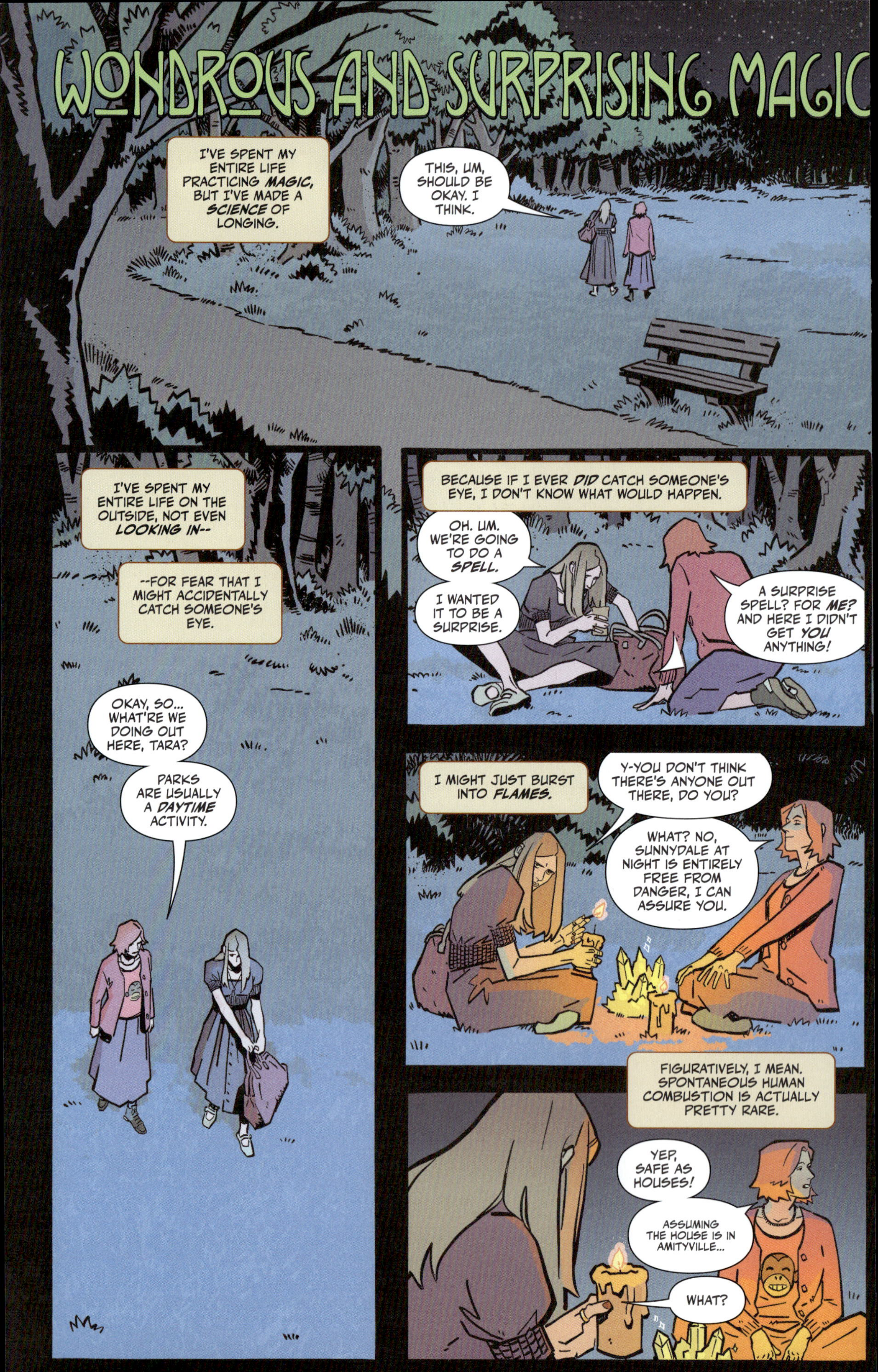
WONDROUS AND SURPRISING MAGIC
I'VE SPENT MY ENTIRE LIFE PRACTICING MAGIC, BUT I'VE MADE A SCIENCE OF LONGING.
THIS, UM, SHOULD BE OKAY. I THINK.
I'VE SPENT MY ENTIRE LIFE ON THE OUTSIDE, NOT EVEN LOOKING IN--
--FOR FEAR THAT I MIGHT ACCIDENTALLY CATCH SOMEONE'S EYE.
OKAY, SO... WHAT'RE WE DOING OUT HERE, TARA?
PARKS ARE USUALLY A DAYTIME ACTIVITY.
BECAUSE IF I EVER DID CATCH SOMEONE'S EYE, I DON'T KNOW WHAT WOULD HAPPEN.
OH. UM. WE'RE GOING TO DO A SPELL.
I WANTED IT TO BE A SURPRISE.
A SURPRISE SPELL? FOR ME? AND HERE I DIDN'T GET YOU ANYTHING!
I MIGHT JUST BURST INTO FLAMES.
Y-YOU DON'T THINK THERE'S ANYONE OUT THERE, DO YOU?
WHAT? NO, SUNNYDALE AT NIGHT IS ENTIRELY FREE FROM DANGER, I CAN ASSURE YOU.
FIGURATIVELY, I MEAN. SPONTANEOUS HUMAN COMBUSTION IS ACTUALLY PRETTY RARE.
YEP, SAFE AS HOUSES!
ASSUMING THE HOUSE IS IN AMITYVILLE...
WHAT?

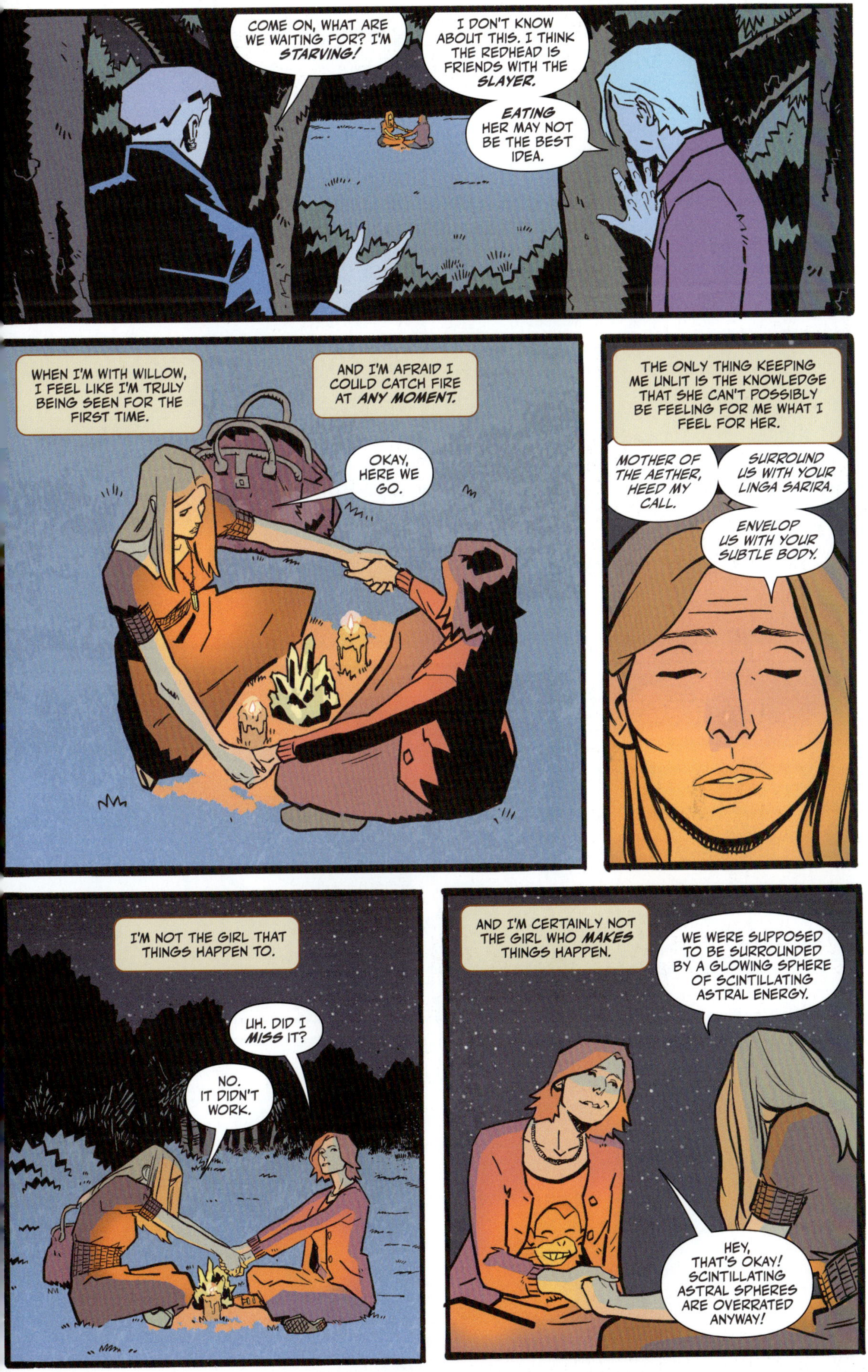
COME ON, WHAT ARE WE WAITING FOR? I'M STARVING!
I DON'T KNOW ABOUT THIS. I THINK THE REDHEAD IS FRIENDS WITH THE SLAYER.
EATING HER MAY NOT BE THE BEST IDEA.
WHEN I'M WITH WILLOW, I FEEL LIKE I'M TRULY BEING SEEN FOR THE FIRST TIME.
AND I'M AFRAID I COULD CATCH FIRE AT ANY MOMENT.
OKAY, HERE WE GO.
THE ONLY THING KEEPING ME UNLIT IS THE KNOWLEDGE THAT SHE CAN'T POSSIBLY BE FEELING FOR ME WHAT I FEEL FOR HER.
MOTHER OF THE AETHER, HEED MY CALL.
SURROUND US WITH YOUR LINGA SARIRA.
ENVELOP US WITH YOUR SUBTLE BODY.
I'M NOT THE GIRL THAT THINGS HAPPEN TO.
UH. DID I MISS IT?
NO. IT DIDN'T WORK.
AND I'M CERTAINLY NOT THE GIRL WHO MAKES THINGS HAPPEN.
WE WERE SUPPOSED TO BE SURROUNDED BY A GLOWING SPHERE OF SCINTILLATING ASTRAL ENERGY.
HEY, THAT'S OKAY! SCINTILLATING ASTRAL SPHERES ARE OVERRATED ANYWAY!

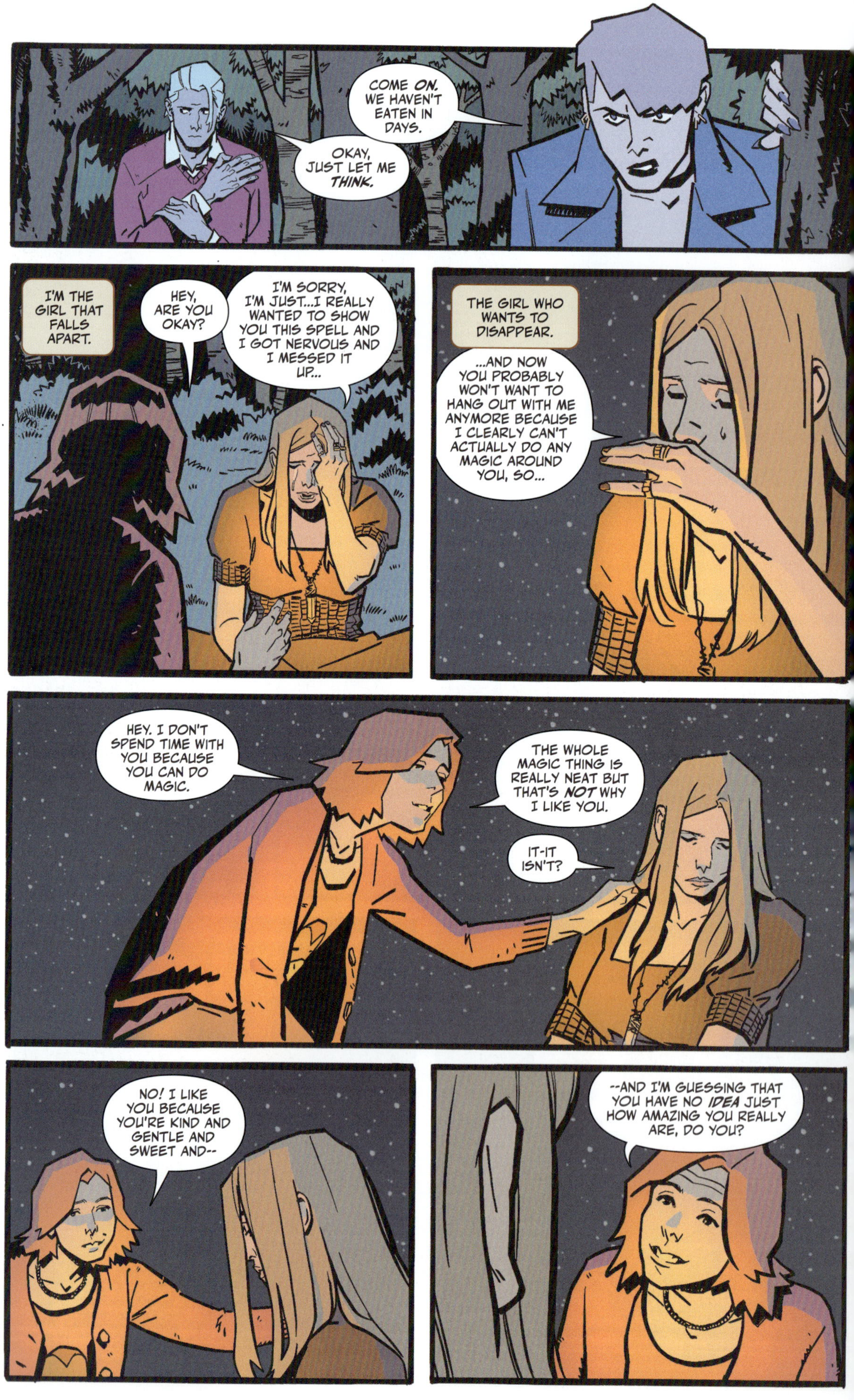
COME *ON.* WE HAVEN'T EATEN IN DAYS.
OKAY, JUST LET ME *THINK.*
I'M THE GIRL THAT FALLS APART.
HEY, ARE YOU OKAY?
I'M SORRY, I'M JUST...I REALLY WANTED TO SHOW YOU THIS SPELL AND I GOT NERVOUS AND I MESSED IT UP...
THE GIRL WHO WANTS TO DISAPPEAR.
...AND NOW YOU PROBABLY WON'T WANT TO HANG OUT WITH ME ANYMORE BECAUSE I CLEARLY CAN'T ACTUALLY DO ANY MAGIC AROUND YOU, SO...
HEY. I DON'T SPEND TIME WITH YOU BECAUSE YOU CAN DO MAGIC.
THE WHOLE MAGIC THING IS REALLY NEAT BUT THAT'S *NOT* WHY I LIKE YOU.
IT-IT ISN'T?
NO! I LIKE YOU BECAUSE YOU'RE KIND AND GENTLE AND SWEET AND--
--AND I'M GUESSING THAT YOU HAVE NO *IDEA* JUST HOW AMAZING YOU REALLY ARE, DO YOU?

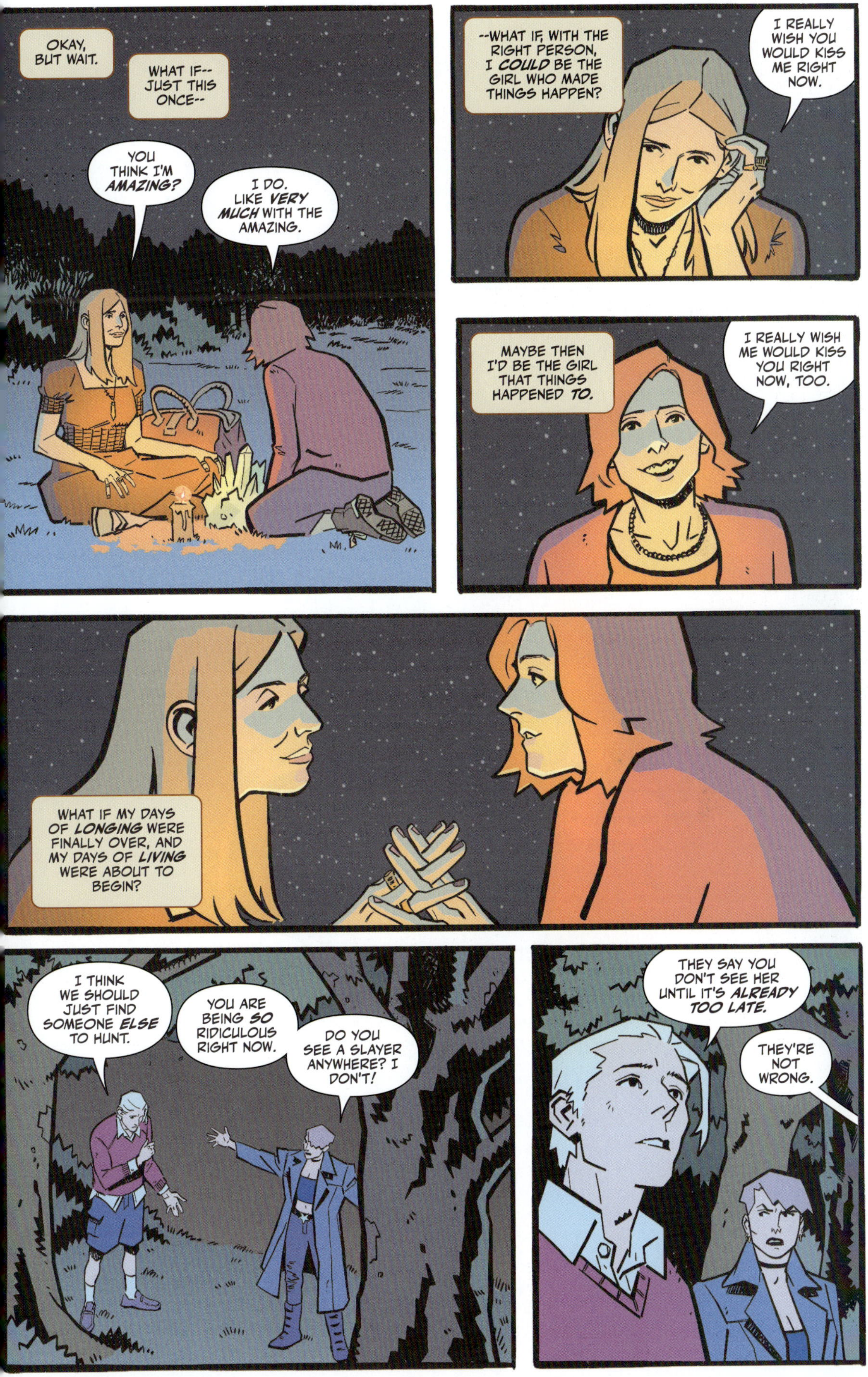
OKAY, BUT WAIT.
WHAT IF-- JUST THIS ONCE--
YOU THINK I'M AMAZING?
I DO. LIKE VERY MUCH WITH THE AMAZING.
--WHAT IF, WITH THE RIGHT PERSON, I COULD BE THE GIRL WHO MADE THINGS HAPPEN?
I REALLY WISH YOU WOULD KISS ME RIGHT NOW.
MAYBE THEN I'D BE THE GIRL THAT THINGS HAPPENED TO.
I REALLY WISH ME WOULD KISS YOU RIGHT NOW, TOO.
WHAT IF MY DAYS OF LONGING WERE FINALLY OVER, AND MY DAYS OF LIVING WERE ABOUT TO BEGIN?
I THINK WE SHOULD JUST FIND SOMEONE ELSE TO HUNT.
YOU ARE BEING SO RIDICULOUS RIGHT NOW.
DO YOU SEE A SLAYER ANYWHERE? I DON'T!
THEY SAY YOU DON'T SEE HER UNTIL IT'S ALREADY TOO LATE.
THEY'RE NOT WRONG.

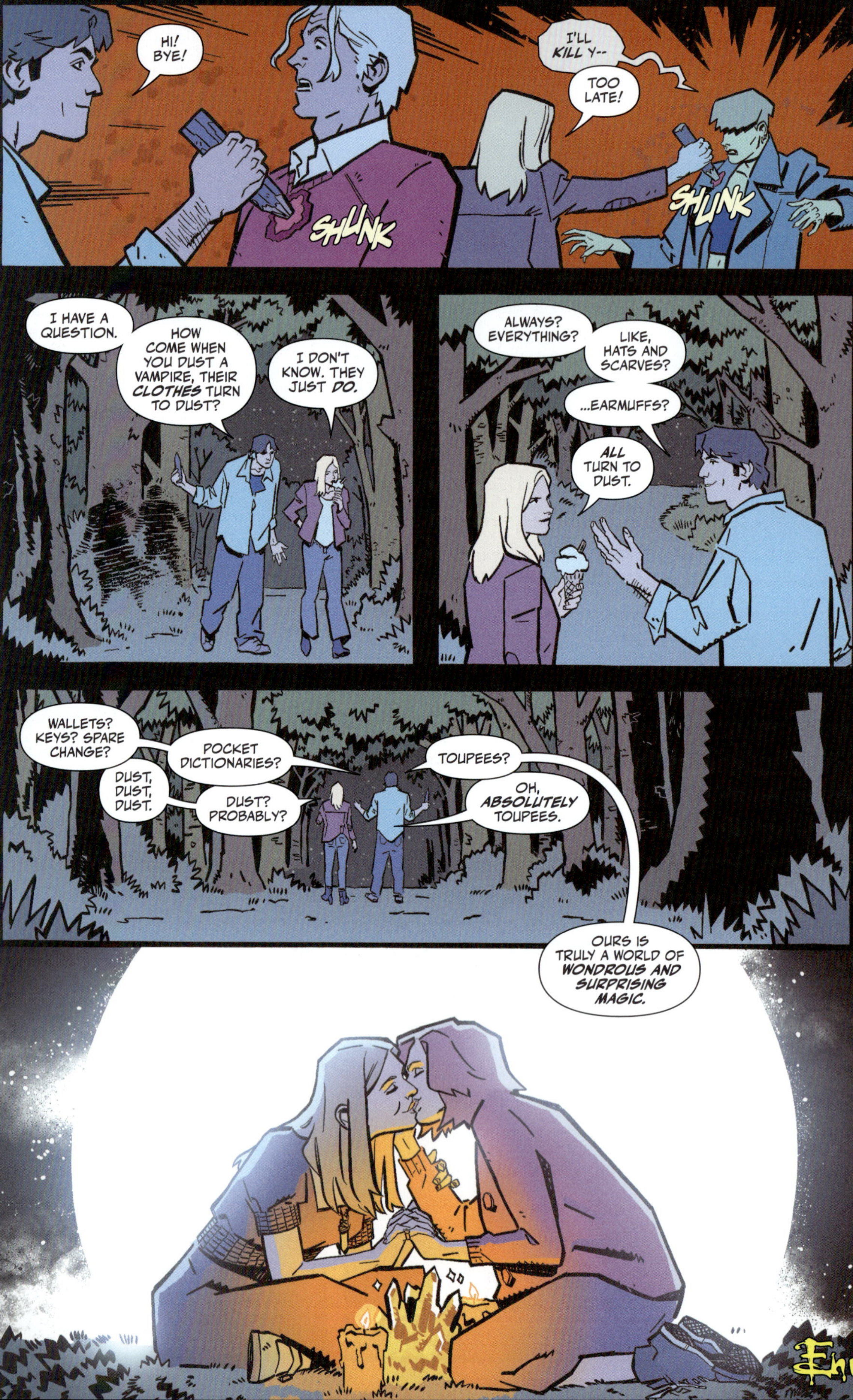
HI! BYE!
SHUNK
I'LL KILL Y--
TOO LATE!
SHUNK
I HAVE A QUESTION.
HOW COME WHEN YOU DUST A VAMPIRE, THEIR CLOTHES TURN TO DUST?
I DON'T KNOW. THEY JUST DO.
ALWAYS? EVERYTHING?
LIKE, HATS AND SCARVES?
...EARMUFFS?
ALL TURN TO DUST.
WALLETS? KEYS? SPARE CHANGE?
DUST, DUST, DUST.
POCKET DICTIONARIES?
DUST? PROBABLY?
TOUPEES?
OH, ABSOLUTELY TOUPEES.
OURS IS TRULY A WORLD OF WONDROUS AND SURPRISING MAGIC.

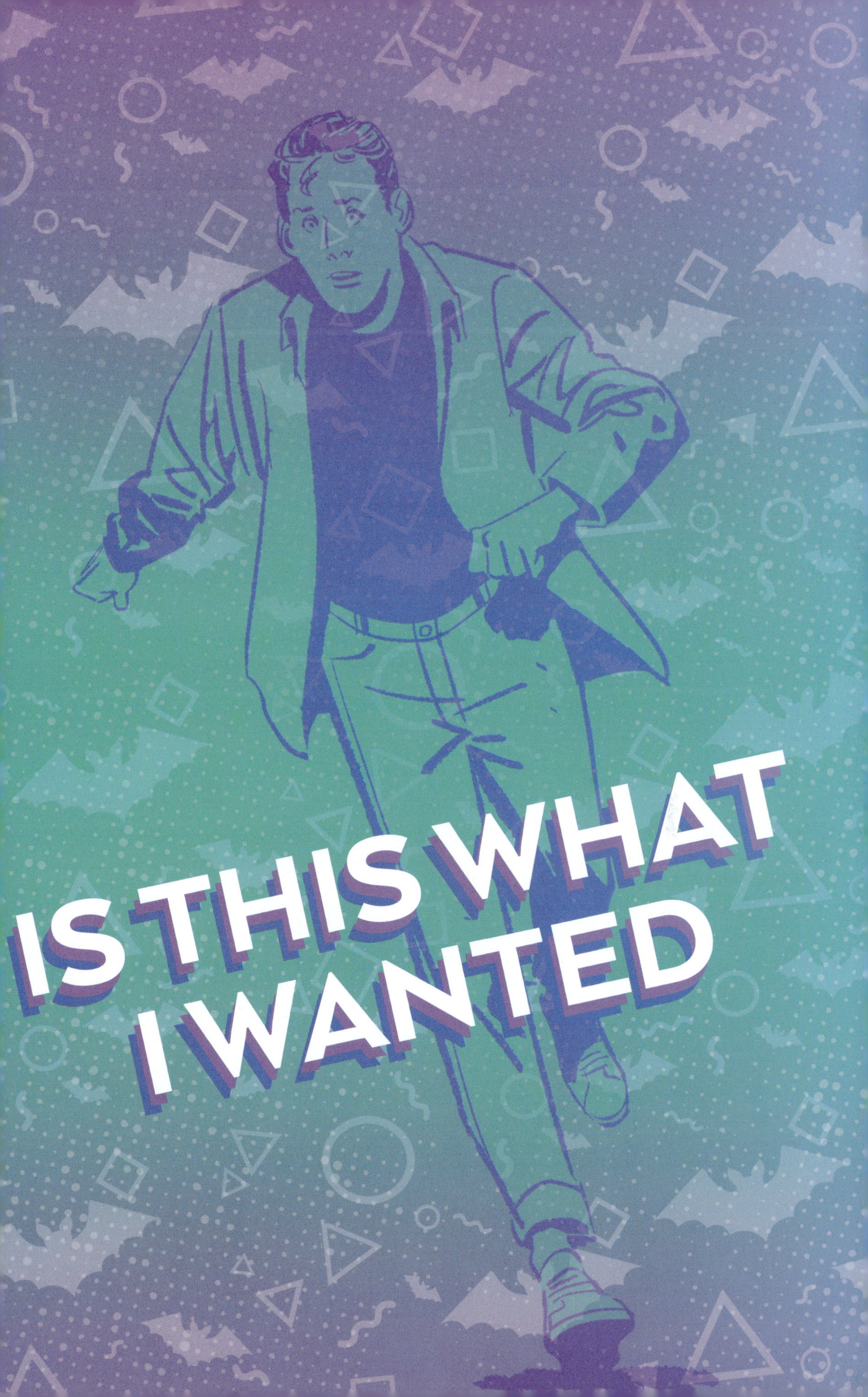
IS THIS WHAT
I WANTED

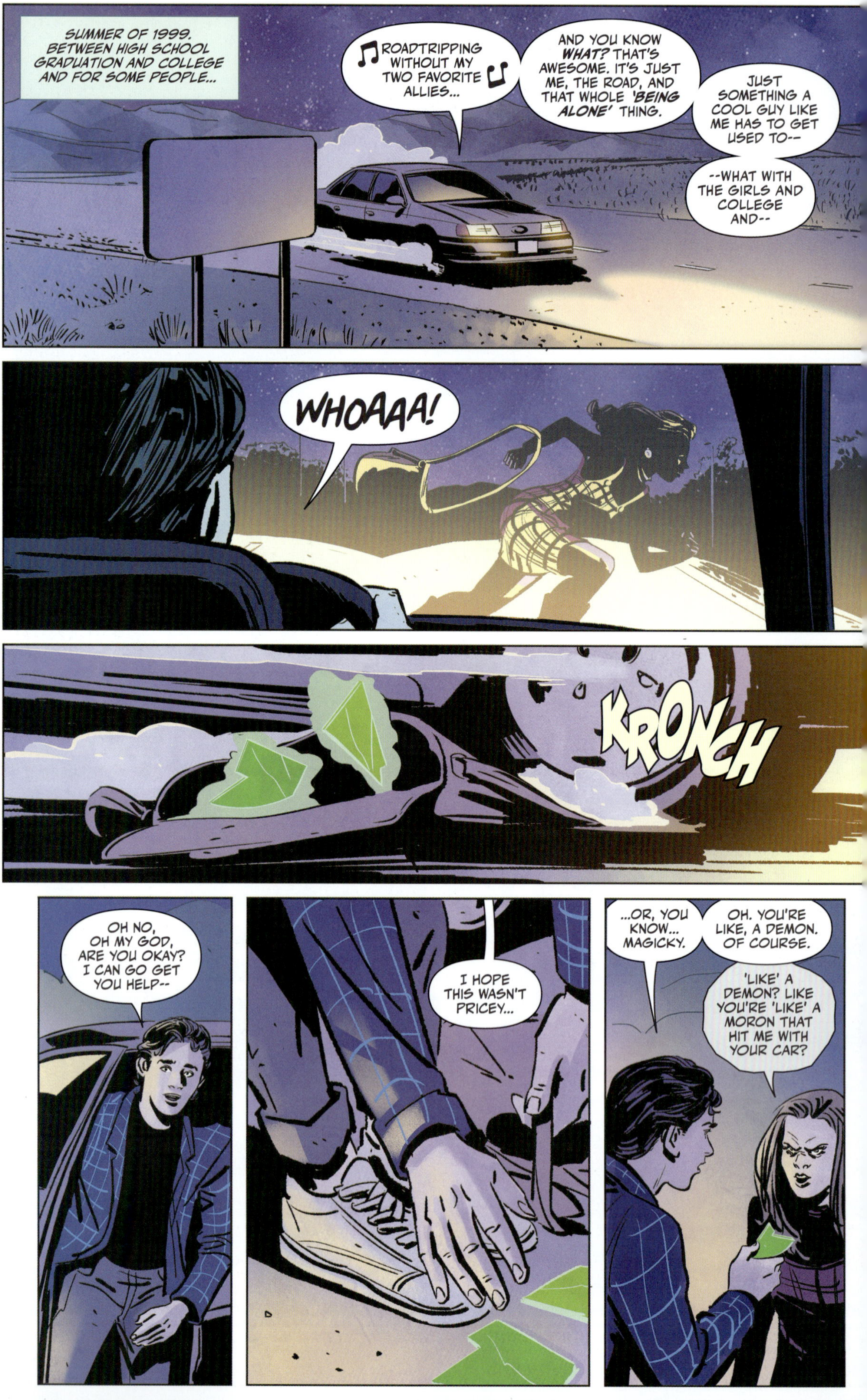

SUMMER OF 1999. BETWEEN HIGH SCHOOL GRADUATION AND COLLEGE AND FOR SOME PEOPLE...
♫ ROADTRIPPING WITHOUT MY TWO FAVORITE ALLIES... ♫
AND YOU KNOW *WHAT?* THAT'S AWESOME. IT'S JUST ME, THE ROAD, AND THAT WHOLE *'BEING ALONE'* THING.
JUST SOMETHING A COOL GUY LIKE ME HAS TO GET USED TO--
--WHAT WITH THE GIRLS AND COLLEGE AND--
WHOAAA!
KRONCH
OH NO, OH MY GOD, ARE YOU OKAY? I CAN GO GET YOU HELP--
I HOPE THIS WASN'T PRICEY...
OH. YOU'RE LIKE, A DEMON. OF COURSE.
...OR, YOU KNOW... MAGICKY.
'LIKE' A DEMON? LIKE YOU'RE 'LIKE' A MORON THAT HIT ME WITH YOUR CAR?

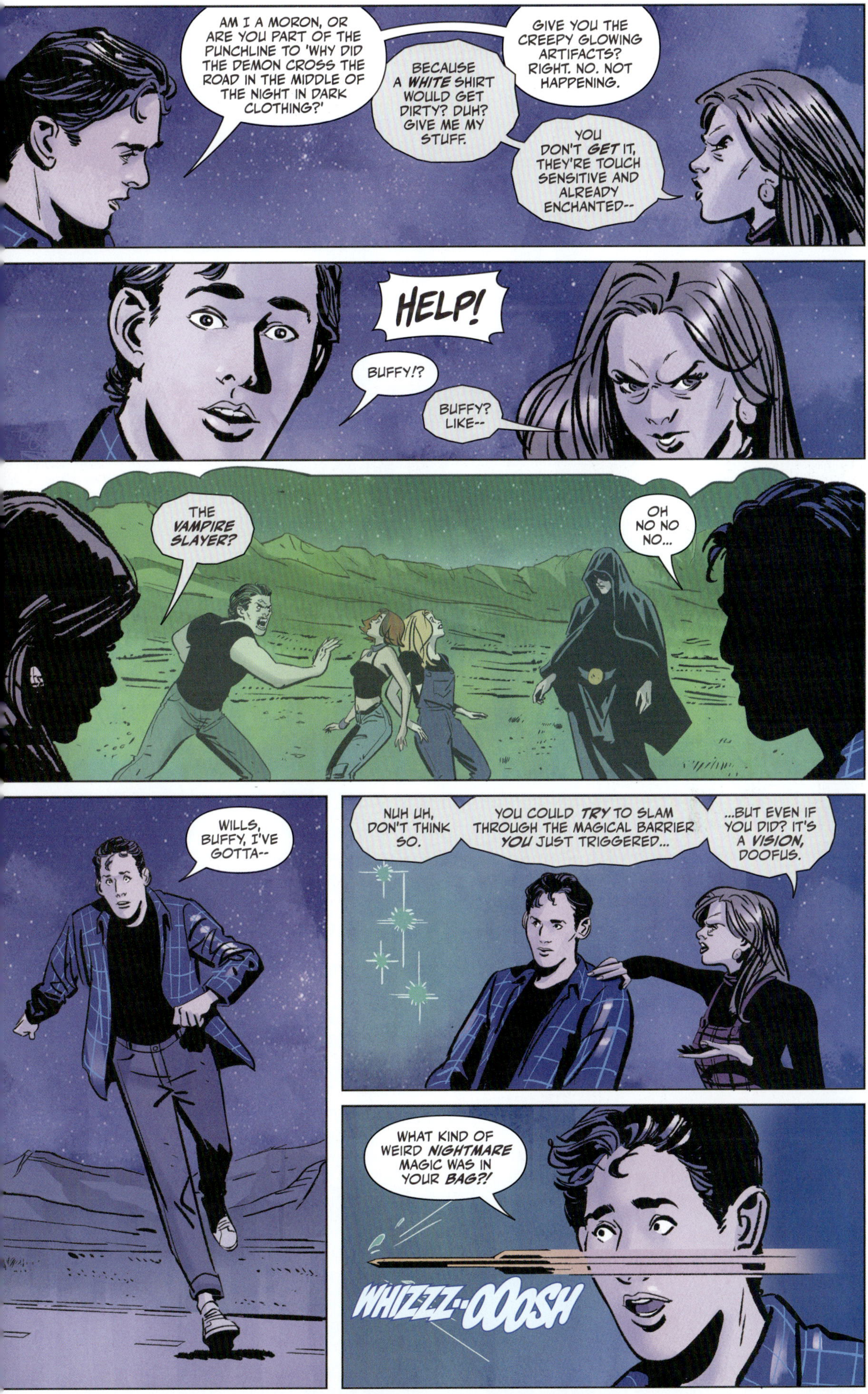

AM I A MORON, OR ARE YOU PART OF THE PUNCHLINE TO 'WHY DID THE DEMON CROSS THE ROAD IN THE MIDDLE OF THE NIGHT IN DARK CLOTHING?'
BECAUSE A WHITE SHIRT WOULD GET DIRTY? DUH? GIVE ME MY STUFF.
GIVE YOU THE CREEPY GLOWING ARTIFACTS? RIGHT. NO. NOT HAPPENING.
YOU DON'T GET IT, THEY'RE TOUCH SENSITIVE AND ALREADY ENCHANTED--
HELP!
BUFFY!?
BUFFY? LIKE--
THE VAMPIRE SLAYER?
OH NO NO NO...
WILLS, BUFFY, I'VE GOTTA--
NUH UH, DON'T THINK SO.
YOU COULD TRY TO SLAM THROUGH THE MAGICAL BARRIER YOU JUST TRIGGERED...
...BUT EVEN IF YOU DID? IT'S A VISION, DOOFUS.
WHAT KIND OF WEIRD NIGHTMARE MAGIC WAS IN YOUR BAG?!
WHIZZZ-OOOSH

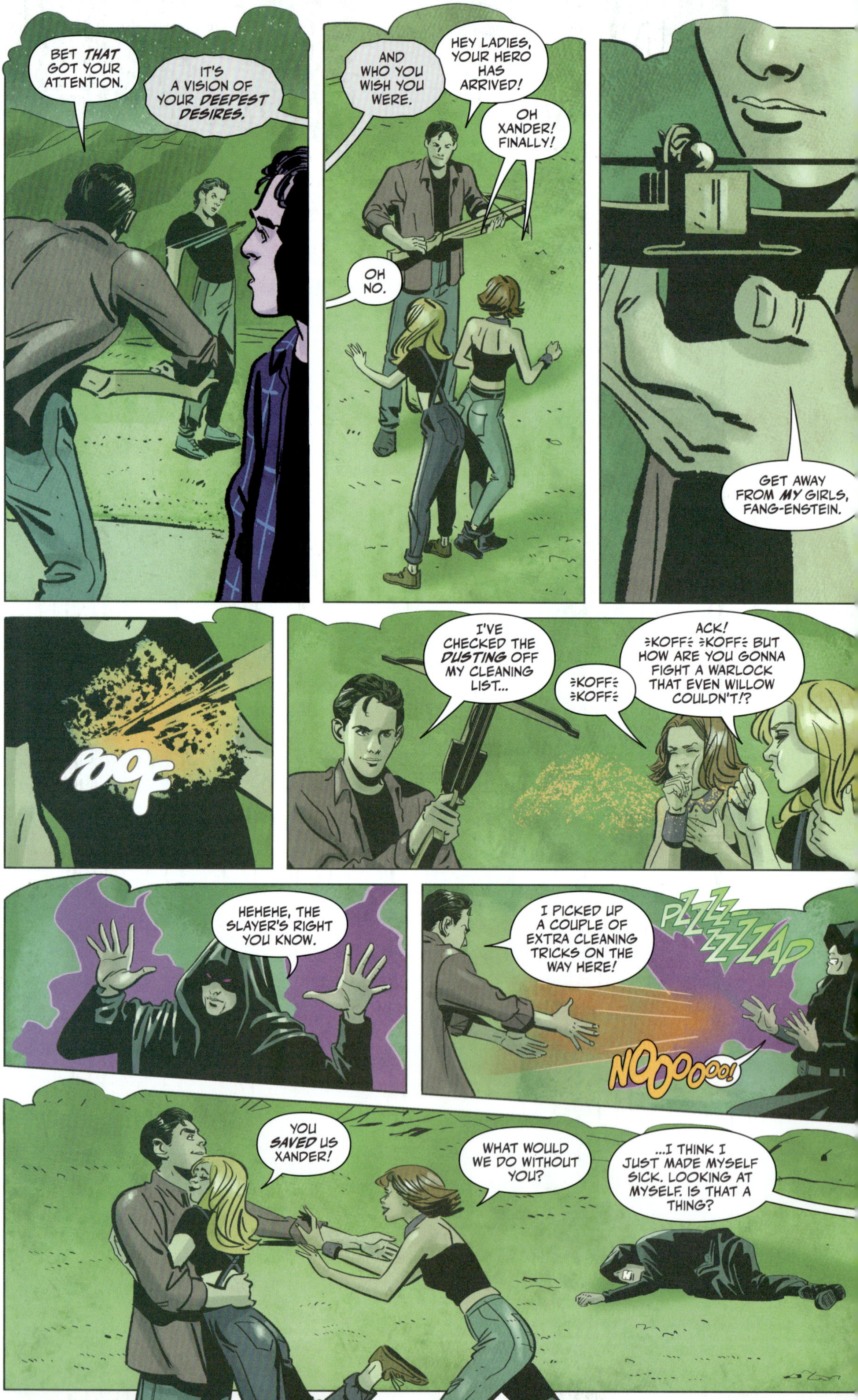
BET THAT GOT YOUR ATTENTION.
IT'S A VISION OF YOUR DEEPEST DESIRES.
AND WHO YOU WISH YOU WERE.
HEY LADIES, YOUR HERO HAS ARRIVED!
OH XANDER! FINALLY!
OH NO.
GET AWAY FROM MY GIRLS, FANG-ENSTEIN.
POOF
I'VE CHECKED THE DUSTING OFF MY CLEANING LIST...
KOFF KOFF
ACK! KOFF KOFF BUT HOW ARE YOU GONNA FIGHT A WARLOCK THAT EVEN WILLOW COULDN'T!?
HEHEHE, THE SLAYER'S RIGHT YOU KNOW.
I PICKED UP A COUPLE OF EXTRA CLEANING TRICKS ON THE WAY HERE!
PZZZZZZZZAP
NOOOOOO!
YOU SAVED US XANDER!
WHAT WOULD WE DO WITHOUT YOU?
...I THINK I JUST MADE MYSELF SICK. LOOKING AT MYSELF. IS THAT A THING?

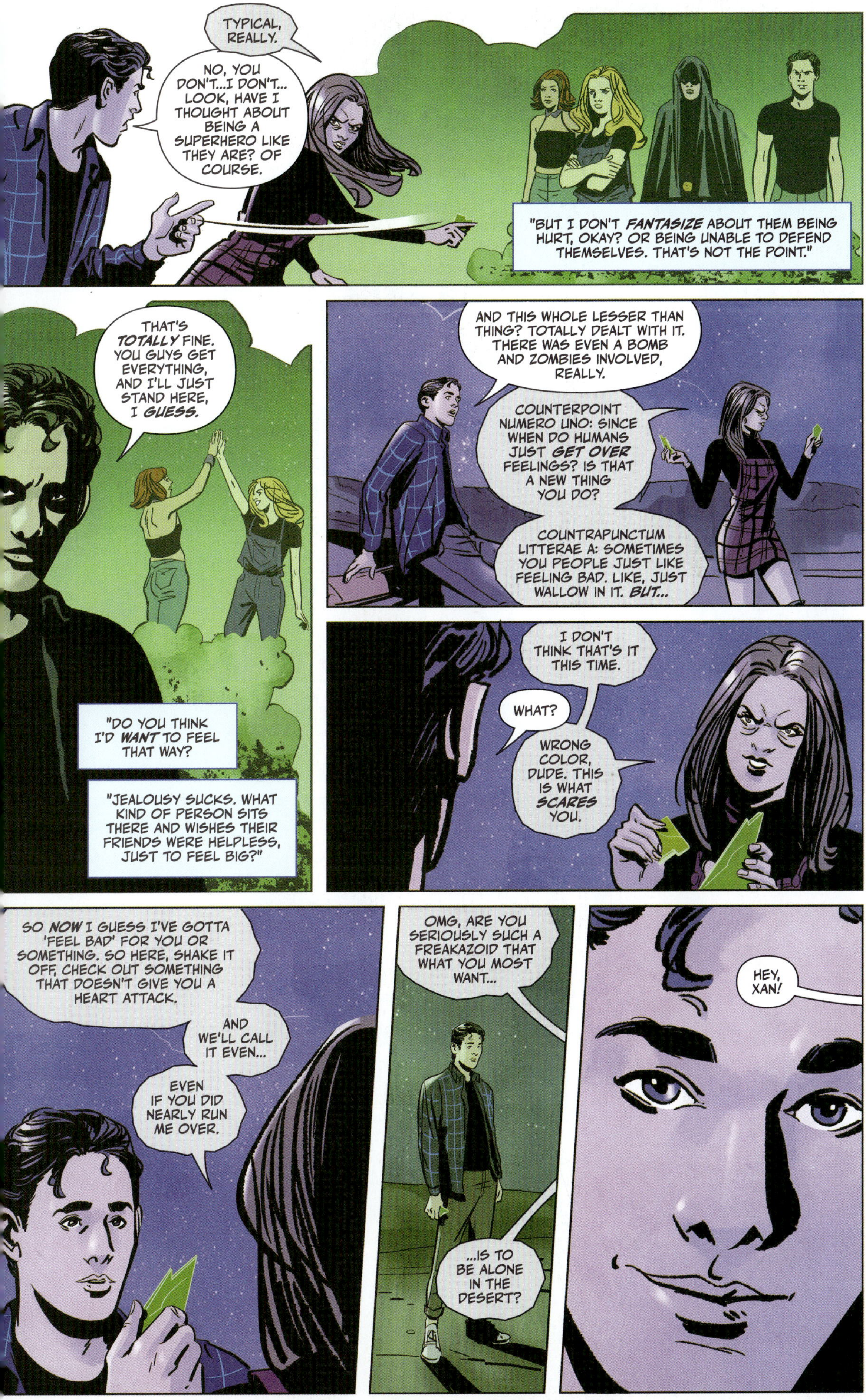
TYPICAL, REALLY.
NO, YOU DON'T...I DON'T... LOOK, HAVE I THOUGHT ABOUT BEING A SUPERHERO LIKE THEY ARE? OF COURSE.
"BUT I DON'T FANTASIZE ABOUT THEM BEING HURT, OKAY? OR BEING UNABLE TO DEFEND THEMSELVES. THAT'S NOT THE POINT."
THAT'S TOTALLY FINE. YOU GUYS GET EVERYTHING, AND I'LL JUST STAND HERE, I GUESS.
"DO YOU THINK I'D WANT TO FEEL THAT WAY?
"JEALOUSY SUCKS. WHAT KIND OF PERSON SITS THERE AND WISHES THEIR FRIENDS WERE HELPLESS, JUST TO FEEL BIG?"
AND THIS WHOLE LESSER THAN THING? TOTALLY DEALT WITH IT. THERE WAS EVEN A BOMB AND ZOMBIES INVOLVED, REALLY.
COUNTERPOINT NUMERO UNO: SINCE WHEN DO HUMANS JUST GET OVER FEELINGS? IS THAT A NEW THING YOU DO?
COUNTRAPUNCTUM LITTERAE A: SOMETIMES YOU PEOPLE JUST LIKE FEELING BAD. LIKE, JUST WALLOW IN IT. BUT...
I DON'T THINK THAT'S IT THIS TIME.
WHAT?
WRONG COLOR, DUDE. THIS IS WHAT SCARES YOU.
SO NOW I GUESS I'VE GOTTA 'FEEL BAD' FOR YOU OR SOMETHING. SO HERE, SHAKE IT OFF, CHECK OUT SOMETHING THAT DOESN'T GIVE YOU A HEART ATTACK.
AND WE'LL CALL IT EVEN...
EVEN IF YOU DID NEARLY RUN ME OVER.
OMG, ARE YOU SERIOUSLY SUCH A FREAKAZOID THAT WHAT YOU MOST WANT...
...IS TO BE ALONE IN THE DESERT?
HEY, XAN!

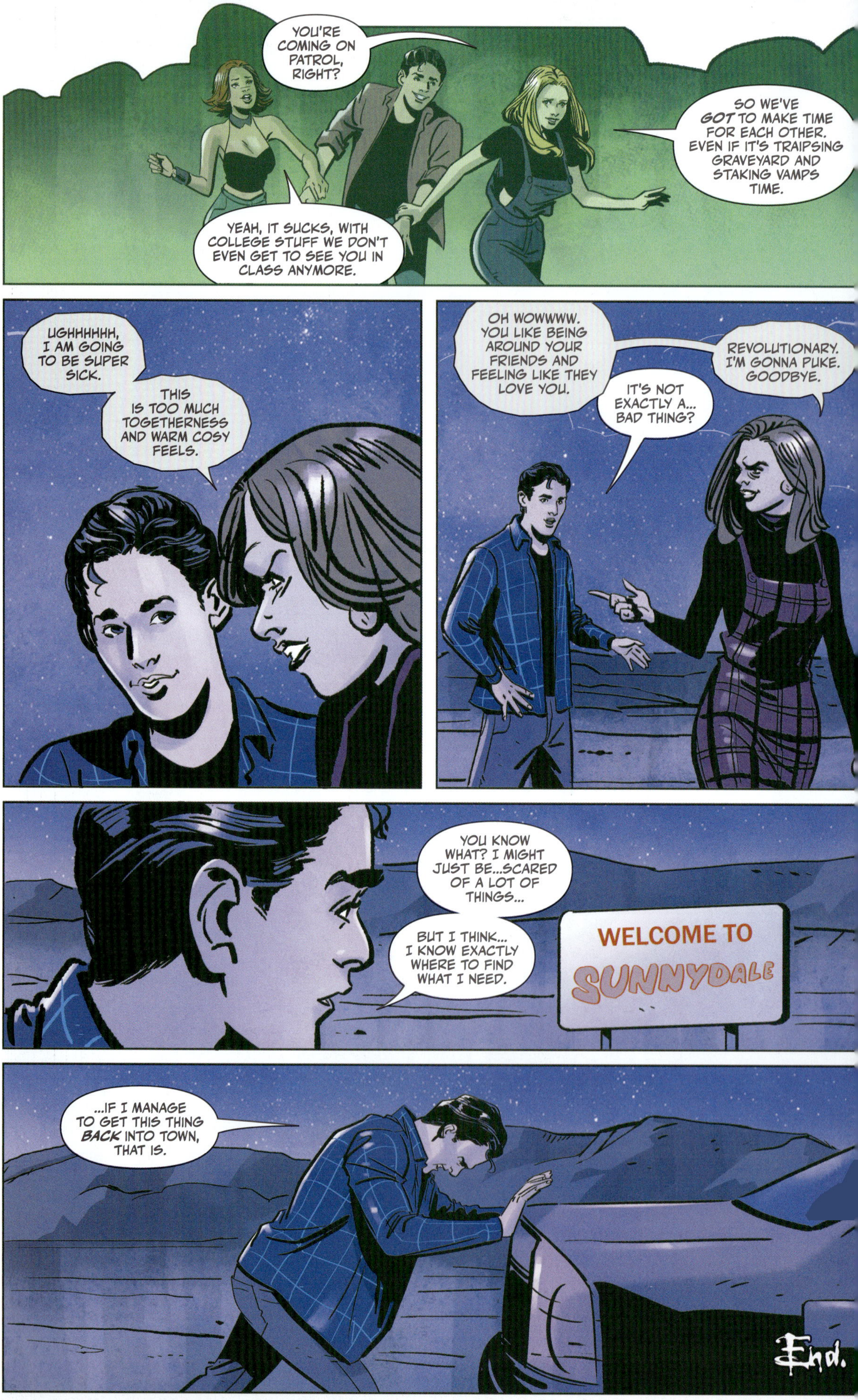
YOU'RE COMING ON PATROL, RIGHT?
YEAH, IT SUCKS, WITH COLLEGE STUFF WE DON'T EVEN GET TO SEE YOU IN CLASS ANYMORE.
SO WE'VE *GOT* TO MAKE TIME FOR EACH OTHER. EVEN IF IT'S TRAIPSING GRAVEYARD AND STAKING VAMPS TIME.
UGHHHHHH, I AM GOING TO BE SUPER SICK.
THIS IS TOO MUCH TOGETHERNESS AND WARM COSY FEELS.
OH WOWWWW. YOU LIKE BEING AROUND YOUR FRIENDS AND FEELING LIKE THEY LOVE YOU.
REVOLUTIONARY. I'M GONNA PUKE. GOODBYE.
IT'S NOT EXACTLY A... BAD THING?
YOU KNOW WHAT? I MIGHT JUST BE...SCARED OF A LOT OF THINGS...
BUT I THINK... I KNOW EXACTLY WHERE TO FIND WHAT I NEED.
WELCOME TO
SUNNYDALE
...IF I MANAGE TO GET THIS THING *BACK* INTO TOWN, THAT IS.
End.

MIRRORS DON'T LIE

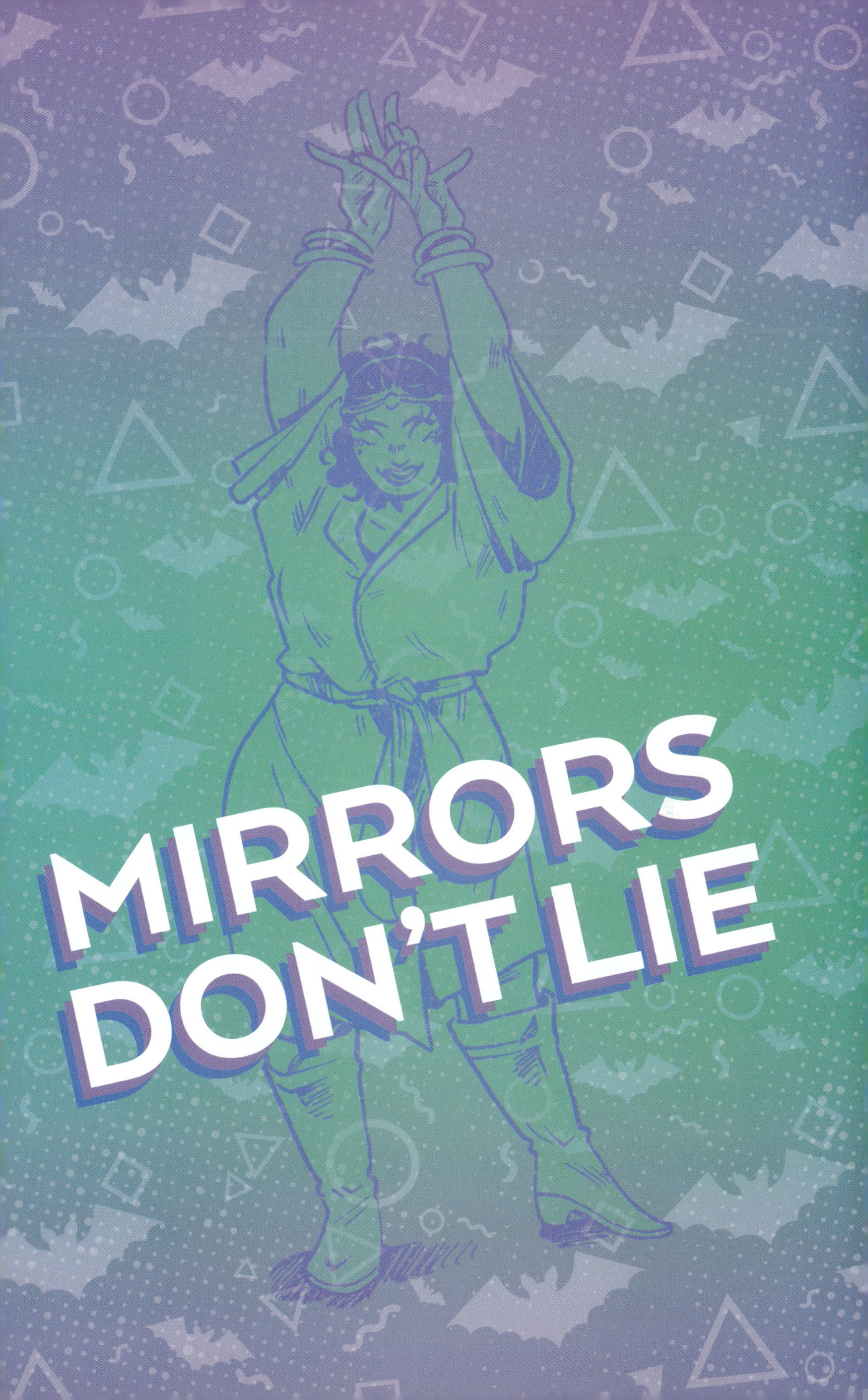

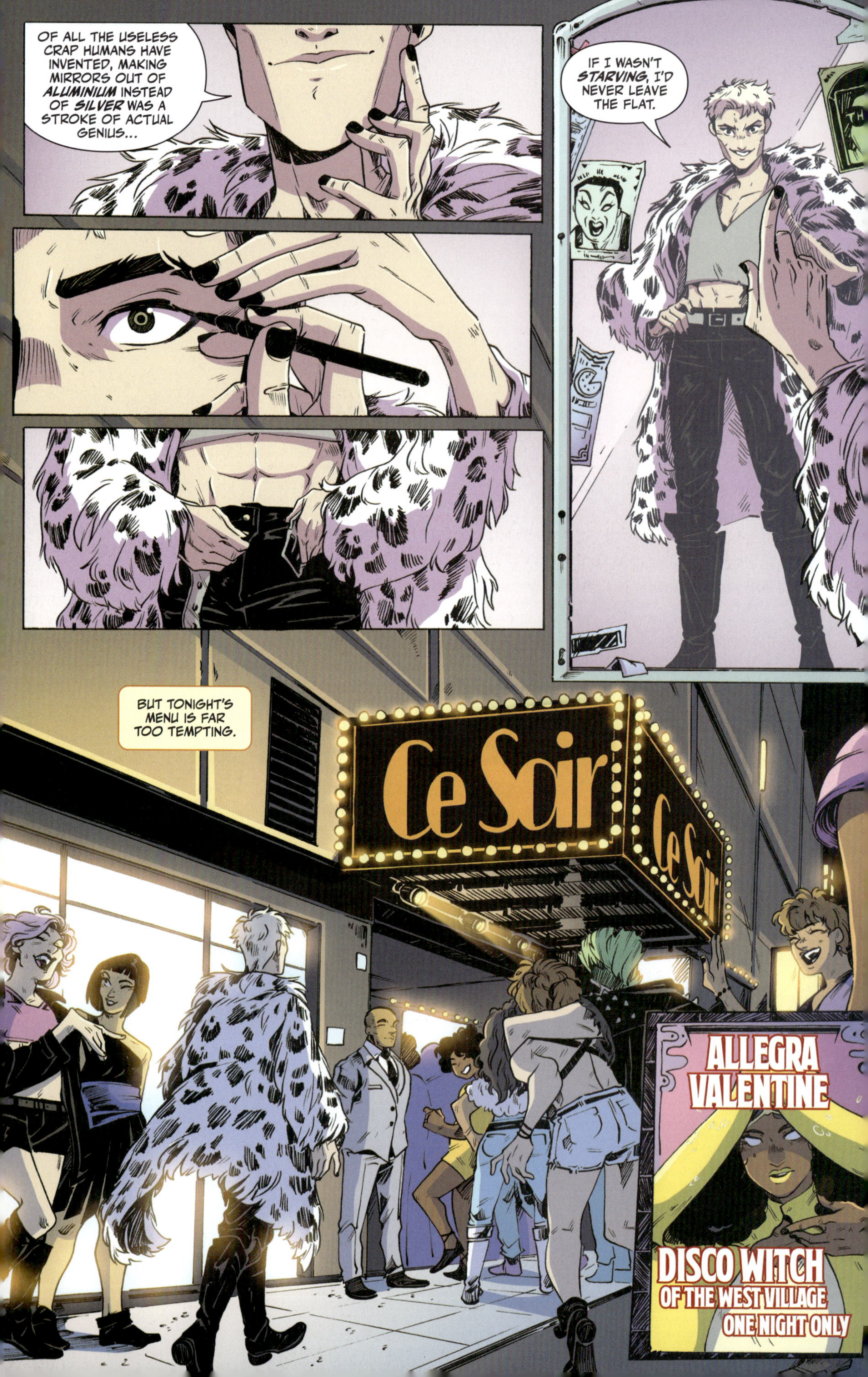
OF ALL THE USELESS CRAP HUMANS HAVE INVENTED, MAKING MIRRORS OUT OF ALUMINIUM INSTEAD OF SILVER WAS A STROKE OF ACTUAL GENIUS...
IF I WASN'T STARVING, I'D NEVER LEAVE THE FLAT.
BUT TONIGHT'S MENU IS FAR TOO TEMPTING.
Ce Soir
Ce Soir
ALLEGRA VALENTINE
DISCO WITCH OF THE WEST VILLAGE
ONE NIGHT ONLY

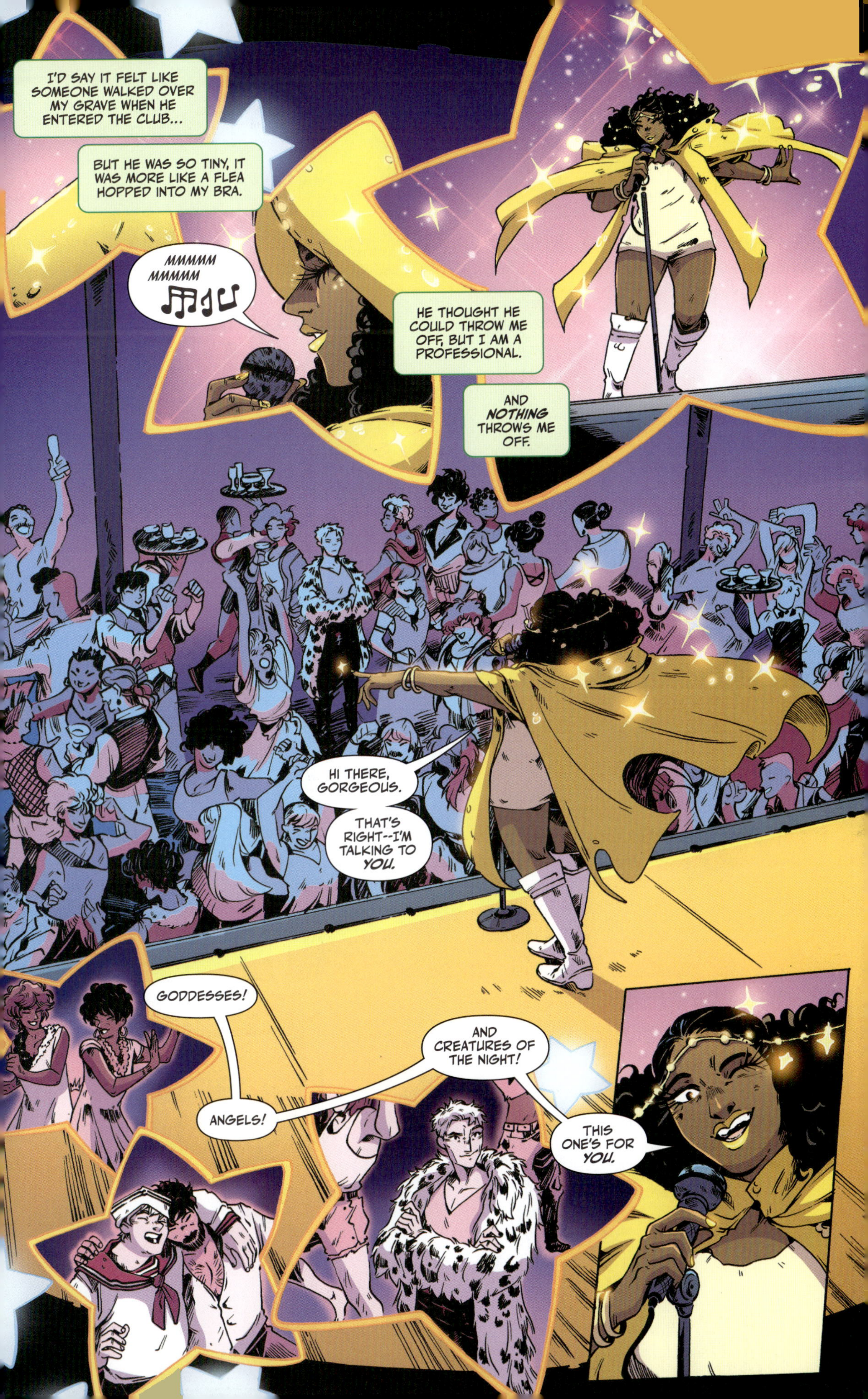
I'D SAY IT FELT LIKE SOMEONE WALKED OVER MY GRAVE WHEN HE ENTERED THE CLUB...
BUT HE WAS SO TINY, IT WAS MORE LIKE A FLEA HOPPED INTO MY BRA.
MMMMM MMMMM
HE THOUGHT HE COULD THROW ME OFF, BUT I AM A PROFESSIONAL.
AND NOTHING THROWS ME OFF.
HI THERE, GORGEOUS.
THAT'S RIGHT--I'M TALKING TO YOU.
GODDESSES!
ANGELS!
AND CREATURES OF THE NIGHT!
THIS ONE'S FOR YOU.

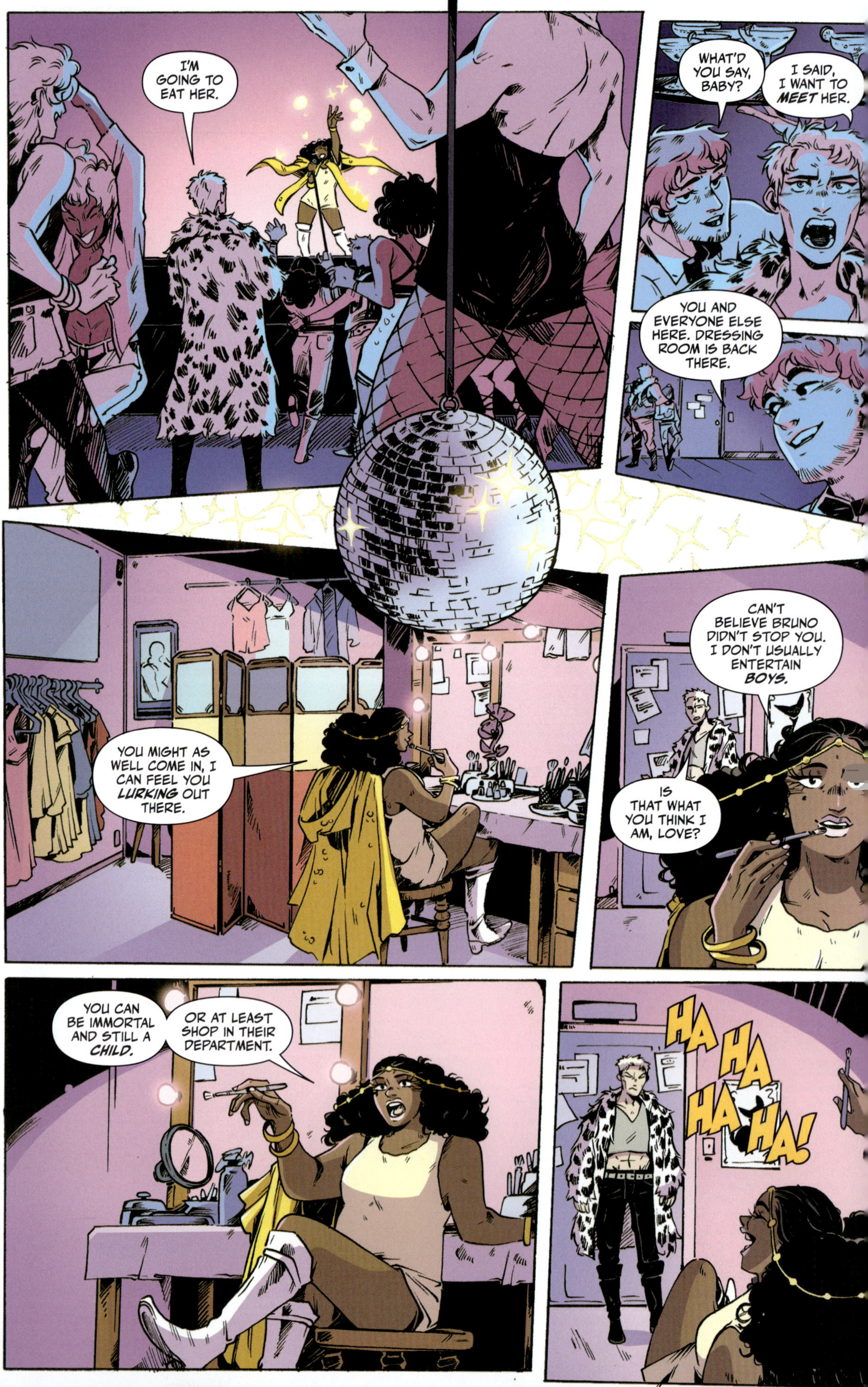
I'M GOING TO EAT HER.
WHAT'D YOU SAY, BABY?
I SAID, I WANT TO MEET HER.
YOU AND EVERYONE ELSE HERE. DRESSING ROOM IS BACK THERE.
YOU MIGHT AS WELL COME IN, I CAN FEEL YOU LURKING OUT THERE.
CAN'T BELIEVE BRUNO DIDN'T STOP YOU. I DON'T USUALLY ENTERTAIN BOYS.
IS THAT WHAT YOU THINK I AM, LOVE?
YOU CAN BE IMMORTAL AND STILL A CHILD.
OR AT LEAST SHOP IN THEIR DEPARTMENT.
HA HA HA HA!

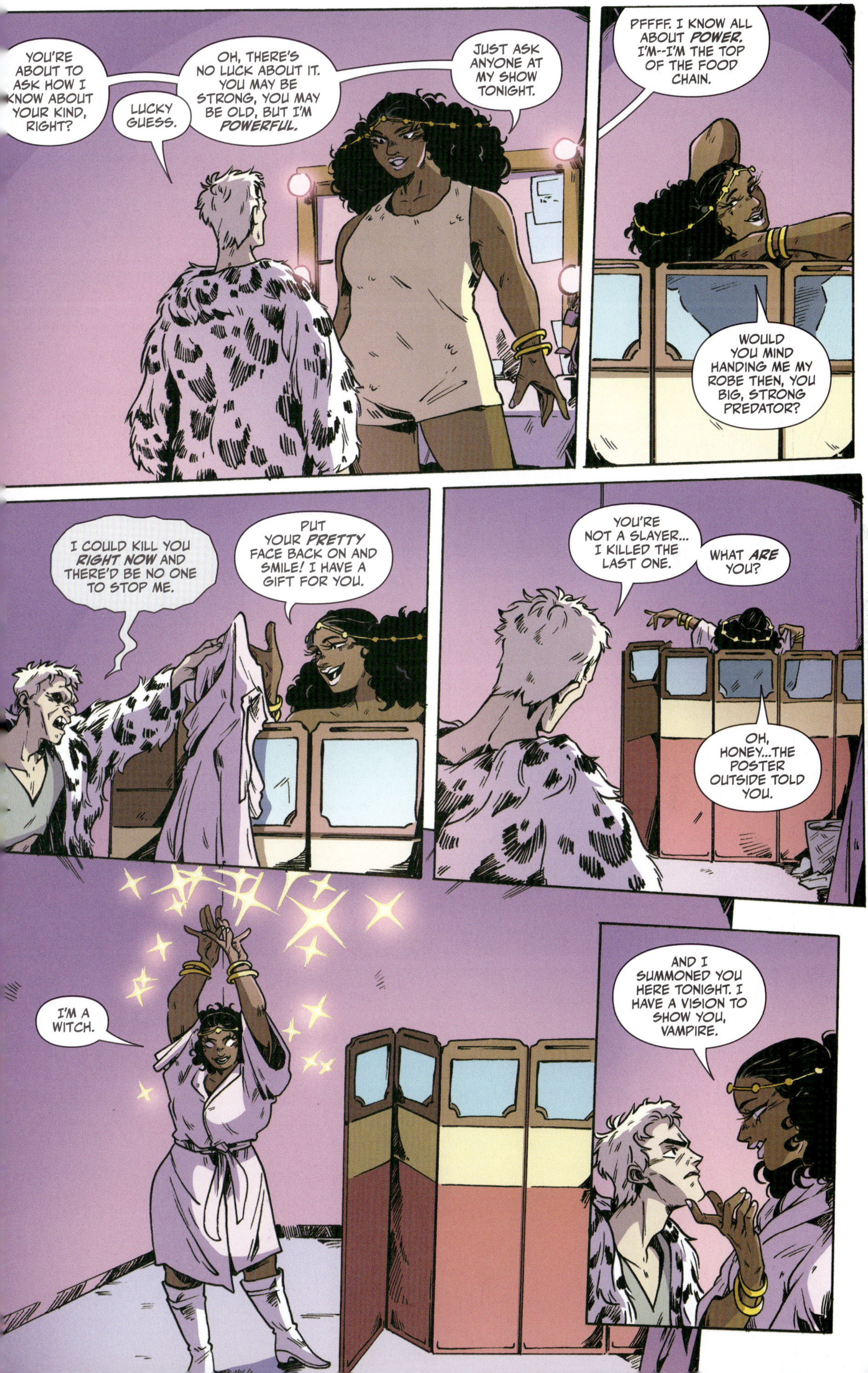

YOU'RE ABOUT TO ASK HOW I KNOW ABOUT YOUR KIND, RIGHT?
LUCKY GUESS.
OH, THERE'S NO LUCK ABOUT IT. YOU MAY BE STRONG, YOU MAY BE OLD, BUT I'M POWERFUL.
JUST ASK ANYONE AT MY SHOW TONIGHT.
PFFFF. I KNOW ALL ABOUT POWER. I'M--I'M THE TOP OF THE FOOD CHAIN.
WOULD YOU MIND HANDING ME MY ROBE THEN, YOU BIG, STRONG PREDATOR?
I COULD KILL YOU RIGHT NOW AND THERE'D BE NO ONE TO STOP ME.
PUT YOUR PRETTY FACE BACK ON AND SMILE! I HAVE A GIFT FOR YOU.
YOU'RE NOT A SLAYER... I KILLED THE LAST ONE.
WHAT ARE YOU?
OH, HONEY...THE POSTER OUTSIDE TOLD YOU.
I'M A WITCH.
AND I SUMMONED YOU HERE TONIGHT. I HAVE A VISION TO SHOW YOU, VAMPIRE.

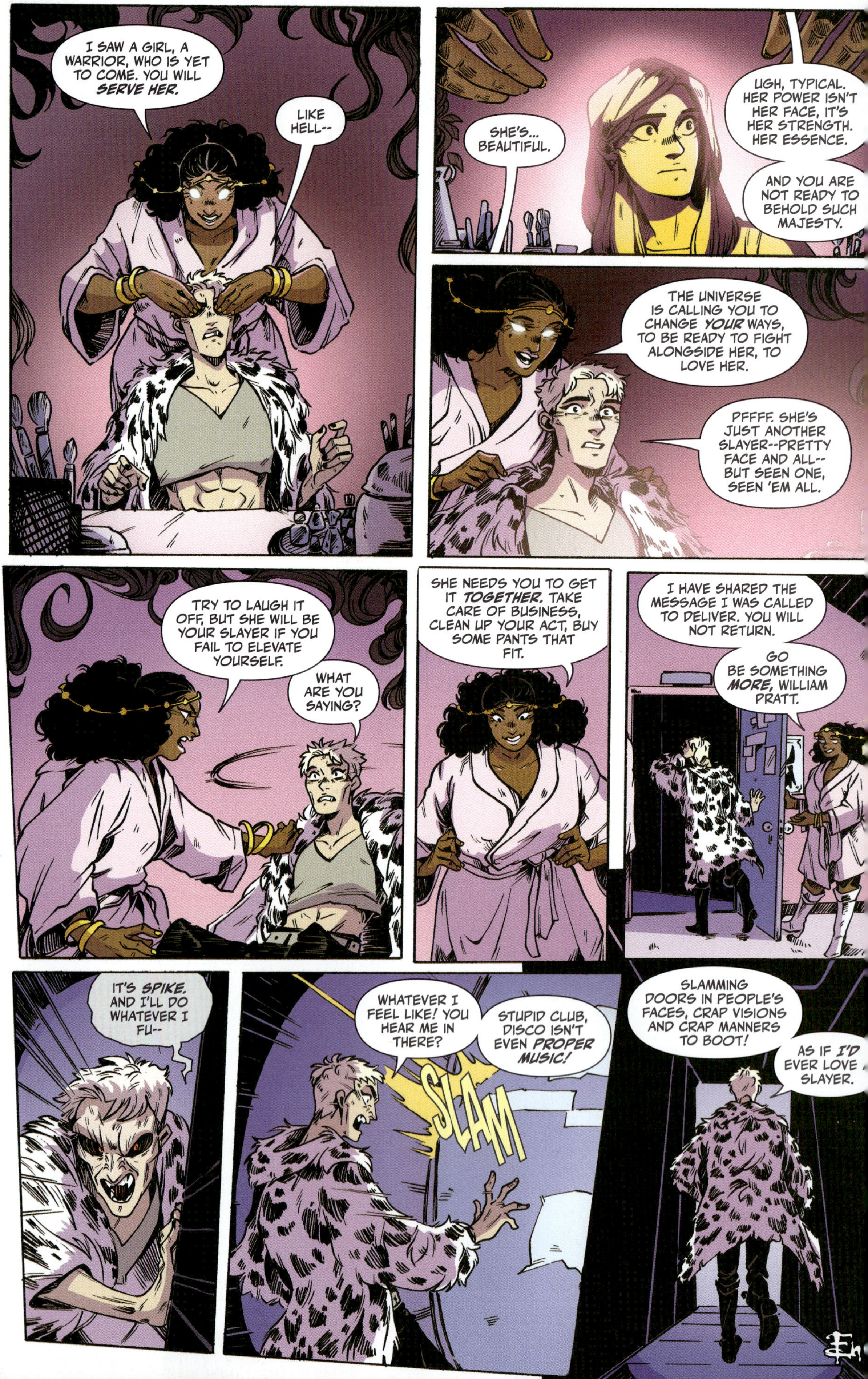
I SAW A GIRL, A WARRIOR, WHO IS YET TO COME. YOU WILL *SERVE HER.*
LIKE HELL--
SHE'S... BEAUTIFUL.
UGH, TYPICAL. HER POWER ISN'T HER FACE, IT'S HER STRENGTH. HER ESSENCE.
AND YOU ARE NOT READY TO BEHOLD SUCH MAJESTY.
THE UNIVERSE IS CALLING YOU TO CHANGE *YOUR* WAYS, TO BE READY TO FIGHT ALONGSIDE HER, TO LOVE HER.
PFFFF. SHE'S JUST ANOTHER SLAYER--PRETTY FACE AND ALL--BUT SEEN ONE, SEEN 'EM ALL.
TRY TO LAUGH IT OFF, BUT SHE WILL BE YOUR SLAYER IF YOU FAIL TO ELEVATE YOURSELF.
WHAT ARE YOU SAYING?
SHE NEEDS YOU TO GET IT *TOGETHER.* TAKE CARE OF BUSINESS, CLEAN UP YOUR ACT, BUY SOME PANTS THAT FIT.
I HAVE SHARED THE MESSAGE I WAS CALLED TO DELIVER. YOU WILL NOT RETURN.
GO BE SOMETHING *MORE,* WILLIAM PRATT.
IT'S *SPIKE.* AND I'LL DO WHATEVER I FU--
WHATEVER I FEEL LIKE! YOU HEAR ME IN THERE?
SLAM
STUPID CLUB, DISCO ISN'T EVEN *PROPER MUSIC!*
SLAMMING DOORS IN PEOPLE'S FACES, CRAP VISIONS AND CRAP MANNERS TO BOOT!
AS IF *I'D* EVER LOVE SLAYER.

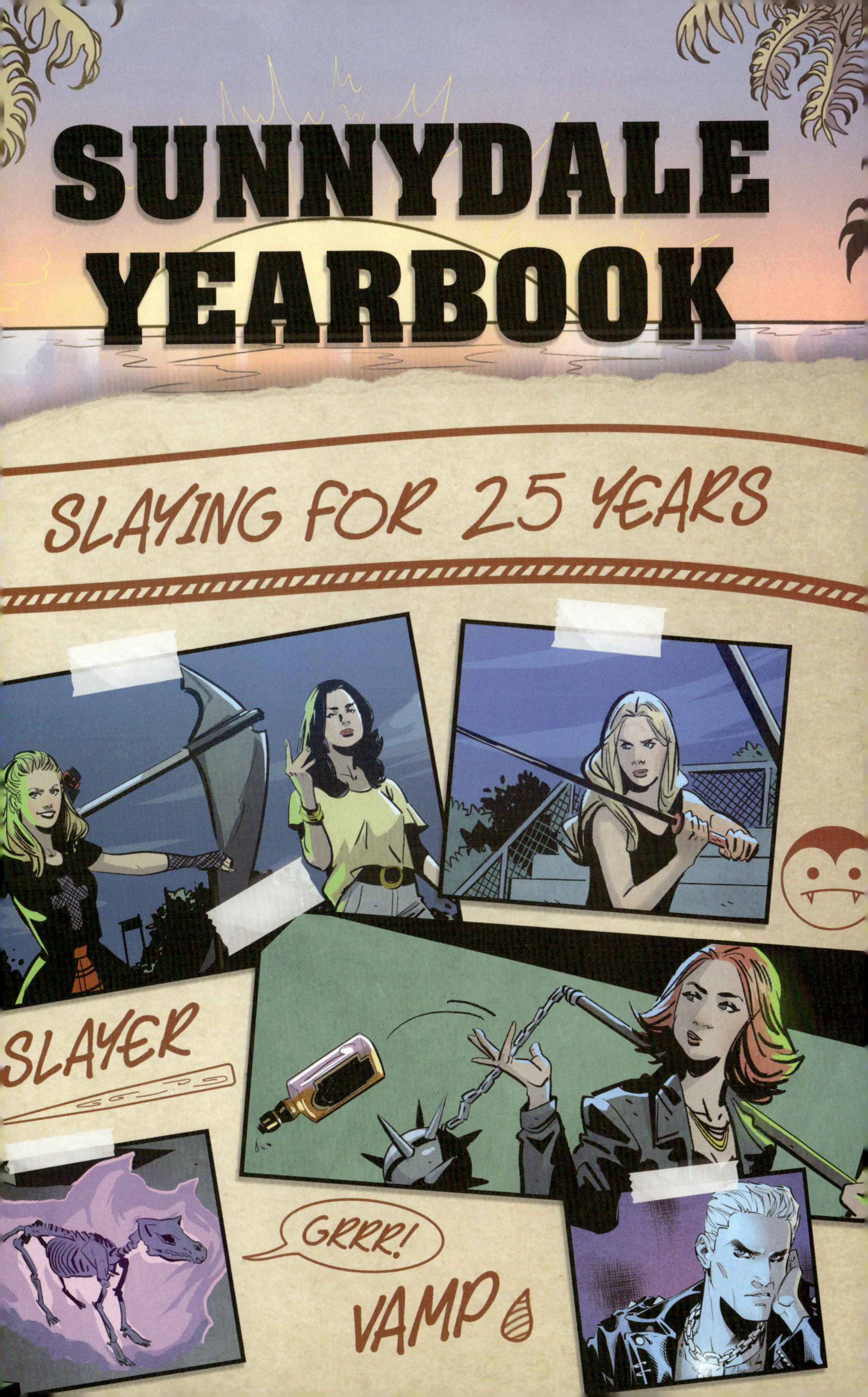

SUNNYDALE YEARBOOK
SLAYING FOR 25 YEARS
SLAYER
GRRR!
VAMP

ANGEL

"There's no Angelus without 'us.'"

ANYA JENKINS

"I often say the wrong thing, so let me think about what my quote should be before I give you an official one."

WINIFRED "FRED" BURKLE

"Stay away from weird sarcophagi. Trust me."

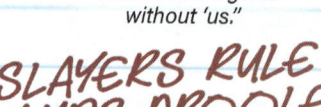

SLAYERS RULE VAMPS DROOLE

KREVLORNSWATH "LORNE" OF THE DEATHWOK CLAN

"What's funny is that I don't even like sweets all that much."

DRUSILLA

"I finally figured out the concept of 'pet food.'"

JENNY CALENDAR

"His first name is WHAT?"

CORDELIA CHASE

"First Tunaverse, then the world."

DOROTHY GILES

"Mummy knows best."

RUPERT GILES

"Why does everybody think Giles is my first name?"

CHARLES GUNN

"I may know every law, but I can't wrap my head around RPG rules."

ALEXANDER "XANDER" HARRIS

"Didn't mean to make dying heroically my thing, but here we are."

TARA MACLAY

"Your shirt…"

ROSE MARTINEZ

"Just out here looking for a girlfriend with a normal job for once."

DANIEL "OZ" OSBOURNE

"Contrary to popular belief, I do NOT play basketball."

ETHAN RAYNE

"Wait, Giles ISN'T his first name?"

WILLOW ROSENBERG

"I'm no longer bored."

SILAS

"Sorry, I lost my head there for a moment."

SPIKE
"[EXPLETIVES DELETED]"

DAWN SUMMERS
"Did you forget I was supposed to be here?"

JOYCE SUMMERS
"I absolutely know what's going on with my daughter and definitely am not completely in the dark, why do you ask?"

ANDREW WELLS
"I can honestly say I learned my lesson."

ROBIN WOOD
"No, I am not jealous that I'm not a Slayer, why does everyone keep saying that?"

WESLEY WYNDAM-PRYCE
"Believe it or not, I did have a functional body once upon a time."

HEY! WHERE'S MY PHOTO?!?!

THE SLAYERS

FAITH LEHANE

"What has eight fingers and is here to kick ass? This guy!"

WILLOW ROSENBERG

"This isn't a mistake. I'm supposed to be on this page."

MONICA SALAZAR

"I promise I am the well-adjusted one."

MORGAN PALMER

"Don't listen to the Council: you're never too old to SLAY."

BUFFY SUMMERS

"We

BUFFY SUMMERS

Are

BUFFY SUMMERS

Not

BUFFY SUMMERS

The

BUFFY SUMMERS

Same

BUFFY SUMMERS

Person."

KENDRA YOUNG

"Contrary to my girlfriend's beliefs, my ideal date is NOT hanging out in a cemetery after dark."

EVENTS

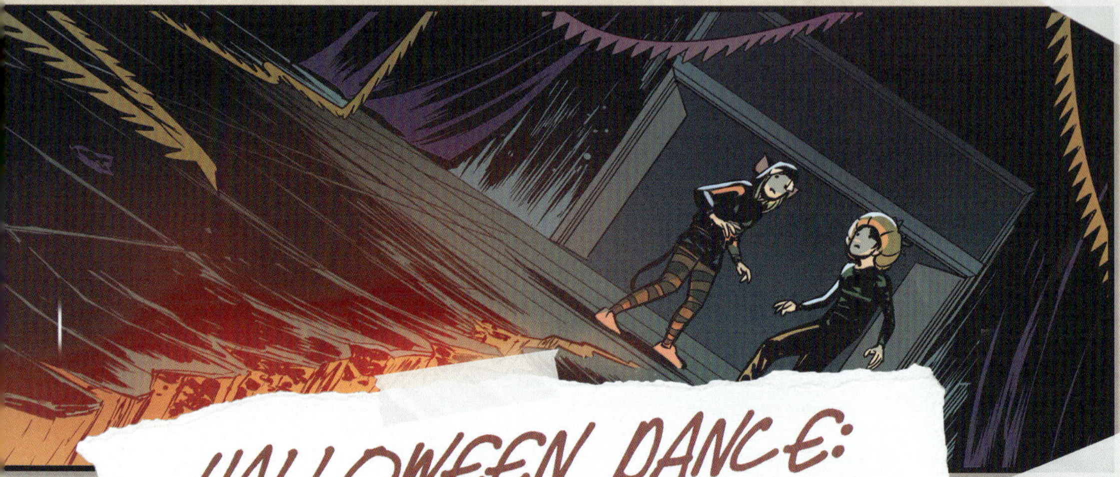

HALLOWEEN DANCE:

OUR BEST DANCE YET! UNTIL THE FLOOR OPENED UP AND TRIED TO SWALLOW THE STUDENT BODY. BUT STILL, THE COSTUME CONTEST WAS A HIT!

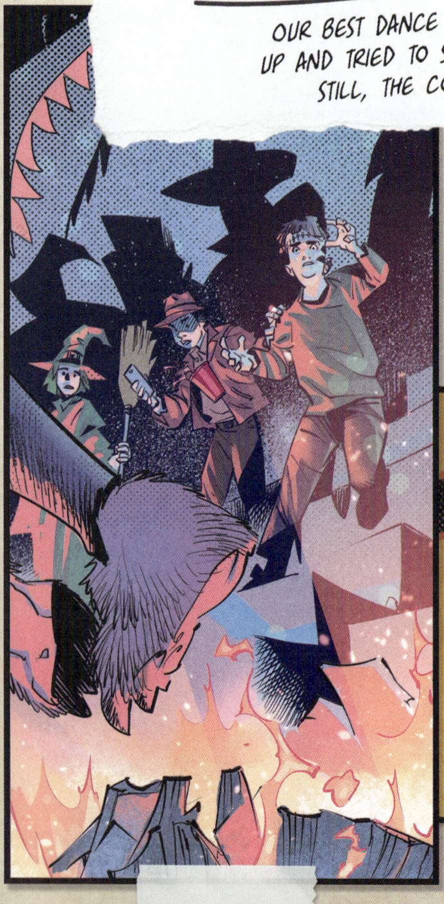

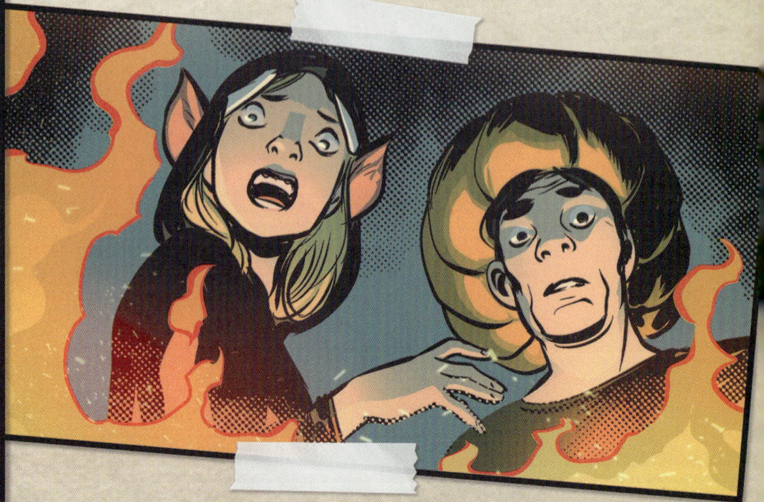

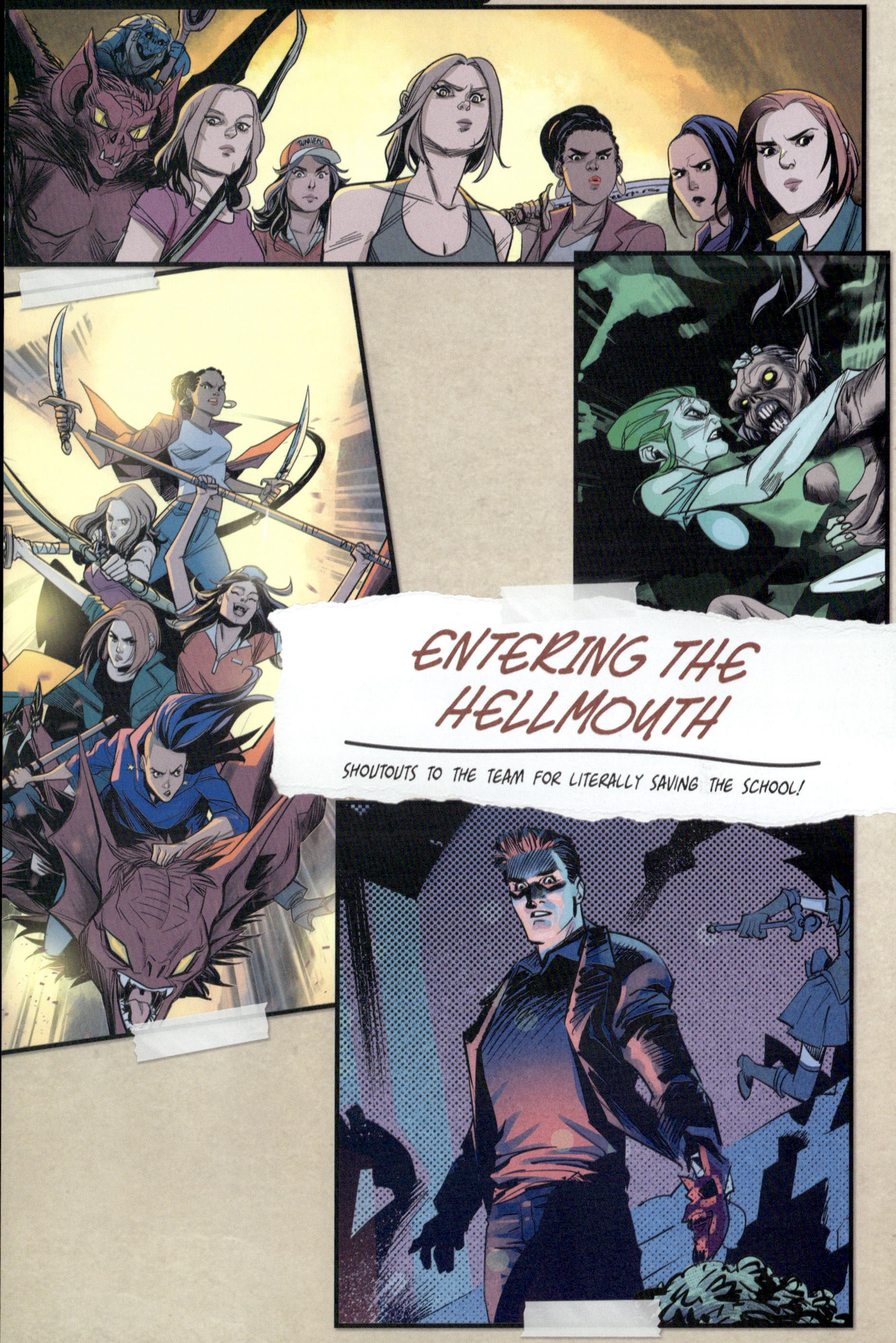

ENTERING THE HELLMOUTH

SHOUTOUTS TO THE TEAM FOR LITERALLY SAVING THE SCHOOL!

SUPERLATIVES

MOST LIKELY TO **BE TURNED INTO A VAMPIRE**

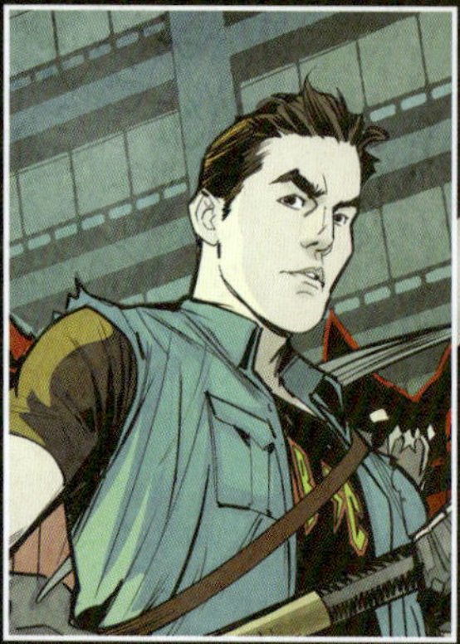

Xander Harris

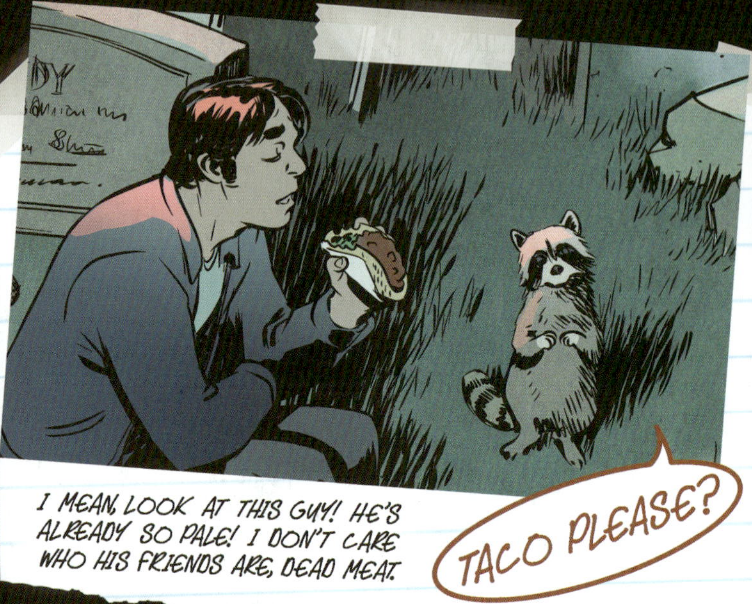
I MEAN, LOOK AT THIS GUY! HE'S ALREADY SO PALE! I DON'T CARE WHO HIS FRIENDS ARE, DEAD MEAT.
TACO PLEASE?

MOST LIKELY TO **BECOME THE MOST POWERFUL WITCH IN THE WORLD**

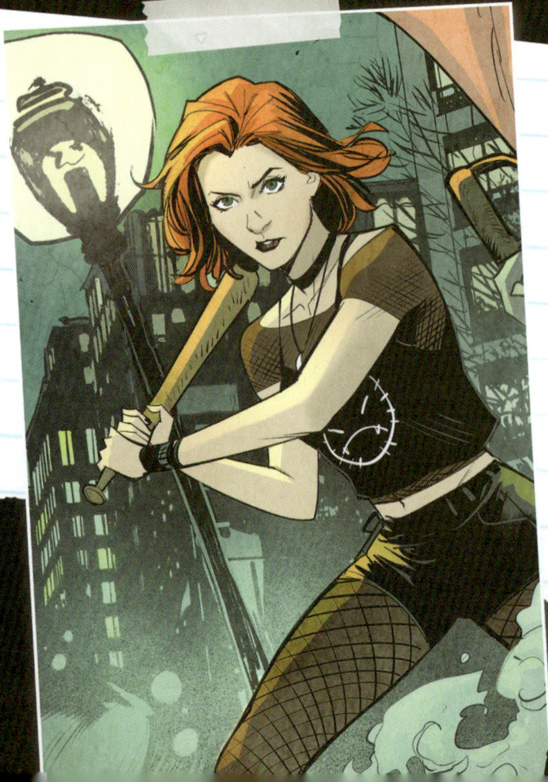

DUH.

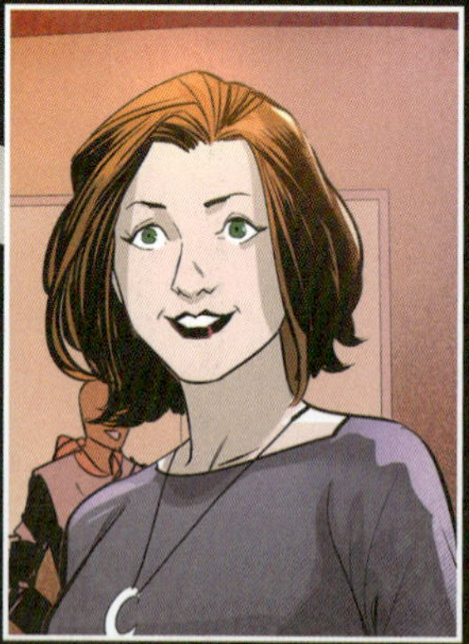

Willow Rosenberg

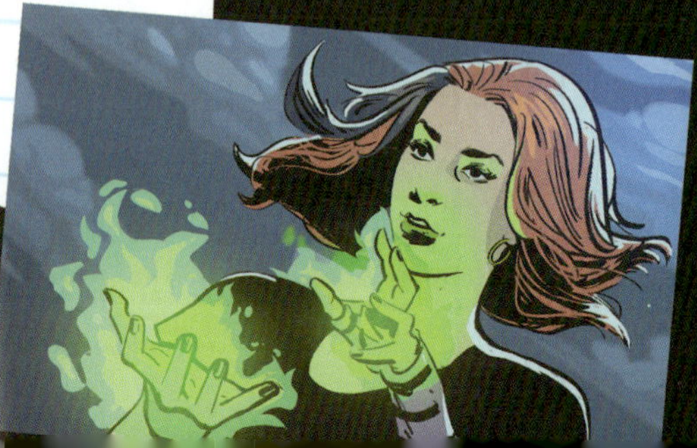

MOST LIKELY TO *OUTLIVE OTHER SLAYERS*

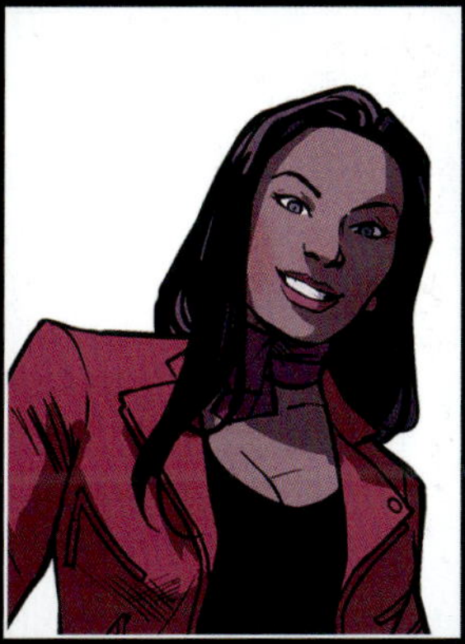

Morgan Palmer

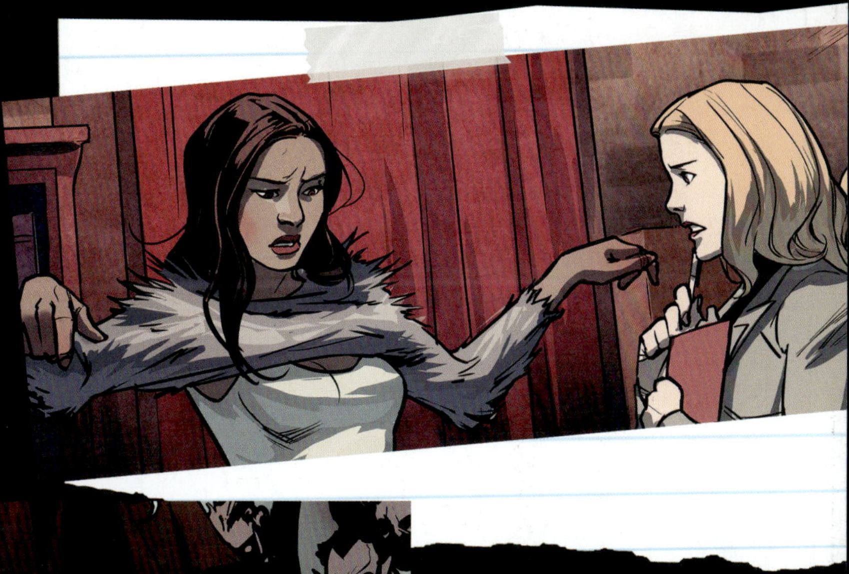

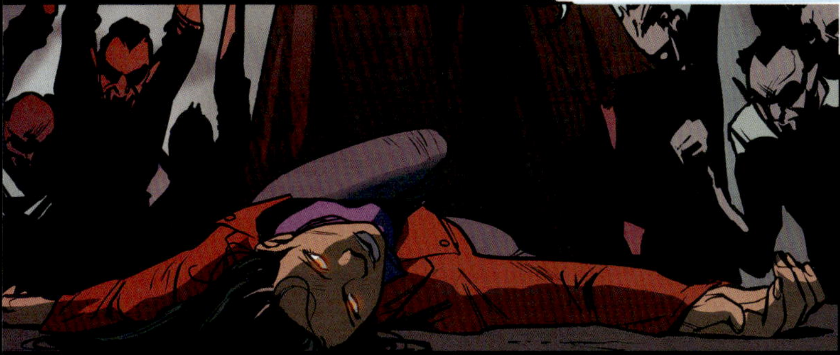

VOTED *PRETTIEST EYES*

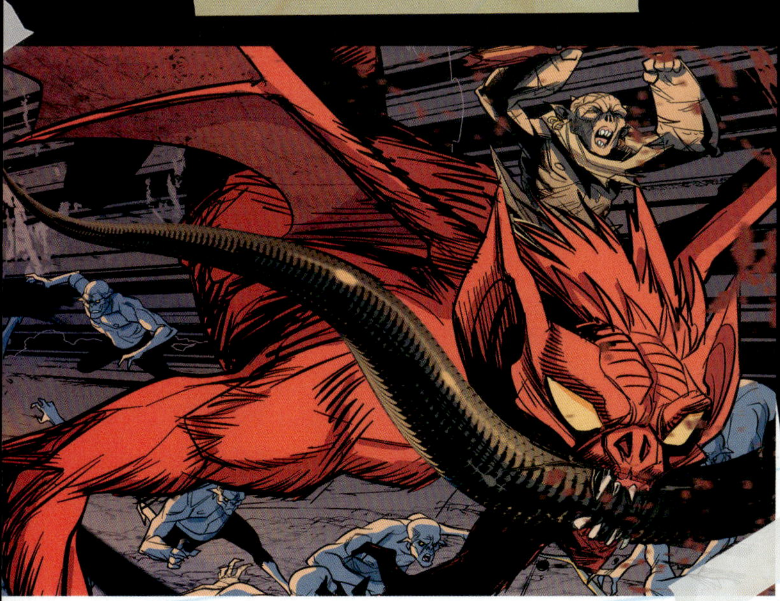

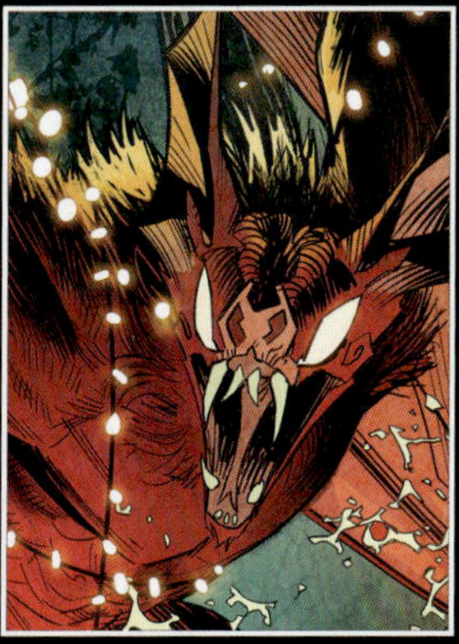

Camazotz

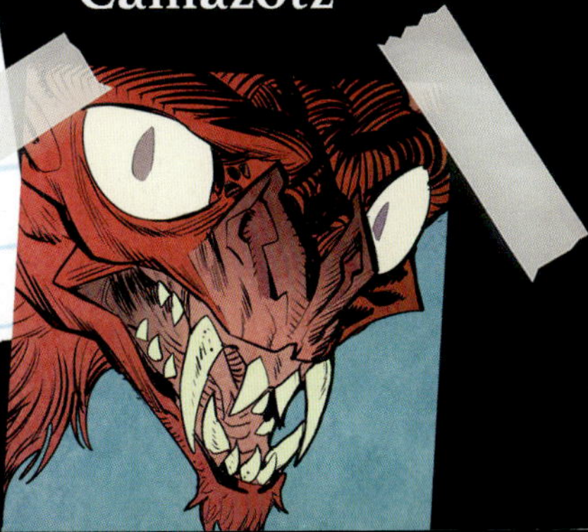

HISTORICAL ANNIVERSARY

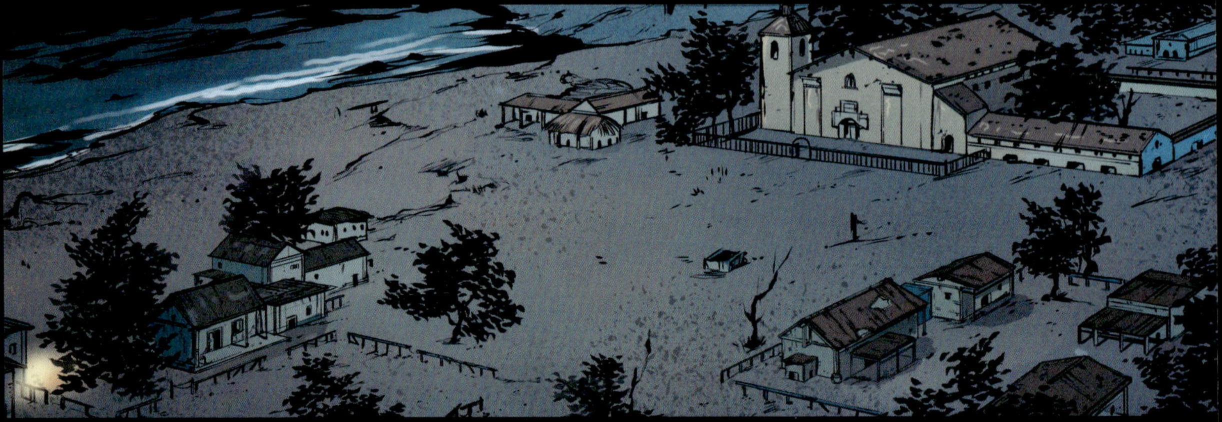

Hundreds of years ago, right on the grounds of this school, the town of Sunnydale was founded!

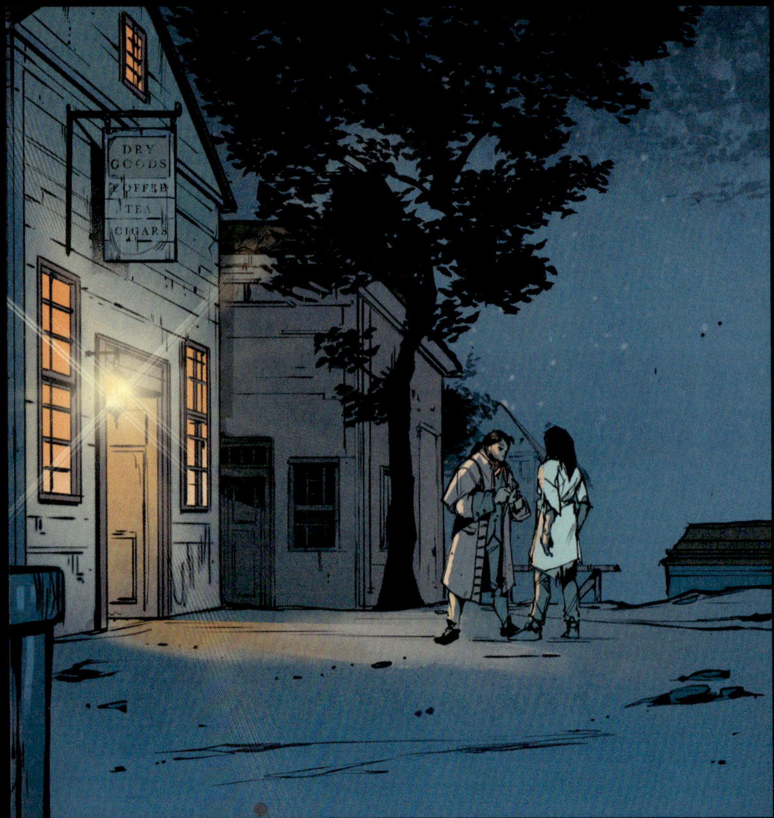
DRY GOODS
TEA
CIGARS

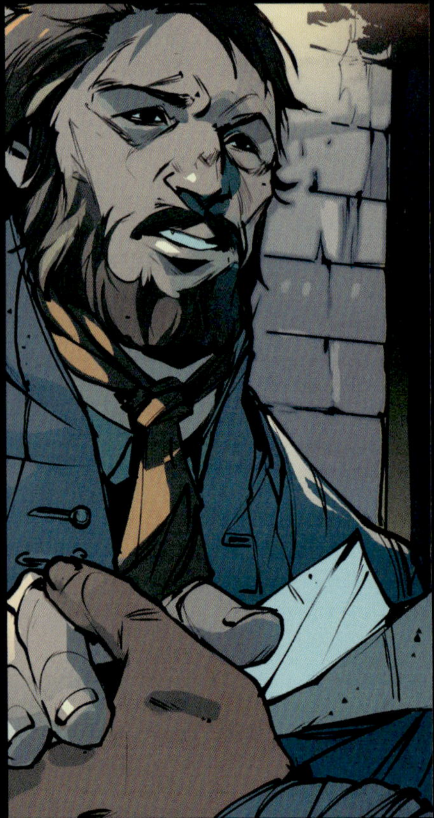

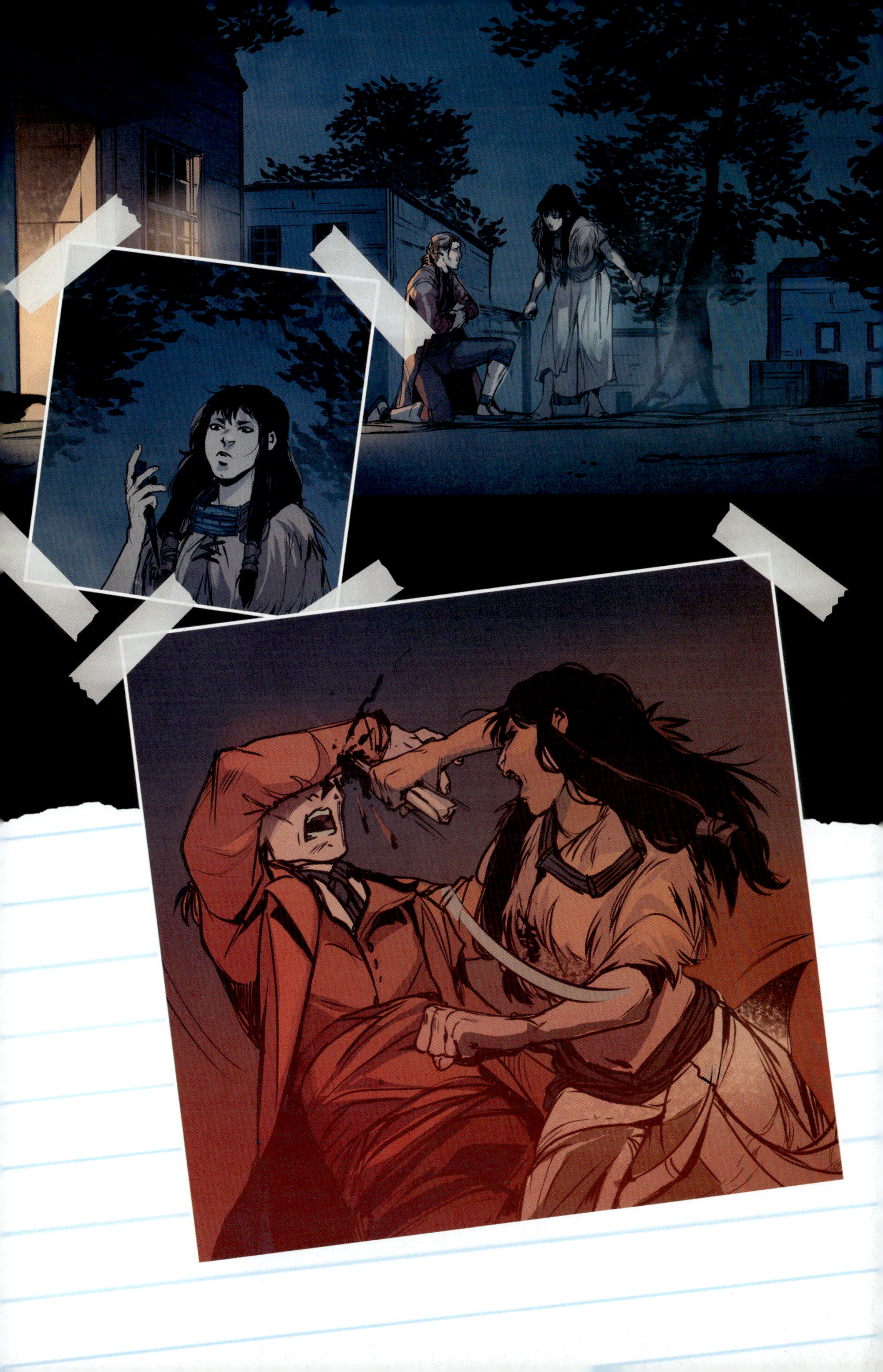

ARE THE TEACHERS DATING:

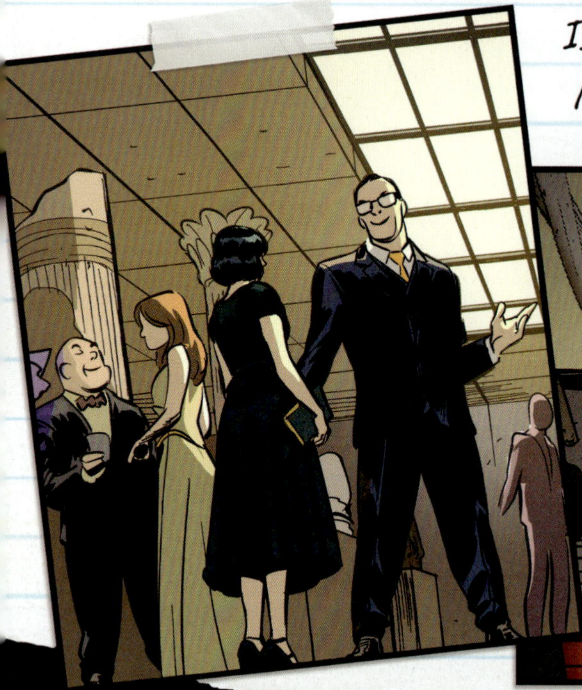

IS THAT MR. GILES THE LIBRARIAN WITH MS. CALENDAR? HONESTLY, AWWWWW!

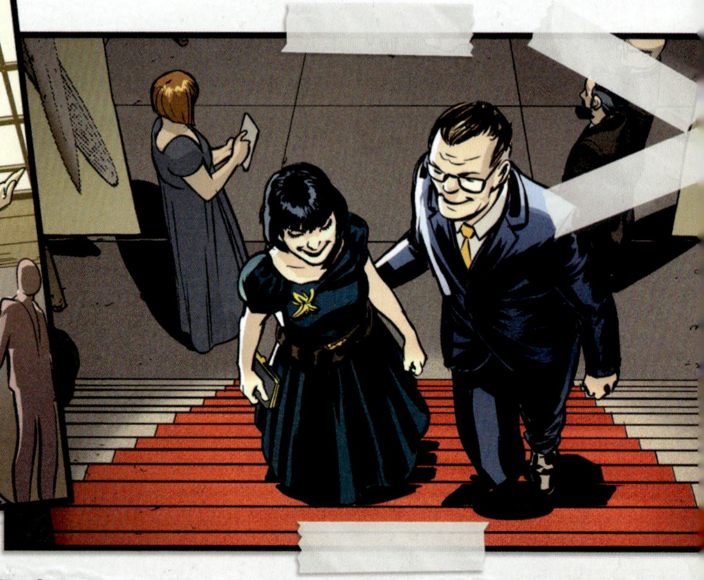

SILAS BATTLE

THE MULTIVERSE GIVES A WHOLE NEW MEANING TO "FOREIGN EXCHANGE STUDENTS."

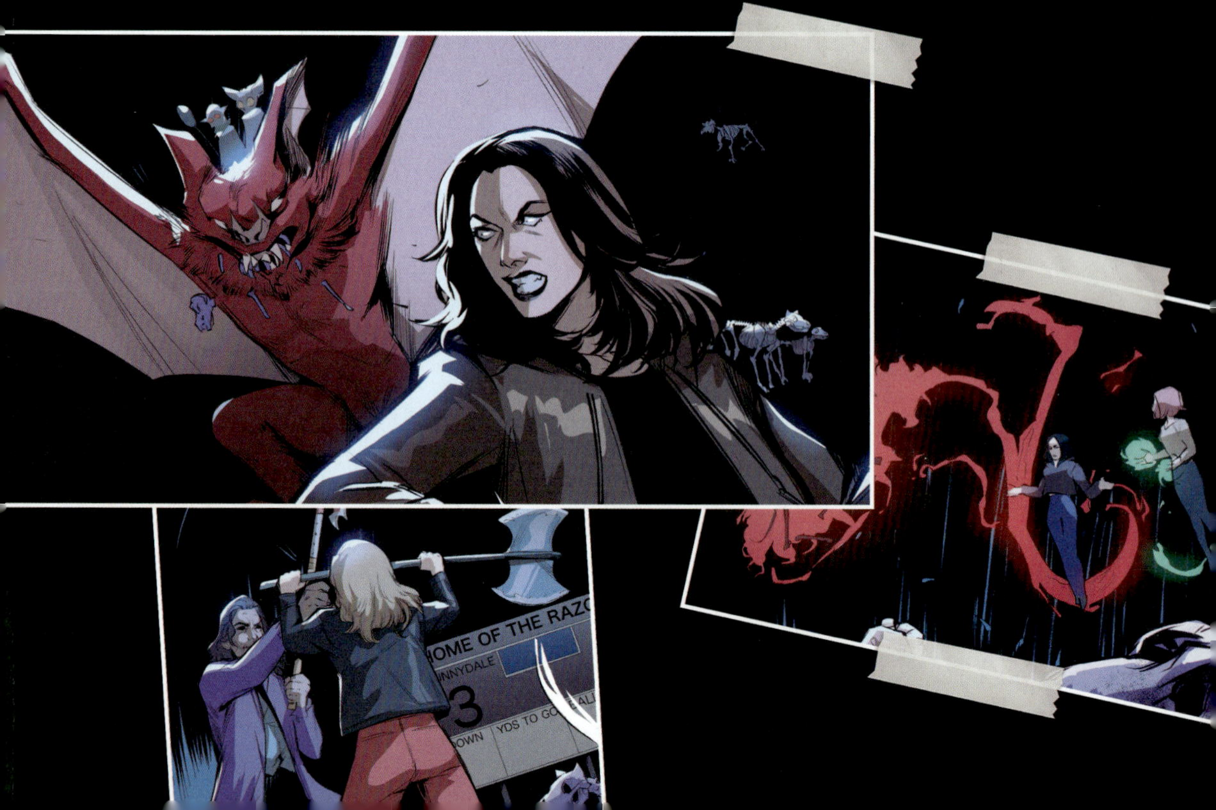

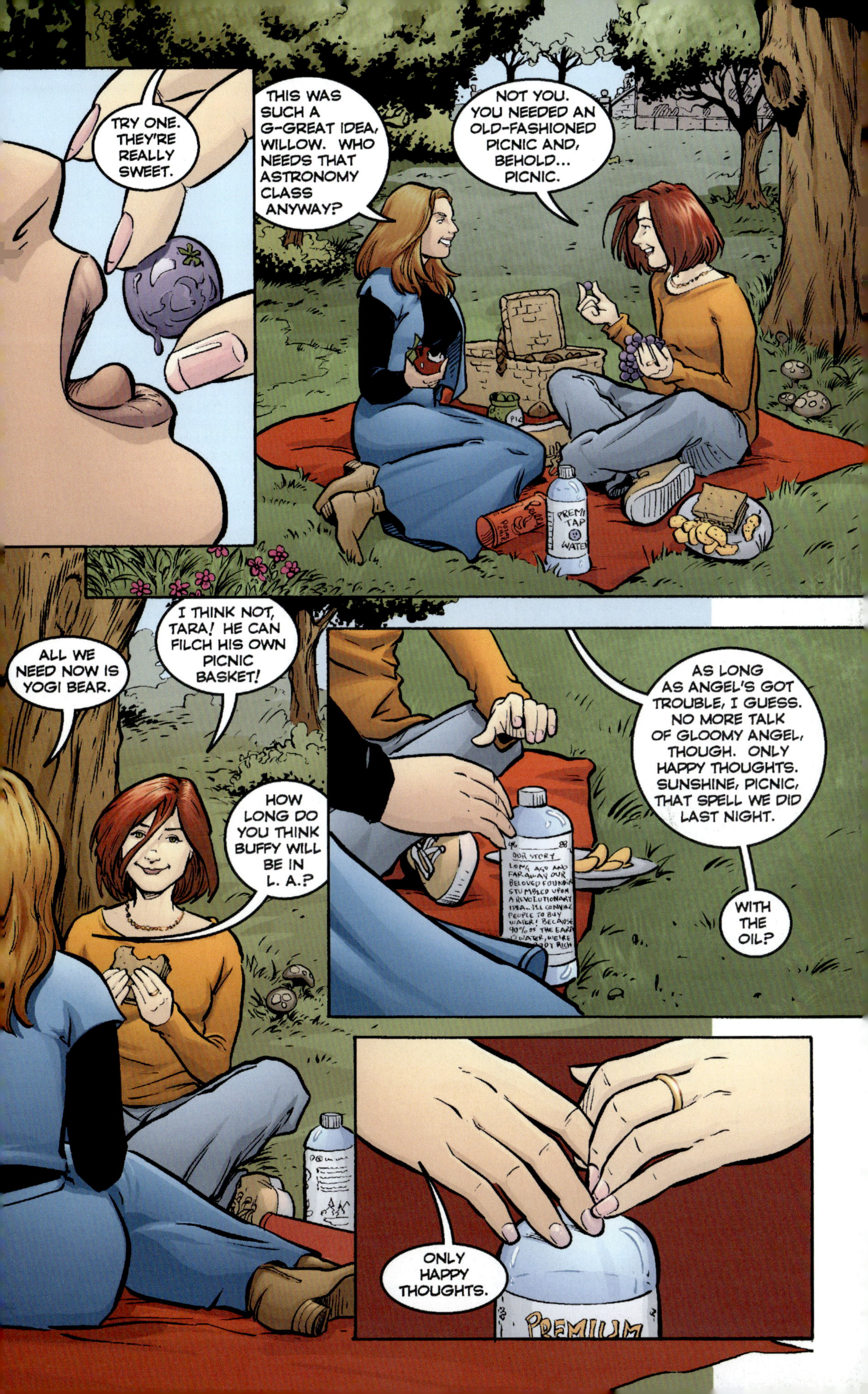
TRY ONE. THEY'RE REALLY SWEET.
THIS WAS SUCH A G-GREAT IDEA, WILLOW. WHO NEEDS THAT ASTRONOMY CLASS ANYWAY?
NOT YOU. YOU NEEDED AN OLD-FASHIONED PICNIC AND, BEHOLD... PICNIC.
ALL WE NEED NOW IS YOGI BEAR.
I THINK NOT, TARA! HE CAN FILCH HIS OWN PICNIC BASKET!
HOW LONG DO YOU THINK BUFFY WILL BE IN L. A.?
AS LONG AS ANGEL'S GOT TROUBLE, I GUESS. NO MORE TALK OF GLOOMY ANGEL, THOUGH. ONLY HAPPY THOUGHTS. SUNSHINE, PICNIC, THAT SPELL WE DID LAST NIGHT.
WITH THE OIL?
ONLY HAPPY THOUGHTS.
PREMIUM

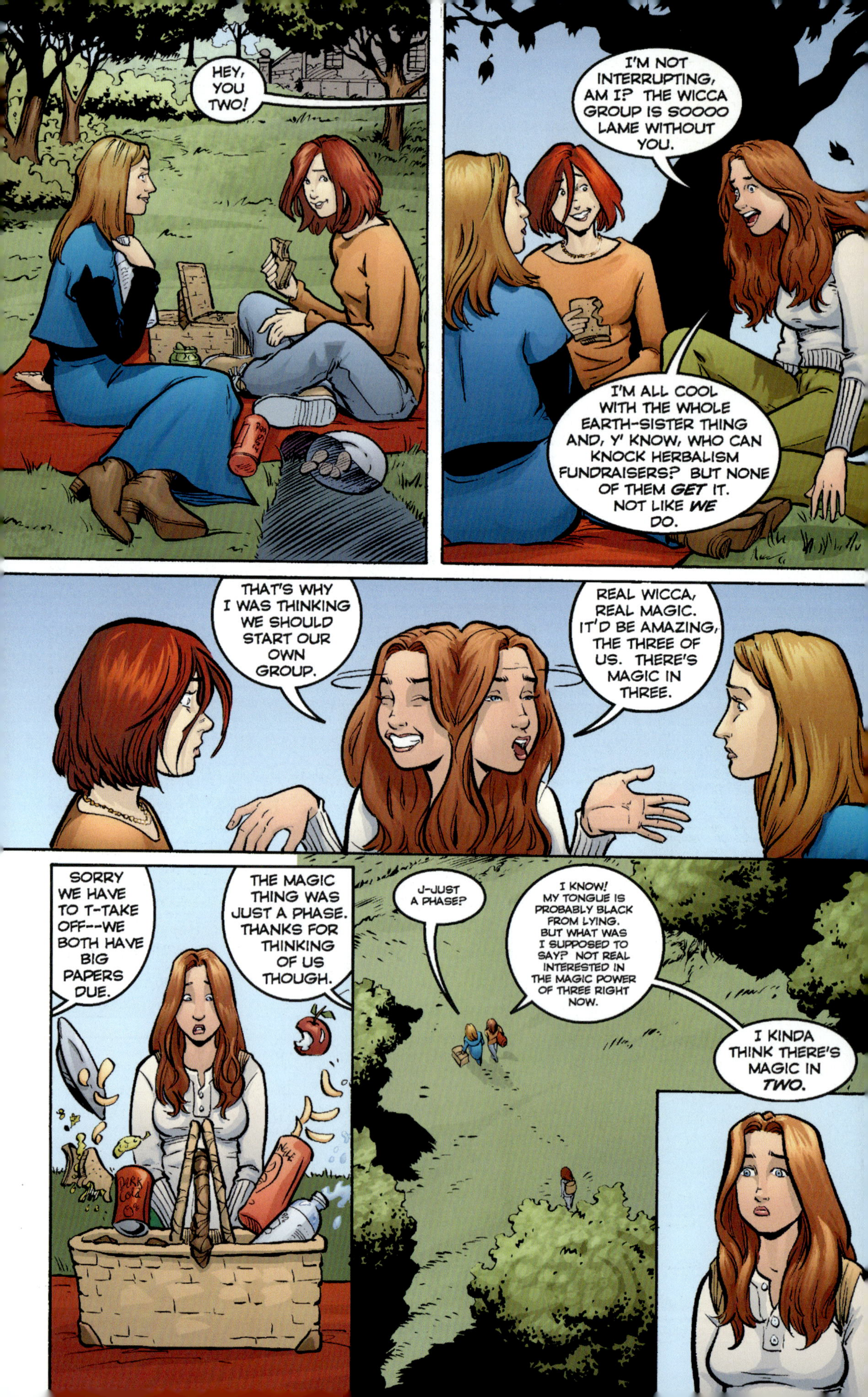
HEY, YOU TWO!
I'M NOT INTERRUPTING, AM I? THE WICCA GROUP IS SOOOO LAME WITHOUT YOU.
I'M ALL COOL WITH THE WHOLE EARTH-SISTER THING AND, Y' KNOW, WHO CAN KNOCK HERBALISM FUNDRAISERS? BUT NONE OF THEM *GET* IT. NOT LIKE *WE* DO.
THAT'S WHY I WAS THINKING WE SHOULD START OUR OWN GROUP.
REAL WICCA, REAL MAGIC. IT'D BE AMAZING, THE THREE OF US. THERE'S MAGIC IN THREE.
SORRY WE HAVE TO T-TAKE OFF--WE BOTH HAVE BIG PAPERS DUE.
THE MAGIC THING WAS JUST A PHASE. THANKS FOR THINKING OF US THOUGH.
J-JUST A PHASE?
I KNOW! MY TONGUE IS PROBABLY BLACK FROM LYING. BUT WHAT WAS I SUPPOSED TO SAY? NOT REAL INTERESTED IN THE MAGIC POWER OF THREE RIGHT NOW.
I KINDA THINK THERE'S MAGIC IN *TWO*.

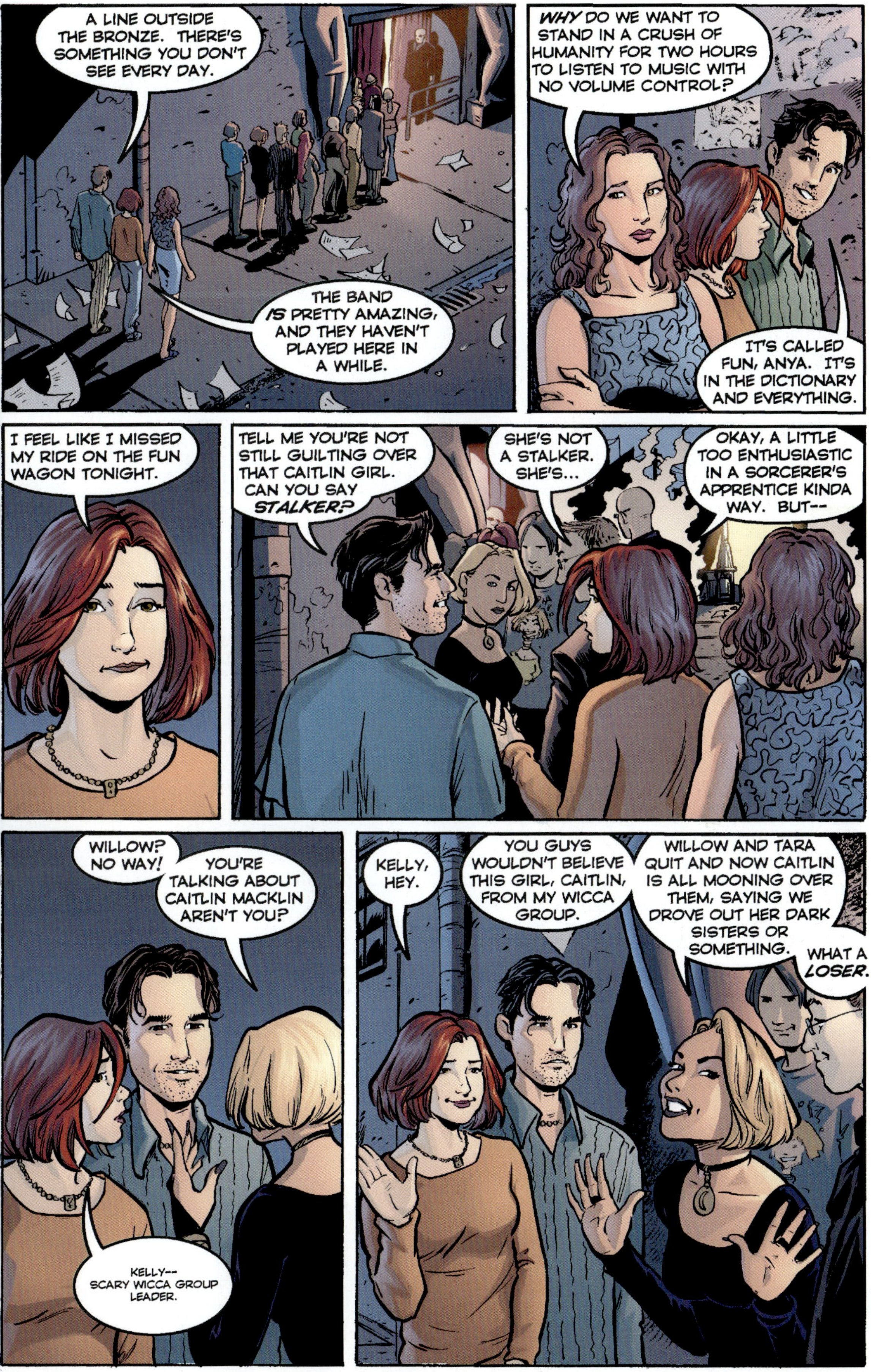
A LINE OUTSIDE THE BRONZE. THERE'S SOMETHING YOU DON'T SEE EVERY DAY.
THE BAND *IS* PRETTY AMAZING, AND THEY HAVEN'T PLAYED HERE IN A WHILE.
WHY DO WE WANT TO STAND IN A CRUSH OF HUMANITY FOR TWO HOURS TO LISTEN TO MUSIC WITH NO VOLUME CONTROL?
IT'S CALLED FUN, ANYA. IT'S IN THE DICTIONARY AND EVERYTHING.
I FEEL LIKE I MISSED MY RIDE ON THE FUN WAGON TONIGHT.
TELL ME YOU'RE NOT STILL GUILTING OVER THAT CAITLIN GIRL. CAN YOU SAY *STALKER?*
SHE'S NOT A STALKER. SHE'S...
OKAY, A LITTLE TOO ENTHUSIASTIC IN A SORCERER'S APPRENTICE KINDA WAY. BUT--
WILLOW? NO WAY!
YOU'RE TALKING ABOUT CAITLIN MACKLIN AREN'T YOU?
KELLY-- SCARY WICCA GROUP LEADER.
KELLY, HEY.
YOU GUYS WOULDN'T BELIEVE THIS GIRL, CAITLIN, FROM MY WICCA GROUP.
WILLOW AND TARA QUIT AND NOW CAITLIN IS ALL MOONING OVER THEM, SAYING WE DROVE OUT HER DARK SISTERS OR SOMETHING.
WHAT A *LOSER.*

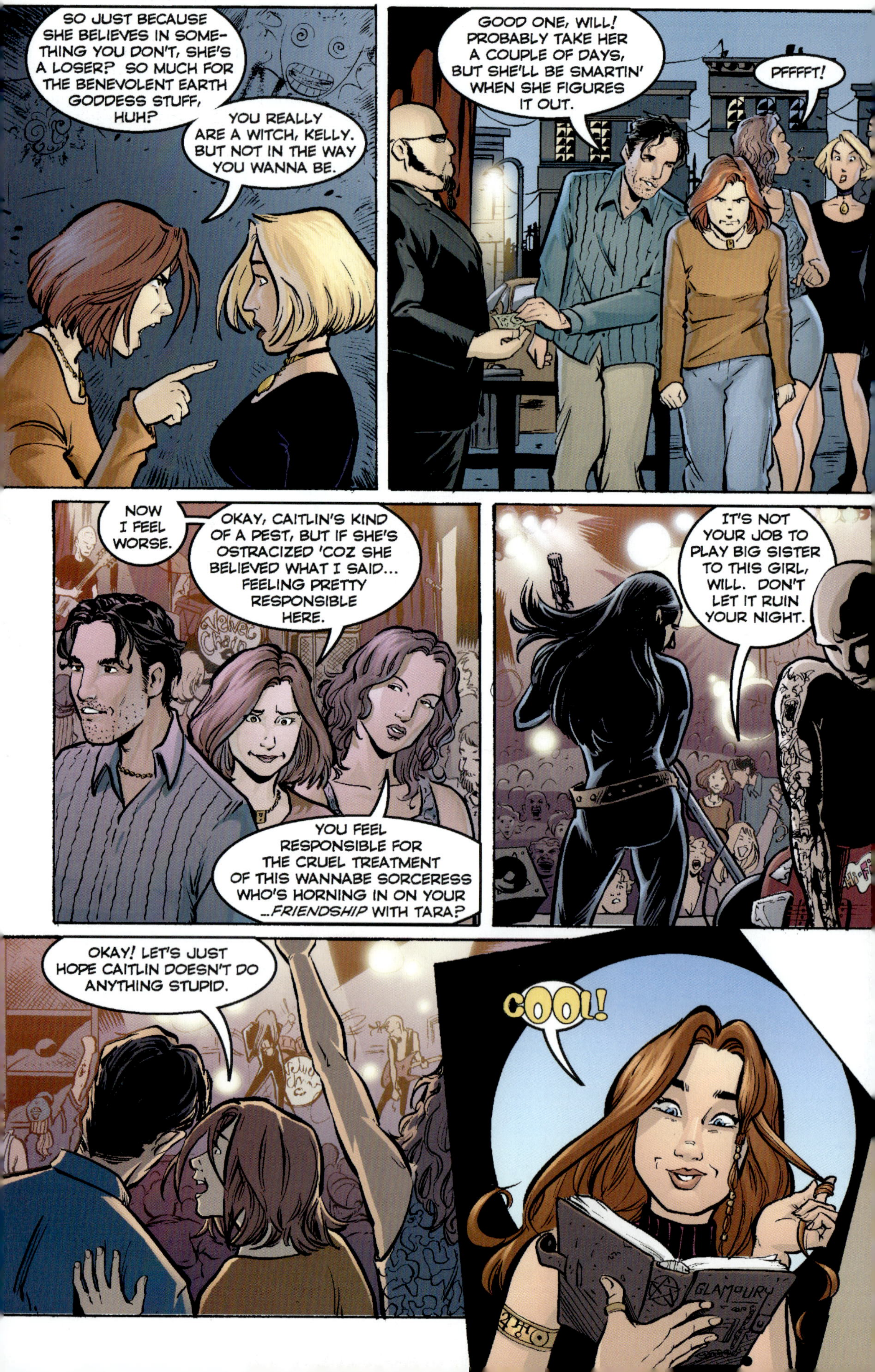
SO JUST BECAUSE SHE BELIEVES IN SOMETHING YOU DON'T, SHE'S A LOSER? SO MUCH FOR THE BENEVOLENT EARTH GODDESS STUFF, HUH?
YOU REALLY ARE A WITCH, KELLY. BUT NOT IN THE WAY YOU WANNA BE.
GOOD ONE, WILL! PROBABLY TAKE HER A COUPLE OF DAYS, BUT SHE'LL BE SMARTIN' WHEN SHE FIGURES IT OUT.
PFFFFT!
NOW I FEEL WORSE.
OKAY, CAITLIN'S KIND OF A PEST, BUT IF SHE'S OSTRACIZED 'COZ SHE BELIEVED WHAT I SAID... FEELING PRETTY RESPONSIBLE HERE.
YOU FEEL RESPONSIBLE FOR THE CRUEL TREATMENT OF THIS WANNABE SORCERESS WHO'S HORNING IN ON YOUR ...*FRIENDSHIP* WITH TARA?
IT'S NOT YOUR JOB TO PLAY BIG SISTER TO THIS GIRL, WILL. DON'T LET IT RUIN YOUR NIGHT.
OKAY! LET'S JUST HOPE CAITLIN DOESN'T DO ANYTHING STUPID.
COOL!
GLAMOURY

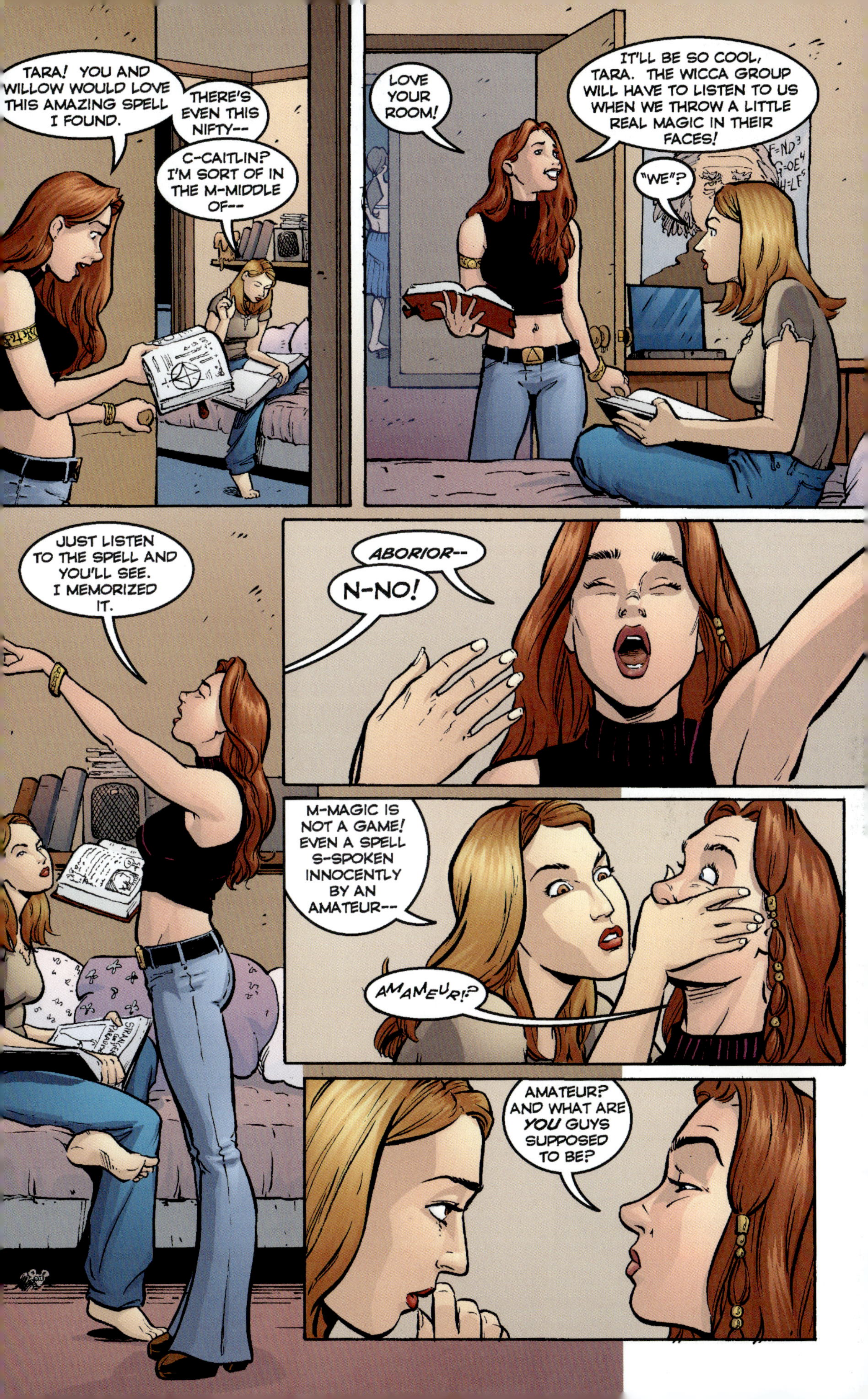
TARA! YOU AND WILLOW WOULD LOVE THIS AMAZING SPELL I FOUND.
THERE'S EVEN THIS NIFTY--
C-CAITLIN? I'M SORT OF IN THE M-MIDDLE OF--
LOVE YOUR ROOM!
IT'LL BE SO COOL, TARA. THE WICCA GROUP WILL HAVE TO LISTEN TO US WHEN WE THROW A LITTLE REAL MAGIC IN THEIR FACES!
"WE"?
JUST LISTEN TO THE SPELL AND YOU'LL SEE. I MEMORIZED IT.
ABORIOR--
N-NO!
M-MAGIC IS NOT A GAME! EVEN A SPELL S-SPOKEN INNOCENTLY BY AN AMATEUR--
AMAMEUR!?
AMATEUR? AND WHAT ARE YOU GUYS SUPPOSED TO BE?

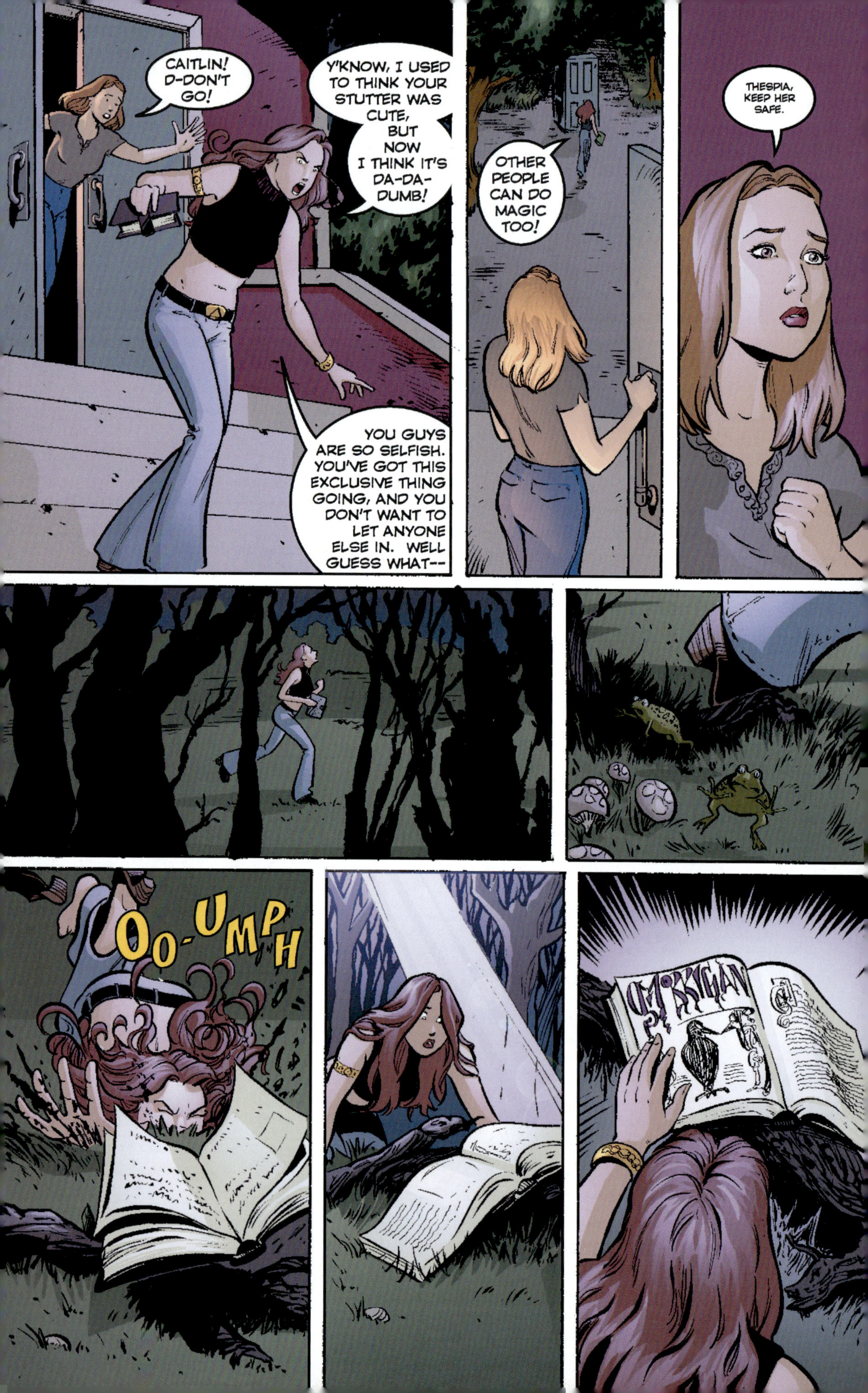

CAITLIN! D-DON'T GO!
Y'KNOW, I USED TO THINK YOUR STUTTER WAS CUTE, BUT NOW I THINK IT'S DA-DA-DUMB!
YOU GUYS ARE SO SELFISH. YOU'VE GOT THIS EXCLUSIVE THING GOING, AND YOU DON'T WANT TO LET ANYONE ELSE IN. WELL GUESS WHAT--
OTHER PEOPLE CAN DO MAGIC TOO!
THESPIA, KEEP HER SAFE.
OO-UMPH

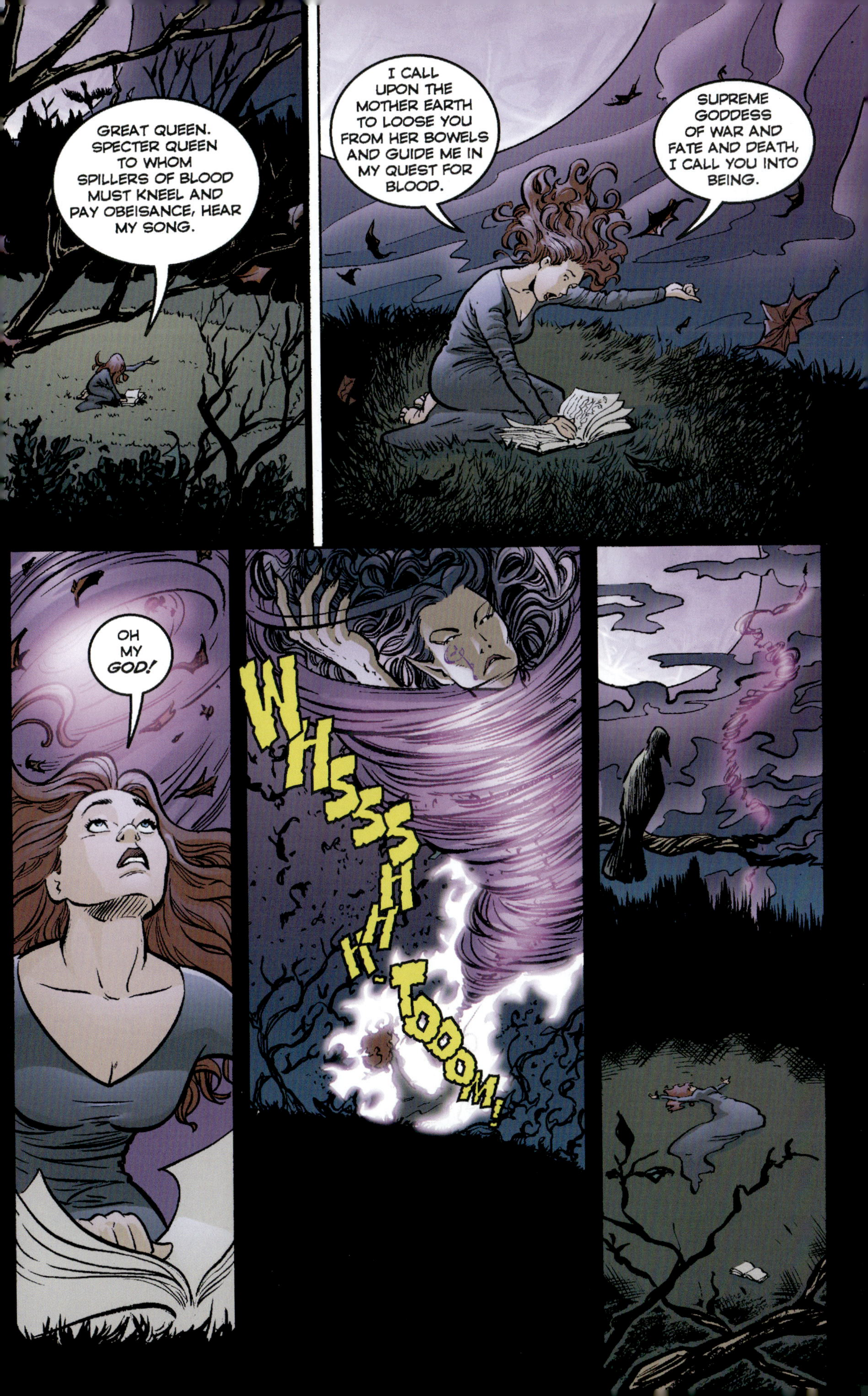
GREAT QUEEN. SPECTER QUEEN TO WHOM SPILLERS OF BLOOD MUST KNEEL AND PAY OBEISANCE, HEAR MY SONG.
I CALL UPON THE MOTHER EARTH TO LOOSE YOU FROM HER BOWELS AND GUIDE ME IN MY QUEST FOR BLOOD.
SUPREME GODDESS OF WAR AND FATE AND DEATH, I CALL YOU INTO BEING.
OH MY GOD!
WHSSSHHH-TOOOM!

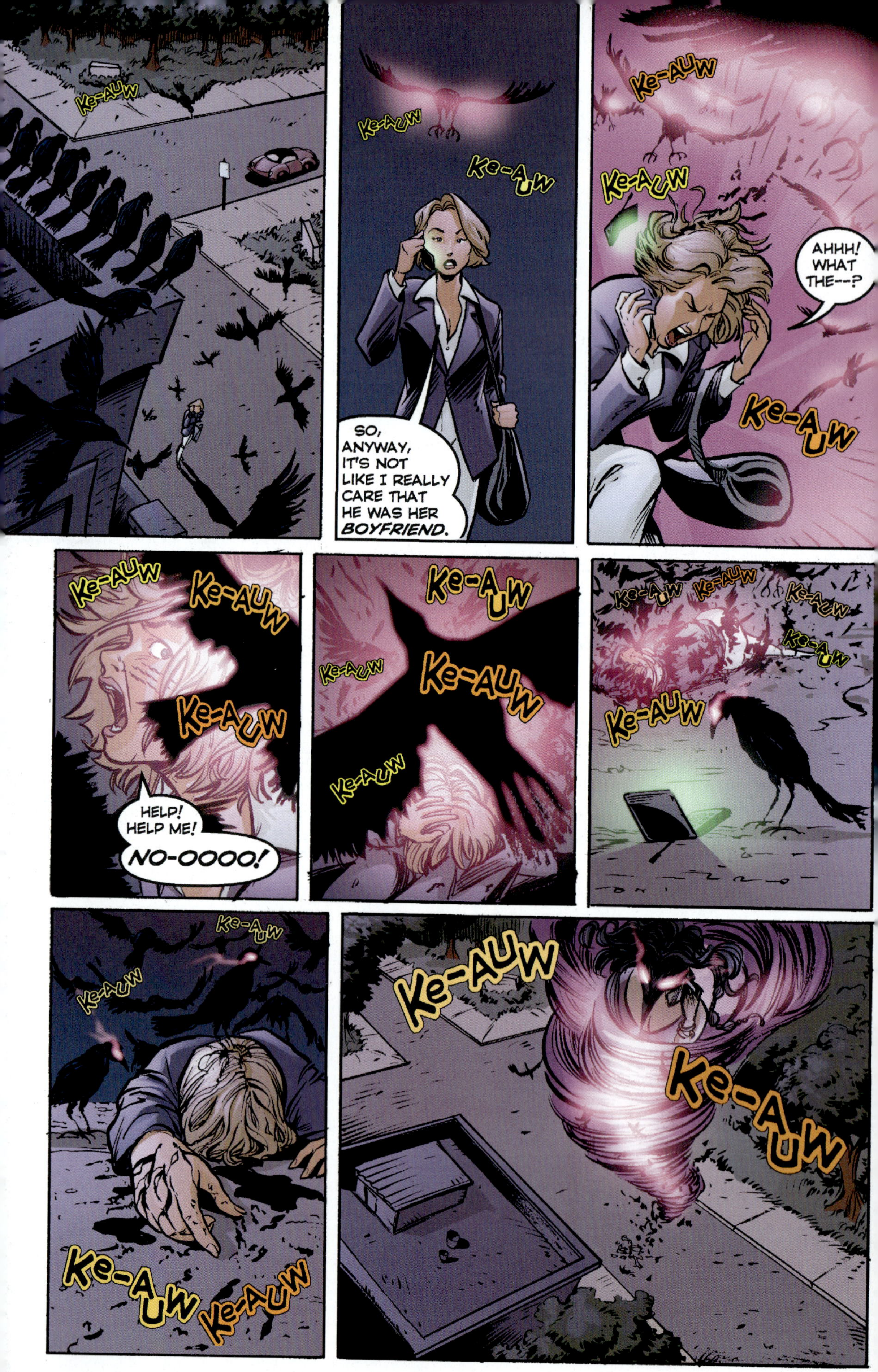
KE-AUW
KE-AUW
KE-AUW
SO, ANYWAY, IT'S NOT LIKE I REALLY CARE THAT HE WAS HER *BOYFRIEND*.
KE-AUW
KE-AUW
AHHH! WHAT THE--?
KE-AUW
KE-AUW
KE-AUW
KE-AUW
HELP! HELP ME! NO-OOOO!
KE-AUW
KE-AUW
KE-AUW
KE-AUW
KE-AUW
KE-AUW
KE-AUW
KE-AUW
KE-AUW
KE-AUW
KE-AUW
KE-AUW
KE-AUW
KE-AUW
KE-AUW

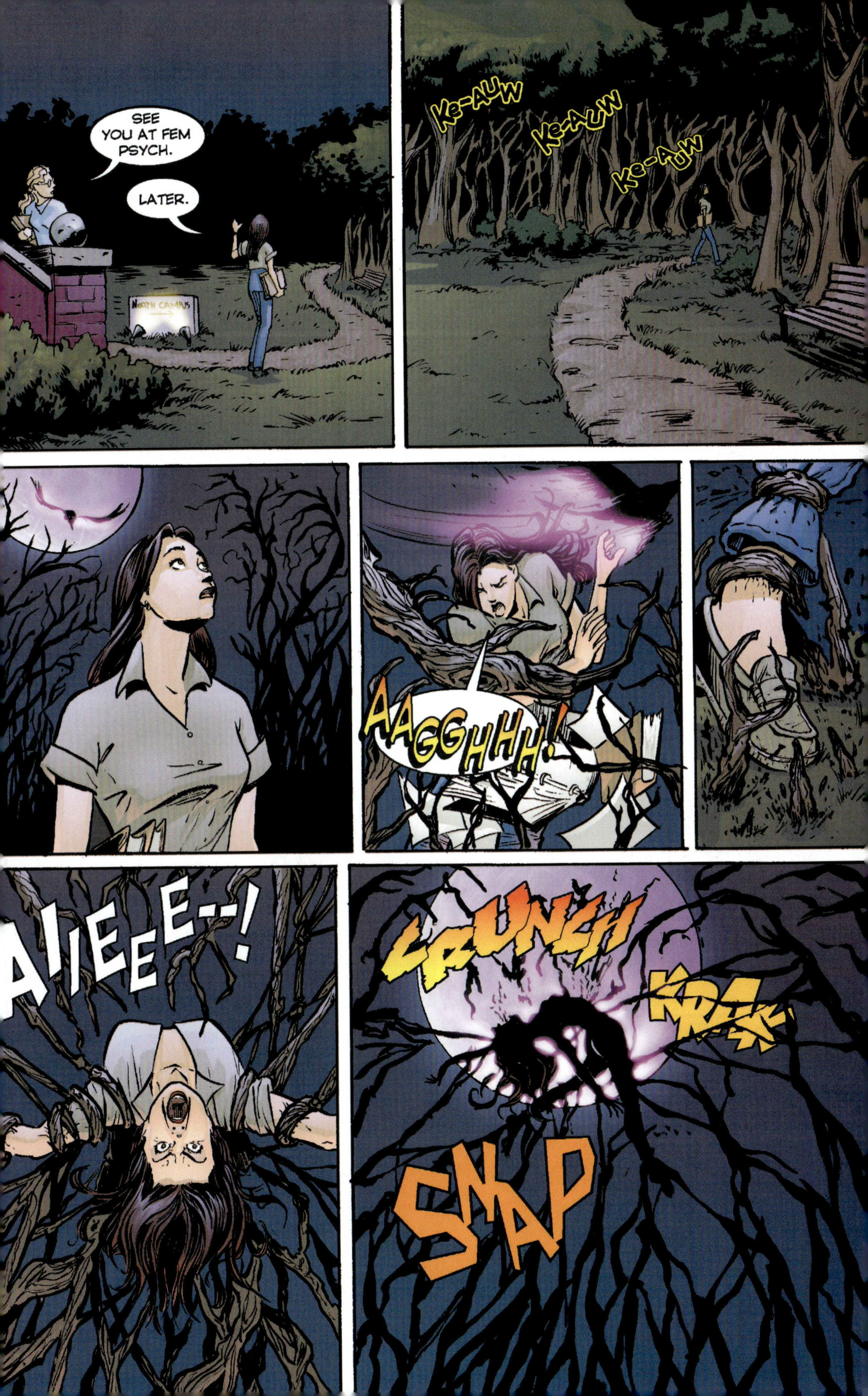
SEE YOU AT FEM PSYCH.
LATER.
NORTH CAMPUS
Ke-AUW
Ke-AUW
Ke-AUW
AAGGHHHH!
AIIEEEE--!
CRUNCH
KRAK
SNAP

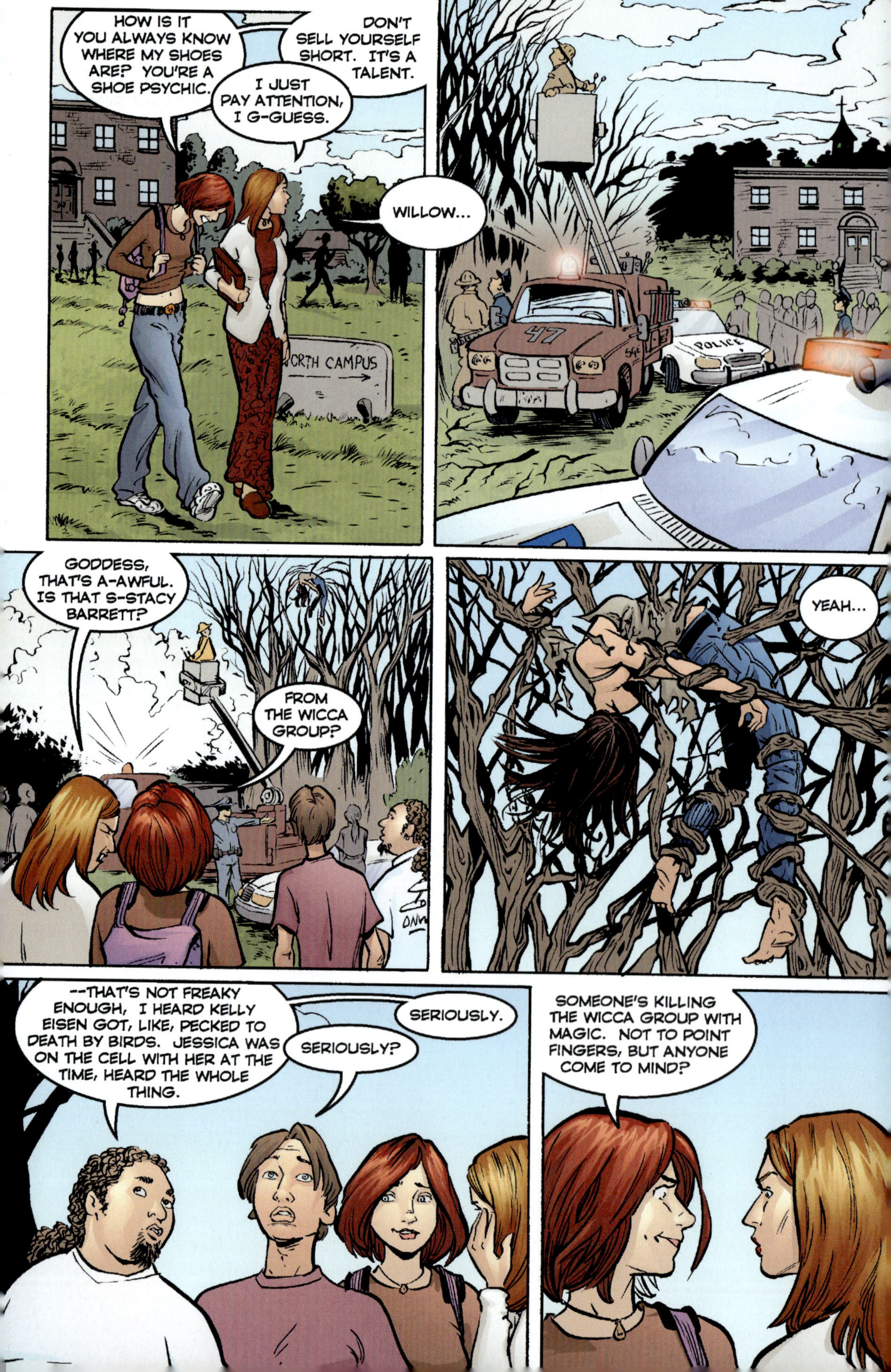
HOW IS IT YOU ALWAYS KNOW WHERE MY SHOES ARE? YOU'RE A SHOE PSYCHIC.
I JUST PAY ATTENTION, I G-GUESS.
DON'T SELL YOURSELF SHORT. IT'S A TALENT.
ORTH CAMPUS
WILLOW...
47
POLICE
GODDESS, THAT'S A-AWFUL. IS THAT S-STACY BARRETT?
FROM THE WICCA GROUP?
YEAH...
--THAT'S NOT FREAKY ENOUGH, I HEARD KELLY EISEN GOT, LIKE, PECKED TO DEATH BY BIRDS. JESSICA WAS ON THE CELL WITH HER AT THE TIME, HEARD THE WHOLE THING.
SERIOUSLY?
SERIOUSLY.
SOMEONE'S KILLING THE WICCA GROUP WITH MAGIC. NOT TO POINT FINGERS, BUT ANYONE COME TO MIND?

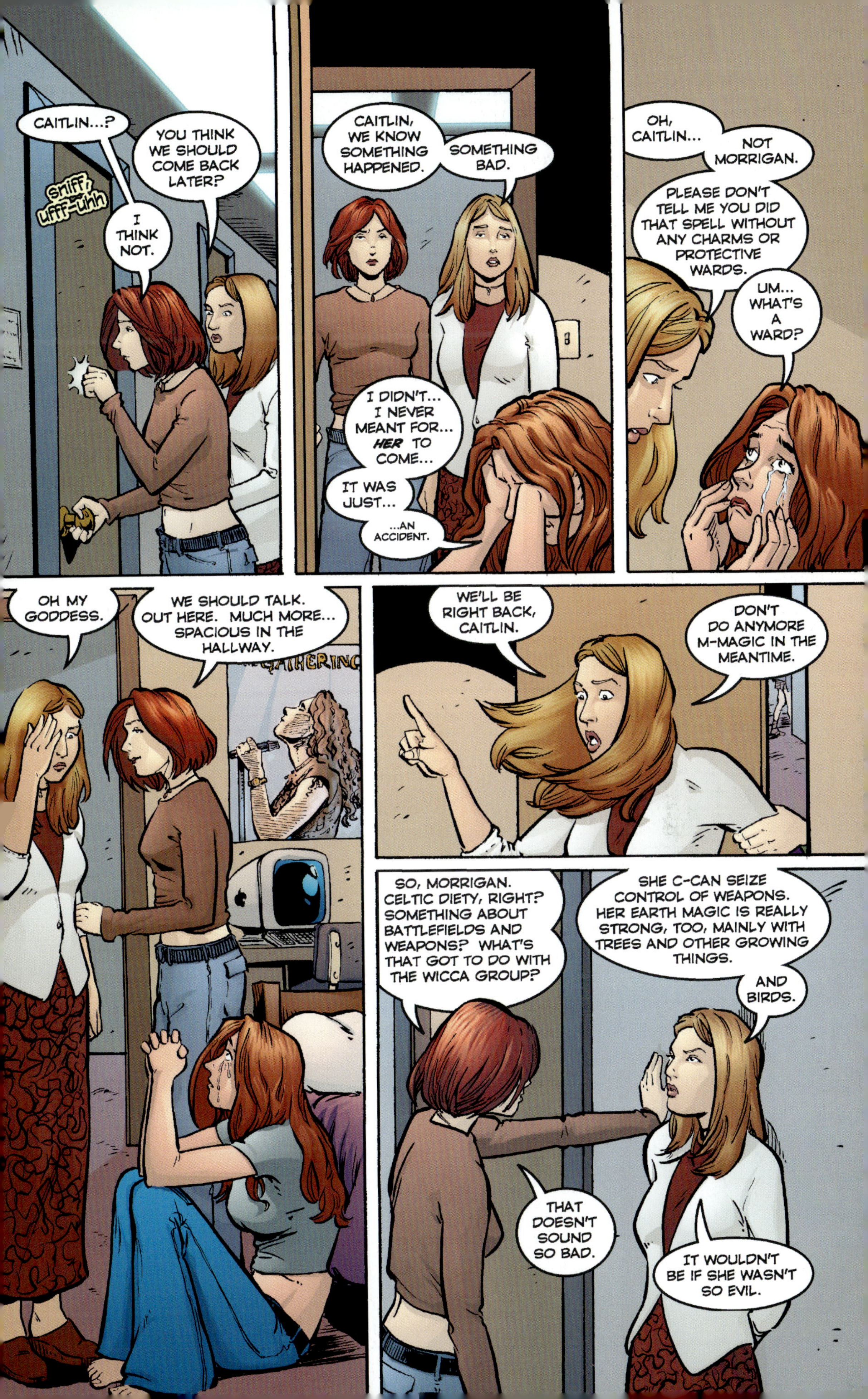

CAITLIN...?
YOU THINK WE SHOULD COME BACK LATER?
SNIFF, UFFF-UHH
I THINK NOT.
CAITLIN, WE KNOW SOMETHING HAPPENED.
SOMETHING BAD.
I DIDN'T... I NEVER MEANT FOR... HER TO COME...
IT WAS JUST...
...AN ACCIDENT.
OH, CAITLIN...
NOT MORRIGAN.
PLEASE DON'T TELL ME YOU DID THAT SPELL WITHOUT ANY CHARMS OR PROTECTIVE WARDS.
UM... WHAT'S A WARD?
OH MY GODDESS.
WE SHOULD TALK. OUT HERE. MUCH MORE... SPACIOUS IN THE HALLWAY.
GATHERING
WE'LL BE RIGHT BACK, CAITLIN.
DON'T DO ANYMORE M-MAGIC IN THE MEANTIME.
SO, MORRIGAN. CELTIC DIETY, RIGHT? SOMETHING ABOUT BATTLEFIELDS AND WEAPONS? WHAT'S THAT GOT TO DO WITH THE WICCA GROUP?
SHE C-CAN SEIZE CONTROL OF WEAPONS. HER EARTH MAGIC IS REALLY STRONG, TOO, MAINLY WITH TREES AND OTHER GROWING THINGS.
AND BIRDS.
THAT DOESN'T SOUND SO BAD.
IT WOULDN'T BE IF SHE WASN'T SO EVIL.

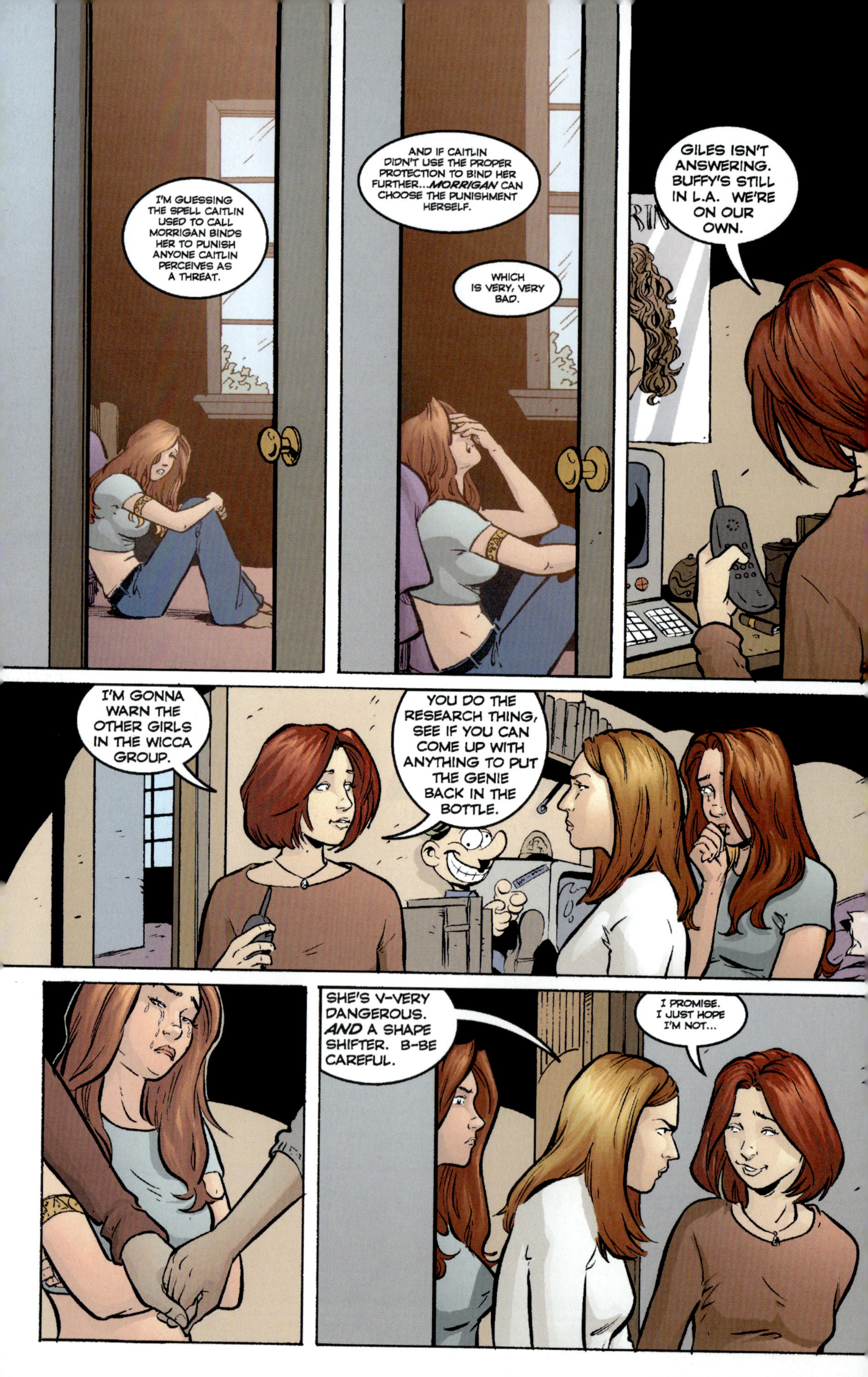

I'M GUESSING THE SPELL CAITLIN USED TO CALL MORRIGAN BINDS HER TO PUNISH ANYONE CAITLIN PERCEIVES AS A THREAT.
AND IF CAITLIN DIDN'T USE THE PROPER PROTECTION TO BIND HER FURTHER...*MORRIGAN* CAN CHOOSE THE PUNISHMENT HERSELF.
WHICH IS VERY, VERY BAD.
GILES ISN'T ANSWERING. BUFFY'S STILL IN L.A. WE'RE ON OUR OWN.
I'M GONNA WARN THE OTHER GIRLS IN THE WICCA GROUP.
YOU DO THE RESEARCH THING, SEE IF YOU CAN COME UP WITH ANYTHING TO PUT THE GENIE BACK IN THE BOTTLE.
SHE'S V-VERY DANGEROUS. *AND* A SHAPE SHIFTER. B-BE CAREFUL.
I PROMISE. I JUST HOPE I'M NOT...

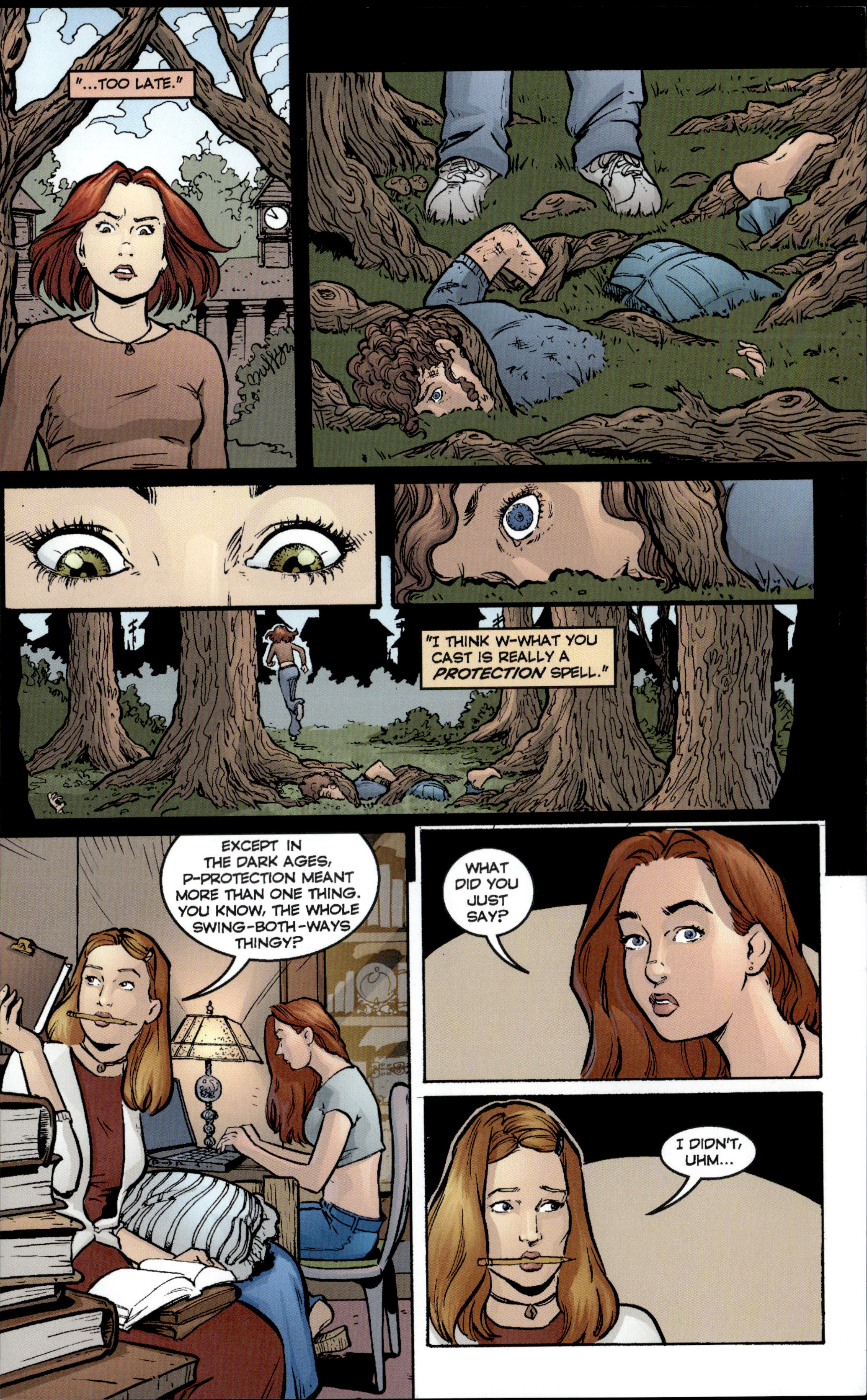

"...TOO LATE."
"I THINK W-WHAT YOU CAST IS REALLY A *PROTECTION* SPELL."
EXCEPT IN THE DARK AGES, P-PROTECTION MEANT MORE THAN ONE THING. YOU KNOW, THE WHOLE SWING-BOTH-WAYS THINGY?
WHAT DID YOU JUST SAY?
I DIDN'T, UHM...

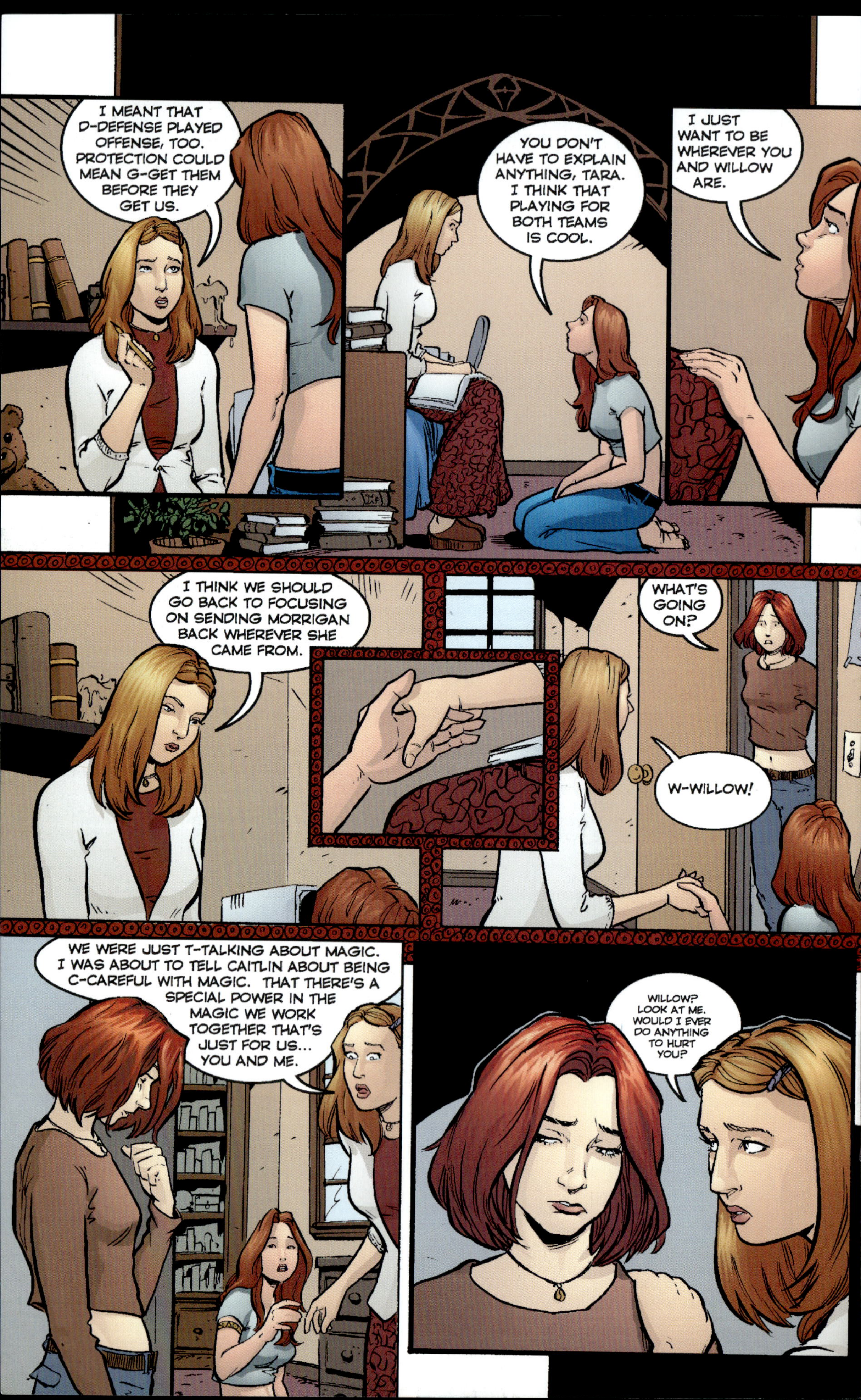
I MEANT THAT D-DEFENSE PLAYED OFFENSE, TOO. PROTECTION COULD MEAN G-GET THEM BEFORE THEY GET US.
YOU DON'T HAVE TO EXPLAIN ANYTHING, TARA. I THINK THAT PLAYING FOR BOTH TEAMS IS COOL.
I JUST WANT TO BE WHEREVER YOU AND WILLOW ARE.
I THINK WE SHOULD GO BACK TO FOCUSING ON SENDING MORRIGAN BACK WHEREVER SHE CAME FROM.
WHAT'S GOING ON?
W-WILLOW!
WE WERE JUST T-TALKING ABOUT MAGIC. I WAS ABOUT TO TELL CAITLIN ABOUT BEING C-CAREFUL WITH MAGIC. THAT THERE'S A SPECIAL POWER IN THE MAGIC WE WORK TOGETHER THAT'S JUST FOR US... YOU AND ME.
WILLOW? LOOK AT ME. WOULD I EVER DO ANYTHING TO HURT YOU?

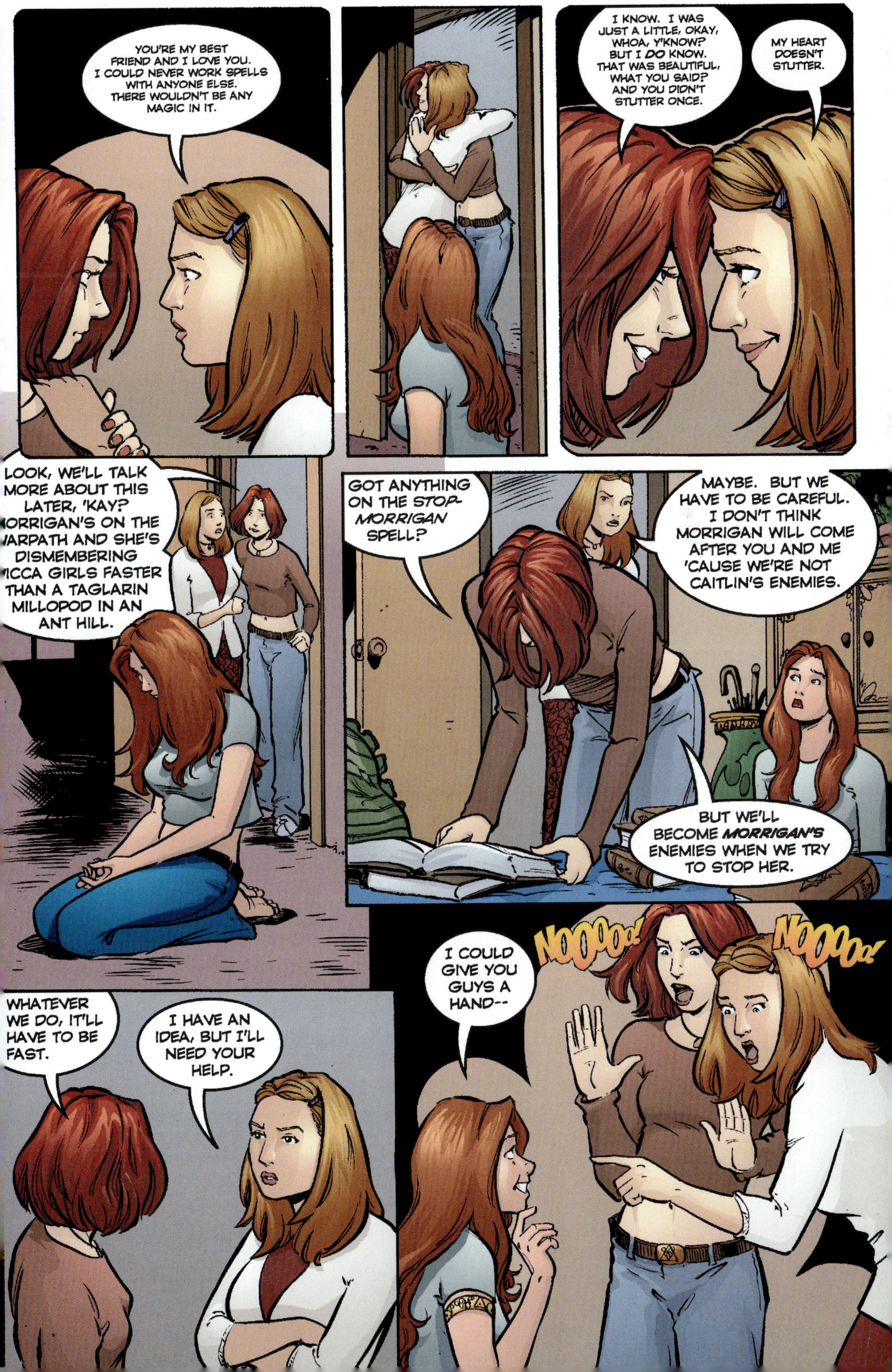
YOU'RE MY BEST FRIEND AND I LOVE YOU. I COULD NEVER WORK SPELLS WITH ANYONE ELSE. THERE WOULDN'T BE ANY MAGIC IN IT.
I KNOW. I WAS JUST A LITTLE, OKAY, WHOA, Y'KNOW? BUT I DO KNOW. THAT WAS BEAUTIFUL, WHAT YOU SAID? AND YOU DIDN'T STUTTER ONCE.
MY HEART DOESN'T STUTTER.
LOOK, WE'LL TALK MORE ABOUT THIS LATER, 'KAY? ORRIGAN'S ON THE ARPATH AND SHE'S DISMEMBERING ICCA GIRLS FASTER THAN A TAGLARIN MILLOPOD IN AN ANT HILL.
GOT ANYTHING ON THE STOP-MORRIGAN SPELL?
MAYBE. BUT WE HAVE TO BE CAREFUL. I DON'T THINK MORRIGAN WILL COME AFTER YOU AND ME 'CAUSE WE'RE NOT CAITLIN'S ENEMIES.
BUT WE'LL BECOME MORRIGAN'S ENEMIES WHEN WE TRY TO STOP HER.
WHATEVER WE DO, IT'LL HAVE TO BE FAST.
I HAVE AN IDEA, BUT I'LL NEED YOUR HELP.
I COULD GIVE YOU GUYS A HAND--
NOOOOO!
NOOOOO!

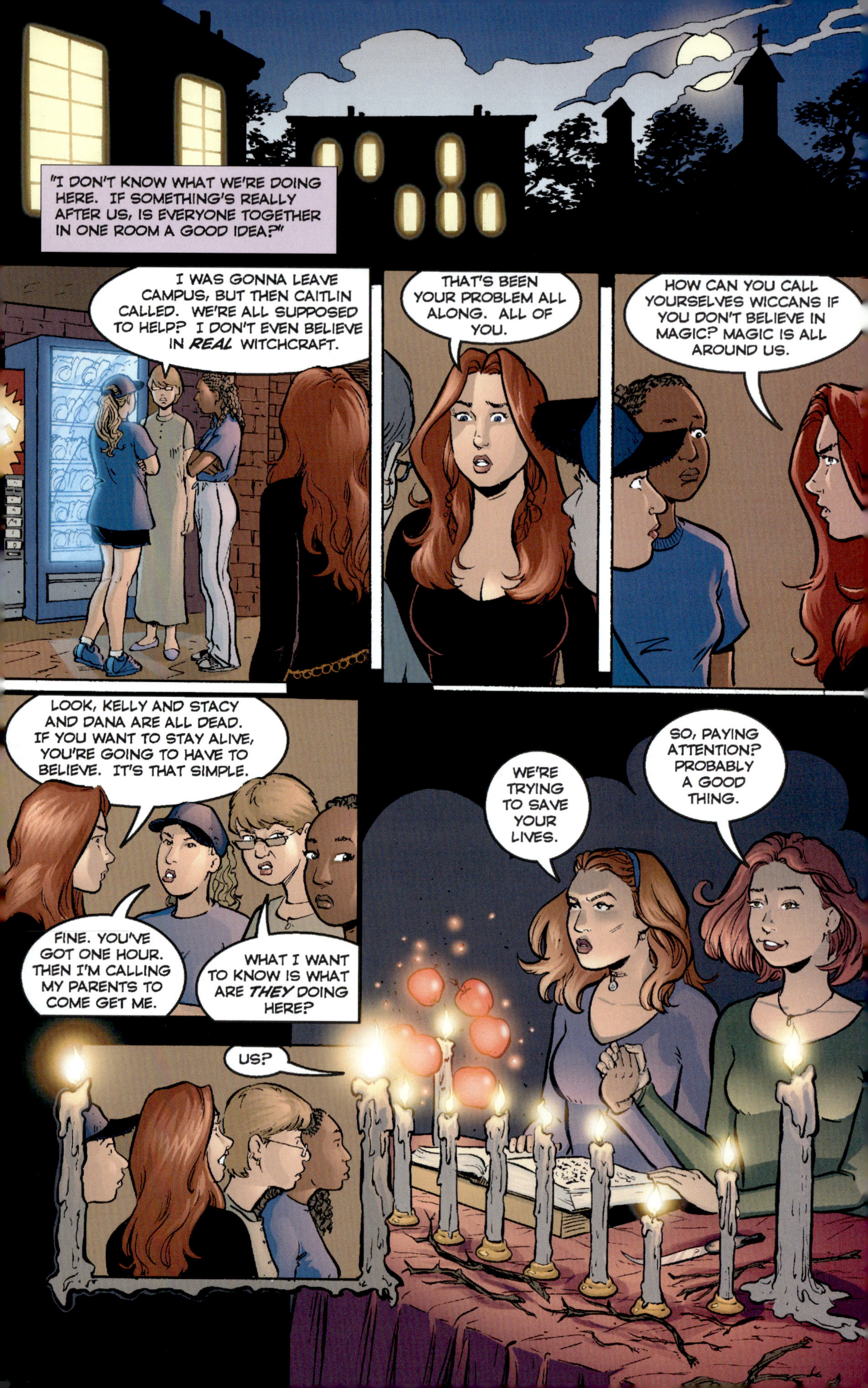

"I DON'T KNOW WHAT WE'RE DOING HERE. IF SOMETHING'S REALLY AFTER US, IS EVERYONE TOGETHER IN ONE ROOM A GOOD IDEA?"
I WAS GONNA LEAVE CAMPUS, BUT THEN CAITLIN CALLED. WE'RE ALL SUPPOSED TO HELP? I DON'T EVEN BELIEVE IN *REAL* WITCHCRAFT.
THAT'S BEEN YOUR PROBLEM ALL ALONG. ALL OF YOU.
HOW CAN YOU CALL YOURSELVES WICCANS IF YOU DON'T BELIEVE IN MAGIC? MAGIC IS ALL AROUND US.
LOOK, KELLY AND STACY AND DANA ARE ALL DEAD. IF YOU WANT TO STAY ALIVE, YOU'RE GOING TO HAVE TO BELIEVE. IT'S THAT SIMPLE.
FINE. YOU'VE GOT ONE HOUR. THEN I'M CALLING MY PARENTS TO COME GET ME.
WHAT I WANT TO KNOW IS WHAT ARE *THEY* DOING HERE?
US?
WE'RE TRYING TO SAVE YOUR LIVES.
SO, PAYING ATTENTION? PROBABLY A GOOD THING.

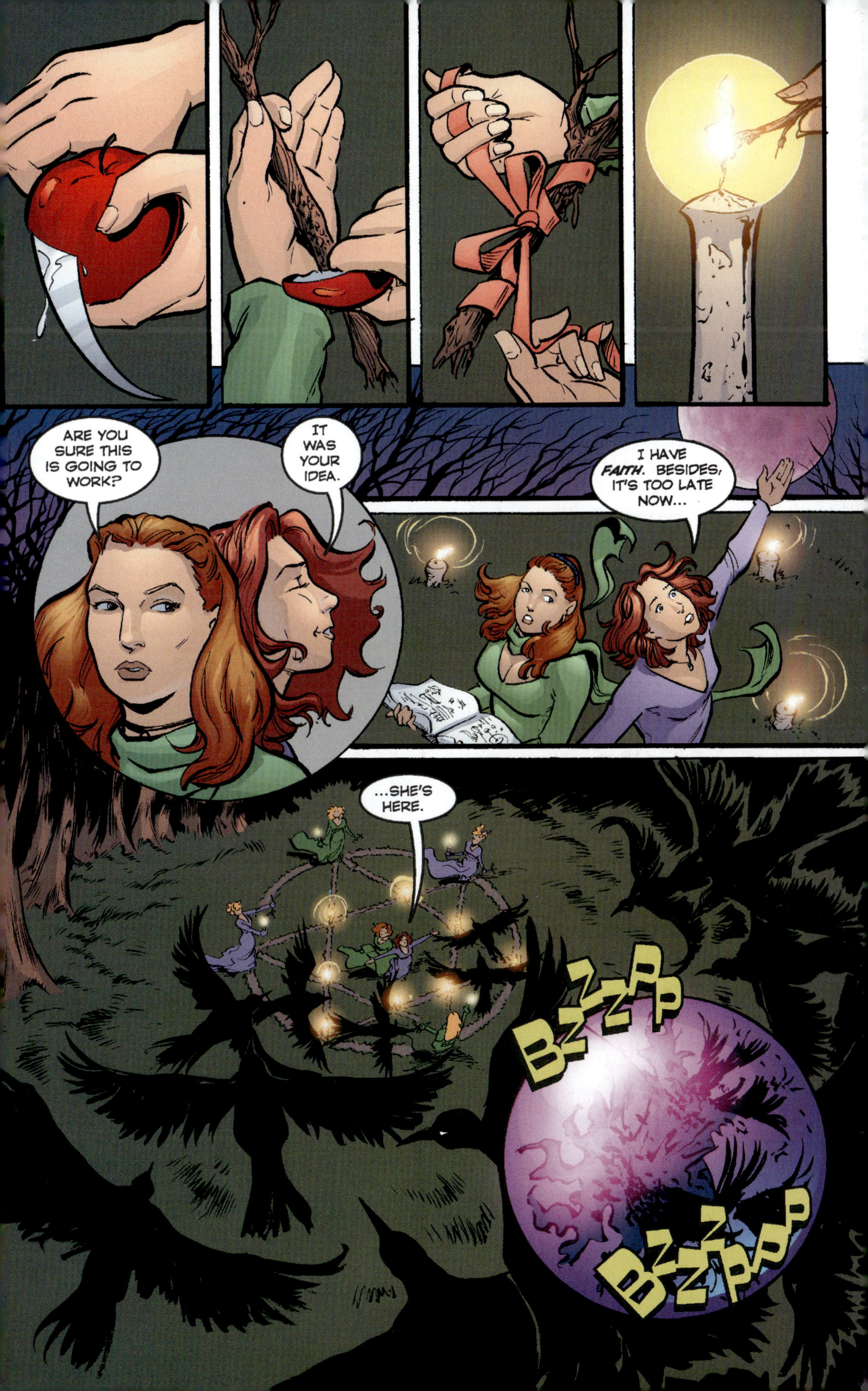
ARE YOU SURE THIS IS GOING TO WORK?
IT WAS YOUR IDEA.
I HAVE *FAITH*. BESIDES, IT'S TOO LATE NOW...
...SHE'S HERE.
BZZZAPP
BZZZPOP

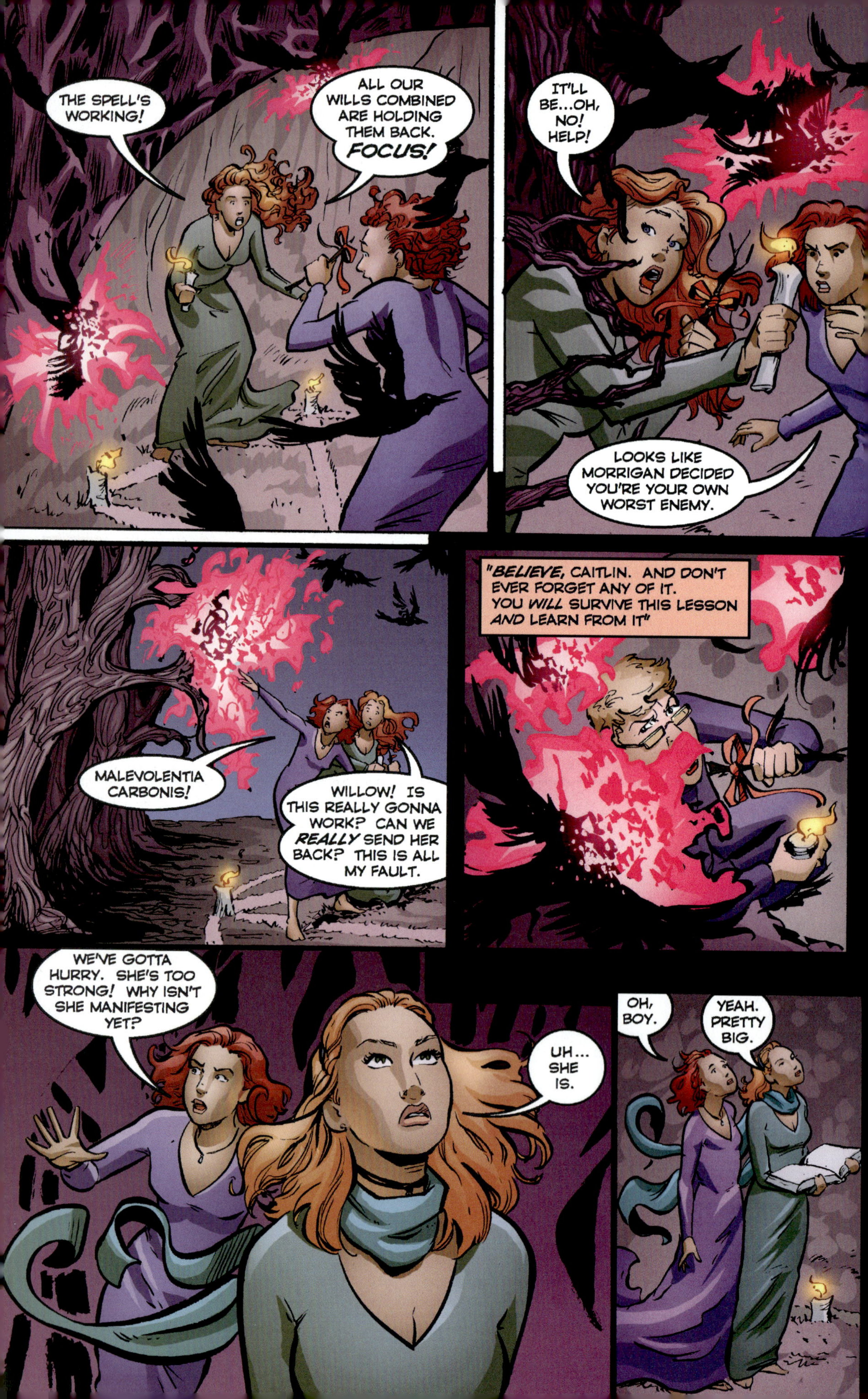
THE SPELL'S WORKING!
ALL OUR WILLS COMBINED ARE HOLDING THEM BACK. FOCUS!
IT'LL BE...OH, NO! HELP!
LOOKS LIKE MORRIGAN DECIDED YOU'RE YOUR OWN WORST ENEMY.
MALEVOLENTIA CARBONIS!
WILLOW! IS THIS REALLY GONNA WORK? CAN WE REALLY SEND HER BACK? THIS IS ALL MY FAULT.
"BELIEVE, CAITLIN. AND DON'T EVER FORGET ANY OF IT. YOU WILL SURVIVE THIS LESSON AND LEARN FROM IT"
WE'VE GOTTA HURRY. SHE'S TOO STRONG! WHY ISN'T SHE MANIFESTING YET?
UH... SHE IS.
OH, BOY.
YEAH. PRETTY BIG.

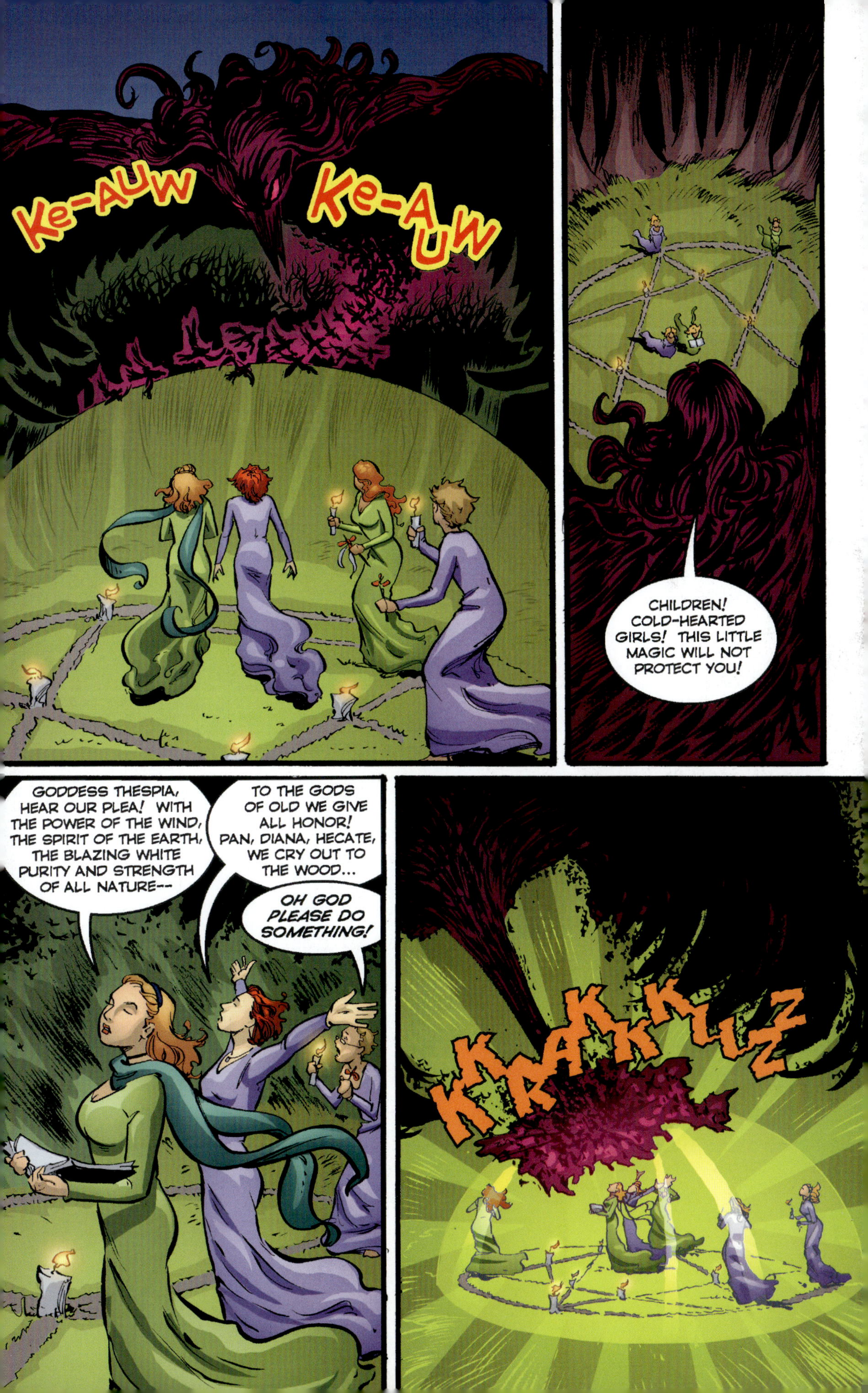

KE-AUW
KE-AUW
CHILDREN! COLD-HEARTED GIRLS! THIS LITTLE MAGIC WILL NOT PROTECT YOU!
GODDESS THESPIA, HEAR OUR PLEA! WITH THE POWER OF THE WIND, THE SPIRIT OF THE EARTH, THE BLAZING WHITE PURITY AND STRENGTH OF ALL NATURE--
TO THE GODS OF OLD WE GIVE ALL HONOR! PAN, DIANA, HECATE, WE CRY OUT TO THE WOOD...
OH GOD PLEASE DO SOMETHING!
KRAKKKLUZ

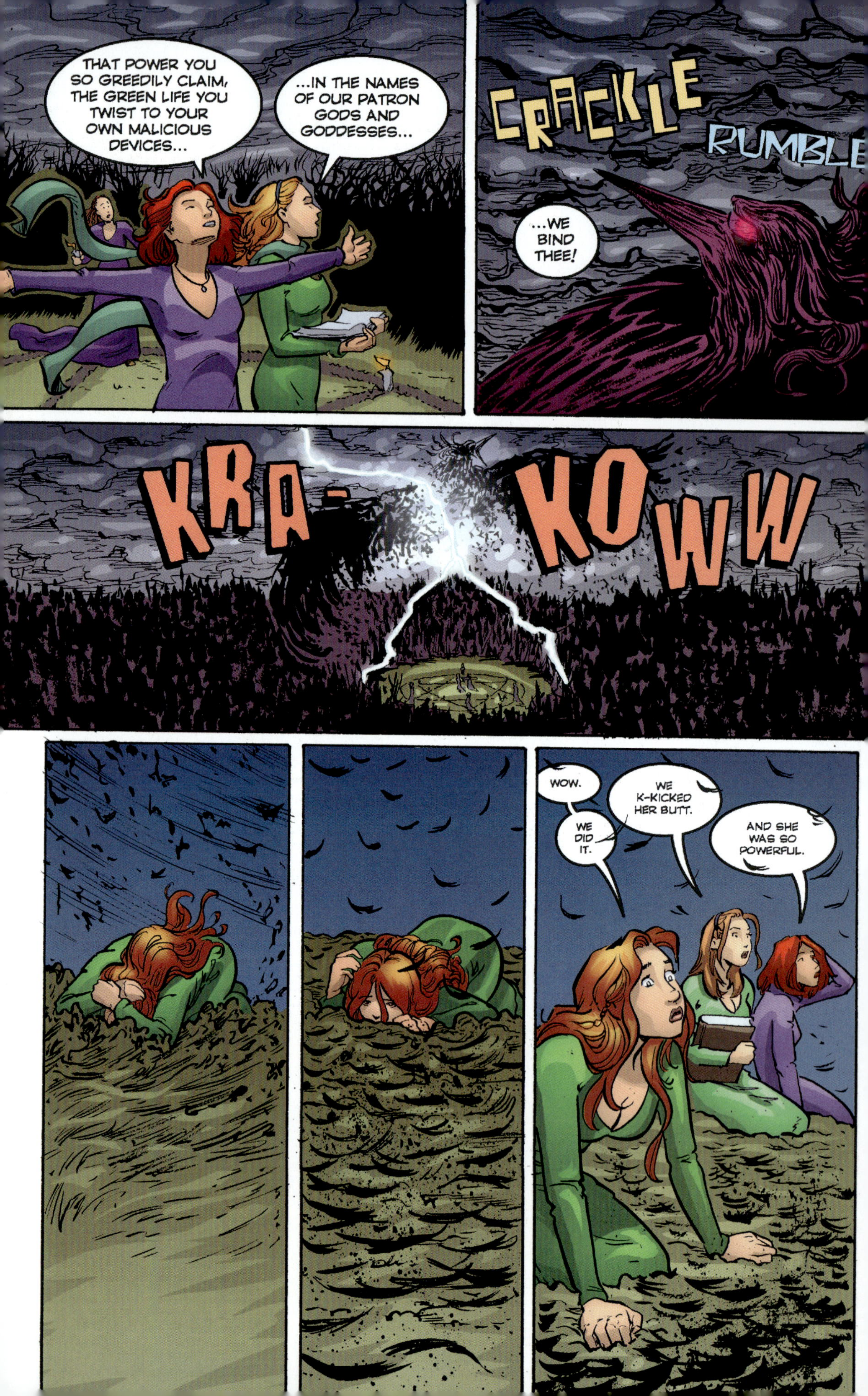
THAT POWER YOU SO GREEDILY CLAIM, THE GREEN LIFE YOU TWIST TO YOUR OWN MALICIOUS DEVICES...
...IN THE NAMES OF OUR PATRON GODS AND GODDESSES...
CRACKLE
RUMBLE
...WE BIND THEE!
KRA-KOWW
WOW.
WE DID IT.
WE K-KICKED HER BUTT.
AND SHE WAS SO POWERFUL.

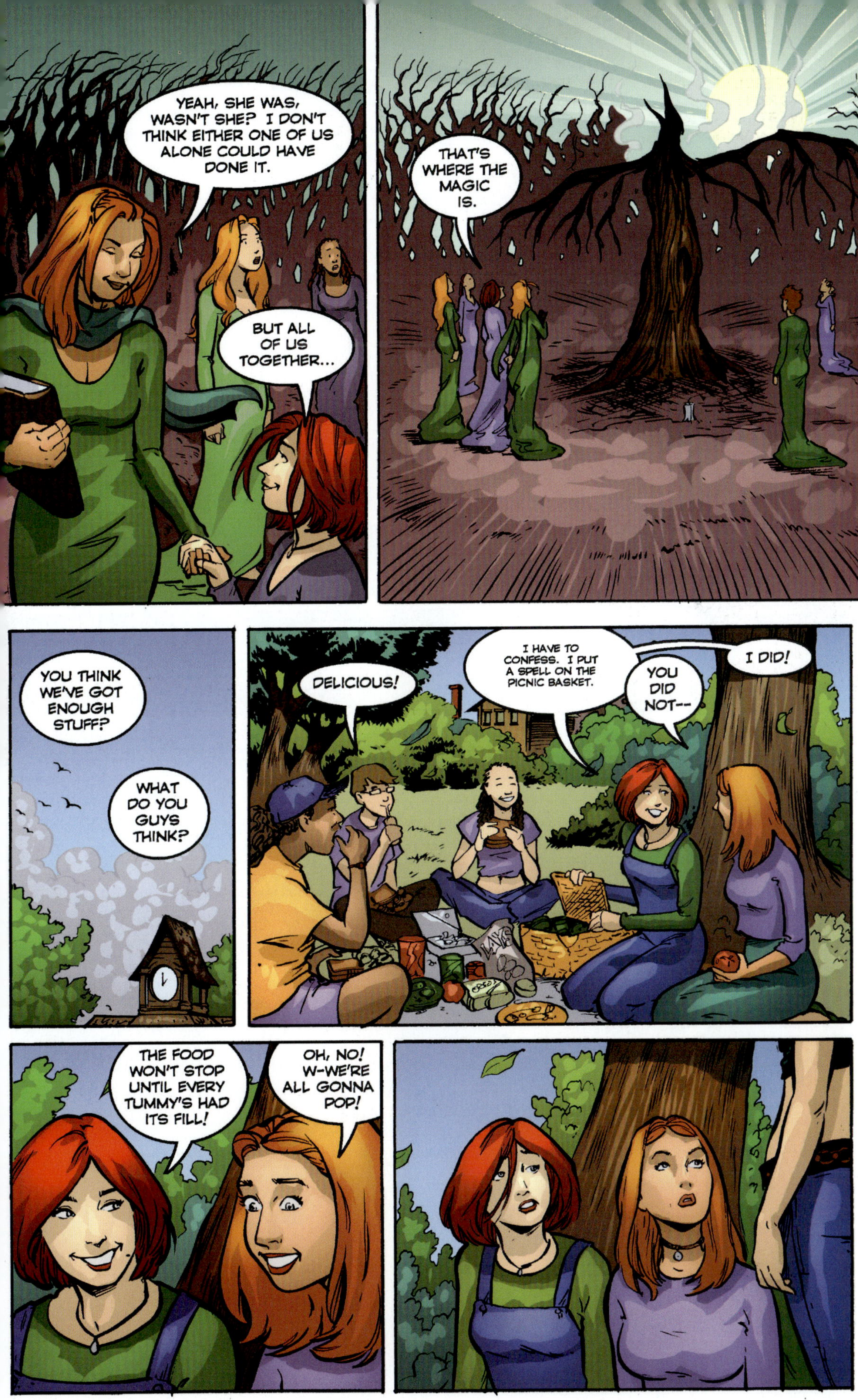
YEAH, SHE WAS, WASN'T SHE? I DON'T THINK EITHER ONE OF US ALONE COULD HAVE DONE IT.
BUT ALL OF US TOGETHER...
THAT'S WHERE THE MAGIC IS.
YOU THINK WE'VE GOT ENOUGH STUFF?
WHAT DO YOU GUYS THINK?
DELICIOUS!
I HAVE TO CONFESS. I PUT A SPELL ON THE PICNIC BASKET.
YOU DID NOT--
I DID!
THE FOOD WON'T STOP UNTIL EVERY TUMMY'S HAD ITS FILL!
OH, NO! W-WE'RE ALL GONNA POP!

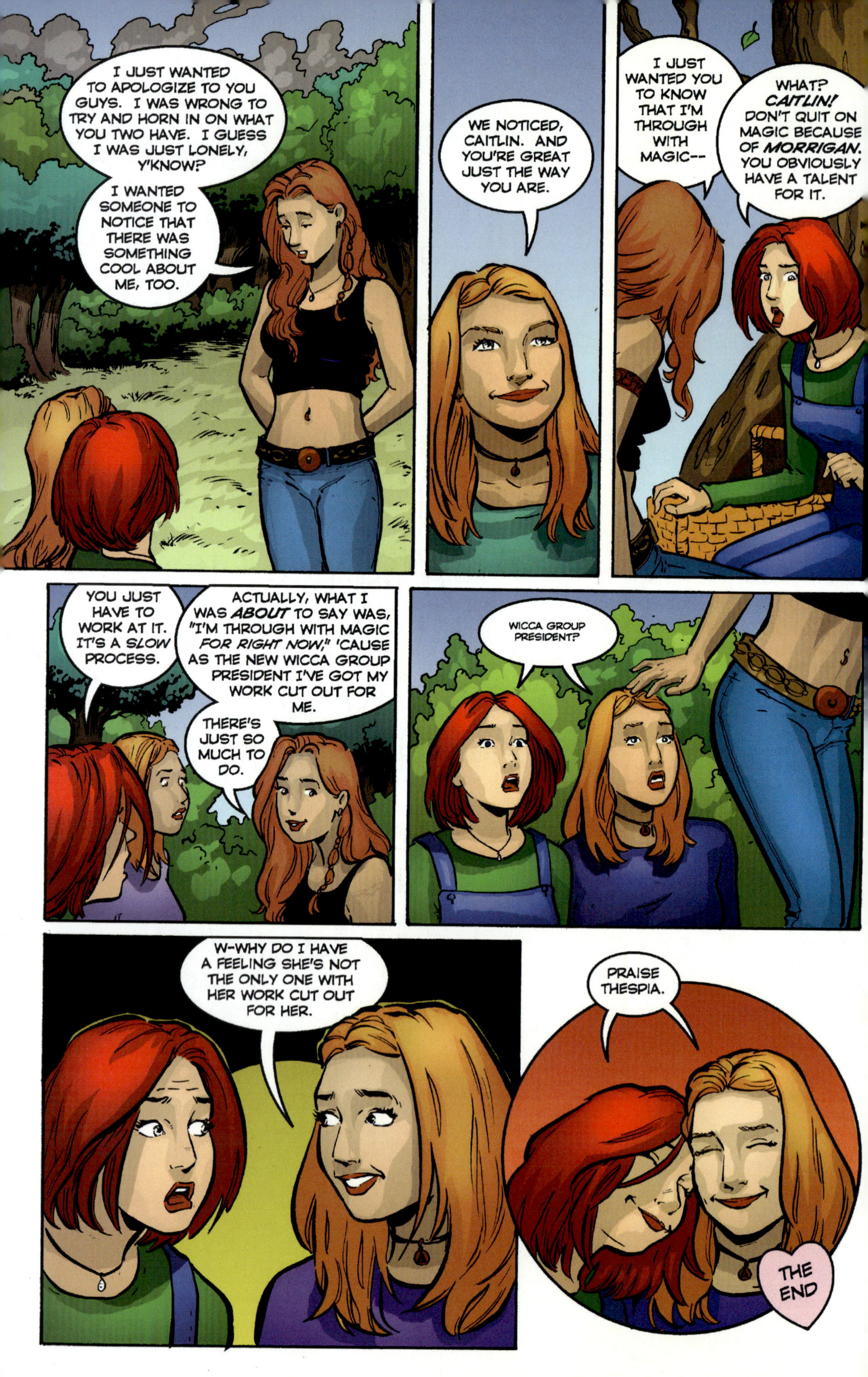
I JUST WANTED TO APOLOGIZE TO YOU GUYS. I WAS WRONG TO TRY AND HORN IN ON WHAT YOU TWO HAVE. I GUESS I WAS JUST LONELY, Y'KNOW?
I WANTED SOMEONE TO NOTICE THAT THERE WAS SOMETHING COOL ABOUT ME, TOO.
WE NOTICED, CAITLIN. AND YOU'RE GREAT JUST THE WAY YOU ARE.
I JUST WANTED YOU TO KNOW THAT I'M THROUGH WITH MAGIC--
WHAT? CAITLIN! DON'T QUIT ON MAGIC BECAUSE OF MORRIGAN. YOU OBVIOUSLY HAVE A TALENT FOR IT.
YOU JUST HAVE TO WORK AT IT. IT'S A SLOW PROCESS.
ACTUALLY, WHAT I WAS ABOUT TO SAY WAS, "I'M THROUGH WITH MAGIC FOR RIGHT NOW," 'CAUSE AS THE NEW WICCA GROUP PRESIDENT I'VE GOT MY WORK CUT OUT FOR ME.
THERE'S JUST SO MUCH TO DO.
WICCA GROUP PRESIDENT?
W-WHY DO I HAVE A FEELING SHE'S NOT THE ONLY ONE WITH HER WORK CUT OUT FOR HER.
PRAISE THESPIA.
THE END

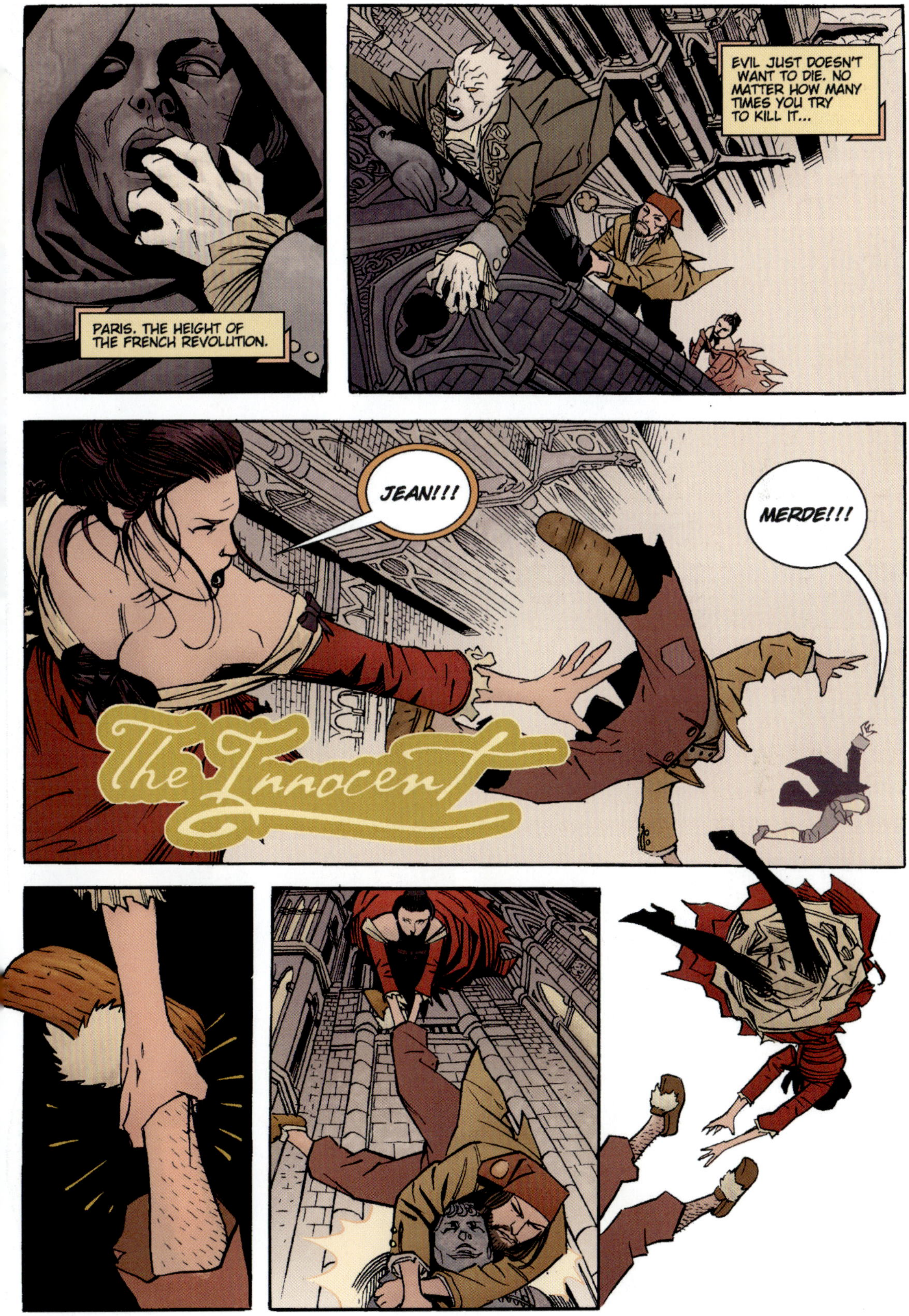
PARIS. THE HEIGHT OF THE FRENCH REVOLUTION.
EVIL JUST DOESN'T WANT TO DIE. NO MATTER HOW MANY TIMES YOU TRY TO KILL IT...
JEAN!!!
MERDE!!!
The Innocent

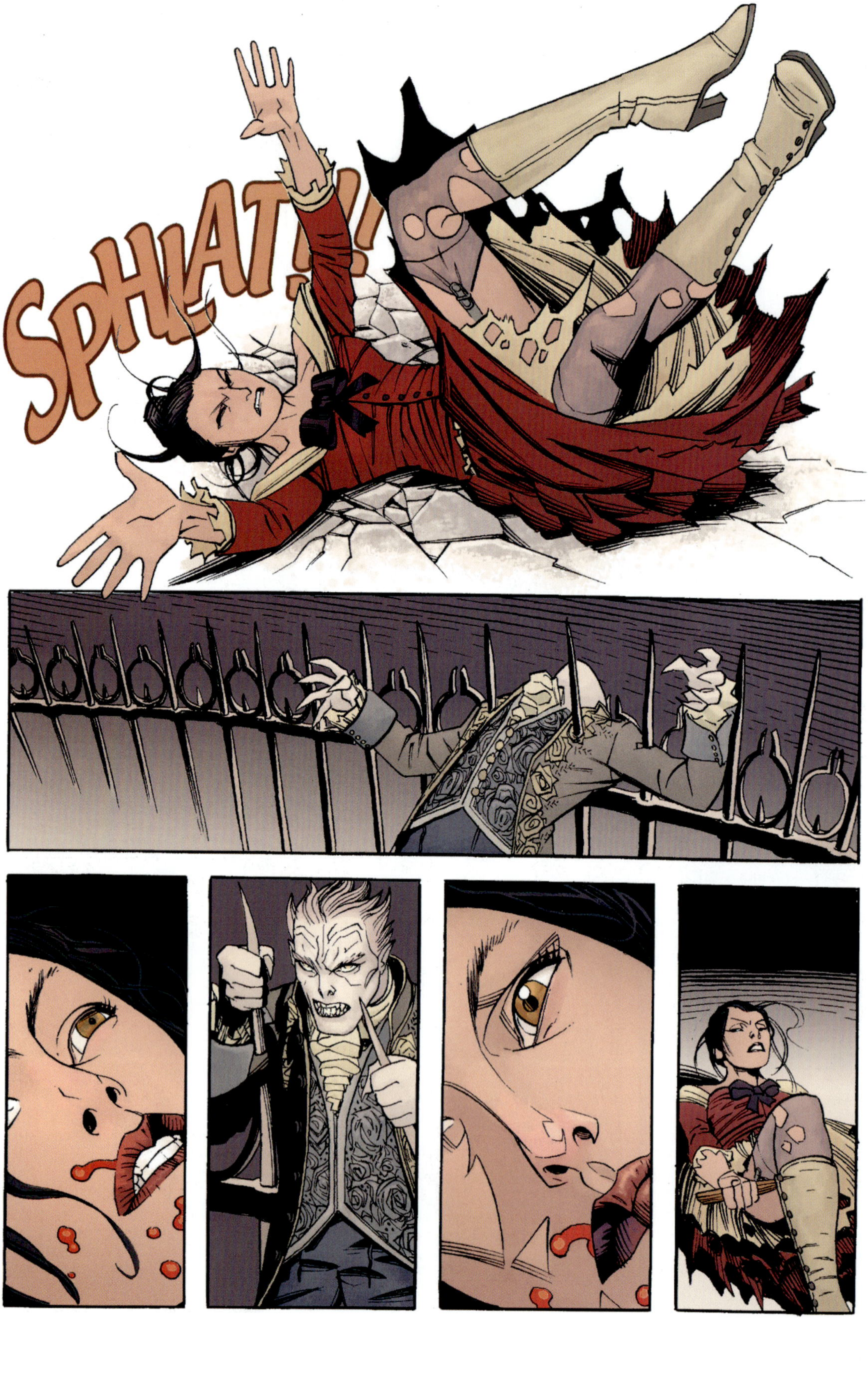
SPHLAT!!

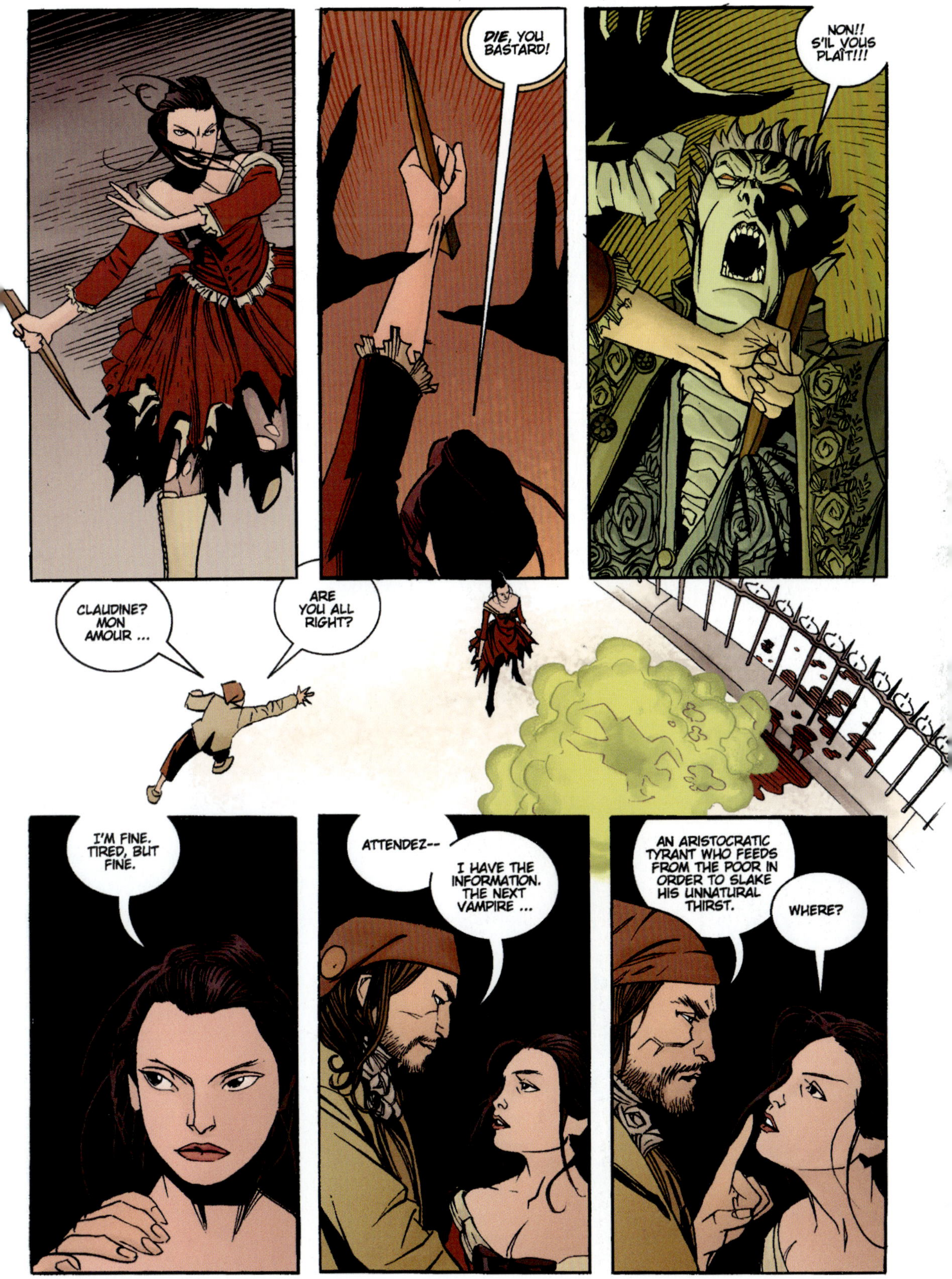
DIE, YOU BASTARD!
NON!! S'IL VOUS PLAÎT!!!
CLAUDINE? MON AMOUR ...
ARE YOU ALL RIGHT?
I'M FINE. TIRED, BUT FINE.
ATTENDEZ--
I HAVE THE INFORMATION. THE NEXT VAMPIRE ...
AN ARISTOCRATIC TYRANT WHO FEEDS FROM THE POOR IN ORDER TO SLAKE HIS UNNATURAL THIRST.
WHERE?

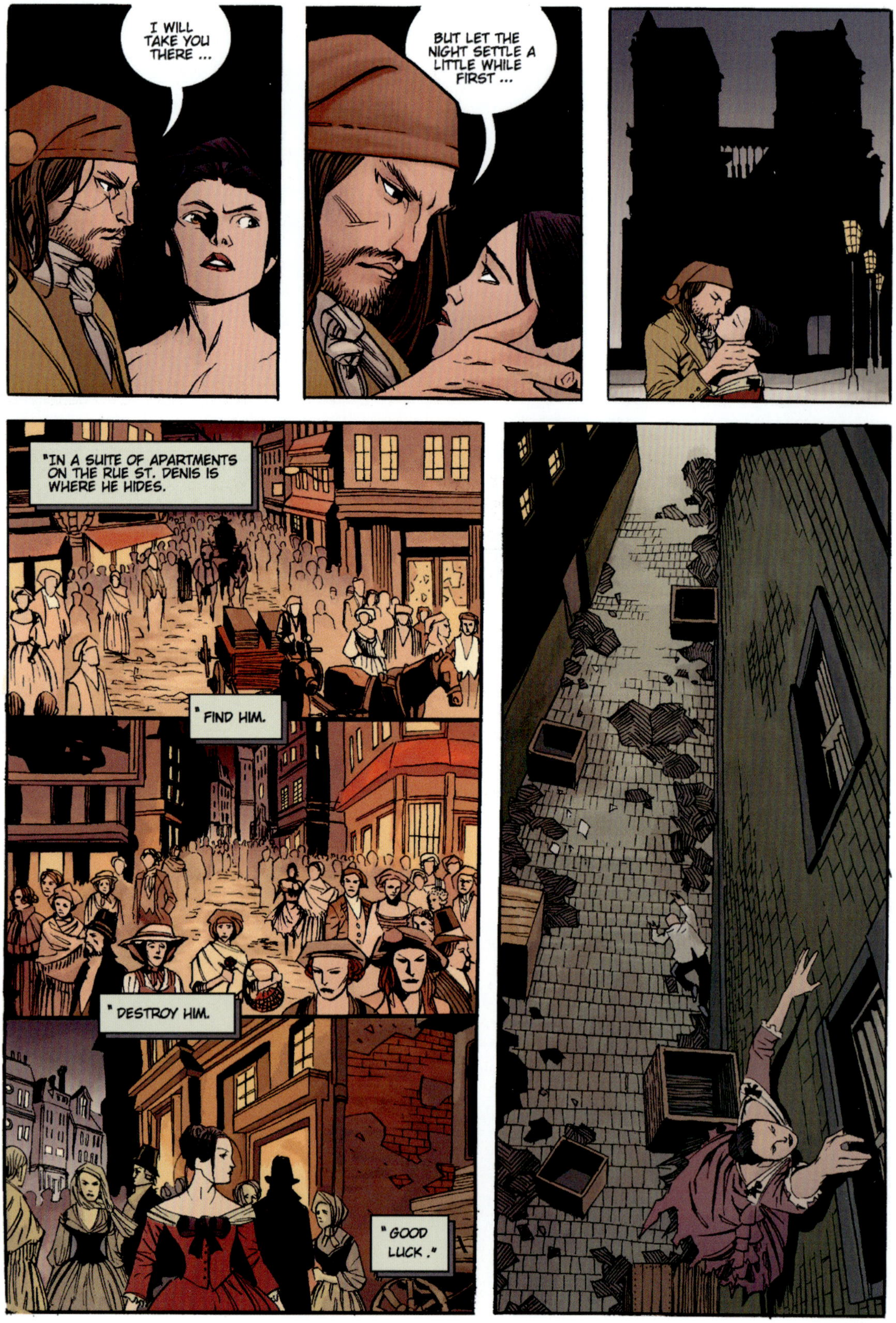
I WILL TAKE YOU THERE ...
BUT LET THE NIGHT SETTLE A LITTLE WHILE FIRST ...
"IN A SUITE OF APARTMENTS ON THE RUE ST. DENIS IS WHERE HE HIDES.
"FIND HIM.
"DESTROY HIM.
"GOOD LUCK."

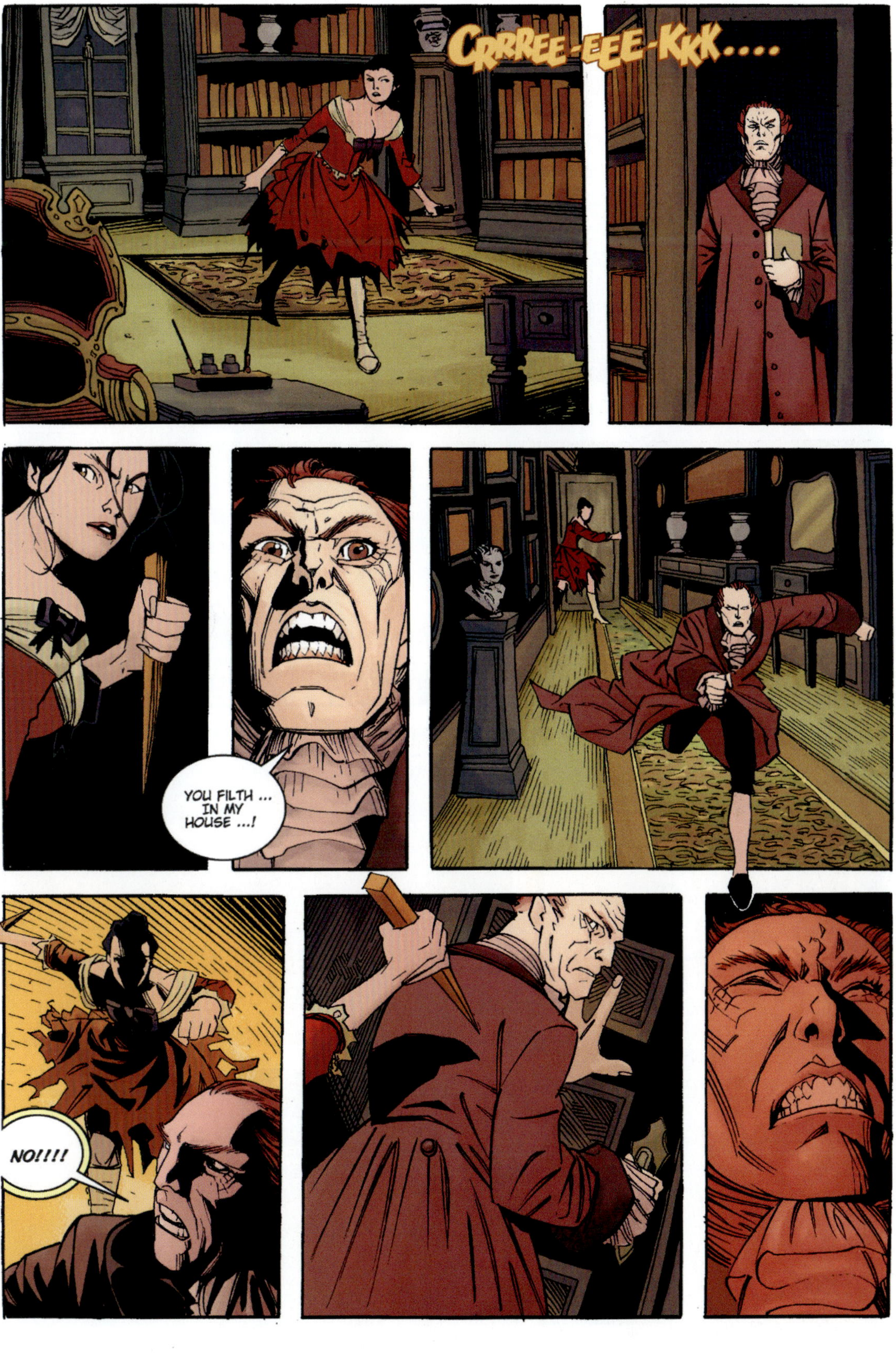
CRRREE-EEE-KKK....
YOU FILTH ... IN MY HOUSE ...!
NO!!!!

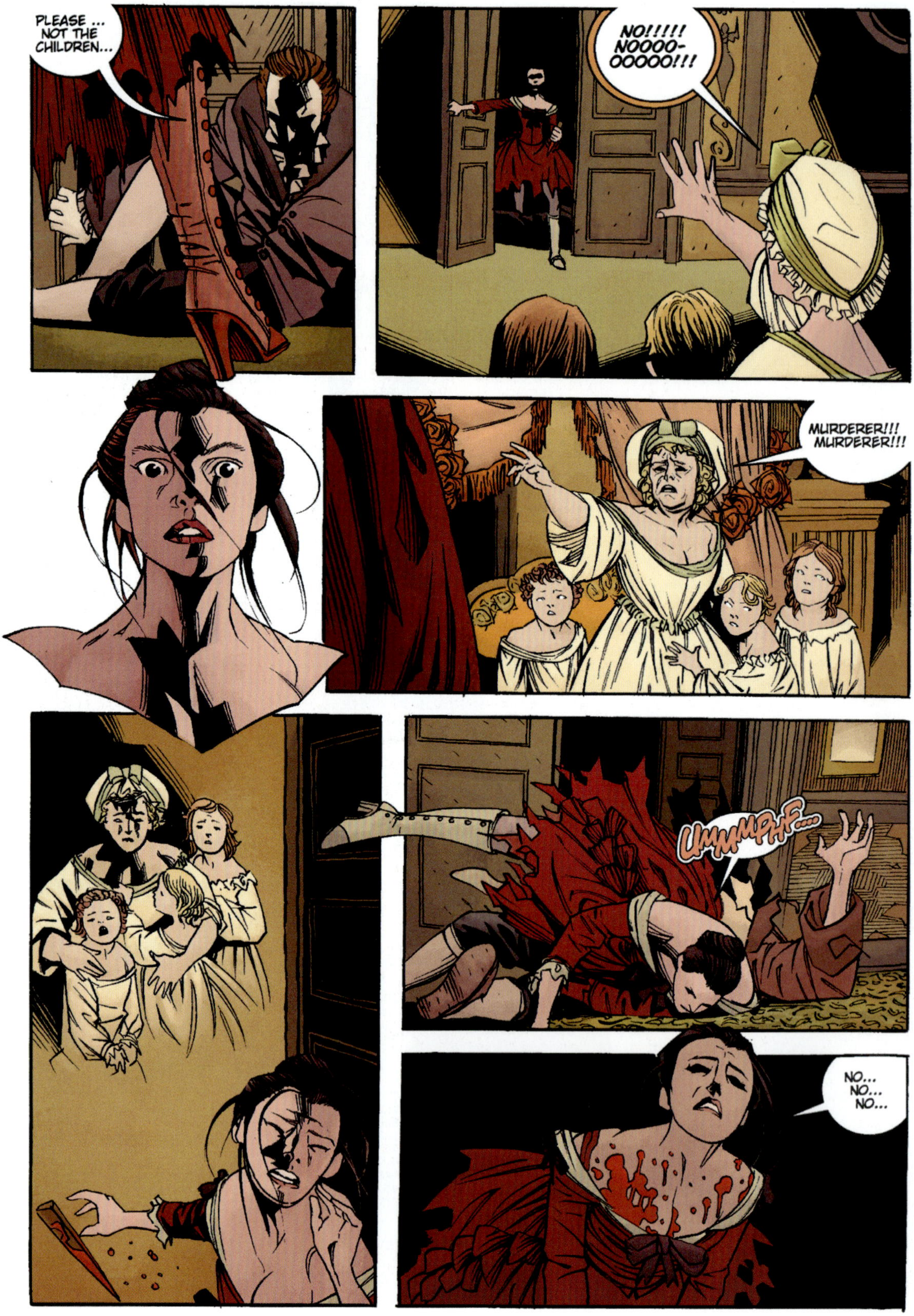
PLEASE ... NOT THE CHILDREN...
NO!!!!! NOOOO-OOOOO!!!
MURDERER!!! MURDERER!!!
UMMMPHF....
NO... NO... NO...

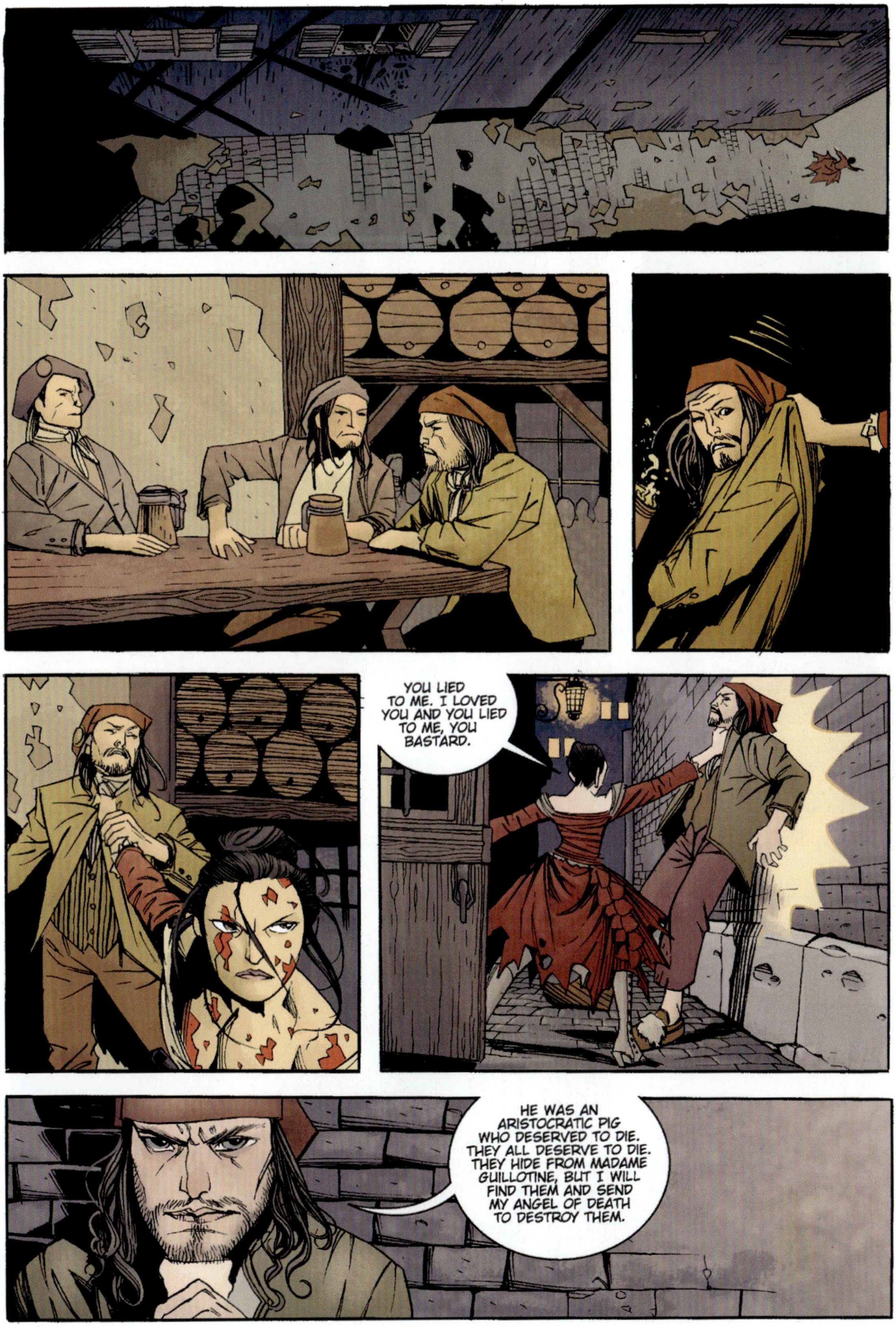
YOU LIED TO ME. I LOVED YOU AND YOU LIED TO ME, YOU BASTARD.
HE WAS AN ARISTOCRATIC PIG WHO DESERVED TO DIE. THEY ALL DESERVE TO DIE. THEY HIDE FROM MADAME GUILLOTINE, BUT I WILL FIND THEM AND SEND MY ANGEL OF DEATH TO DESTROY THEM.

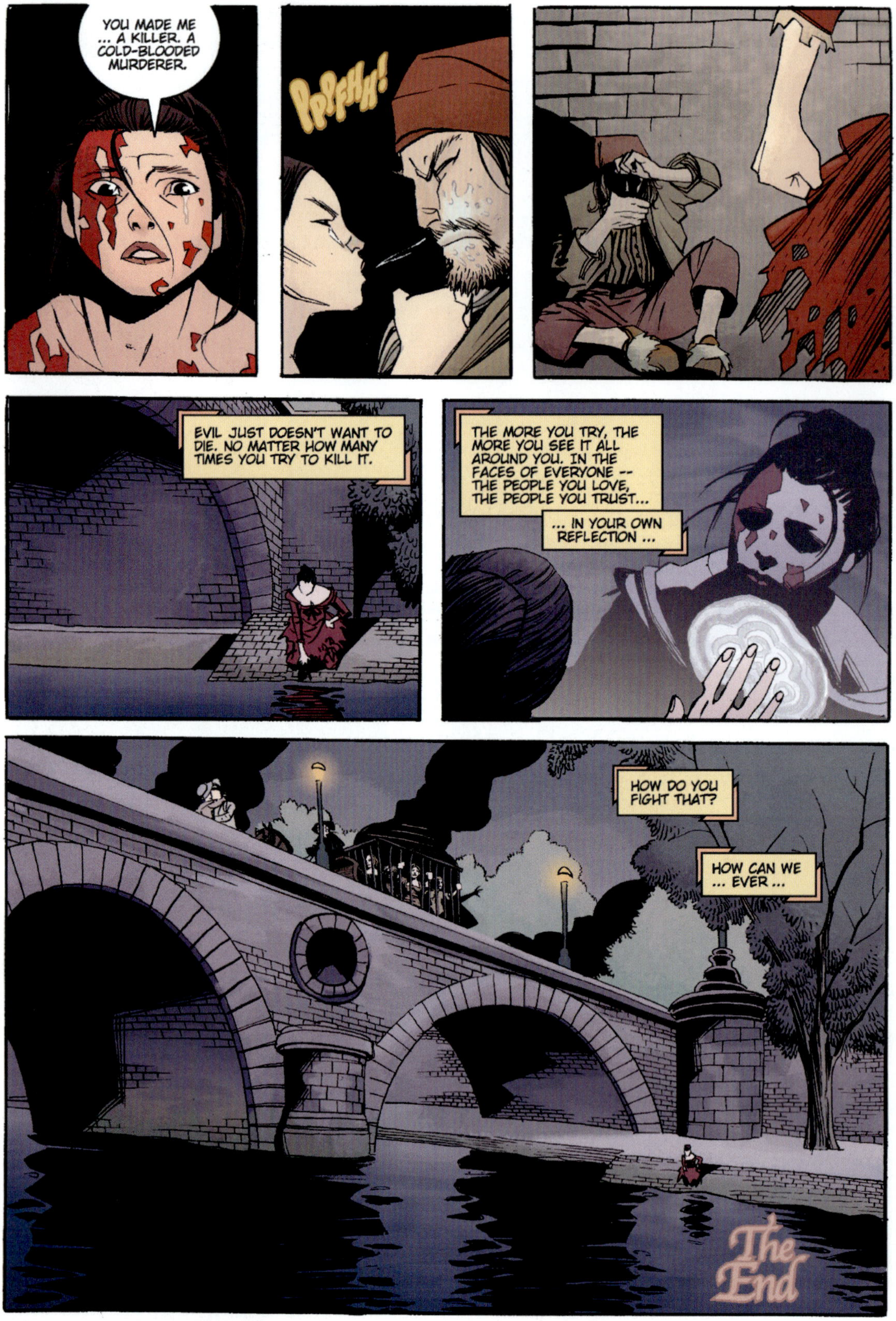
YOU MADE ME ... A KILLER. A COLD-BLOODED MURDERER.
PPPFHH!
EVIL JUST DOESN'T WANT TO DIE. NO MATTER HOW MANY TIMES YOU TRY TO KILL IT.
THE MORE YOU TRY, THE MORE YOU SEE IT ALL AROUND YOU. IN THE FACES OF EVERYONE -- THE PEOPLE YOU LOVE, THE PEOPLE YOU TRUST...
... IN YOUR OWN REFLECTION ...
HOW DO YOU FIGHT THAT?
HOW CAN WE ... EVER ...
The End

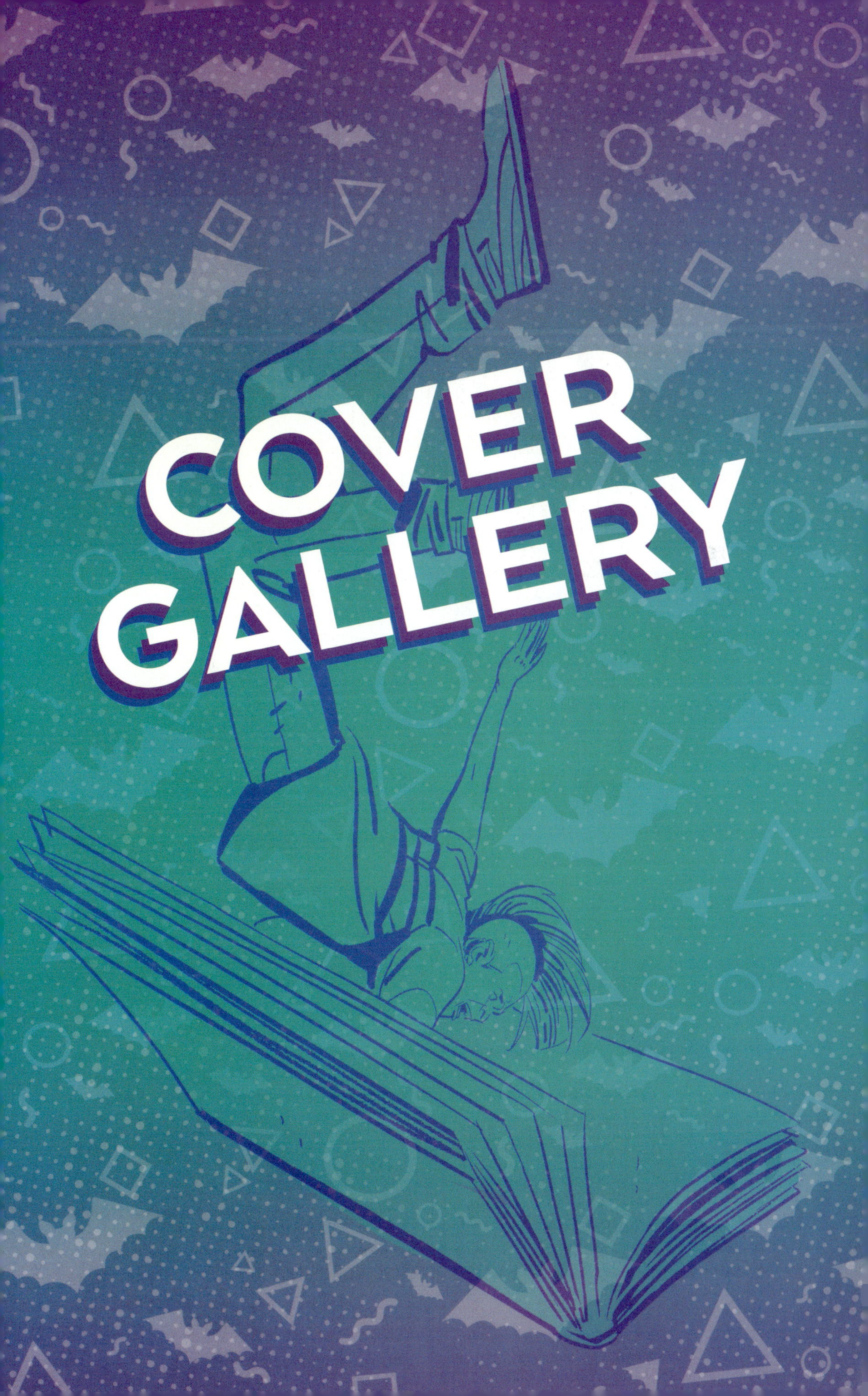
COVER
GALLERY

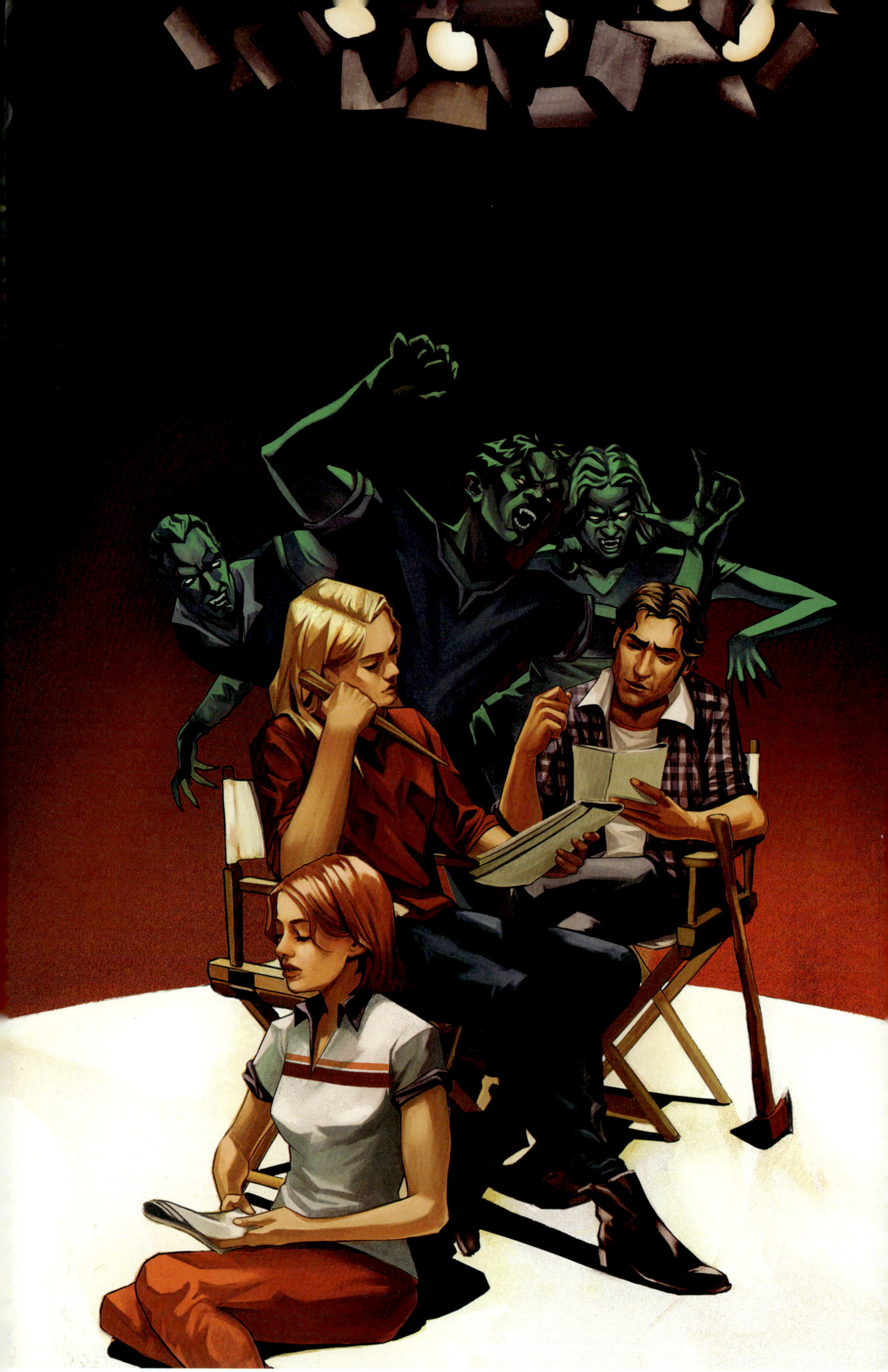

Buffy '97 Main Cover by **Qistina Khalida**

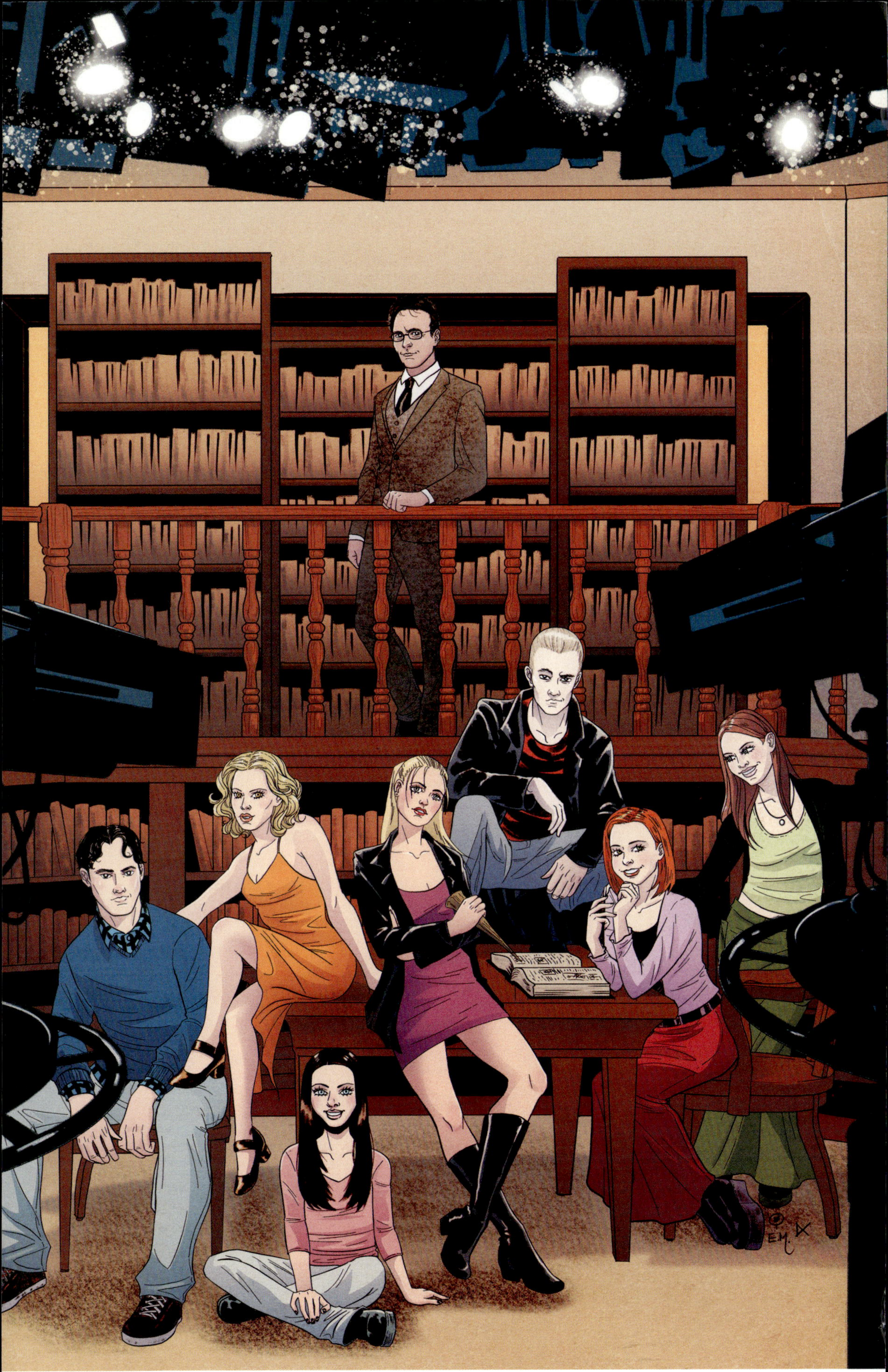

Buffy '97 Variant Cover by **Megan Hutchison-Cates**

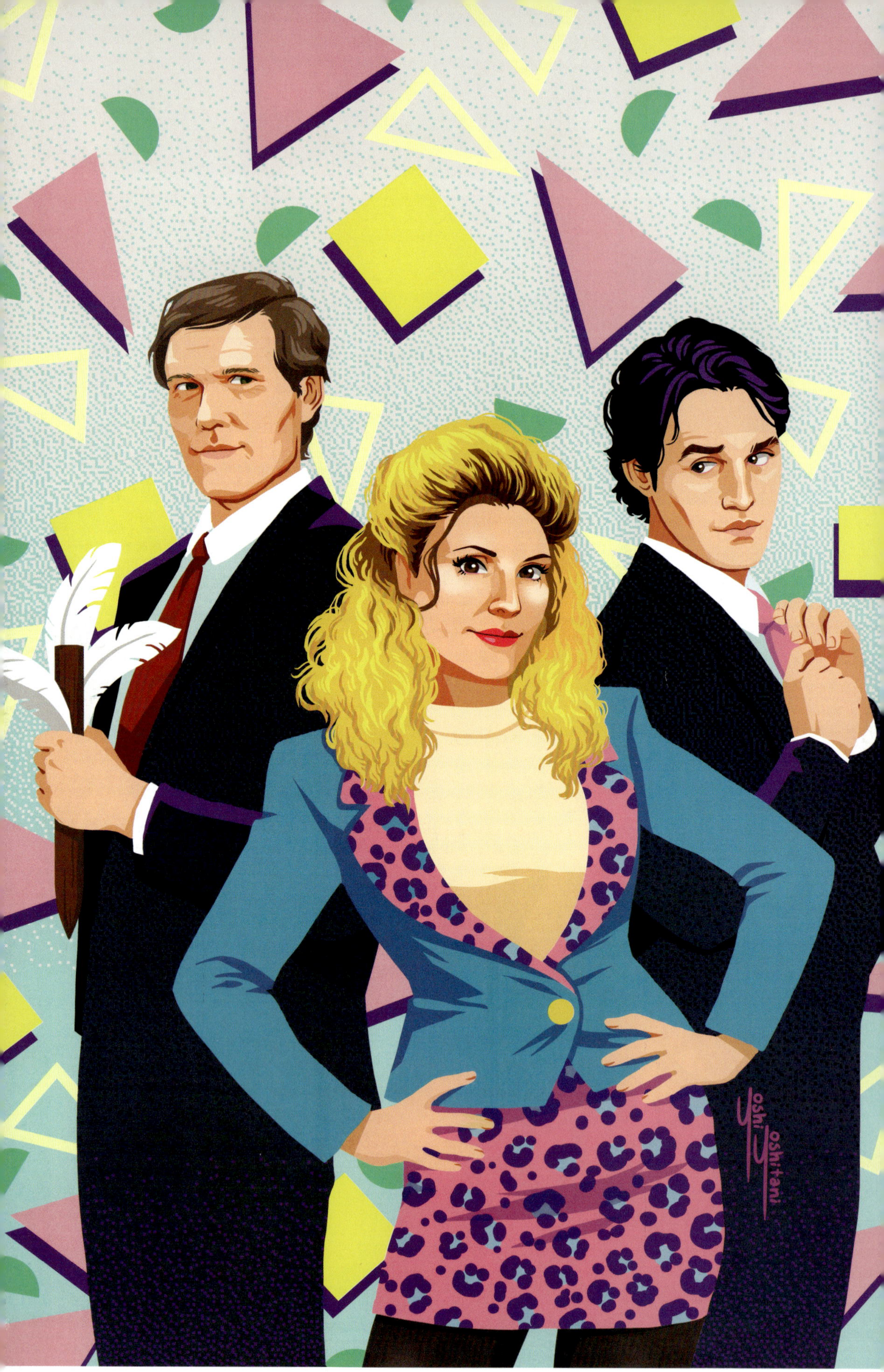
Yoshi Yoshitani

Buffy '97 Variant Cover by **Yoshi Yoshitani**

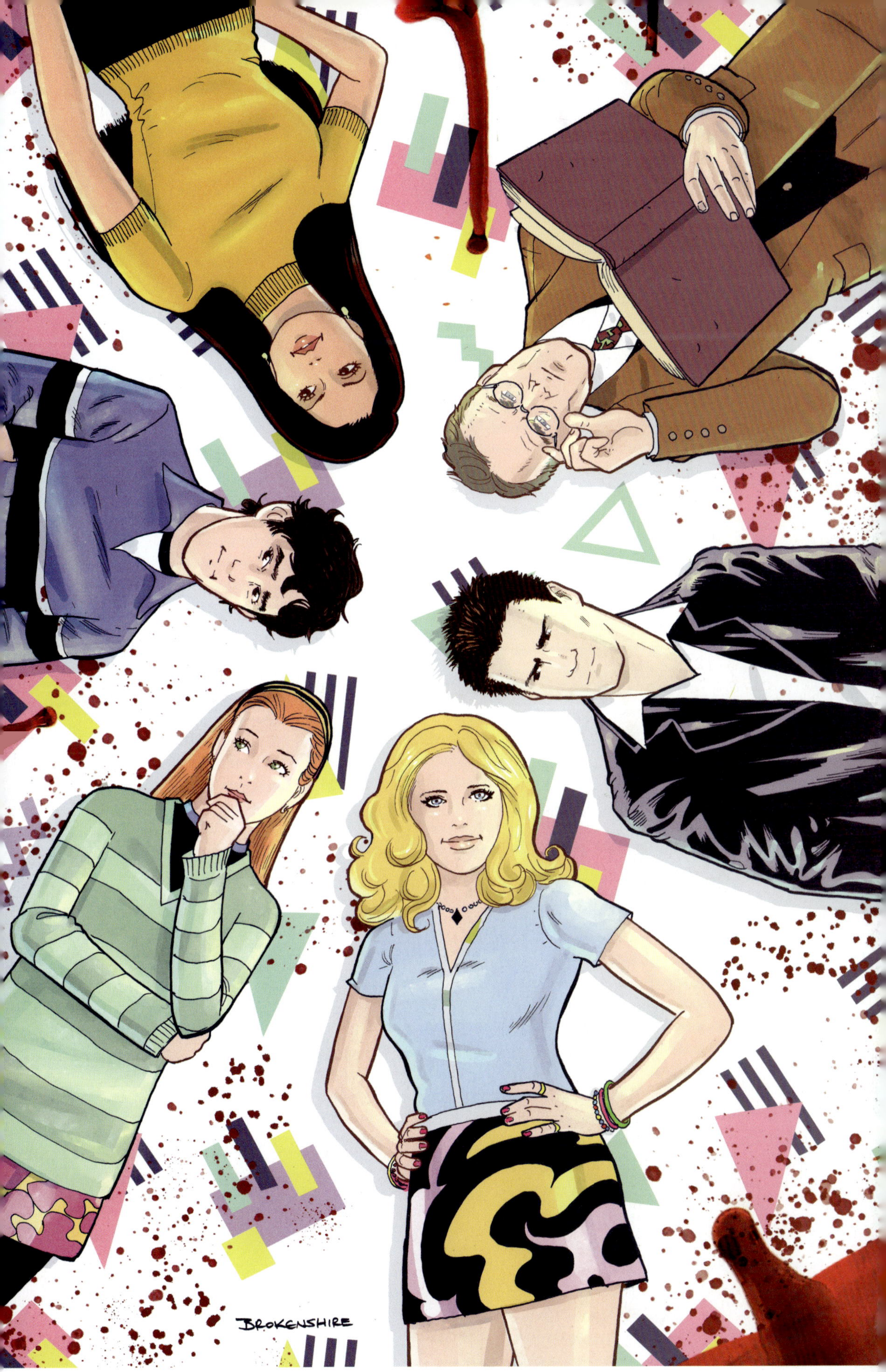
BROKENSHIRE

Buffy '97 Variant Cover by **Nick Brokenshire**

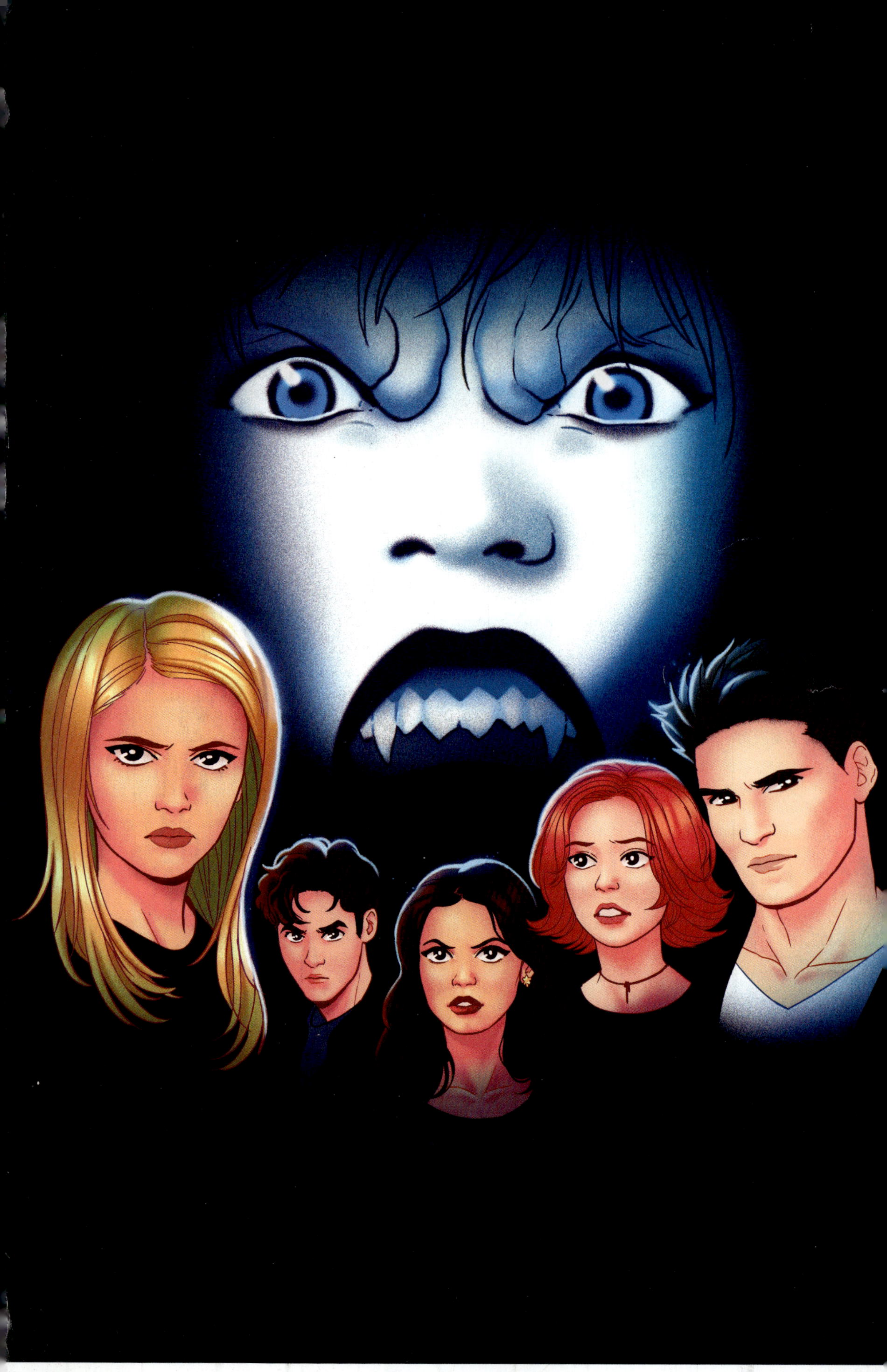

Buffy '97 Variant Cover by **Paulina Ganucheau**